Also written by S.T. Upton

Death Dot

First published in Great Britain
in 2017

This edition, published in Great Britain in 2018

ISBN

978 1 61947 316 4

DREAMNEST
RETROSPECT

QUANTALORE

*For Alison, Glen
and John*

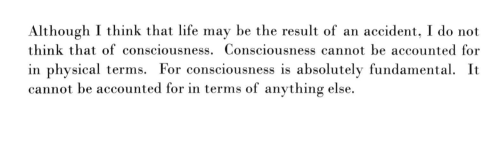

Although I think that life may be the result of an accident, I do not think that of consciousness. Consciousness cannot be accounted for in physical terms. For consciousness is absolutely fundamental. It cannot be accounted for in terms of anything else.

Erwin Schrödinger, *Physicist*
As quoted in The Observer, 11 January
(1931)

Chapter One

Mutating

'Tell them,' Wil said firmly. However, his voice came as a slurred whimper. '*Tell* them,' he demanded, grimacing again into his pillow.

He shouted the words once more, waking himself, and felt only febrile and disorientated from the ordeal he could not remember.

Wil sat downstairs at 2am on Blake (Dad's favourite leather chair) while the green hue of the energy-saving bulb ripened to a warm yellow beside him. It seemed leg cramp was what woke him this time. Or a fever. In any case, he swallowed two painkillers, grunted for the remote and aimed it at the new telly Dad genially named Sonya and introduced to Blake only two days ago. He pressed the little red button.

Matte black instantly became brilliant white, obliterating the pathetic light in the room, forcing Wil to squint at the wide screen. His eyes quickly adjusted, leaving him transfixed by the astonishing detail of five circles within circles, emblazoned suddenly onto his retina. They appeared to dangle in front of him off a smooth, transparent, mucous-green surface.

Intrigued, Wil leaned forward, turned up the volume slightly and stared with fascination as the camera angle changed.

'There are five antibiotic concentrations within the tray here,' a lab technician declared, moving her hand mechanically over what Wil quickly realised was a coffee-table-sized petri dish. 'Each is divided by a ring. The further out, the stronger and more specific the antibiotic treatment. As you can see, the bacteria start here.' She pointed to the middle circle already culturing brown spots. 'Without treatment, you'll see in the time-lapsed video how easy it is for the colonies to spread to the first sample.'

Footage ran, demonstrating her point, showing the brown spots multiplying, filling the untreated centre then moving onto the next circle with no sign of difficulty.

'Here, the broad-spectrum antibiotic has had little effect.'

The blotchy patch moved through the next two circles, slowing only as it breached the barrier of each new section. This fascinated Wil, for while it seemed the tiny organisms were dying off, really, division and mutation ensured the survival of generations; mutants withstood the higher concentration while their counterparts became sacrifices, succumbing to the weapon designed specifically for them. The rogues multiplied, became invincible, dominant.

'These are the very antibiotics our doctors have at their disposal,' the woman went on, 'and if you imagine each section is a more specific or stronger treatment, resistance *is* inevitable.'

The time-lapsed footage carried on, and as Wil watched the brown spots build up around the edges of the last barrier he thought for a second that the final concentration had won, but the video hurried along until a few bacterial specks leached out then spread just as vigorously as their ancestors.

'I'm afraid this antibiotic is our last. There is no other manufactured or available at this time to overcome this particular strain,' the woman said gravely, her freckled brow crimping. 'What you have just witnessed here is biological evolution, and we are quickly running out of options unless we can tackle the problem some other way.'

The footage replayed from the beginning and Wil sat with eyes wide as the mouldy patch broke through the deterrents—every antibiotic concentration known to man—mutating and resisting until it survived. It was so complex... yet so simple.... *Inspiring.*

A sudden commercial break darkened the room momentarily, like Sonya had been turned off, and Wil consciously appreciated just then how enchanting Blake's new companion had become in those few minutes. It was only last month that Dad seemed shocked by the bad reception and little selection on the old tube telly. A gradually appearing picture never seemed to bother him before, and neither did that annoying high-pitched noise it emitted that disturbed the cat. Of course, Wil couldn't forget that it was *he* who argued with Dad over there being no point in getting the 4K replacement, not when internet, laptops and handheld devices were all the family ever used for entertainment anyway. But having seen her, having experienced Sonya... sprawled there along the top of the entire sideboard like a shameless lounge singer atop a piano, luring you into an escapist's paradise.... And having noticed her glossy frame when he stood at the kettle yesterday morning, and saw the panorama of the open-plan downstairs reflected across her dimensions.... Again, he let out a wry sigh.

Without thinking, he whizzed through a dozen or so channels and started noticing how obvious contact lenses had become in actors' eyes. Then... how clumpy mascara was even on superstars, and that their faces all had strange lumps and dimples. Even the excessive layers of movie make-up couldn't hide those facelift scars. Not from 4K resolution.

Just then, Wil stopped at a sweaty, out-of-breath televangelist drawling into a microphone. The mesmerised crowd waved their arms side-to-side to a lulling chant and the camera focused on a mousy-faced woman emerging from the back row, limping down the centre aisle to the stage at the front. Flushed and panting, she quickly joined the queue of people apparently waiting to fall over like dominoes.

Wil felt his distaste already justified as the camera panned and showed disturbing images of the elderly falling while onlookers held bewildered children. Only, the miracle madness knew no bounds as a 1-800 number suddenly flashed on the screen, urging viewers to call and be healed at home—unless you were outside the Continental United States (miracles in that case could *only* be attained from the website). As Wil smirked wearily, grateful he lived in England, a banner slid across the screen, making it clear which miracles viewers were entitled to, based on their donation: *Illness Anointing... Addiction Release... Grief Relief... Wealth Blessing.... $100.*

Just turn over, he told himself, raising the remote to the screen.

An abrupt shock wave from the front of the queue suddenly pushed the flushed woman off balance and into a railing, directing Wil's wrist back to his knee. Briefly unsettled, she reclaimed her place on the steps and regained her desperate, hopeful expression. It was enough to make him feel a little disgusted with himself for watching, and he even tried looking away, spotting the sooty residue on the wall at the far end of the sideboard that remained of the unnamed telly he could turn away from at the slightest impulse. *Not so with Sonya*, he concluded ruefully, managing only a second or two before sliding his eyes with cynical anticipation back to the woman.

Something about Dad's new toy was beginning to bother Wil as he took into account his viewing experience of the last fifteen minutes. Somehow, it had managed to display both illusion and reality at the same time. Like watching a magic show *without* the sleight of hand, cool misdirection and clever suggestion. In *this* show, the magician's box with hidden compartments… it was *just a box*. The mirror, an empty wooden frame. The magic re-appearance? A pathetic struggle up a step ladder through a stage trapdoor. The Ultra-high-definition resolution of a billion shades with a 14-bit colour depth, compared to the old inferior box they use to watch their movies from, had ruined the journey of the imagination for Wil, and now the crude reality behind creating the flawless impression of television was exposed in the scars, movie make-up and contact lenses he hadn't ever seen before. It was too much information: the illusion revealed. There was, however, something about Dad's splurge and HD Wil dared to like though, seeing the truth maybe. Clearly. But there was an ugliness about it he wished he hadn't seen.

The heal-frenzied man gave hopeful words to a palliative cancer patient. Words about a place with no pain or tears, no sun or sea or mourning. He then admitted that God would not allow him to use healing powers on the cancer, rather a blessing, which left the young man in the wheelchair looking only more desperate as they wheeled him out of the shot. The woman was next. Wil missed what her ailment was, but the dripping man palmed her forehead and sent her falling over backwards, glasses askew, into the arms of an assistant waiting behind. She quivered for a few seconds with the miraculous healing, then was led away, joyfully sobbing as the camera pulled back.

Wil too felt himself disengaging from the experience and quickly remembered the bacteria from the other channel.

'One single bacterium from a deadly strain won't kill you,' a more enthusiastic woman insisted. 'But that one divides, then *those two* divide, and so on,' she gestured with her hands. 'When population density reaches a certain level, they detect chemically that they are vast in numbers and excrete toxins in unison. But if we block their communication receptors, so they think they're the only ones, then they are completely harmless.

They can't detect their neighbours and they don't launch a united attack.' A diagram of a single-cell organism filled the screen and something about quorum sensing inhibitors....

Wil had had enough. As soon as he turned off Sonya, a strange relief settled over him. It followed him up to bed until finally, when he had closed his eyes atop his sheet and let the breeze from the sash send a chill picking its way down his spine, his mind went to that place of bliss and anguish, where Sadie sat in front of him in class, and he could watch her from a short distance, creating unlikely scenarios that might make her turn and notice him. This was a place mixed with fantasy and reality, where he could undo his wrongs and maybe muster the courage to try again in real life. This time though, he simply wished he could do Thursday over again, *without* the stunned look, because seeing her there... turning to him to put her cardigan over the chair... making eye contact, then smiling as she wafted her fragrance his way with knitted cotton and cashmere... (Yes, he noticed the label poking outwards: *Handwash only.* How he wanted to be delicate fibres, *her* delicate fibres, kneaded and wrung.... *Worn*....) ...he simply wanted to go back and smile in return. Do *something* to encourage her to turn once more.

Wil exhaled. *She'll be there tomorrow,* he told himself, swallowing hard, as if fear and apprehension could be rid of so easily. Then flopping his arm over his eyes, he kicked the duvet across his legs and wondered how he had been so impervious to matters of romance the last five years. To think of all those times he secretly pleased himself with sport and politics, dodging the sticky relationships his mates complained about. What good was any of that to him now, now when he felt wholly unprepared to even *greet* the girl who sat diagonally from him in Psychology?

Exhausted now, Wil allowed the same cool breeze that came through his window to materialise into that dreamlike classroom where he boldly assumed the seat *next* to Sadie. Here, the air swept over her body and then brushed across his, making him feel connected to her somehow, because despite his decision to sit beside her, she could not see him in these half-dreams, for there was a freedom in not being seen.

His mind lingered... the pages in her open textbook turned slowly, lifting, resisting the air with a quiver, only to fall to the other side with a strange as-though-sighing gentleness. For a time, they both sat in silence and watched until all the pages were still, and Wil entered deep sleep with the overwhelming feeling he had shared something meaningful with Sadie.

Disorientating white fog pressed in on him from all directions.

'Hello?' His voice sounded as though it had been absorbed in the padding of a soundproof room. *'Hello...?'*

But wait—

'You there!'

Oblivious.

A man and woman, maybe ten metres away, stood there in the haze. They seemed to be unaware of each other, for the man crouched slightly with his hands on his ears, and the woman stood right beside him, ignorant to this fact. Wil squinted against the bright white, desperate to see their faces, but the thick fog curled between them, obscuring their forms completely. Just then, a thinning gap allowed him to see how clearly distressed the man was. The woman however appeared calm. It seemed too that maybe her eyes were closed. Was she deaf? Deaf to the distress the man beside her was in, for he was clearly crying out, shouting even. Wil realised at that moment that he couldn't hear shouting, not across the ten metres through the fog. Unnerved by this, he looked warily over his shoulders and hurried towards the pair, only to find that despite his efforts, he made no progress whatsoever in reaching them.

Confused, he stopped.

Just then, something flashed through the fog on his left, in the corner of his eye. *Was that a lighthouse beam?*

Was he by the sea? On a cliff? Another flash came, on his right. And another, ahead. Always where he didn't expect it.

A few more sightings and he realised he had seen... *a person*. Or at least, something *human-like*, blurred, flashing by. The two ahead clearly hadn't seen it, for the man still crouched, holding his hands over his ears, and the girl, she hadn't moved at all. *But surely they saw it....*

A chill crept up Wil's neck. Sensing the bright form beside him, he twisted around to catch a glimpse of it, but it was gone.

Then... he *did* see it.

The iridescent, pale face no longer evaded Wil and instead stared intensely at him. Marbled blues, pinks and greens there in the flesh of that human-like presence were surely a trick of the light—an illusion from the misty vapour surrounding them. Only as Wil contemplated this, he knew it could not be the case, could not be possible, and he became afraid.

Just then, a deep droning pervaded the fog. The thing standing before Wil flashed away, leaving him to listen as the ominous noise came low, like the static of an amplifier, then quickly increased in volume and intensity. Within seconds, the sound waves beat against Wil's skin, making his chest feel like the inside of a drum as the droning resonated deep inside him. A strange sensation came up out of his throat and changed the pattern of his breathing, stifling it so that he seemed to fight against the vibrating waves simply to breathe. Each time he exhaled, a staccato, breathy, guttural sigh came like the call of some primal beast. The battering gradually increased, covering him... filling him, until his ears tickled and itched. Involuntarily, he found himself pressing his hands to his ears and swallowing the sound down, for it caused his uvula to tremble like an insect was loose in his mouth.

Then partially hunched and fearful, waiting for the noise to stop, Wil became aware of the radiant figure close beside him again. This time though, he got a strange impression, like the thing was trying to communicate with him, and *he* in turn was trying to do the same—like they both knew the other was there but neither would be able to do anything about it.

Lowering his elbows a little, Wil turned slowly, hoping to catch just a glimpse of the creature's legs there next to him, but in that instant, the incredible sound intensified, crumpling him, forcing him to his knees. Sound penetrated his body, whisking away at his insides, his blood, his organs, churning the buoyant contents of his stomach until it seemed he could take it no longer.

Wil closed his eyes tightly and cried out, suppressing the overwhelming urge to be sick.

An odd feeling came over him just then. Not of sickness, but more of disorientation. Like he was falling and didn't know which way was up.

All had become quiet.

Wil opened his eyes and sluggishly propped himself up on an elbow. He tasted dread as a sudden release of excess saliva filled his mouth, and quickly, he threw the duvet back and dashed for the toilet down the hall.

Chapter Two

Droning

Wil ambled back to his bedroom, imagining a colony of bacteria taking over his stomach as it had in the petri dish he watched only hours before. There was no way he could go to class now. Not at the risk of vomiting in front of Sadie.

Not looking like this either, he decided, cringing in front of the mirror. He pushed his heavy cascade of fine brown hair across his forehead. Darkened sockets made his tired blue eyes stand out like two moons veiled in the cloudy night sky. He leaned in closer to his reflection and tugged at a lower lid, inspecting the red capillaries shattered there. Disgusted, he recoiled, recognising the unusually sparse crop of stubble, noticing too that his cheeks appeared deeper, as though scooped out by a tablespoon. His cheekbones had become quite prominent, like two bewildered sentries keeping watch over the changes in his face, yet helpless to do anything. The disappointing inspection took him to his more obvious good points. Unfortunately, Cognitive Psychology provided little opportunity to highlight muscular arms and broad shoulders, especially if you arrived early to sit unnoticed in the back.

After texting Ben, Wil slunk into bed and within minutes, fatigue lured him back to the foggy dream.

The haze of brightness appeared like a dense summer fog under a beating sun, causing Wil's eyes to tear up and squint shut. There were no buildings or objects around. Disorientated, he put his arms in front, faltering to keep balance.

'Hello?' He wiped a steady stream of tears from his cheek. 'Is anyone there…?'

White noise whooshed around him, like maybe he was safely in the middle of a windy field, or high above on the unguarded roof of a skyscraper.

'Hello?' he called out again, unnerved. Only, his words sounded dampened like he was listening with his ears covered.

The peculiar nature of the fog tugged at the more conscious layers of Wil's dream state and he found himself reasoning that none of this was making any sense—that he couldn't possibly be on some rooftop—that it was all… *like a dream.*

Suddenly, with eyes watering and narrowly open, Wil spotted a blurred version of that bright human-like thing he had seen from before, only he had no memory of before. And there too, something else caught his eye. Off in the distance. A couple. The girl stood strangely still, oblivious-like, and the bloke crouched next to her with his hands over his ears.

Slightly afraid, Wil raised his voice to them. 'Hel—' But before he could finish the word, an ominous sound penetrated the air, cutting him short.

Droning.

A deafening bass ensued, just as before, only Wil could not recall it here from this dream. It itched his gums, vibrating into the very roots of his molars until he threw his palms over his ears, clenched his teeth and staggered amid the swirling fog for a way out as though for the first time.

'Please, *help me.*' His voice was a mere mumble. '*Please…!*' Again, the word sounded like it was only in his head.

The strange shape whizzed by.

'Stop! Just *stop!*'

The vibrating bass, the tormenting bright light… the strange sense of being somewhere both safe and dangerous, protected… yet on the precipice of peril however did not stop. It carried on, gaining a scary momentum around Wil as his sight, his hearing, his balance… all wildly escaped him. After a few minutes, the droning eased, giving him only brief respite from his aching teeth. But then, it started again, sounding a bit like Morse code, with quick determined beats now. Beats of five. It quickly dulled, becoming a new sound altogether. Something less painful but louder... closer... more urgent... like a hollow... beating drum.

Ben's freckly, overly-tanned face was inches away.

'I'm awake. I'm *awake!*' Wil pushed him off and rubbed his now tender shoulder. 'What are you *doing?*'

'You were *shouting*. I thought something was wrong.' Ben sat his burly frame into the window seat opposite, clearly agitated by his best friend's lack of gratitude. 'Your mum said you were asleep... I was hanging out downstairs and then I heard you shouting....'

Wil wasn't listening though. He sat up, prodding his jaw, unable to let go of the surreal, physical sensations of the dream. But when it all seemed so oddly ridiculous, he caught Ben's unpleasant glare.

'What?'

'Nothing.'

But it was something.

The silence was a little uncomfortable.

'What time is it?' Wil asked lightly.

'Four o'clock-ish.'

'*Four?*'

He turned his clock radio around. *4:08pm.*

'Four,' he absorbed, feeling robbed of a day. Feeling something else too.

Mulbryn.

Mulbryn was the place where dream after dream the magnification of his thoughts and feelings couldn't be stopped. Only when his situation changed at Mulbryn did his dreams finally follow suit. But so far, there were only two dreams in the fog he now remembered clearly. Tonight might be nothing at all. *Nothing at all.*

However.

They didn't feel like nothing. Just like last time.

'I think I'm having those dreams again,' Wil confessed, hoping that telling Ben about them might somehow purge him of their unpleasant effect on him, '...they were so real. They *felt* real, even after I woke.'

'You don't say,' Ben muttered sarcastically, scratching a ginger sideburn.

'Seriously. Two of them. One early this morning and another just now, when you woke me. They were practically the same dream twice.'

'That *is* how they work,' Ben remarked sardonically to the floor, crossing his arms.

'Well, I don't like it.' It became clear to Wil just then as he watched Ben poke the stack of MOJO magazines under the edge of the bed with a toe that his friend couldn't be less interested in hearing about the dreams.

'There was this weird alien thing,' Wil enticed, 'but it looked like light. And this horrible noise.... I forgot about that after I woke up and was sick.' The top two issues slid towards Ben's foot. Carelessly, Ben flicked them off. 'That's when I texted you,' Wil added, a bit more determined, though annoyed now.

'If you actually threw up, then you really are ill,' Ben insisted dryly. 'Just as well, class was cancelled anyway.' He hesitated, clearly wanting to say more, though maybe deciding against it. Only, he could never resist. 'Of course, you must be disappointed.' His words hung there, like wriggling bait off the end of a hook. Like an ugly little worm, wrenched and awkward for hiding the barb. Ben picked at the seam running along the outside edge of his jeans and cast a suspect glance at his rousing friend.

'I'm sorry,' Wil said indignantly, forgetting all about the dreams, 'I must be *disappointed*? What's that supposed to mean?' But he knew exactly what it meant. Ben had no idea about Sadie, so he couldn't possibly have meant her. The unwarranted accusation was about someone else.

'Is this about *Shellie* again?'

'The *whole class* saw it. You two… all *beside* yourselves.'

'I wasn't *beside* myself,' Wil spat, hating the idea of rehashing all this again. 'She said something funny... I didn't even realize it was *her* saying it!'

'Listen, I told you before, just forget it.'

'No—*I* told *you*, I'm not *interested* in Shellie,' Wil said incredulously, shaking his head. '*Yes*, she happens to sit near me in class. *Yes*, she chose to be in my group and *yes*, she looks at me in that funny way, but did it ever occur to you that I might be interested in *someone else*—or maybe the fact that *you're my best friend*… do *any* of those things enter your mind when you decide to come up here and start making accusations?' Furious, he set his jaw and exhaled, nostrils flaring. 'Honestly, don't you think I've considered the implications of going out with someone you're interested in, Ben? And in all the time we've been friends, have I *ever*?' Wil abruptly smoothed the wrinkles in the duvet over his lap as though swatting crumbs.

Ben was quiet for a minute.

'So you've… *thought* about going out with her,' he said sheepishly, 'that it would…hurt me…?'

Wil's eyelids weighed with disgust.

'You've *got* to be kidding me—*no I haven't thought about going out with her!*' Incensed, he forced himself to look at the scruffy lump on the window seat that still held the beginnings of a wounded frown. 'Not until you accused me of it! *THEN* I thought, *how ridiculous for you to even think I would think that!*'

'Is that your underhanded way of saying she's not good enough for you then? That I'm being *ridiculous* in thinking *you'd* consider her?'

Wil scoffed. 'What is *wrong* with you? Have I just said that? It has nothing to do with *Shellie*. I'm talking about *principles* here.' Leaning his head back, Wil stared in exasperation at the ceiling, then after a minute began with greater restraint. 'You know what, Ben? Don't come round here taking your frustration out on me because you're not getting anywhere with Shellie…because it's not my fault.' Waiting a beat, he presented the door using a sweeping gesture of the arm and indignantly eyed Ben's sweaty toe prints all over his MOJO magazines.

Ben shifted uncomfortably in the window. Then,

'Sorry,' he said finally, under his breath.

'*Pardon?*'

'Sorry,' he said a little louder, obviously more flustered with himself than Wil. 'You're right,' he said desperately, leaning his head against the alcove. 'I'm just frustrated with this thing with Shellie. It's not about you. I need to let it out on the field or something….'

'*Something,*' Wil retorted. 'You just do that.'

'Sorry,' Ben repeated with a self-loathing his best friend could identify with. '…I know you'd never steal my interest… it's just I'm always the second choice. I make a move and… they think it's a way to you. *Let's just be friends…*' he imitated. 'Do you know how *old* that gets?' Of course, Wil did. It was about as old as all the times he was accused of making these situations happen. About as old as the sorrys that followed them.

'I know this is nothing new,' Wil tried to make it sound different from the times before, 'but whenever you've told me that you like someone, I've done whatever you've asked when you thought it would help. And I'm not reminding you of this because I've got a problem with it—I don't, but I disappear… I invent a girlfriend… I lie… because we never betray interests, and I never want you to think that I would, that I would betray you.'

21

'I know....' Ben accepted with a tired smile. He sat there for a minute, looking like he was daydreaming. 'Remember Samantha?'

Wil rolled his eyes. Suggesting that you might be gay to ward off a girl no doubt had been stupid. At the least, mean.

'Seriously though,' Ben huffed, 'that's just it. Every time it gets to the point that you have to do *that*—to set a boundary or just say you're not interested—they lose all interest in me. If you could call it that,' he said glumly, fiddling with his hand. 'I'm not saying it's your fault, Wil. I mean it's silly really.' He shook his head and shrugged. 'Why would I want to be with someone who doesn't want to be with me in the first place?'

'It's not silly, Ben. You're just trusting that they're being honest with you, and they haven't been. No wonder you second-guess everyone's motives.... And for the record, Shellie seems nice. I don't have anything against her, but I'm definitely not interested in her, all right?'

That familiar truce-pause sat between them for a few seconds.

'Now, do you want to hear about my dreams or what?'

'Go on then, with your stupid dream.'

'*Dreams*,' Wil enunciated, emphasizing the plural.

'I don't think you've got a sleep condition,' Ben said simply afterwards. 'More like a virus or something. I don't mean to sound rude, but you do look a bit on the rough side, and if you were sick earlier....' He scooted his bum towards the wall, giving himself greater distance from his friend, apparently just realising a potential contagion. 'And that Mulbryn stuff was brought on by stress,' he recalled. 'You're not stressed are you?' Wil didn't think he was. 'Yeah, see? You obviously needed the rest and you probably just need to let whatever you're trying to fight work its way out of your system.'

One

Wil wandered along his usual thinking-circuit after Ben's brief visit, taking the path along the southern ridge of fields on the outskirts of the village, then back down alongside the stream. Whatever took hold of him in the morning, it had completely gone, because he felt fine. And knowing class had been cancelled, that it wasn't his own decision that kept him from seeing Sadie today, allowed him to focus his thoughts on her again and eventually forget about the dreams altogether.

He headed back towards the dense middle of the village where stone cottages, grassy verges and oaks lined the narrow, gravelled roads. The lowering sun threw brilliant linear arms between the branches and Wil heard young children laughing in back rooms, trampolines creaking behind walls and fences, pensioners clipping, cutting and clearing their gardens, a farewell-to-summer tidy. He decided to take the shortcut home.

Wil turned up Wide Way, the only street in the centre of Darlingdon wide enough to accommodate a footpath either side of it. While the street itself was sizable, convenient for those coming and going to the village school, church or pub, the Georgian terraces hemmed in along its stretch were so narrow and compact that only widows and young singles inhabited them. This contrast was not the only that struck Wil each time he walked this way. The quirky thatched cottages, grass-banked stream and unpaved lanes that made up the picturesque middle of the village suddenly disappeared down

Wide Way and made you feel like you weren't in Darlingdon anymore. Wil didn't mind this so much because he knew that in a few minutes' time, the roads, wide or narrow, would all be behind him.

He went down a concealed alleyway after the first terrace on the left, strolled between two withering gardens and came to a 'T' in the path where a high stone perimeter wall towered above him. It ran the entire length of Wide Way behind the terraces.

Wil stood for a moment in its cool shadow. Then, a few doors down to his right, the dull spray of a hose into the hollow of a watering can hurried him to the left, along the wall. He carried on down the dirt path deeply marked by wheel barrow and bicycle tires from muddy days, on through the overgrowth of bramble and nettle... and found the gate. It was a gate one could easily overlook, steadying their gait amid the thorny vines encroaching the path, or the muddy troughs and stony mounds, but if you caught it in the corner of your eye, you most certainly would do a double-take.

The intricate detail carved into the thick oak planks epitomized everything that was beautiful and charming about Darlingdon. A wildly sinuous tree, taller than Wil, set chiselled into the grain, and out of its contours came shrunken natural knots, cleverly left to look like severed boughs. And flowers and honeybees, scrolling vines and delicate butterflies, they adorned the empty spaces. Though their edges were rounded now, given over to the changing seasons of at least 200 years, their mossy protrusions and swelled crevices in the winter and spring... and porous texture that paled and split with ease in balmy summers... it made the beautiful garden scene look as though it too had a life of its own, changing with every new season. Not only did Wil feel the privilege of seeing such a gate, he secretly pleased himself every time he used it. As far as he knew, he was the only one who did.

He turned the handle, an iron ring made to look like a vine, and pushed it open until the sagging wisteria growing along the top of the wall prevented him from opening it any further. Ducking under the canopy, he slipped through the gap sideways and closed the gate behind him.

From under the foliage, the manicured lawn of The Common Garden sprawled away from Wil and he emerged from the greenery enticed by the magnificence of the Georgian manor house as it dazzled with the warm glow of sunset in the excess of windows on the upper floors, and gilded insects flashed about over the pathways like petering sparks. Every time he came this way, he imagined this house, in its entirety, his. Then, of course, he looked down at the geometrical paths of gravel laid out, leading off in three directions, and was reminded of how such a beautiful place had been changed for modern living.

Three families now lived at The Manor House and it was so cleverly divided up that the Stokes never even saw the other inhabitants outside common spaces such as these. Everyone shared the main drive, flanked by an ailing apple orchard and parked in the gravelled area at the front. They each had their own private entrance, marked by evergreen hedges or stone walls supporting rose and clematis, and they disappeared behind these to their respective quarters (or thirds in their case). Each enjoyed their own small private garden with little gates that led to this: The Common Garden. Sadly, no one ever seemed to come here. It was nothing grand but gave the impression that maybe it once had been. Shaped conifers dotted the far end of the lawn near the house, paths converged in the middle where a neglected stone fountain bred generations of mosquitos. The gathered ruins of a Gothic folly stood in a patch of uncut grass to the right of Wil and though it all seemed a little sad, it made it that much easier to believe it was all his.

Wil crunched slowly along the path, imagining again the old Lord of the manor turning in his grave if he could see what had become of his estate, its vast grounds sold off and developed, cutting it off from the immediate countryside. And maybe more disturbingly, its halls and staircases stopped up with false walls, like arteries, blocked, ending an existence that had become outdated and impractical. The life the manor once led had been swallowed up by progress and consumed by the defunct nature of the passing of time. Whatever it had been built for, it was now only a skeleton of that. Bones.

Wil kicked a little stone off the grass and onto the path. Despite its demise, he loved the building, the enclosed Common Garden, the fragmented use of the house and the history that went along with all of it. The fact that it could be scavenged to suit the needs of modern living gave him a little hope that it wouldn't just cease to exist one day. He looked up to the glowing sashes feeling it was all a shame and a marvel at the same time.

At the end of the path, to the West, Wil went through the private garden gate and entered what used to be the main hall through the French doors along the terrace. This part of the manor was now a vast lounge, dining and kitchen space with the only other main ground floor room Mum's favourite: a sizable pantry off the kitchen. She spent hours in there, folding laundry on the long pine table, unpacking groceries and hiding them away in the ceiling-to-floor cupboards that lined the entire west wall. Everything went in them, from dry goods to household supplies, and despite telling everyone where they could find things, Mum seemed to be the only one who really knew where any of it was. Wil often thought standing in front of those 36 doors to find a new razor or deodorant was actually like playing a round of *Deal or No Deal*. When she beckoned him in there last month, he assumed she had re-arranged things again and simply wanted to show him where to find the essentials. Instead, she proudly pointed out replacement knobs with little creatures on and a corresponding laminated card: '*A list,*' she said, '*just in case. So now when you ask me, Mum, where's more printer paper... I can say, check the woodlouse cupboard.*' She pointed to the enamelled knob with the grey crustacean. '*And if I'm not here, you've got this.*' She snagged the card's ribbon on a nail nearby.

'*That still won't stop me from asking, you know.*' Wil smiled a little, recalling his words as he closed the French doors behind him.

'*You can ask as much as you want—it's the having to come and find it for you that I'm trying to avoid.*'

She was due home any minute now with another load to store away, Wil felt certain, slipping off his shoes. The floor was still warm under his feet and he realised he had just missed that time of day when the evening sun turned the honey-coloured flagstones across the lounge and kitchen a glowing gold. In the hour he was gone, the grids of light slanting through the windows had moved up the room and now cut the main hall in two, dividing it into darkness and light.

Wil went over and sat down in front of Sonya, faintly aware of the impression she left him in the early hours. Strangely, in the light of day, none of it really mattered now.

He grabbed the remote.

'*Ugh...*' he recoiled. Blood-encrusted stitches, puss, and poorly healed skin flaps filled the screen. The battered and swollen faces of celebrity before-and-afters then featured. 'Why do people cut their faces like that?'

'I didn't think you knew I was here...' a voice from behind him spoke with surprise.

Chapter Four

Annie

Wil took a second to register the voice then slowly looked over the back of the couch in the direction of the pantry. Though it was dark, he could still make out the silhouette of Annie, his sister's best friend, scribbling away on a sketch pad.

'Where's Steph?' he asked, irritated. The fact that she was there and he hadn't known was easily hidden in his annoyed default tone toward her.

'She's still at the studio.' Annie spoke with a coolness that defied her age.

'Why are you here then?'

'I twisted my ankle. She gave me the key to wait here until I could get a ride home.'

You twisted your ankle but walked all this way...? Wil rolled his eyes and turned his back on her.

An uncomfortable heaviness came into the room just then, reminding him of why he hated being alone with Annie. At 10, she made outrageous claims about bumping into famous people no one could verify—not even her own family. At 12, she got away with saying she had a 16-year-old boyfriend, but only because no one ever *saw* this Murphy. *No one.* In fact, her family decided he must have been Charlie, her imaginary childhood friend: *all grown up and nowhere to be seen.* Of course, everyone forgot about him until Annie became predictably awkward at the going-away party and declared herself pregnant at the age of 13:

'*Well, most of you remember Murphy,*' she explained, delighted, scooping dip with a tortilla chip as her mother stood there horrified.

Murphy? Wil thought to himself at the foot of the stairs as the room became uncomfortably quiet and fidgety. *We remember you talking about him, but none of us has actually ever* seen *him!*

'*...Murphy and I didn't want the Stokes to find out second hand... you know, while they were in London.*'

How considerate, so instead, you decided to crash their going away party with this load of rubbish! Wil folded his arms angrily on the couch, stilling wishing he had said those words aloud.

'*Two years is a long time and they'd get quite a surprise when they got back....*' The gloating, crazed look on Annie's face when Steph stormed off to her room seconds later burned in his mind, for his sister clearly only learned of the pregnancy that night, right along with everyone else. Steph was devastated at the thought of Dad's job dragging them off to London for two years while her closest friend was turning into a parent. She didn't even think to question Annie's honesty. Wil thought of the spate of late nights afterwards, when he walked down the hall past Steph's room and heard mum soothing her at all hours over the distressing issue of teenage pregnancy. But Annie didn't seem bothered. She was characteristically elated at the effect her news had on people, seemingly oblivious to scepticism and disappointment. Right up until they left, Annie was getting *twinges* in her stomach. It wasn't long after that that her mum had had enough. She took Annie down to the GP and got her to take a blood test. No one but Steph was surprised to find it had all been a ruse—the whole lot, including Murphy. Who knows what Selena had to do to get the truth out of her.

The memory of all that... just over three years ago... it caused Wil to seethe discreetly just now as Annie frantically abraded the tip of her charcoal pencil against the paper in the dark.

'Do you have to be so loud?' he huffed over his shoulder at her.

'Why, am I *bothering* you?'

'Never mind,' he said, shaking his head a little.

It occurred to him that he could just go to his room. Then again, she was known to follow him up there and make him uncomfortable, standing in his doorway chatting about nothing. He turned over to the news channel and dropped the remote in his lap.

'Would you be still?' she asked, making out like she was erasing a mistake, swiping her pad.

Wil clenched his teeth, despising the idea that he was the subject of one of her little drawings.

'I never did show you that charcoal one I did of you,' she said, sounding deep in thought.

'*Really?*' he pretended to care. 'I'm not interested.'

'Everyone's interested.'

'Have you called your mum to come and get you?'

'She's on her way…. Why? Are you trying to get rid of me?'

He turned around and slung his arm over the back of the couch, confrontational. '*What do you think?*'

'You'd be shocked at what I think,' she warned, scribbling away. 'Unless, of course you've already been inside my head and now you're just being coy.' She stopped herself and glared at him from under her black, fine eyebrows like she was trying to catch him out on something. 'I can't seem to get inside yours,' she said, narrowing in on him before returning to her sketch.

What's that supposed to mean? Wil rolled his eyes and backed down. It wasn't worth it. He turned to the telly again, but wasn't actually watching because his mind was suddenly dumped with all the things that annoyed him about Annie. From all those silly little lies that started back in primary school and hinted at the person who sat behind him in the pantry, annoying him… *for what? Attention?* From what he knew of Annie, she could never have enough.

Flash mobs suddenly came to mind.

Just before Wil and his family came back last summer, Ben sent frequent texts about Annie being up to her old tricks. The rumour was she had become obsessed with flash mobs. At first, Ben's sister Zara said she spotted Annie in the mall at Cribbs Causeway singing *The Sound of Music* at the entrance to John Lewis. And not just singing respectably, as one would imagine. Then more rumours alleged she made trips up to London, showing up on the tube, at station platforms and railway stations, singing her heart out. Again, nothing complimentary. Wil thought people were just being mean, exaggerating on social media, but then photos and video clips started appearing. His initial reaction was to feel sorry for Annie, knowing she picked some moment, climbed a flight of stairs and started singing as loud as she could as passers-by hoped they were witnessing the beginnings of a massive professional performance. Heads surely looked around… suspecting others nearby… waiting for someone else to carry the tune…. But no, it was just Annie. She had to be oblivious to the reaction of those around her to have carried on for the length of time in those clips. To imagine, the disappointed looks of disgruntled commuters—and in Cribbs Causeway's case—annoyed shopkeepers and confused security guards. And to do it over and over again, for six months, meant she didn't even care. Yes, his initial reaction was to feel sorry for her, but it quickly moved from that to disgust. He had no patience for Annie when they returned to Somerset. If he didn't know better, she tried to make them all enemies before they even got back. Of course, Steph couldn't be deterred, despite the number of times she was upset because of some insensitive thing Annie did, or didn't do. She'd spend the night crying her eyes out in her bedroom, then emerge the next day certain of a thing or two about Annie, modifying her expectations and just trudge on. Like a true friend.

'Can you change over?' Annie asked plainly from the other room, startling Wil from his thoughts.

'What do you want to watch?'

'Anything but this. It's just speculation now.'

He flicked to the next channel.

'My favourite,' she said sarcastically. 'Antiques.'

'You said *anything but the news….*'

'No, I didn't.'

He hated it when she did this. 'You said anything but *this*, and *this* was the news.'

Annie zipped the pad and pencil box away in her bag and came over and sat down on Blake, measuring Wil up. 'So we're clear, you could have turned it to another news channel and I wouldn't have minded. And no need to be defensive,' she said crossing her legs slowly, 'I did say antiques were my favourite.'

Wil glared at her knowing full well that they weren't and suddenly noticed the length of the outside of her thigh exposed to him. 'Well, that may have been what actually came from your mouth,' he acknowledged, frustrated, wishing she hadn't seen him looking at her legs, 'but I know all about this little thing you do… twist words so you can get off on a technicality. I'm not an idiot, Annie.'

'You're the only one here mentioning idiots,' she said dismissively as she ran her fingers along the hem of her skirt, straightening it, though not pulling it down to cover her legs. She checked to see if Wil's eyes were wandering, but they weren't. Instead, he was glaring right at her, unprovoked by her suggestive gaze.

'You know what? I'm not bothered,' he decided contemptuously as he grabbed the remote and tossed it beside her in the chair, ruffling her. 'I'm getting a drink.'

He didn't dare go back to the sofa and instead took his glass of water to the French doors, just the other side of the large built-in bookcase dividing the dining area from the lounge space. Standing here meant he didn't have to look at Annie, but could have a general idea of where she was until someone came home. Predictably unpredictable, and with that look she just gave him in the chair, he knew it was better to keep his distance because she had a way of saying things without saying them... and who knows what she'd say after half an hour of being alone in the house with him—in the same room even. Wil closed his eyes tightly and swallowed his mouthful hard. She was 16, but he was 18. He wished again that she hadn't seen him looking at her leg.

C'mon Mum... hurry home.

Wil's mind churned with the Annie-things that affronted him. As he looked out onto the garden, he suddenly thought of Annie's Great Aunt Margaret, living in that idyllic country cottage in Dorset somewhere, knitting happily in her tartan wingback chair. Annie once produced a picture of her relative, sitting petite and erect, skeins on her lap, posing with needles jabbed into the loops of an emerging scarf, giving the camera that same perverse coy smile that Annie had just given him. It was neither genuine nor pleasant, rather, sickly sweet. Evil sweet. The image stuck in Wil's head like a protruding thorn and every now and again, he'd snag it, like now, and it created that unbearable prickle that made him see a formidable gene passing through Annie's family. They seemed a strange bunch, the lot of them, even the kindlier ones, like Great Aunt Margaret, who would offer to keep Annie a few weeks every summer. That is, until last summer.

Wil rolled his eyes the other side of the bookcase, disliking the fact that Annie's great aunt just happened to be too old to have her niece the summer he and his family returned from London. He took another gulp from his glass and watched two sparrows flap around in the bird bath by the shed. As far as he was concerned, Annie was a liar and that was enough to remind him that she was an attention-seeking danger. And as he stood there thinking of good old Steph, honest and trusting, giving away the house key and sending her hobbling friend down the road to rest a poorly ankle, his sarcastic inner monologue came back to the same place whenever he thought through the annoyances of Annie:

Why is Steph still her friend?

Anytime he saw his sister next to Annie for the first time in a while, he wondered what she needed, or was getting out of their friendship that she couldn't get out of someone else with fewer whims and more sense.

Wil wished London had been that severing event, especially with Ben's sister Zara taking Steph's place for awhile there, but no. They were all back, and so was Annie. Right where she left off.

Annie turned off the telly the other side of the bookcase just as Wil began to wonder what sleight she was planning next. The flash mob fetish was clearly behind her now, but there was always something. The art of ambiguity. Pretend pregnancy. Imaginary boyfriends. He couldn't be sure what she was up to this season because it wasn't obvious like before. Not yet, at least. That mysterious, controlled, guess-what-I'm-thinking air she carried that blew out the window the minute she became annoyed didn't fool him. Last summer, she started dressing in vintage tailored clothes and chopped her long dark brown hair into a blunt bob with a thick fringe cut a little too short over her eyebrows. A drastic measure to welcome old acquaintances. As far as Wil was concerned, it was her attempt at making it *all about her* again. She kept the look. Seeing her shadow just then move across the floor the other side there, Wil couldn't decide if this prolonged masquerade was yet another phase, making Annie even more dangerous in trying to appear older than she was, or if it was the honest beginning of her outgrowing those rebellious eccentricities. Either way, he didn't like it lurking around in the shadows of his pantry or suddenly making the room silent.

'Shouldn't you be putting ice on your ankle or something?' he asked her, intensely annoyed now.

'I have.'

Of course you did. 'When's Steph getting back?'

'Any minute now,' she said sweetly, snidely.

Just then, they heard the key in the lock. Wil felt a wave of relief pushing his shoulders down already. Steph and Mum came in with groceries and cheerfulness, whisked Annie away straight through to the other room to put food into cupboards while chattering about the fall in the dance lesson and what to have for dinner.

Chapter Five

Pearls

'Hel-*loooo...*' a forced-happy voice piped down the hall from the front door. It was Selena Bodhan. Come to collect her daughter. Well after dinner time, of course.

Her waif-like frame slunk through the archway and already the clash between her mannerisms and her appearance grated on Wil. He scrutinised everything about her for some clue as to why Annie was the way she was. With her high heels, power-dressing trouser suit, creasing layers of make-up and that bouffant hairstyle pinned up at the back, she gave the impression that she was high maintenance. While she tried to be light and airy, pleasant, her face strained as though she smelled something foul and hoped to conceal it—that maybe it was coming from her.

'So sorry I'm late, Liz,' she gushed, 'I didn't get your text until after work... and the signal there's *awful.*'

Selena made a gangly, lazy movement of her arms and shoulders that reminded Wil of an exasperated child. He imagined this infantile body language used in an ugly exchange with Annie, only Selena's face didn't display the leering happiness he saw just then across the room there.

'And I see you fed her.... What would I do without you, Liz?' Throwing her head back as though the answer wasn't worth contemplating, she added, 'You're like a second mum to my little Annie...' and hurried her daughter to gather her things with silent nods and a talon that prodded the air, pointing to bags and clothing.

Annie responded promptly as her mother inched back under the archway.

'It's not a problem,' Mum assured, laying a cardigan over Annie's holdall full of dance gear. 'She's no trouble. Let's just hope that ankle's not going to cause any problems for the routines coming up.'

'I'm sure it'll be fine,' Mrs Bodhan said dismissively.

Annie mumbled something to Steph, loaded herself up and thanked Mum on her way down the hall.

'Lovely, then,' Selena declared, fiddling with her keys and catching a glimpse of Annie already out the door. 'Well, it was nice seeing everyone. Briefly.' She gave a more intense smelling smile. 'Thanks again!' And they were gone.

Wil closed his eyes slowly, the Annie-creeps already subsiding, and retreated upstairs for the night.

The chaotic state of his room reminded him that he hadn't found his old journal and the wake of the weekend search left clothes everywhere: books on the floor, baskets turned out into merging piles of trinkets, sports gear scattered in amongst childhood memorabilia.

Tidying, he thought of Steph, how they used to be inseparable once, but now... his dislike for Annie made it difficult for her to even speak to him when the three of them were in the same room.

Standing there with a hanger dangling off the crook of his finger and a pile of shirts draped over his arm, it occurred to Wil that if he were to have any sort of relationship with his sister he'd have to tolerate her best friend. Because if he didn't, all he was really doing was just abandoning her to Annie.

Resolved of this, Wil shoved the remaining hangers into the shoulders of the last three shirts, stuffed them into the old compactum wardrobe and was stopped halfway through compressing it all along the rod by another thought:

What if I have another one of those dreams tonight? And what if this time it seems more real, like the Mulbryn ones?

'They're just dreams,' he quickly mumbled, sidestepping piles to the opposite side of the room. He brushed pens off his desk into the open drawer and pushed the loose darts scattered there deeply into the cork target hanging from his bedroom door. Without thinking, he tilted his head and stared at the bull's eye, feeling oddly positive about the dreams. Vivid dreams were interesting, he determined. Motivating. Another odd feeling percolated, something like déjà vu, for as Wil squared with the target there in front of him, the anticipation of the dreams felt vaguely significant, yet completely trivial.

A compressing fidgetiness took over him. He was certain now those dreams would come again. This was the same peculiar feeling that stayed with him every disturbing night for nearly six months, until one day, like a profound finale, or redemption of a sort, everything finally stopped.

As Wil kicked the rugby ball into the corner, he remembered what Ben said about stress bringing the dreams on before. Presently, the only stress that truly drove him to the point of panic... was Sadie. Failed attempts at talking to her. But if the dreams were some sort of measuring stick to show just how much of an effect she had on him,

'Then dream away...' he decided under his breath.

By the time Wil finished his room and got into bed, he did truly appreciate the imposition of the dreams, and his adamance conjured that familiar image of Sadie, this time alone on a bench. In the park. A rush of wind stroked and flicked at her. The trees moved. Dried leaves, clumsy and disorientated, rambled this way and that. And just so, words bumbled around in Wil's head. He imagined himself sitting there with her and at the same time, he imagined that she could not see him—that she thought herself alone. But he is there, she just doesn't know it. He cannot tell her he is there because he hasn't the courage to speak.

Loathing himself yet again, the lines across Wil's forehead deepened.

Words appeared all of a sudden behind his eyelids, gleaming out of the blackness as he lay there. They stung a little as they came, like hot tears, mocking the frustration of this daydream. The frustration of all his daydreams. He was always there like a fly on the wall, too small and insignificant to play a speaking part. As the words came to him, he considered them in a phrase but they were trite, awkward or too contrived. None made it to his lips and so he sat beside the Sadie of his daydream, invisible.

She suddenly looked over her shoulder in disgust, right on cue, as if to remind him that even thinking words provoked her offense. She stared this time, in his direction, in complete and utter disbelief, but he knew she could not see him because he chose not to be seen—though when she did this, it always felt like she was looking right at him. This was where he held his breath and shrivelled up inside like a snail on the hot pavement. His mind instantly emptied and all those words disappeared. Sadie's expression became vacant too, as if she were looking for something that wasn't there, or maybe she had forgotten something.

The Sadie on the bench thwarted him every time from showing his face and he could rely on her to strip him of hope and courage. She seemed to know his worst fears yet didn't mind wounding even the ghost of him.

When the wind calmed and the bench dimmed to nothing, all she left him in these pathetic fantasies was alone, exasperated and discouraged for having said nothing. This wounded feeling however healed quickly. As quickly as Wil could vindicate himself with the words he meant to say when invisible and mute.

Just as he had hoped, the beginnings of a poem took shape in his mind. Everything she provoked and stole from him— exasperation and discouragement... hope and courage—they justified one another. Opposed, yet equal. These possessed Wil until winding together, binding tightly like the unique strands in a rigid cord, he could not tell one from the other anymore, couldn't *feel* one from the other anymore.

Images came to mind like pearls just then, glossed and lovely in their singularity. The hypnotic leaves blowing... Sadie's exquisite form waiting there on the bench... her vacant expression, so inviting... each picture distinct, encapsulating a gritty core, redeemed the contrary strands and all they represented so that Wil now felt their meaning afresh.

Finally, after a few moments, it all came together. That taut cord pushed itself through every aspect of the disappointing daydream... piercing the middle of every emotive image... until there came a beautiful, gleaming composition.

Quickly, he turned on the light, pulled his journal from the drawer next to his bed and held it over his chest. Sadie sitting there on the bench burned against the insides of his eyelids one last time. After a minute he rolled over onto his stomach and began.

September 27
When words are but breath
Like wind and air
You feel it
Yet nothing's there
Feel my silence

36

Eloquence hiding
Toiling to tell you
Love residing.
—Thoughts of Sadie. One day I will speak to you.

Wil read the words over and over again, satisfied. He took great care to write when he was inspired, avoiding it at all cost when he was not; mediocre scratch never took him to that same place twice. He grew to love the cryptic nature of these short succinct poems, adopting the style more recently, just before they left for London. He wished now that he had always used it, especially back when his little sister threatened to find his journal and share it with her friends after he started secondary school. While he knew now she never would have actually done it, he felt certain the suggestion of such an invasion dramatically limited his candour. The restraint in some of those earlier prosaic entries... the ambiguity... presented nearly lies.

Wil thought once more of where his old journal might be, only to be grateful *this one* hadn't been lost. He never had to defend the content of his compressed confessions before. However, defending the practice of poetry-writing itself... well, there was only the one time:

'*What's this?*' Ben teased, swivelling in the desk chair, nonchalantly flicking through the notebook on the desk.

'*My journal, thanks.*' Wil remembered snapping it up.

'*Sorry,*' Ben said snootily, sniggering away.

'*What?*'

'*Nothing.*' Five seconds later, '*I didn't know you write* poetry,' he mocked.

'*You can sit over there and poke fun,*' Wil began calmly, '*but lots of blokes do it. Men have been writing poetry for thousands of years. Think about it. The Odyssey—an entire book. The epic poem Beowulf.*' The argument Wil had developed in his head over the months, for a moment just like this, came tumbling out of him. '*Seriously Ben, just to name a few, there's William Byrd...Thomas Morley, from the Renaissance. Thomas Gray and Robert Burns from the Restoration. Then Byron... Keats... Shelley... T.S. Eliot—D.H. Lawrence.... And I've only mentioned a few... and can you even imagine a world without Shakespeare?*' He turned to his freckled friend questioningly. '*Can you?*'

Ben appeared slightly impressed. '*I'm not saying men didn't write* poetry. *I'm just saying it's a bit weird. Maybe a bit girlie.'* But he didn't seem sure of himself. Then swinging his knees side-to-side and clicking the end of a pen he found off the desk, *'It's like heels,'* he decided. *'Men used to wear high heels… it was the fashion.'*

'Yeah—and they still do! Are you saying they're not men?'

'No…I mean… yes. …NO!' he insisted, confused. *'What I mean is, they're not what I'd call… manly men.'*

'Well, manly men still write poetry today, Ben. Think about all the rap artists. Poetry is no different from music lyrics. You wouldn't think the Beatles less manly—or Drake… or Ed Sheeran, would you?' Wil waited a beat, *'Surely, you're not saying making words rhyme is a woman's art?'*

'Okay…' Ben mumbled, exasperated, *'so you write poetry…'* as if it were no big deal.

Wil figured that if he could convince Ben it was okay, he cared less about what others thought after that. He stoked this resolve at the thought again of his misplaced journal and surprisingly wasn't too bothered if Steph borrowed it. Or Mum. Not that he believed they would.

Annie?

He sighed, considering the fact that she had been alone here in the house before he found her in the pantry, an occurrence that wasn't uncommon these days. *Would she be that bold and invasive?* Perhaps that's why he wanted to find the thing, because he couldn't actually remember now why he had been looking for it in the first place. Wherever it was, he felt almost certain it couldn't be far. He just had to look in the right place.

Wil closed his notebook and put it back into the side table. With the light out, he lay there thinking of those words regarding Sadie, thinking of how silly he had been to worry about any dream, for he always woke in the end, and it wasn't long before he was there in the fog, just as before.

Chapter Six

Spiralling

Wil stood there, uncertain. The white was like a vise, keeping him from straying too far—or anywhere for that matter—and he could easily imagine a huge hole a step away in front of him, or a drop hundreds of metres down either side. If he took the wrong step, he would surely wake. *That wouldn't be bad, would it?*

A peculiar feeling came over him just then. It was like he wasn't properly there in the fog anymore. In fact, he began to sense the loosening grip of fortitude as consciousness and unconsciousness struggled to change shifts... like his eyes were in this dream, but his mind wasn't... and both wrestled with each other in the haze until one gave way. Wil's impression of reality became diluted, and finally, he made one last effort to reclaim what little conscious thought had emptied from his mind, like involuntarily patting himself down and digging in his pockets for a set of keys he knew should be there, but weren't. *They had to be somewhere....* *Where...?*

Where am I...? He looked around, bewildered. That dismissive resolve he thought he could bring into the dream, it left him completely now and fear filled its place... fear of some unknown... yet known thing.

Expecting something to surprise him at any moment, he adopted a defensive stance, moving his eyes to the far right and left, surveying his deserted surroundings, hearing the absence of sound flow densely around him like the sigh of a motorway far off in the distance.

Suddenly, there in front of him, maybe ten metres or so, two darkened figures appeared. *The couple.* The bloke stood beside the girl but then doubled over with his hands to his ears and it was then that a panicky urge to assemble with them took over Wil. Quickly, he kicked away the billowing swirl of white winding around his legs like an affectionate feline, convinced it had something to do with the man's difficulty. Then sliding each foot steadily in front of him, he noticed the black shine of asphalt beside his heel. The glossy flecks of quartz-like material was a deep black, like a freshly laid out road.

'Hello there!' He said this more to the woman than to the man, for the man now appeared only as a head and shoulders in the thickening fog. '*Hello?*' he called out again, ten or so steps away. But she didn't even flinch, and *he*… well, *he* looked like he was looking desperately for something on the ground, yet found it so distressing in the fog that he squeezed his head between his hands in despair of it. The blonde, with her eyes strangely closed, just stood there, completely oblivious as he came within arm's reach.

Wil studied her, trying to understand the dynamic. She had a peaceful arrogance, despite the loud white noise whooshing around them, while her partner was entrenched in discomfort. She looked 25 maybe, with posture erect, ready for something. She wore a white T-shirt and jeans that seemed overly casual for her long coiffed hair. It occurred to Wil that maybe she wasn't real. Maybe she was a mannequin or a prop person. He leaned even closer to her face, inspecting its translucence, only to fear she might pop open her eyes and reveal a horrifying pair of white marble-like orbs. Quickly, he withdrew from her.

The man caught Wil's attention with renewed whimpering and writhing. His hands, pressed firmly over his ears, were no apparent comfort.

'Are you all right?' Wil got no response as the man's elbows quivered from squeezing his ears so tightly. 'Are you okay?' This time, Wil tapped on that jerking, squirming shoulder. The stranger immediately looked up with relief.

'Turn it off!' his beleaguered voice rasped.

A quizzical expression came over both of them.

'Go on…' the man urged. '*Please*, turn it off…!' But Wil was obviously confused. They exchanged equally frustrated expressions and the man croaked finally, 'Just *do it,* Wilden…!'

'Do *what?* Turn off what?' Wil shrugged with an effort to understand, but it was no use. Already, he could see the disappointed and helpless form curling back into itself, retreating to its misery.

'It's too loud... *too loud...*' the man enunciated silently to himself, grimacing as the fog came into, and out of his mouth. It swirled around him indiscriminately as though unaffected by anything he felt, yet seemed to somehow contribute to, or cause his pain.

'You *can* stop it, Wilden...'

But there was nothing to stop. *And how do you know my name?*

Just then, that poor crumpled figure became an unexpected reference point. A landmark. Like coordinates on a map Wil apprehensively watched the cupping of the ears, the tensed muscles along the neck, shoulders... that fighting against something deep inside the head.

A noise.

A noise Wil himself could imagine. Or *felt*... once before.

Comprehending the man's affliction entirely, Wil took a guarded step away from him and scanned the white around. A leaden certainty sunk to his middle as the fear of that most terrible noise reverberated into his memory. It had to be on its way now... to wrench him in half, right to his very core! Just like last time....

Last time.

How had he forgotten?

Staring at the anguished stranger, Wil suddenly saw himself at an imprecise point in the recent past, in that very state, writhing and helpless. Mentally, he retraced his steps between then and now, unable to extract even one thought that filled the space between the two dream experiences. All he could do was imagine himself *there...* and *here*. Life didn't seem to exist outside these two points.

Confounded, Wil shook his head and glanced at the girl. How could she just stand there when the noise was coming? She wasn't *dead*. Obviously not. Small movements in her stance—a slight sway and minuscule muscle twitches around the eyelids—they indicated life in there somewhere. The noise wasn't traumatizing her yet, but she was occupied by something. Perhaps, totally incapacitated by this place.

'Hello—*you there!*' Wil took a step closer. 'Can you *hear* me?' he shouted. Just then, as he reached to poke her shoulder, something bright passed between the small gap of his index finger and the girl's sleeve.

That thing!

Like the noise, Wil wondered how he could have forgotten that luminous human-like thing. And just as he referred back to that original event in his memory, right back to the place just the other side of the void, even as he stood here in the midst of its likeness… his two worlds began to feel equally unreal. And thinking outside his two points of existence, Wil dared to reason that maybe *he* wasn't real—that he was in some other place altogether.

This feels like a dream, he told himself, becoming vaguely conscious of being unconscious, unaware this limbo state became him whenever the rousing world distorted his dreams with bird song, cars along the drive, someone down the hall using the bathroom…. He forgot that he had experienced this peculiar existence thousands of times already.

All of a sudden, the flash came again, snatching away all suggestion this place was a dream, because Wil saw it—saw it *properly* for the first time! Only for a second—but he saw it.

What… was it…?

It was human. Probably. It looked human, at least. It was the most captivating human he had ever seen if that were the case. Indeed, this creature had all the fleshly attributes of humanness… arms… legs… body and head… but with something more. Was it colour? Light? Substance?

Depth.

The swirling, hypnotic flesh of the creature had strange depth. It was on… and around him. It *was* him. But in colour. The colour was deep… as if space were in it—like a nebula of pearly shades—greens, pinks and blues. And the astonishment of seeing the eyes… the face… to witness the expression of someone—some*thing*—so mesmerising…. And to think, the face of this creature expressed something meant for Wil. Was it pleasure? Anger? Curiosity? He didn't know. The face of this light form was unlike anything alive or possible.

After briefly mulling over the striking creature, Wil felt an incredible slingshot release mentally, as though his mind had been jettisoned beyond the two points of existence he had been confined to, and with casual ease, he determined that he had to be dreaming.

Just then. A whisper came from behind his shoulder, 'You are not dreaming.'

He shot around in the dream to catch the figure but saw no one. Even the couple became obscured by the fog and Wil found himself back where he started, looking at his feet on the road, hearing nothing, seeing nothing, but feeling an incredible sense of having experienced something very real.

The feeling consumed him as he woke.

Motionless in his bed, all Wil could think about were those eyes. That face. Looking at it, eye-to-eye. The expression, it was neutral. Acknowledging. Or maybe warning. From this comfortable distance, Wil wished the dream hadn't ended and knowing he couldn't go back, an urge to preserve it somehow got him reaching for the notepad under the side of his bed.

'The eyes...' he uttered, sketching lightly, '...magnetising.' The pupils were different from his own. Bigger. *No—smaller.* He sketched madly, rebuilding a poor image of what was almost impossible to recreate in 2-D because a strange fractal pattern about the eyes made them appear both large and small at the same time... like a spinning galaxy. They seemed to draw you to their centre, like looking through a kaleidoscope, ever-expanding, ever-shrinking. Wil placed two tiny spots for pupils into the frame of the eyes, but the real difficulty was in the irises. There, dark colours seemingly moved in a spiralling pattern. Wil couldn't possibly recreate the effect in his sketch book, so instead, he simply drew two shadowy circles around each pupil, then lines coming out, giving the illusion of a tunnel, or depth. He pushed the pad from him and looked at the eyes, marginally satisfied they held something of the real encounter.

He then built a more accurate facial profile to fit, swiping faint lines across the page to represent the jawline, pronounced, and the chin, small and pointy.

The nose....

Absolutely nothing came to mind. It sat as a void on the page, throwing every other feature off kilter, forcing Wil to smudge a bit of pencil dust down the corners of the eyes and above the lip to give the vague impression of a nose.

The hair....

That bit was easy. A dark brown mass worked in crazy slow-motion around the head with a life of its own, as though under water. Wil let fire-like waves lick over the page as he sketched away, capturing the snaky writhing from the dream with undulating lines.

The skin of the creature...

It was tan. An unremarkable tan that confined a myriad of changeable hues beneath the surface as if to dull their eye-catching movement. He couldn't draw that either, but unlike the nose, he wouldn't be able to forget it.

Wil sat back and looked at the picture in its fullness. It wasn't amazing, but it helped him hold onto the image already slipping back to the realms of his unconsciousness.

He focused in on the eyes again with a vacant stare.

A tanned water pixie. That's what it looked like.

'Tanned water pixie.' He suddenly regretted saying it, as if such a declaration might be offensive to someone overhearing. 'Don't be ridiculous,' he caught himself. 'It was a *dream...* just another vivid dream.'

He looked over at the clock.

6:36am! He needed to be at the station by 7!

Wil shot out of bed and within fifteen minutes was showered and dressed, stuffing a muffin in his mouth downstairs, ready to catch the train to Exeter.

Chapter Seven

Mediocrity

The train pulled away, groaning through an ascending scale of flat notes as it picked up speed through the unseasonably crisp air. The next one on the screen was headed for Bath. Wil watched the end of the Bristol train in the distance with an empty wide-eyed stare, thinking of his early-morning school routine his last year at Mulbryn.

London wasn't all bad. But it wasn't mostly good.

He certainly didn't miss feeling like a pervert every morning on the Underground, crushing himself against the passively hostile backside of any male or female who assumed his motive was to take advantage of the close quarters during peak travelling times. And he didn't miss the sooty residue from public transport that seemed to always stick to him and infuriate what little acne he did have.

The paradoxes. He didn't miss those either.

It was incredible the number of people in such a city, yet you could feel totally alone. And the pursuit to be entertained... he didn't miss how his peers had to always go out and *do* something. Something that no doubt ended up costing money. Lots of it. He resented the fact that going to a posh school gave the impression you had money to spare, but he and Steph only got in because Gran left a large sum with all those strings attached. Wil poked his tongue into a molar there on the platform, removing muffin as he shook his head a little. *The money is to be spent on education* was the translation he and Steph understood. Unfortunately, it could only be given to an educational institution of Gran's choosing.

The list of secondary schools and universities came in the post from the solicitor a few months after she died. '*A mine field*,' Dad insisted to Steph and Wil, letting the sheet of paper slip from his hands with the same blasé discharge with which he allowed Gran to disappear from their childhood. The three universities on her list were soon out of the question: Westricton College for Boys, Westricton College for Girls (the word strict hidden in the name however was not hidden on the website's Code of Conduct), St. Mary's Immaculate Conception College (the Stokes weren't Catholic—though Gran was), and Somerset's Agricultural College. Wil remembered trying to figure that last one out. All they could come up with was Steph's obsession with horses when she was... *five*.

Dad said one could only guess what Gran was thinking. Saving the inheritance for a college degree was not an option. However, as Gran was a generous trustee for a posh public school in North London—local compared to the other choices she listed—and considering Dad decided to take the two-year contract at the Royal National Orthopaedic Hospital... it seemed the obvious choice. Confirmation came after surrounding boroughs advised they had no spaces for two new students at such short notice.

Looking back, that money was a bittersweet pill for everyone. The minute Dad and Mum resorted to Gran's list, everything began to change and before Mulbryn even started, Wil felt the incredible pressure to do well there, to make Gran's money worth its investment—and to make sure Dad didn't have second thoughts, because really, there were no other options. Wil's mental prod that first year was the image of Gran sitting up there in heaven, reading her *Daily Mail*, and putting it down to smile on him and Steph, congratulating herself for achieving the results of her wily scheme: both grandchildren finally right where she wanted them. But by the second year, secretly, in the shadowy alleyways and dim common rooms, Wil cursed her. As far as he was concerned, her only relevance in their lives was through the splurging of money. Aside from the scant details of rare early-childhood visits, he only remembered her profoundly age-*in*appropriate gifts, cards that patronized and her seemingly incessant demand for thank you letters that always stopped him from playing with Lego on a Sunday. By the time he finished his first year at Mulbryn, he had become tired of her generosity.

Steph, on the other hand, wished for more of it. She kept on about what she could have done with her £40,000, partly because the pressure to spend at Mulbryn was infectious. Obscene amounts of money to join clubs, take trips, attend events, and keep up with the social pace of those in your year divided peer groups into the Haves and Have-Nots as quickly as sign-up lists went round. Seeing this, term after term... event after event... it eventually widened the chasm between Wil and his peers. He regularly off-loaded his frustration using a tongue-in-cheek philosophical banter that inevitably irked the more serious students. One such conversation came to mind as he waited for the Exeter train, causing him to self-consciously smile.

Rupert Sinclair was an exemplary student who epitomised the ideology Wil was up against, and he was a big fan of the school motto: *In Omnia Excellentia*. Excellence in all things. He dutifully adopted it as his own personal mantra as if it could atone for his entire life's shortcomings and get him through Latin and Chemistry. Equipped with everything he needed to do well at Mulbryn (connections, money and the scholarly devotion equal to an assembly of Oxford dons) Rupert consistently became the metaphorical punching bag with which Wil used to remind himself of how ridiculous—and impossible—*excellence in all things* was.

Sitting opposite Rupert in the library late one night, Wil suggested mildly over open textbooks, 'What's wrong with mediocrity anyway? I mean, in most things, and maybe excellence... in a few?' He had heard, over and over again, that any form of mediocrity was the result of one not applying oneself. Of just getting by. The question was like waving a red rag to a bull in this particular instance, but Wil didn't care. For him, it was a liberating right-hand swing.

'Don't be so absurd *Wilden*,' Rupert insisted, narrowing his eyes in that don't-be-such-an-idiot way which actually made him look like an idiot. 'Why would one *choose* to be mediocre at anything when they can be excellent at everything—the best?' The defiant gleam in Rupert's eyes reflected a bright day replaying itself over and over again—a day of recognition—a day of being the best at not just something... *everything* in fact, and lots of people seeing it.

'Everything?' Wil said doubtfully. 'That's quite a margin for failure, don't you think?' He knew the mention of the word would be a sore spot for ol' Roops, who, earlier in the week, lost out on Mulbryn's elite termly trophy for The Lauded Learned (that's Learn*ed*, otherwise known as the Putz Prize in some circles). 'Of course, you must know how disappointing it is to *not* be the best.'

Rupert gave an unguarded expression of incredulity, however he quickly composed himself and coyly sunk his head into his books. 'I know what you're up to Wilden,' he said curtly, 'and if you're not going to study, then go away.'

'Think about it though,' Wil urged more seriously, adopting the same gleam he just trounced upon, 'there will always be someone who comes along and is better at something than you are.' He paused for a second, imagining a crowd of Mulbrynians hearing this morsel of truth, taking it on board for the first time: some angry, stomping on textbooks, others crying with joy, stripping off school robes and giving away their piles of Learned trophies... and some just standing there stunned, stuck in that boggy place of truth where the lie was so much easier. *Now what do I do?* they seemed to be asking themselves.

Rupert looked up from his books, annoyed. 'Just because *you* never got a pencil and eraser from the head teacher for a job well done doesn't mean you should try and crush those who actually make an effort.'

'Wait a minute, I'm not suggesting trophies are *useless*. They're great motivators....'

'*Then what*?' Rupert spat. 'What *are* you suggesting? Because *all I hear*, all year long, is this nonsense about *mediocrity*. And *why*?'

'Because excellence in everything is a lie,' Wil answered, as though it were obvious. 'The whole thing is a mistranslation anyway, and it's just *not possible*. If you try to be the best at three things, you're three times more likely to encounter failure. I mean, look at you Roops. How many things have you tried to be the *best* at?'

Rupert glared, refusing to give an answer.

'*Everything*,' Wil answered for him, nodding gravely. 'You can say it, it's not a secret.' Ducking down, he leaned towards the table. 'But I'll tell you something,' he whispered, waiting for Rupert to meet him halfway.

Rupert rolled his eyes. 'This better be good,' he threatened, slumping between two stacks of library books.

'If you're going to be the absolute best at even *one* thing,' Wil confided, 'you better bloody well enjoy it. Be sure it's something you love doing. Something you see yourself doing every day—maybe even until you *die*.'

'All right Wilden,' Rupert noted, unimpressed, retreating back to his Latin.

'Seriously Roops, think about it….'

'Don't call me that.'

'Sorry. But hear me out… it's about passion. *Your* passion. I mean, do you even *enjoy* all this?' Wil frowned with disgust at the volumes of textbooks stacked between them, the notebooks and loose pages of study material surrounding Rupert.

'Are you suggesting I put all this away *and not even try*?'

'Not at all. You don't see *me* failing all my classes, do you?' In fact, they both knew he was actually doing well, even in his most difficult subject: Classical Greek. 'What I'm suggesting are two things: that you ditch the lie that you can be excellent in everything—*including* Latin. And that you find something you actually love doing—and be really good at it.' But Rupert again put his head to his books, rejecting Wil's plea.

'I know you think I'm a bohemian, but if you do what you *love*… one day when that better person comes along—*because they always do*—it won't matter… because they can't steal that passion from you… like they steal all those Lauded Learned trophies and certificates and all that public recognition.' Wil waited a beat, seeing if that made ol' Roops think twice. 'You know, all that stuff everyone here wants….' He suddenly imagined that crowd of Mulbrynians again (pre-enlightenment) scrumming on the pitch for The Lauded Learned Trophy… robes and limbs everywhere and couldn't help but chuckle a little. 'Seriously, it's *one* cup—you can't *all* have it.'

Rupert seethed over the page, trying hard not to engage, but Wil could tell from his opponent's strained face that he was sitting there finding offense in every little idea Wil had chucked his way. *Mediocrity… love… passion…* they were those arbitrary words that meant nothing alongside definitive exam results. Consequently, this was where the chasm widened between Wil and Rupert and their demographic profiles. *Love* had limited space in Rupert's life. And as for *passion*…not even the likes of Elenore Porter (so desperately in love with Rupert) could get an interested glance unless she was handing him the *Best at Everything* award for Mulbryn's *perfect prat!*

Despite the frequency of these potent encounters, Wil and Rupert both knew, even as they sat at the table in the library that evening, that these conversations helped to confirm what really mattered to each of them as they honed their convictions off one another. And both secretly concluded that the other was ridiculous for believing what he did. By the end of the first year, it was obvious to Wil that most people at Mulbryn found it difficult, impossible even, to admit to being average at something. And mediocre? *Scoff!* Were they not *Mulbrynians*?

Were they not *human*?

For Wil, being average, ordinary, was a fact of life. Mediocrity, he accepted it, identified with it and would never have found his passions and discovered his motivations without it. It tempered his life and gave him contentment—bringing fulfilment in the things he was good at. Things he *wanted* to be good at. Every bright Mulbrynian who was conned into thinking they had the capacity to be excellent in every single thing they did… Wil was convinced they would walk out of those school gates and one day end up embittered and unhappy. And that's exactly what Rupert already was.

Wil expected him to look up any second, like he always did, and come out with one of his rhetorical questions: *All right then, Wilden, define passion.* Or the favourite, *You excel at being mediocre, so what's your point?* But as Wil watched Rupert dutifully skim through a page of notes, resisting the debate for the first time, it suddenly occurred to him how embittered and unhappy his study partner actually was. At that moment, Wil was overwhelmed with compassion and wondered how he hadn't seen Rupert's genuine suffering before. He had been so busy indignantly disarming the ideology of the masses that he never even saw the individual. Right there in front of him.

'Don't you see?' Wil lightened his tone. 'You can't ever be a failure if you pursue your passion, Rupert.'

Rupert agitatedly turned the page of his notebook.

'Can you imagine,' Wil carried on more meaningfully, 'a life with contentment?'

'*Contentment?*' Rupert sneered all of a sudden, his eyes glazing with an anger Wil had never seen before. 'I'm quite *content* to strive for excellence, thank you very much. And your theories of passion may work for the artist,' he said sharply, 'but have you even given any thought to the person whose passion *it is* to excel in all things?' Rupert's eyes bore into Wil, pinning him into silence. 'Maths,' he spat, getting louder, 'science… Latin? Honestly, Wil, who's passionate about *Latin?*' he demanded, scoffing. 'But *someone* has to be the best at it. *That* is my passion. *Excellence in all things.* I don't need to *love* everything to be the best….' Heads began turning and anonymous eyes peered at the study partners from behind book covers. Their usual banter had clearly turned into something else.

Wil tried hiding his surprise and feigned resignation. 'Then, I'm afraid, you'll be quite disappointed,' he said soberly, gathering his books, 'if you aren't already,' he added. '*No one* can be the best at everything, Rupert.' He stood up with a doubtful expression, 'Honestly, do you know anyone who is? In *all* things?' and walked away disheartened.

Rupert Sinclair waited for a moment, thinking. He then shouted across the silent room, 'That could be *me*—you idiot—*ME!*'

There wasn't an ounce of sarcasm in that declaration and Wil shook his head at the ruinous absurdity of it. Sometimes a right hook didn't feel as relieving as he thought it would be.

Smiling regretfully on the platform, Wil wondered whatever happened to ol' Roops. Probably on his way to Oxford or something.

That conversation was a turning point for Wil and his case for mediocrity. He got out of that musty old library and made for Aristotle's statue in the courtyard just opposite, thinking of the desperate words Rupert threw at him. Whatever happened to the pompous quips and rhetoric under a façade of certainty? That was how they always debated. Argued. Not only had Wil seen something different in Roops that evening, but he heard something different too. *Maybe it's too soon to have these discussions after losing out on The Trophy*, he thought to himself, hoping the dissolve was just bad timing. But then again, whenever exam results came out, Rupert was always up for a good argument. It was his calibration curve and they both knew he regularly used the mediocrity pitch to motivate himself to try harder for the next Trophy. *But sometimes you just can't try any harder.*

Wil sat there on the great philosopher's plinth and cast a long spiteful glare at the school motto chiselled above the library entrance, convinced the words were as good as poison, mistranslated or not. *Why isn't anyone else seeing it?* He suddenly wished he never mentioned the word mediocrity before. His overt campaign just felt like a mockery when he compared it to the discreet subversion of *excellence in all things*. It was so much more effective, the attractive lie. That's why no one else saw it. They *wanted* it to be true.

That could be me—*you idiot*—ME!

But maybe Roops was having doubts. Why else was he defending excellence so vehemently? He never had before.

A niggling hope squirmed in the pit of Wil's stomach. Could Roops really be on the cusp of transformation? It was either that or destruction.

The thought burdened Wil further and for a moment he believed that if he could save Rupert from his inevitable demise into perpetual disappointment, he wouldn't be helping only Rupert, but the *whole* world. It was a lofty idea and he sniffed at the thought of it after the moment passed, but accepted that there was something to be said for rescuing a person. Just *how*, he wasn't sure. Here, he crossed his arms and leaned restively into the folds of Aristotle's tarnished robes as the engraving on the plaque beside him caught the evening sun and glinted in his direction. Absent-minded, he read:

Some vices miss what is right because they are deficient, others because they are excessive, in feelings or in actions, while virtue finds and chooses the mean.

...Chooses the mean....

Wil considered these words—just as he had done before when he sat in this very spot, and for the first time, he appreciated them. Coupled with that shameful mediocrity pitch grinding around in his head … and Rupert's desperate declarations slipping into the pauses… they told him exactly how he could save his study partner from self-destruction.

First thing: go back in there and study.

Wil jumped from the plinth and ran for those chiselled words as if they could save the both of them and began an excruciating process that threatened to destabilize everything he believed about passion.

In that one decisive moment, he remembered Rupert's angry words, *Just because* you *never got a pencil and eraser from the head teacher for a job well done doesn't mean you should stomp on those who actually make an effort,* and an image popped into his head. *Scales.* Rupert sat on one side, weighed down with all his textbooks and trophies. And on the other side, Wil saw himself, lifted high above, with nothing. Not a book, not a pencil or eraser. That image struck him most profoundly: *No wonder no one takes me seriously.* Rupert was never going to listen to a laid-back rebel who couldn't appreciate the privileged education he was getting, and seeing the situation in this new light, Wil realised how much he needed those books to weigh him down, because the only way to help Roops was to be right there with him.

Over the following months, Wil advocated excellence in all things, certain all that stuff about contentment and compassion would redeem his charade, proving the pursuit of excellence in all things tipped one over to insanity trying. Once he could convince Rupert, *then* he could embrace mediocrity again. But quietly, not like before.

Unfortunately for Wil, astonished peers, who had already heard his views the previous year, refused to believe his numbers were creeping up the assessment lists posted outside the form room—until he earned The Lauded Learned Trophy for Winter term. Rupert was just as surprised yet complimentary, seeing what it took to become first, having studied diligently with Wil every step of the dramatic turnaround. Everyone else, however, dismissed Wil as a hypocrite—having *pushed the passion* when he was actually seen regularly slogging it out over books in the library. The fiercely competitive students simply accused him of playing mind games to reduce competition.

Near the end of Spring term however, results started coming out and Wil was exhausted. Whatever he intended that evening on the plinth, it seemed to evolve each day and all he knew was that he had to look as though he could keep it up indefinitely, that exhaustion wasn't the reason for rejecting excellence and turning to mediocrity. *No... because that would be... giving up.* And he couldn't give up on Rupert. He was only just becoming his intellectual equal. Why he needed to gain his study partner's respect and plead with him one more time once the scales were even, he didn't really know anymore. But every night, after the studying ceased, Wil found himself driven by two distinct things: hope and dread. *Hope* that Rupert would one day look up from his books with an enlightened smile—the futility of it all dawning on him.

And the *dread*. Since his epiphany with Aristotle, Wil woke every morning having dreamed that Rupert had been found drowned somewhere along the Thames. And someone needed to go out there and identify him. Someone who knew him well. Wil did it, every night, squelching along the bank under Waterloo Bridge to meet phantom police officers and identify... his friend. The feeling in the dream was never clear. Had he jumped or not? (There was that incredible ambiguity.) And there was that overwhelmingly tragic feeling Wil woke with—the dread— that became almost intolerable, especially every time he knew Roops was already on his own somewhere buried under books.

The plan, as it evolved over its final days, was to stop the charade when it looked too easy to finish, too easy to get that second Lauded

Learned. Somehow, intuitively, Wil knew this was essential in saving Rupert and that such perfect timing would allow his study partner (already in line as #2 for their year and mimicking Wil's stamina with mechanical fury) to easily have the prize he had always wanted.

On the morning of term exams, Wil woke from yet another of his disturbing dreams and took a moment outside their early study time to carefully tell Rupert what he thought about excellence again, confiding in him that he intended to bungle their last assessment for the term, making Rupert next in line for The Trophy.

'But you can't,' he declared. 'You're well ahead of me. You'd have to fail the entire exam quite spectacularly.'

'I can do that,' Wil said easily, sparing all tone of arrogance.

'But you're the best in our year.... *Why?*'

'I'm just not bothered anymore,' he said, shrugging, already feeling the weight of six months lifting off him like textbooks sliding one-by-one off his shoulders. 'I meant what I said before about passion. And all this,' he pointed to the sheets of notes in front of them, 'I can still do all this without sacrificing everything else. I just won't be the best anymore.' He looked at Rupert thoughtfully and asked, 'You wouldn't think I'm a failure if I give up a trophy, would you?'

'No,' Rupert said hastily, then considered his answer. 'I don't think you're a failure, because you're *choosing* to give this one up,' he reasoned. 'You had already earned it. It was yours.'

'Even so, I don't want it. That doesn't make me a failure.'

'No...' Rupert agreed, hesitating. 'But why come this far... and give up?'

'I'm not giving up,' Wil said plainly. 'It just doesn't mean anything to me anymore, so someone else can have it.' He gestured with an open hand, implying that Rupert would be that someone. 'I've spent the last six months slowly giving up everything I enjoy to earn a piece of metal that says what? I'm *clever?*' He rolled so-what eyes and shrugged. 'Actually, I'm unhappy. And I don't need The Lauded Learned Trophy dictating my life anymore. You and I have spent hours together, every day, and did you know I love writing poetry?' Rupert looked a little surprised. 'Don't laugh. I also love spending time with my family. And I have a friend back home who is the only person who knows what I've been through to get a useless award that I've stupidly allowed to steal nearly everything that's important to me.' Wil pushed his notes towards Rupert. 'Not anymore.

You'll get that trophy Rupert whether you do well in this Greek exam, and when you do, you'll see what I mean. It'll feel like you're walking away with someone else's prize and you can't appreciate it the same way again.'

'That's because I *will* be walking away with someone else's prize. *Yours*.'

'No. It'll feel like someone else's because you worked so hard to get it, yet it could have been yours *or* mine. Don't you see? We worked the same hours every study session. We researched... we shared notes and used every mnemonic we could get our heads round. Whether *you* get it or *I* get it is neither here nor there. It's about who *wants* it.' He smiled soberly. 'And I don't.'

Rupert nodded faintly, understanding. After a few seconds his eyes brightened and his lips stretched across his face into a wicked smile. 'One could argue... that we *both* earned it,' he suggested. 'And seeing as I don't want it half as bad now—now that it's just a hand-me-down...' he teased.

Wil chuckled. The sight of his friend sitting there across from him, beaming, with their books and study material pointlessly scattered about... it felt so ridiculously relieving all of a sudden. Students nearby glared and huffed as the two began chortling and giggling the more they tried to keep quiet in the library. Eventually, they wound down and Roops started packing the books away.

'What are you doing?' Wil asked, surprised, expecting to finish their session, at least for Rupert's peace of mind.

'We've studied enough, Wil,' he decided, shoving notepads into his back pack. 'Too much, in fact. Shall we go find something in the dining hall?'

'Definitely.'

Rupert did get his trophy. He humbly took it there on the stage as if accepting it on behalf of someone else. No speeches or indulgences whatsoever. Soon, Wil couldn't find him huddled over notes in the library as he often did and when the Summer term accolade line-up was announced, Rupert hadn't even tried to fit into the top three. He decided he rather liked cricket and eventually stopped having a study partner altogether. Wil's dreams along the Thames stopped too. The fear of finding Roops down on the banks... it had gone completely the day Wil watched him humbly collect his cup.

Chapter Eight

Voices

Wil surveyed his recent thoughts as another train came and went. All that stuff about Roops hadn't popped to mind when he stood here last week. No doubt, it was the dreams, stalling the mind into a bizarre loop now as they did back then, revealing the subconscious under some great pressure.

Exhaling a deep breath, Wil created a white cloud in front of him in the cool morning air and couldn't help think of the fog. But as the vapour curled away and disappeared, he found something reassuring in it. The dreams would disappear one day, just as they had before, but Sadie most certainly would be more than a passing infatuation.

Wil wiped the side of his nose nonchalantly with his thumb and leaned his shoulder against one of the pillars along the platform. Remarkably, those dreams on the Thames were exactly the same each night—exactly—with the exception of the last. But even that final one carried with it the same fear and anguish of all the others as Wil walked along the water's edge, at low tide, toward the floodlights and that ironic little tent surrounding the body. 'What's this for?' he asked each time, like it was his first go. 'For protection and privacy,' the faceless officers answered. 'And the dignity of loved ones, of course.' He slunk inside with that feeling of déjà vu, that feeling of chest-splitting regret. That final month, he'd trudge back up to street level, wishing desperately that it had been himself instead of his study partner. But on the last night he'd ever have the dream, he came away from that sickening tent with such relief… because the face in the mud wasn't Roop's. It was someone else's. Someone Wil didn't even recognise. He inhaled nervously at the thought of that unfamiliar, pale face, luminous like a ghost, for dawn brought that strange glow to the tent in the last dream. Oddly, the sun hadn't come up in any of the others. All the reason more he couldn't forget that face.

Losing contact with Roops wasn't planned. They didn't leave on bad terms, it just sort of happened those weeks before school ended. Everyone was focused on university and college by the end when all Wil could think was getting back home to Ben. Dad lead the moving vans to Taunton that last day of school and Wil remembered finding himself quietly elated to see his best friend again. It was Ben, with his invaluable outsider's perspective, who motivated the final stretch in the charade to excellence, pushing when there seemed no point. And in a place where many competed ruthlessly against their friends, and friendships were stepping stones to elite circles,he was that essential breath of fresh air.

Wil smiled wryly, feeling slightly indebted to his best friend.

Again, Justin Salinsky came immediately to mind. Chuckling discreetly there on the platform, Wil was certain he and Ben might never have become best friends had Justin been ignorant of the circumcision in Year 4.

Justin was one of those iconic playground bullies who established that sick pecking order where the fattest, meanest, most obscene kid was the most revered, out of fear, of course, and the smallest, cleverest, politest child was positioned submissively at his feet, ready to receive sporadic abuse. When Wil returned to school after his two-week convalescence, Justin promised to give him his notorious *crotch-crunch* as a welcome-back present at lunch time. Wil wasn't in any state to defend himself from the swift kick meant for him. However, standing there amid that curious little crowd, shielding his groin with his Star Wars lunch box, Wil was suddenly grateful to Ben, who threatened their adolescent tormentor with a dose of his own medicine. It only took a second and before anyone could believe what had happened, Justin had become a wailing, snivelling heap on the floor, having received the only crotch-crunch delivered that day. In fact, the only the rest of that year as it turned out.

It was Wil's smooth talking later that kept Ben from exclusion and once they defeated the common enemy, they were inseparable.

The train came in, whooshing Wil back onto his heels, squeaking to a stop. He quickly got into an empty carriage on the end, slammed the door behind him and took a window seat with a table. Doors banged shut along the other carriages as he wrestled off his backpack. After a short wait, the train lurched forward and he slouched into the chair, leaned his head against the window and closed his eyes.

Without trying to think of the strange pixie, it came vividly to mind as though Wil were asleep, but of course, he wasn't. He held his breath, astonished, for the form seemed to move beyond the scope of his daydream imaginings and stopped in front of him, staring most curiously, eye-to-eye. Seeing the pupils clearly, there was brightness and darkness there, present and distant, finite within the space of the eyes... yet composed of what seemed... infinite depth. Mesmerised by this paradoxical appearance, Wil felt himself lured, compelled with bewilderment, to reach out. And seeing himself doing so in this daydream, lifting his hand... his arm... the illuminating thing in his mind suddenly disappeared. He involuntarily grasped for what had already gone and felt his head jerk downwards in his haste.

He repositioned himself against the glass, annoyed for having nodded off.

'You are not dreaming,' came audibly from behind him.

Wil popped his eyes open, lucid, and pricked his head up over the line of seats.

No one was there.

But he *had* heard someone. *Heard* them.

He got up, sunk a knee into his chair and leaned over the high back of the seat, expecting to see someone—anyone—crouched down behind him.

No one.

Agitated, he walked the aisle, checked every row, but again, no one. Back in his seat, the words came to him once more. *You are not dreaming.* This time though, they were just the memory of what he had heard and the distinct difference between the two became unnerving.

The train swept along the countryside at high speed, rocking smoothly side-to-side and Wil shifted in his seat and watched as the landscape flashed by.

The announcement for St David's station blared suddenly over the intercom. Startled, Wil opened his eyes, grabbed his bag and headed down the aisle for the nearest door.

Twenty minutes gone, like that? He hadn't even heard the calling for Tiverton Parkway halfway. *Surely I didn't check these seats,* he tried convincing himself, glancing beneath the tables, certain now that he couldn't have walked the carriage this direction already this morning in a frantic state to find some unlikely person winding him up. His memory became so muddled as he strode out of the station that by the time he made it to class, he pushed the journey from Taunton to the back of his mind, convinced anything troublesome about the experience had been nothing more than a dream.

After class, he met Ben for breakfast in a cafe at Princesshay.

Ben led the way to a table in the front window overlooking a busking violinist. Wil stood back with the loaded tray and watched his friend straddle a rickety, wrought iron chair. Ben's typical rugby-player build defied the strength of most fold-up chairs and as this one in particular creaked under 18 stone of dense muscle, Wil winced,

'Are you sure you want to sit here?' He cast a glance at the two armchairs over his shoulder in the corner.

'Yeah, why not?' Ben shrugged, seeing no potential danger whatsoever. 'It's a good spot,' he insisted, looking enthusiastically out the window as if to show what they'd miss if they moved.

'All right.' Wil took the equally flimsy chair opposite, pleased Ben wasn't the slightest bit dejected from yesterday. In fact, he seemed happy.

'So...' Wil started delicately, moving sandwiches and drinks from the tray, 'have you figured out what you're going to do about Shellie?'

Ben folded his arms and smiled at the violinist, trying to catch her eye. 'Oh, I've got a plan,' he said confidently.

Too confidently.

'*Have* you? I mean, you *have*—a plan that quickly?' Ben never came up with anything quickly, outside of a double decker sandwich and his impeccable rucking technique.

'Of course I do.' He took his eyes off the girl jabbing the air with her bow. 'I just needed to figure out how to get rid of *you*.'

Wil recoiled, not sure how to take that.

'I mean that in the nicest way possible,' Ben tried assuring. He then poked the handle of his mug with a single finger, filling it, and took a sip like a gorilla learning etiquette. 'The thing is, how will I get her attention with you around?'

Wil had to remind himself that Ben sometimes came out with

statements culminating from a long internal conversation between himself and his perceived opposition. Every now and again, Ben would be deep in thought, uttering something emphatic—playing an audio track of what was going on in his head, rehearsing clever answers. Wil imagined Ben in the bathroom mirror talking to his reflection regularly, facing his foe. In this case, it was his best friend—that obstacle between him and Shellie. Knowing Ben drew incorrect conclusions, Wil figured the best thing in these circumstances was to ignore hurtful or offensive statements and to delve into the erroneous premise they were built upon. It was a toilsome task.

'And... what does this plan involve?' Wil asked, oblivious to his own doubtful tone.

'Well, it doesn't involve you...' Ben started off, but then noticed the dubious look on his mate's face. 'What I mean is... I *realised*... I need to do something that allows me to *see* Shellie... but without you as a distraction.'

'Nicely put.'

'Thank you. Since it's really only the start of term, I thought I'd sign up to the Wednesday activity she's doing and then we'd have something in common.' He took a bite from his panini, evidently smug at his brilliance. 'Then, it would only be *natural* for us to gravitate towards one another, out of shared interest.'

'And what exactly *is* her Wednesday activity?'

Ben's facade cracked a little behind that contentedly chewing face.

'Well you know. The Wednesday one.'

'So what you're saying...' Wil closed his eyes, both amused and annoyed, 'is you have *no idea* what she's doing?'

'No *exact* details more like, but does it matter? I'll get them. Besides, Wednesday activities only need to be signed off. And to be honest, I don't really *care* what it is.'

'*Basket weaving?*'

'Why not?'

'C'mon. *You?*' Wil chuckled.

'That's not going to happen, and you know it,' Ben said indignantly. 'Now don't be such an idiot.'

'Oh *I'm* not being the idiot here.... You have no idea what she's taking and you're ready to sign yourself up!'

'Well do you have a better idea?' Ben brusquely pushed his plate a few inches away. 'Preferably one that doesn't *involve* you...?' He was serious now. Serious enough to find his lunch unappetising. Resting his folded arms on the edge of the table, rocking it a little, he stared, confrontational.

Wil knew he had to choose his words carefully. However many times Ben plotted and schemed, it always ended up a mess, and though Wil often swayed him from even greater disasters there was something about this time... Ben wanting to keep him so blatantly out of the picture maybe... that proved to be a bigger challenge than before. That look on Ben's face did seem rather desperate.

Wil squared with Ben's expectant glare, but before he could say a thing, he had the overwhelming urge to invest, to show Ben that he was genuinely on his side, that he wasn't working against him... that he wanted to see him happy. That he was in fact taking this whole Shellie infatuation seriously.

I could tell him about Sadie. It would definitely take a bit of the edge off Ben's insecurity.

Wil leaned forward apprehensively, cupping a fist in his hand as he put his elbows on the table. Just as he was about to speak, Flika Finch and the science project shot through his mind.

'*A project...?*' he could still hear Ben blurting in that corridor outside Mr Briggs' classroom like it was yesterday. And those awful quote-fingers thrown in the air.... '*...More like snogging session! Good going, Wil—don't be shy!*' It was unfortunate that Flika was waiting in that room. And that the door was open. And that Ben's contribution to damage control was a '*Sorry mate, she probably didn't hear that,*' as he waved animatedly in her direction. The disgusted expression on her face... Wil imagined it was no different to his own at the sight of his best friend scuppering off down the corridor like nothing happened....

But that was years ago, Wil rationalized quickly, ridding himself of any hesitation.

'Listen Ben, I have no better plan,' he offered sincerely, instantly undermining his friend's resistance. 'Whatever you scheme on a Wednesday... it won't matter as long as you're honest with Shellie.'

After a moment, Ben unfolded his arms and took his plate back, looking a little irritated by the inconvenience of having to give it up in the first place.

'Speaking of honesty...' Wil tried being subtle, 'I haven't told you, but I'm really interested in Sadie.'

Ben's eyes widened as he pulled his sandwich from his face, leaving a string of mozzarella to fill the gap like a fine white hair. He then hurried to swallow his bite. 'Psychology Sadie?'

Wil nodded and immediately looked onto the street, avoiding a discussion about it.

'You're not telling me this so I'll end up telling Shellie and put her off you....'

'No....!' It hadn't even occurred to him. 'But if you think it'll help....'

'Don't flatter yourself,' Ben sneered. 'I've learned my lesson from that one.'

'Okay. But have you learned the lesson about signing up for stuff you're not really interested in?'

'She'll see what lengths I'll go to be closer to her... and she'll only be *flattered*,' Ben defended.

'Or think you're stalking her,' Wil said with a smile, making it difficult for his friend to be upset. 'Why don't you just go up and talk to her? Invite her to something? I don't know...just bypass the scheming altogether?'

Ben didn't say anything straightaway and instead turned thoughtfully with his little mug in his hand to the busker. She noticed him watching and smiled, to which he returned the same, raising his latte.

'Wilden, you're always coming to the rescue. But I've got this one, okay?' He turned, his smile gone, and gave Wil a long, meaningful stare.

'Of course you do,' Wil accepted respectfully.

'By the way, I won't be needing a ride in the morning, I've got Nan's car. Enough about me now.' Ben slugged back his froth and wiped his mouth with the back of his hand like a five-year-old. 'So Sadie, huh?'

Please no. Wil smiled and nodded.

Splitting his thumb and forefinger across his brow, he suddenly regretted telling Ben.

Chapter Nine

Humiliation

'Wi—*IL*...' came the familiar whine from the other side of the door. 'Sorry...' he called out, squirting shampoo into his hand, 'I missed the alarm... I need to be gone by half past.... I'll be out in five minutes....'

Quickly he worked a lather through his hair, and as he dropped his chin to his chest, watching the steam thicken around his legs this side of the glass, he realised the couple weren't there in his dream last night, and he didn't see the tanned pixie either. It was just him... and the fog.

'Hurry up, Wil...' Steph's muffled whine came again.

'*Two minutes*....' He blindly reached down for a bottle of shower gel and knocked near-empty containers off the ledge like dominoes. The clatter around his feet was somehow satisfying, loudly conveying the hurried state his sister might not otherwise appreciate from the other side of the door. 'Seriously, I'm done!' he lied, still rinsing.

Wil squeezed an excessive amount of gel over his chest. As he washed frantically, he found himself amazed at how dreams could be so troubling and reassuring at the same time, even within the same dream there could be such strong opposing emotions as disappointment and pleasure. Or like on the Thames, such dread. And in the end... relief.

'Wi-IL! Seriously! Would you just get out?'

Squeak... squeak... squeak.

'Nearly there...' he hollered, grabbing the towel and toothpaste.

'I'm just a bit naked at present,' he threatened, as freshmint saliva foamed down his chin and into the sink. There wasn't time to shave.

Throwing open the door, 'See! Done,' he said magnificently, buttoning his trousers then yanking his T-shirt over his damp chest.

Steph looked at him dubiously. 'Did you touch my makeup?'

'No. But I did pick up the razor you left on the floor like a bear trap.'

'I need to finish getting ready,' she huffed, squeezing through the doorway. 'You should take a look in the mirror. Your *bedroom* mirror.' With that, she pushed him out into the hall and latched the door.

'*What?*' Staring at the unnaturally dark circles in his reflection, it looked like he had literally rubbed his eyes with one of his sister's eye shadows. He leaned in closer, inspecting the actual pigmentation of the skin and wondered where all that brown and purple could possibly have come from. *No wonder she asked if I touched anything.*

'Never mind...' he breathed.

Ten minutes later, he was parked near Ben's mini at the Taunton campus. Up in East Wing, the third floor was quiet. In an hour the place would be teaming with students and professors, the ones who found the 8:50am start too early. As Wil quickened his pace towards the classroom, four doors down on the left, with its door propped open, he could already hear voices coming from the room: a sarcastic chuckle from a male and a few female voices agreeing. Ben's voice chimed in. Wil stopped dead in his tracks.

Ben's confidence sounded volatile. He was clearly psyched to get Shellie's attention with whatever plan he had in mind from the café yesterday. Wil suddenly regretted telling him about Sadie, knowing there was no way he could go in there and quietly admire her from the back of the room again. From now on, Ben would be watching him, trying to give him pointed eyes from three rows up, unable to be in the know without giving *something* away.

Ben's now hyper silence screamed of his impatience for Shellie, so Wil lingered at the notice board outside the classroom, hoping he could just go in when the professor arrived.

Waiting, he heard someone coming up the stairs and pretended to be interested in the small print of a flyer posted there in front of him. He hoped it was Shellie, getting there well ahead of him, because the last thing Ben needed to see was the two of them arriving together. The landing doors suddenly swung open and after a few seconds, hearing steps coming towards him, Wil nonchalantly looked over.

Sadie!

He swallowed hard and continued his pointless perusal of the noticeboard. Shifting his weight, he felt a stray tack under the toe of his shoe and glad to be doing something other than just standing there, picked it up and casually stuck it into the margins of the cork.

She was almost passing him now. He looked over his shoulder at her and smiled—the same smile he had practised a million times—only she caught the deflating last half of it because she was distracted by something on the wall. But at the very last second, when Wil started to feel uneasy—like this was one of his daydreams and that she *couldn't* actually see him—Sadie raised her eyebrows quizzically and gave him a beautiful grin.

He watched her go into the classroom and gave himself a collecting second to face Ben.

Just then, the words "Gonorrhoea" and "Chlamydia" jumped out at him. His eyes flitted around the pages pinned there on the board he had just pressed the tack into: "Who has gonorrhoea? Chlamydia?" The line-up of apparently healthy men and women stood underneath an enormous font with the shocking words shrieking across the page. Wil looked around at the other ads. Symptom trackers. Advice lines and local clinics. It was all related to sexually transmitted diseases!

No. No...no...no.... The blood in Wil's extremities felt like it was all receding back to his heart, weighing it down so that it dropped deeper and deeper into his chest. The embarrassment became debilitating, and unable to move, he just stood there. He couldn't go back down the stairs... or walk into the classroom...or stare blankly again at the ads as though interesting. *No....* His focus ended in the general direction of his feet and carried a dumbfounded expression which no one, thankfully, could see.

There was no denying it. Sadie had read the board. That's why she raised her eyebrows and smiled the way she did, drawing conclusions.

Wil sighed a defeated sigh.

'Hey!' Ben said cheerfully, having stuck his head out into the hall. 'You coming in?' Without even thinking, Wil walked towards him, nodding as he recovered from his minor humiliation. 'You all right?' Ben asked, concerned. 'You've got massive circles around your eyes.'

Wil had forgotten about them. 'I'm fine,' he moaned, parting from

Ben to take his seat—the one to the right of Sadie, a row behind—exactly where he imagined himself in his page-flipping daydreams. He was so embarrassed he hadn't the foresight to sit further away and instead sat where he always did, feeling small. Any hope of speaking to her today was lost. There was just no way.

Ben ambled over from his seat halfway up the front and sat in the empty seat beside Wil. He had that prowling idleness about him that always made him look like he was spoiling for trouble. Mischievously, he flickered his eyes over in Sadie's direction and smirked.

Don't... Wil mouthed, widening his eyes in rebuke as a plump little woman came into the room and stood there at the front. She watched the class chattering away and cleared her throat.

'Apologies, Class,' she interrupted.

Wil had seen her before in the department office. A little head behind a desk. With her dense brown bob and bulgy pale neck, he often thought she resembled a mushroom wearing bifocals, cultivated in the dim and dank corners of the Psychology floor.

'Professor Smith is still poorly,' she announced, 'and his classes have now been cancelled for the week.' She peered down at a scrap of paper and began reciting, 'All reading assignments should be followed on the syllabus and will carry on from next week. Expect the topic assessment on Tuesday as scheduled.'

Books began closing and students started packing up their bags. The Mushroom Lady answered a quiet question or two from the front row and repeated her answers loudly, for the benefit of the whole class. She seemed to enjoy the role, dismissing everyone, having done none of the actual work of teaching, yet she stood there delighted with herself as if she had.

'See you next week...' she squeaked to a small crowd filtering out the door. Scribbling the cancellation onto the white board, she then stuck a notice on the outside of the door and left.

'Well, *I've* got something to go and sign up for,' Ben gloated, making it clear again that he was on a solo mission as he got up and went back to his seat.

Wil was again filled with the embarrassment of looking all too interested in a sexual health board and pulled out his phone. He focused on it intensely while Sadie slowly clicked and zipped a few things shut: the little purse with lip gloss he liked watching her use and the neon-yellow banana pencil pouch she curiously wrote the words *FIND ME* on last week in huge letters with a permanent marker.

'I'll see ya later,' Ben said, stuffing pads and clothing into his bag.

Wil nodded modestly in his direction, unable to engage, unable to pretty much do anything. It didn't occur to him to make a hasty move *with* Ben until he was already gone, and with no Ben to buffer his existence Wil just sat there looking at his phone, pretending to be interested in it as the class started to feel suffocatingly sparse, like oxygen disappeared with each person walking out that door.

There were a few students left in the room now: two older women seated in the first row and a man waiting for them in the doorway. With all the vacant chairs, Wil suddenly wished he was at the front, so Sadie could be certain he wasn't watching her from this distressing proximity. He hadn't the capacity to even pretend to draw out his packing-up routine, much less start it.

The two women went out the door, suggesting a few places on campus to spend the next hour. The man wholeheartedly agreed with one of them for reasons that quickly fell out of earshot and Wil found himself, for the first time ever, alone with Sadie. He was aware that now was the perfect time to say something to her, but his mouth seized, right along with this mind.

She rummaged around in her handbag at a painfully slow pace, as though *trying* to torture him, and eventually dropped her pens into the side pocket of her book bag. She closed it up with a finality that relieved him a little, slung it over her shoulder then turned in her seat towards him, prompting Wil to bring his phone close to his face.

She didn't move.

Surely she was getting her coat off the back of the chair or something, but he didn't dare look, still feeling her eyes on him. After a few more seconds, Wil threw a self-conscious glance in her direction.

She was staring *right at him*.

'You all right?' It was light and sincere and it was all that he could manage as he found the courage to look at her face-to-face.

'*I* am,' she assured, as though it were obvious. 'Are *you* all right?'

Wil hesitated. 'Yes....' he said uncertainly, not catching her meaning. He searched her playful grin for some explanation. And then it hit him.

The noticeboard! Who has gonorrhoea? Chlamydia?

Whether she was joking or not, Wil wanted to clear that up while he had the chance.

'About the notices outside...' he pretended it was all a funny misunderstanding, 'I was just standing there deciding whether to come to class or not.... I hadn't actually *seen* what was up there... I haven't *got* gonorrhoea or—'

'I don't mean *that*,' she quickly clarified, amused.

'What then?'

She lifted the flap of her bag and took out the *FIND ME* pencil pouch. Opening it, she then presented a small orange container and held it out to him.

Gingerly, he took it.

'Thanks,' Wil said, unsure of what she had just given him.

'Well, you look like you could use them.'

Now he really was curious. 'Do you want this back?'

'No...' she laughed, as though doubtful it was a good idea. 'Just let me know if they help.' She slung her bags over her shoulder, got up and walked to the front of the class. 'I guess I'd be able to tell anyway,' she remarked, heading for the door, her neon banana pencil case still in hand.

'Seriously, thank you.' He didn't want her to go all of a sudden.

She threw him a smile over her shoulder, 'See you later' and was gone.

Wil turned the container over end-to-end in his hand a few times, feeling a dull bumbling around of something inside. He peeled off the cap and let it dangle as he emptied two new orange earplugs into his hand.

How odd, he thought.

Chapter Ten

Intruder

Approaching the manor, Wil spotted the elderly neighbour standing in her upstairs window again, keeping watch at the end of the chalky drive. Her distinct features, hair, skin and beige-taupe clothing, they became a whitened silhouette whenever he glanced at her from a distance; her striking form poised in that central window, like a ghost warding off visitors. He waved anyway when he got out of the car, and forced a smile, just like he always did, but she just stared in his direction, defying all politeness.

He set the orange canister on his bedside table, smack in the middle of a faint mug ring and took off his jacket. Catching a glimpse of those dark circles around his eyes in the mirror, he realised all of a sudden, *That's why she gave them to me.* That's why she said he looked like he could use them.

He plopped the entire length of his body onto the bed, took the canister and peeled off the lid. No marks, and sadly, no personal messages. However, he dumped the contents into his hand and rolled the foamy pellets between his thumb and forefinger, believing sleep was precisely what he needed. Pushing the plugs into his ears, he imagined Sadie turning around in her chair their next class and asking if her little gift did him any good.

A world of good, he thought, feeling them swell. He closed his eyes long enough to let go of the morning's events: the noticeboard… his dark circles... Ben's smirk in Sadie's direction, the Shellie plan.... It was all now... in the far reaches... of...

Wil's mind filled with the dense white fog. It was heavy and humid, pressing against his trousers like a damp towel.

Just then.

A figure approached. He had seen it before. It was the strange tanned pixie he remembered drawing in the recent past. Where and when, he wasn't sure, but a surreal feeling, made up of surprise and familiarity, it reminded him that he had seen this captivating being not long ago.

It came out of the distance and walked directly towards Wil, staring boldly at him.

'Look,' the creature said in a heeding voice as he walked right past, their shoulders almost brushing. For a second, Wil was too amazed to even take in the meaning of the word, but as the man-like thing moved behind his shoulder, Wil instinctively turned around to find it had vanished. Instead, Sadie was there, in the distance. Feeling the urge to go to her—to call out to her—he noticed the creature too, next to her, unveiled suddenly by a shift in the dense vapour. Wil could only see the back of the tanned form as it put its hands on her shoulders, seemingly reassuring her in some way, but it was this interaction that made him realise Sadie was upset, anxious. Her head sunk a little, she nodded and closed her eyes as though accepting something disappointing the creature was telling her. Or maybe she was preparing for something difficult. Maybe he was making her do something she didn't want to, Wil couldn't help suspect.

Their dark forms amid the pale scenery disappeared all of a sudden and it was at that moment that the fog began to move purposefully around Wil, disorientating him. He tried finding some way out, a thinning gap, but everywhere was white, suffocating white. *Where is this place?* he couldn't understand, still trying to spot Sadie, worrying what that thing wanted with her.

'Sadie?' he called out, searching the fog. '*Sadie...?*'

'I told you I'd see you later.'

Startled, he shot around to find her smiling coyly. The relief of her presence hustled every disconcerting thought he had about this place, and the creature, immediately to the back of his mind.

'I need you to do something for me, Wil.' She promptly took his hand and walked through the fog as though she knew exactly where she was going. And before Wil knew what was happening, his legs began to feel heavy, drawing along behind him. She then let go of his hand.

'Wait...' he said to her, squinting to try and see his lower half through the blanket of white, '...something's happening to my legs....'

Then almost as quickly as the heaviness came, his lower half felt back to normal, and Sadie was ahead of him, sitting down... on grass... in a field... under the gnarled, rheumatic extensions of an aging oak tree. It was summertime. Rapeseed afar filled the air with a comforting sweetness and everything felt lovely and sunny and trouble-free.

Wil looked over his shoulder, bewildered to find the fog was nowhere to be seen. In fact, all that was left of anything vaporous was a thin veil hanging around down by a pond at the bottom of the field.

'Wil.' Sadie patted a spot on the ground, indicating that he needed to join her. She appeared intent. Determined. Maybe even pressed for time.

He gingerly sat down next to her.

'Are you pleased to see me?' she asked nonchalantly, but then searched his face for something he felt might be too soon to reveal.

'Of course.' His answer was guarded.

'And were you *hoping* to see me?'

Her expression was hopeful slightly, on the verge of being hurt whatever he said. All he could do was laugh a little and momentarily looked away, embarrassed. When he turned back, she was deadly serious. No faint smile or anything. 'I guess,' he admitted awkwardly.

'Good,' she said, recalcitrant, though appearing a little relieved. 'That will help.'

'Help what?'

'Help you to remember. Things have become complicated and we can't trust the same people anymore. When you wake, you need to remember that.'

He had no idea what she was talking about. *Wake?*

'Complicated? What's become complicated?' he asked, neither feeling nor remembering anything outside this dream.

Sadie's eyes darted over to the wisp hovering above the pond and Wil's eyes naturally followed.

'Do you see that?'

'Yes.' The white patch swirled and lilted oddly with a life of its own, like a writhing knot of snakes made from cloud. Wil watched attentively as its sinister and beautiful motion seemed to stretch over the pond completely, like a disk, floating maybe a foot above its surface.

'I can't explain all of it now, because of *that*, but if you remember any of this when you wake, then come and find me. We're on the same side, Wil.' The fog churned in a uniform manner, becoming more solid in appearance, and it lifted slowly, condensing, so that Wil saw the reflection of the clouds far off down the valley on the edge of the water's surface.

'We haven't much time now,' Sadie determined, watching as the white patch seemed to have woken and looked like it was creeping up this way.

'What *is* that…?' It sounded like it was buzzing, humming.

'Don't look at it, Wil,' she put her hand onto his knee, which he couldn't help glance at. 'Just remember what I've told you—when you wake, come find me, okay?'

There she said it again. *Wake*. 'What do you mean *wake*?' he asked confusedly, his eyes drawing from her hand there on his knee. But Sadie's shoulders fell at the question and her desperation seemed to change the whole feel of the field and the surrounding countryside. Colours muted. The warmth was suddenly gone. It was as if a huge cloud passed over, affecting light and temperature, making the breeze uncomfortably cool now.

'*Please, Wil,*' she squeezed his leg, 'you *need* to remember, *we're on the same side.* Don't do anything but *find me.*'

'Find you….'

'*Yes*,' she insisted, looking over to the foggy patch that was definitely on its way. 'You're going to forget all this, but if any are on our side, you'll remember. You'll look for me. Even if it doesn't make any sense, just do it, Wil. Find me. Okay?' She looked fretfully down the hill and took her hand from him. The fog had come halfway, like a waft of smoke determined to envelop them. He couldn't take his eyes off it now.

'Please try, Wil,' she said quietly, desperately, beside him.

'Okay,' he uttered, transfixed by that droning thing rolling towards the oak. It was maybe a few feet thick, in a slightly smaller shape to the pond's surface, and it tickled the odd grassy strand like it was pulling itself closer. 'I promise. I'll try.'

Suddenly, it stopped and retreated, then crept its way back down the hill. Relieved, Wil looked over at Sadie, but she had gone. So too had the tree and the field—in fact everything now was white again like before.

All of a sudden, Wil tried thinking of the field again, but his mind went blank and he found himself in his room, awake from his nap. He rubbed the earplugs out of his aching ears, Sadie's image… her words… already fading, and that keenness he felt to understand the creeping fog somehow transferred to the events of this morning; all Wil could see in his mind was Sadie holding that canister out to him... all he could feel was the *keenness* to know what was inside it. Any *eagerness* to remember what had just happened was replaced by that eagerness he felt to get home and think through his first proper encounter with Sadie. In fact, as she and the field disappeared completely from his mind in those few seconds, everything Wil still felt as he woke slotted right back to an identically emotive point in his day—a point before the dream with her. And with this concealing shift, all impulse to remember left him completely.

Relieved, Wil was glad to find there was nothing so pressing or troubling after all that he could have forgotten about his day, about anything Sadie had said to him.

That's exactly what she said, he suddenly recalled, not sure what he was remembering, or from where. *You're going to forget all this....* He clearly remembered her speaking those words. It wasn't when she handed him the earplugs... it was *just now*, when—but all of a sudden, Wil heard a strange clatter downstairs.

It was well after noon on the clock. *No one should be home at this time.* Sitting bolt upright, Wil saw the improvement under his eyes in the mirror as his mind could only think of one person.

Annie.

He watched his own reflection ferment to anger.

Carefully, he poked his head into the hall and listened to what his sister's best friend got up to when she thought no one else was around. He crept past the closet on his right, hearing music coming through from the neighbour next door. Classical, it sounded. As he moved slowly to the landing, it grew faint until he could only hear what was going on downstairs. Sliding his hand quietly along the bannister, it occurred to him that Annie would have seen his car in the front. She could have at least had the decency to ring the bell. *Unless it's not her....*

It occurred to Wil that anyone could be down there. And if they didn't know which part of the manor his car belonged to....

Making his way silently down the steps, drawers opened and closed frantically in the kitchen with the kind of force that wasn't Annie's. In fact, it sounded like someone was looking for something, riffling through anything with a knob or a handle. Wil suddenly wished he had something—a cricket bat or ski poles from the hall closet. Without making a sound, he moved his foot to the first step, then the next, and the next, aware it was now visible to whoever was down there, and slowly—very slowly—he bent down and peered just below the ceiling level. There... *was Ben*, rummaging away with his backside poking out from the fridge door.

'Oi vagrant!' Wil hollered, to which Ben dropped a yogurt and squeezy mayonnaise bottle as he stood to attention with ham, cheese, and a loaf of bread in his arms.

'Why do you *do* that?' he demanded, wilting at the sight of Wil coming down the steps.

'Why do *you* do *that*?' Wil quipped, eyeing the lot in his arms. 'How did you get in here anyway?'

Still shaken, Ben began putting his refrigerated plunder on the island counter with apparent relief. 'Your mum showed me where the key was,' he confessed. 'Garden gnome wheelbarrow.' He went for the ham and ripped the packet open, then picked up the mayo and squirted it shamelessly onto bread.

'And you're sure that wasn't just for emergency access?' Wil asked suspiciously.

Ben stuffed a corner of a sandwich into his mouth and started chewing quickly. 'Hey, I was hungry,' he said after a hard swallow. 'What, you want me to *create* an emergency and *starve* before I should use the key...?' He filled his mouth again.

Wil smirked and shook his head incredulously on his way to the kettle. 'My mum has no idea you come and raid the cupboards. She thinks it's *me*.' He grabbed his mug from the draining board and dried the outside of it with his shirt. 'Cuppa tea?'

Ben moaned the affirmative and was already making his second sandwich when Wil turned around and pulled up a stool with their drinks a few minutes later.

'You get my text?'

'Sorry, no.'

'I've sorted something with Shellie. You'll never guess what I'm doing on Wednesdays with her.'

'Well from the look on your face, you've clearly managed to avoid basket weaving,' Wil said, watching Ben prepare the rest of his lunch at half the speed now.

'You have guessed correctly my friend,' he declared triumphantly. 'Seriously though, have a guess.'

'I don't know.' Wil was slightly impatient at the thought of a guessing game. 'What?'

Ben puffed up his chest. '*Planetarium technician.*'

'And what does that involve?'

'I have no idea, but if it means being in the dark with Shellie....' Wil threw him a doubtful sideways glare. 'I met the head and professor this morning, to show I was keen you know, and he's showing me the ropes tomorrow.' He tipped his head back and filled his mouth with meat and cheese slices straight from the packets. 'You wouldn't... believe it,' he said, carrying on in a staccato rhythm as he chewed between words, 'they needed... a bloke.... *Two* people... but no one signed up.'

'Just *chew*,' Wil urged, to which Ben nodded and swallowed.

'I think the class needs *me* as much as I need *it*. Plus, it sounds awesome. I'll learn all the constellations and do like... these little shows and stuff.'

'And you're sure Shellie is signed up?'

'There's no question.'

'And how do you know?'

'Because I asked! *Who is the other person helping?* He told me *Shellie Sanders.* So,' he mouthed the words *I think I'm okay* like he was telling a secret over the turned head of a child.

'Ben, your plan sounds like it's going well then.'

'Uh-huh,' he said smugly, shovelling lettuce into his face.

'Hey, I didn't tell you, but this morning in class, after you left, Sadie gave me some earplugs.'

'Oh yeah, they were giving those out earlier this week to get people to sign on to a sleep study. One of the Psychology classes is doing it.'

Ben said it so casually that it completely caught Wil off guard.

'And here I was thinking I was something special,' he joked. Partly.

'Sorry mate. She probably meant well though. Did she just *give* them to you?'

'She said I looked like I needed them.'

'You do. A bit. I mean, you look better now than you did earlier.... She was probably just trying to be nice....'

'Thanks,' Wil said flatly.

'You know what I *mean*. She was probably looking for an opportunity to talk to you.' He had a terrible way of smoothing things over when he was too happy with his own affairs to care for those of others around him. 'I mean, you've never even *talked* to her before, and she goes out of her way to *give* you something….' He directed his white eyebrows pointedly at Wil. 'If *I* were you, I'd jump on the possibilities.' Ben seemed quite pleased with his pep talk and started putting things back into the fridge. 'You want any of this by the way?'

'No. She did wait til everyone in the class had gone before she gave them to me.'

'Ex-actly. She was obviously waiting for the right moment.' He stopped eyeing the contents of the refrigerator and looked over his shoulder with the door wide open, 'Mind you,' he said glumly, 'if she waited for everyone else to leave… that could be interpreted in two ways.'

Wil glared. '*How*? Are you saying she didn't want to be *seen* giving them to me?' He was beginning to feel more like a receptacle for unwanted items than potential boyfriend material. 'Is she even in that class, the one doing the study?'

'No idea.' Ben pushed the door closed. 'But if she is… maybe that's her edge: corner a guy so he can't say no.'

'Sadie didn't corner me so I'd join a sleep study,' Wil insisted. 'She just gave me the earplugs. Maybe someone gave them to her and she couldn't be bothered to bin them.'

'Maybe.' Ben however appeared doubtful. 'My advice would be to forget all about *why* she did it and use them to start talking to her. Shall we HD until your mum comes home?' He didn't wait for an answer, flumped down on the couch, put his feet up on the coffee table and poised the remote like he had done this a hundred times before.

'How often do you come here when nobody's home?' Wil asked, to which Ben gave a wicked smirk from over the back of the couch.

'Only once or twice.'

Chapter Eleven

Steph-Annie

Wil watched Ben's taillights disappear off the end of the drive before turning back to the house, where again, the old woman next door stood and watched from her wide, arched window, the moonlight barely making her visible. He didn't wave this time and went back inside, turned off all the lights and went up not long after the others. Steph was in her room, and as he passed by, he heard the radio on low and considered knocking, then decided not to. But by the time he got halfway down the hall, he changed his mind again, went back and knocked gently three times.

Steph, in her pyjamas and wearing her hair in a messy ball on the top of her head, opened the door wide so that her lengthy arms stretched between the doorknob and doorjamb, like a barricade. This time though, without Annie somewhere on the other side, her posture seemed less of an affront.

'Hel-looo,' her voice lilted pleasantly with a hint of surprise. There was an awkward moment between them as she leaned her head forward a little, waiting expectantly for him to say something. However, Wil said nothing. He just stood there, blankly apprehensive, wondering why he hadn't thought of even a remotely justifiable reason to disturb his sister. Any other time he came to the threshold of this room and actually knocked, it was to simply relay a usually cryptic message from Mum, and occasionally receive one to take back. And most of the time, he just shouted through a closed door from the neutrality of the hall. But now, without Annie... or dispatch from Mum... and the door wide open, what legitimate thing could he say: I want us to be friends again, like before...?

'Wanna come in?'

'Sure,' he said quickly, impressing Steph with the actual acceptance of her offer.

She dropped her arm from the door and let him head straight for the only vacant chair in the room. The papasan in the corner with a small patchwork quilt draped over it he hadn't seen since their childhood.

'I can remember us making dens with this,' he said, delighted as much to see the thing as he was in having something to talk about. He sat down and rubbed the patches tucked around the rattan frame and made himself rigidly comfortable in his sister's room—the only room in the house, he now realised, that he avoided at all cost some days. He found himself looking around for signs of Annie's influence.

'I remember you wrapping me in it and rolling me across the floor... calling me a *piggy-in-a-blanket*,' Steph accused, standing there like she just might ask him to leave.

'I don't remember that...' he said vaguely, trying.

Glaring playfully at him, Steph closed the door. 'Course you don't.'

This was the last thing he came here to do, to be sarcastic and light or make veiled objections like he and his sister usually did when they communicated. Already, he felt liberated crossing the threshold and he felt slightly exuberant knowing that coming here spited Annie in some way, but he didn't really want to make trouble. Even in jest. The mocking remarks and cold quips, however harmless they were meant to be over the last year, they were what seemed to fill the absence of depth between him and Steph now. And quite honestly, it was the stuff of Annie and he was tired of it.

Unwilling to match his sister's sarcasm, Wil imagined himself committing his offense against her... of rolling her across the lounge floor in the colourful quilt... laughing and pushing... calling her a piggy-in-a-blanket as her muffled eight-year-old voice cried out for him to slow down... and he confessed to her just then with a surrendering grimace,

'Unfortunately, it sounds exactly like something I'd have done. I know it's probably a bit late for it now... but sorry.'

'Don't worry, I'm not scarred...' she insisted '...*much*.'

Wil exhaled deeply but quietly, finding the Annie-imitation somehow fouler when Annie wasn't around and noticed one of her charcoal drawings of Steph taped to the wall near the desk.

He looked around the unfamiliar room in his house, noting how furniture had changed since the last time he was here, and he wondered how he and his sister could be so close for years, and then, over the last year end up like strangers almost. What he knew of her now came from trivial mealtime tidings or lame one-liners that gave little indication to what was really happening in her life.

So much has changed....

Wil imagined that maybe it might not have if he hadn't let Annie just come and take over. But instead he had allowed her to slowly fill the comforting spaces in his house until there was nothing left. Over the last year, he watched her move from room to room, floor to floor, leaving him with no place he felt confident was his.

The pantry was where it started.

After they came back from London last summer, when Annie wouldn't dare wander off upstairs if Steph wanted to stay downstairs, he hung out in the old Ercol armchair in the corner of the pantry, wasting his time on the laptop. With Mum and Dad not far away in the main room, he at least felt a little protected from Annie's intolerable dramatic streak, knowing she put a lid on it when they were around. Not only that, but his space in the pantry helped him too to defy that urge to retreat to his bedroom where he was certain he'd just end up feeling like a prisoner in his own home. Even Ben liked the gloomy margins of the pantry, enticingly packed out with dry foodstuffs where he easily trolled cupboards, sampled snacks and enthusiastically made suggestions for the week's meals. But then one day, Annie came in and started rearranging things... cleaning... putting stuff away... aimlessly looking for this or that while he and Ben waited for her to leave. And after it happened once, it happened over and over again, just to annoy him, flushing him out, he was certain, whenever she came round. It became increasingly difficult for him to know if she was over or not, the way she lurked around the place after that, and the pantry quickly became another of those no-go areas.

Just like Steph's room.

Steph went and sat on her bed. She crossed her legs, watching him take in the space and he was reminded of the last time he was here. It was before last spring. He walked by late one night, heard the music playing quietly and knocked... for some reason that presently escaped him. A cheerful, familiar voice encouraged him from the other side. Only, when he pushed the door open and started to come in, there was Annie, who he thought left, lying where Steph sat just now, stretched out on her side with a text book open on the pillow. Shocked and confused at the time, he had been certain it was Steph's voice he heard. He even looked behind the door, convinced she was in there somewhere.

'Not expecting me?' Annie said in that antagonising way that made her sound six years old.

'Where's Steph?'

'Out.'

Annie's demeanour suddenly changed as she turned her head slightly towards her slender body and fixed a sideways gaze on him. She then ran her hand slowly along her waist... down her hip... and lifted her leg effortlessly to a 90° angle, all the while focused on him. At this point, he felt uncomfortable, backing out of the room slowly, yet he was somehow transfixed by her strange provocation. 'Do you like babies, Wil?' she said quietly as she slid her hand obscenely down the inside of her leg. '*I do.*' She then let her leg fall with ease to her shoulder.

It was intimidation. But instead of giving her the satisfaction of seeing him awkward or repulsed, he said plainly, as though unaffected,

'I came for Steph.'

'And instead... you found me....'

'Not quite what I was looking for.'

'Then look a bit closer.' She put her leg gracefully back down and subtly batted her eyelids, as though presenting herself to him.

'I don't know what *this* is about, Annie,' he said dismissively, looking a little disappointed in her, 'but you can't possibly believe I'd fall for that....' He cast a disgusted glance along her legs. 'Is that supposed to make me think you're interested in me or something?' Her expression was faultless and she said nothing, gave nothing away, to which he started to leave.

'Next time, don't pretend to sound like Steph if you didn't want me in here in the first place.'

After he shut the door, he stood there in the hall for a second, wondering where Steph had actually gone and heard Annie say aloud to herself, 'Who says I *didn't* want you in here? If only you knew....'

Plucking the frayed threads of the patchwork quilt under his wrist, Wil imagined he had been a disappointment to his sister, turning her over to the wiles of Annie to spare himself. No wonder she had changed. Only because he had. Keeping his distance... turning his back on her. Maybe the sarcasm and cold quips weren't all Annie's fault.

Digressing from his guilt, he stood up to absorb the changes in his sister's room, and spotted a group photo with Annie next to Ben's sister Zara. Zara was a petite version of Steph, easy to recognise and her image was partly cropped away to fit the oval frame.

'Isn't that Annie and Zara?' he asked, bending towards the frame there on the floating shelf.

'Um…' Steph leaned over to see, 'I think so.'

'Weren't they good friends for a while, when we were in London?'

'They were…. I don't think so now.' She was being diplomatic.

'I never really understood from Ben what happened between them,' he commented, hoping she would elaborate. 'I thought Zara was really good for Annie while we were away.'

'Well you'd think with her turnover of friends she might try to keep one, wouldn't you?' Steph said wryly, not making it clear as to whether she was speaking about Annie or Zara. Wil was tempted to ask which, however gave a bemused nod.

'That's quite good' he said, noticing a photo where Steph had taken a picture of her own shadow. It was long and stark, maybe at the end of the day, on a beach, and Annie's actual feet were standing on Steph's head, her shadow head. There was another photo next to it with her and Annie together at some dance event. In this second photo, they were standing side-by-side, wearing identical outfits and name badges. 'Were you two in some competition here?' He smiled over his shoulder at her, but she looked a bit distracted.

'You could say that,' she said sarcastically, sardonic, and Wil got the feeling she wasn't talking about dance. In fact, it was beginning to feel like she was trying to get him to do what they used to so easily, draw the other out in the gentle give and take of intuitive conversation. Only, they hadn't done that for ages and this felt a spoiled likeness. But it was better than nothing.

'I take it you don't mean a dance competition then.' He met her evasive glance with determination. 'What did you mean, Steph?'

She set her jaw, pulled her crossed legs closer and folded her arms. 'Do they not tell you plenty?' she shrugged at the photos. 'People are starting to call us *Steph-Annie*,' she said disgustedly, 'like *Kimye*.'

Wil frowned, realising the badges in the dance event photo boldly displayed the names Steph and Annie in that order. And as his eyes moved from the beach shadow picture where Annie was stepping on his sister's head, back to her sweaty arm draped lazily over Steph's hunched shoulders (because Steph was taller by comparison), these two images spoke volumes about how his sister was feeling just now.

'I hate these by the way,' she determined, getting up and peeling the pictures off the wall. She then tore them to pieces and dropped them in the bin on her way back to the bed. 'She thinks it's funny, but actually, I don't want to be some *extension* of her. I'm my *own* person....' Her focus glazed over momentarily, appearing to mentally recount wrongs, and just as quickly as her mind vacated the room, she arrived again, determined. 'Besides, it would be good for Annie to have other friends.'

Wil seemed to miss a link there when she became distant for that second, but it didn't matter. Steph was obviously considering stepping back from Annie and he had to do his best not to be ecstatic about it.

'What kind of friends do you think she needs then, aside from you,' he proffered.

'The kind who fulfil her little fantasies.' She shot a wildly evasive look at him before composing herself and shrugging it off as though it didn't matter. It struck Wil how uncharacteristic it was for his sister—*his tolerant sister*—to have such disgust and anger towards *anyone,* much less her best friend. She always saw the best in others, giving them the benefit of the doubt.

'Have you two had an argument?'

She started kneading her foot with both hands. 'No. I'm just not as naïve as I used to be.'

The wounded look she had just then resembled the old Steph, and feeling the privilege suddenly of being here again, Wil knew he needed to avoid the temptation to just flagrantly attack Annie's character. She seemed to be damaging it well enough on her own. No, he'd have to assume a more passive role here. He had to be neutral. A safe haven.

'Steph, you've been a good friend to Annie,' he offered sincerely, taking the seat in the papasan again, 'and you put up with a lot.'

'I know,' she said plainly, suddenly finding interest in her cuticles. 'That's why *you're* here... and *she's* not.' A few seconds passed and she tentatively met his eyes. 'I've put up another picture,' she said cheerfully, changing the subject, 'and I think you'll appreciate it.'

Intrigued, he watched as she pulled her pillows away from the toile headboard and contentedly presented a photo pinned low to its fabric.

He got up to have a proper look.

There in the corner, tucked almost below the mattress and obviously covered by the duvet when the bed was made, Wil found an old picture of Steph, age four, holding her hands in the shape of a heart close to the lens of the camera, with a blurry smile shining through the space between her fingers. A flurry of memories stretched happily across his face. It was their little signal. Like a wave in the distance, a code between them. *Good-bye.* But it wasn't just *good-bye.* It was *I love you.*

Wil suddenly felt the sting of tears forcing to the corners of his eyes and he tried hard to hide them with a huge quizzical smile. 'I forgot all about that' he lied, because he had only been thinking of this same gesture between them the other day. And the thought of his sister hiding this very picture in her room from Annie... while he was wishing they could be closer like before... it felt like they were on the same side again.

'I love this picture' she admitted, pushing the pin in deeper. Then looking up at him, 'What is it?'

'Nothing.' But the timing was uncanny. Three years of distance, now this. 'That's one of my favourite pictures of you. I'm glad you've put it up.' He turned from her and quickly blinked away the dampness in his eyes on the way back to the chair.

The two of them beamed in their respective corners of the room, catching the other doing the same, which ensured more beaming, and Wil couldn't help see that little four-year-old's smile coming through those heart-shaped fingers in that photo pour right out of the girl sitting on the bed. It felt like no time at all had been lost.

'I've missed coming here' he admitted.

Steph pursed a smile and gave him a look just short of regret.

'Well, next time you're passing' she brightened, 'just knock.'

'You make it sound so simple...'

'It is. You just mosey your stupid self to my door....' She then shrugged her shoulders, settling the matter.

'Seriously though,' he could, however, already see the dangers, 'I don't want to be a wedge between you and Annie, but I *do* want to feel like I have a sister... that we can talk like this, like we used to.'

'I *am* being serious, Wil. And don't worry about Annie. She'll get over herself. And actually, you'll be doing me a favour showing your face a bit more when she's around.'

'All right then, I will.'

'Okay.'

'*Okay.*'

Wil took in a deep breath, glad he hadn't ignored that niggling feeling he got outside in the hall on his way to his bedroom half an hour ago. It was the beginning of him reclaiming his sister. And apparently, of her wanting to do the same with him.

Wil smiled contentedly and gave a little decisive pat to the quilted arms of the chair as he readied to leave.

'You're not going, are you? It's barely 10:30.'

'I'll be back,' he assured. 'Short and sweet to start.' He got up, opened the door and started closing it slowly behind him. 'And not too long in between,' he said resolutely through the narrowing gap.

'Seriously Wil... *knock.*'

'I promise. I will.'

He sat on his bed and looked at the back of his door. The dart board there, with all its confining rings, no longer reminded him of that trapped feeling he sometimes felt after he passed his sister's room, especially when he heard her giggling and chattering away with Annie. He often saw Steph situated perfectly in the middle, that red circle, and he and Annie were those alternating wedges of black and white, vying, reinforcing that image of barriers to the centre. Somehow, Annie always seemed to be a segment closer to the bull's-eye. A step ahead of him. *Not so now*, he felt certain, because like that little bacterium he saw Monday night... he just broke free. And there would be no stopping him now. Because he and his sister were made of the same stuff... on the same side again.

Suddenly.

We're on the same side....

Only, the words determinedly forming in Wil's mind weren't those of his own internal voice. It was... *Sadie's.* Sadie in his dream. From the nap.

We're on the same side....

'Why was she saying that...?' he muttered, staring hard into the centre of the dart board, certain there was something he wanted to remember.

Needed to remember....

Chapter Twelve

Find Me

Bewildered, Wil lumbered from the fog, his normal-looking legs feeling strangely elongated and heavy. They tingled and tightened as though shrinking back to normal and he found himself on the sloping field again, under the heavy arms of the oak tree, with a ribbon of mist suspended down by the pond. It was all fascinatingly familiar, but he didn't know why, and finding himself drawn to the water, he wandered in its direction.

'You've got a terrible memory,' someone said coyly from behind him.

Sadie? 'Have I?' he asked innocently, turning around. Somehow he knew it would be her.

'Obviously. *I* wouldn't go down there if I were you….'

He glanced over his shoulder at the mist, curious.

'You don't want to go back *now*, do you? We've only just started.' And folding her arms, she glowered at him. 'So, how many times are you going to make me do this Wilden?'

'Pardon?'

'We were in a hurry last time, and my opportunities are disappearing. I'm relying on you to *remember* this one.' She sounded more desperate than authoritative. 'Right now you're dreaming, but at least *try* to remember... when you wake up, *find me*.' She walked past him and paused, staring off down the valley. 'I think part of the problem is you don't believe me. Or maybe you don't believe this is really me,' she said thoughtfully. 'So what's it going to take to get you to find me, Wil?'

She narrowed in on him from over her shoulder. 'Neon signs don't work. What about a megaphone? Writing in the sky? Would you find me then?'

'But you're... *right here.*'

Flustered, 'Did you not hear what I just *said*?' She stepped towards him in earnest. 'You're *dreaming* now. *When you wake up...* that's when you need to *find me.* And you mustn't *forget* this time.' She looked back down the field to the white mist and started walking, then running. And it was like she clapped or something, her hands seemed to come together in front of her, and she was gone.

Wil woke immediately with a disorientating beam of sun spreading liberally throughout his room, and having already forgotten his second dream with Sadie, the very most it inspired was that familiar feeling that he needed to be somewhere.

7:48am.

Media! ...Homework!

He grabbed his phone and quickly forwarded the assignment to the professor, watching the data bar creep across to *100%*. With the confirmation *whoosh,* his entire Friday suddenly became free. Cheerfully, he took the one earplug from his ear, the other from beside his pillow and popped them into the bedside drawer, feeling yet again there was something he was supposed to do.

'Morning Sunshine...' he croaked, knocking quietly on Steph's door on his way downstairs, to which a faint 'Morning...' followed. Any of the guilt he felt before standing here, the fear and worry of losing his sister, it faded away as if bleached out by the sun that poured from his bedroom and filled the hall. Anything Annie had over him, he felt certain now, was gone.

Downstairs, he found Mum ready for work, quickly making a large quantity of tea in a Pyrex jug. 'Morning Love. Don't you need to get ready for school?' She glanced at his pyjama bottoms, bare feet.

'It's Media today. I could have joined the online discussion this morning but chose the written assignment instead. I've got a free day now.'

'Well don't be too chipper in front of your Dad,' she warned, poking bloated tea bags with a spoon. 'He didn't sleep well at all last night.' She emptied what was left of the milk bottle into the jug and pulled open the fridge door. 'Is that *really* the last of the milk?' she asked, incredulous.

'I think so....'

'What about the little pantry fridge?'

'No. Unless you count the bottle Ben's been drinking out of.'

'*Ugh*,' she screwed up her face, 'I *used* that last night.... I wish he wouldn't do that.' She shut the fridge door in annoyance and grabbed the box of powdered milk in the cupboard above the kettle. 'Well there's that if we're desperate. I don't imagine he'll chug *that* anytime soon. You wouldn't mind stopping at the shops later, would you? Your Dad and I need to get my car in first thing... and I have no idea when it'll be done.'

'Yeah, sure.'

Dad came down, wearing glasses instead of contacts, and with his greying hair scruffy around the ears, his drawn, weary expression suddenly made him look ten years older.

'Sorry to do this to you Darling,' Mum thrust a flask into his left hand as he stood ambivalent at the bottom step, two slices of toast into his right, 'but we've got to leave pretty much *now*.'

He looked quizzically at his take-away breakfast, then to Wil. 'You're up early. How's your second week of college?' But Mum wasn't about to tolerate the delay and started leading Dad by the elbow towards the coat pegs and shoe pile. 'The one day I can see my son before work....'

'Yes well you've seen him now, *let's go*....'

'Well, perhaps we'll meet again some other time lad,' Dad said wryly, disappearing with Mum down the hall.

Just as the door slammed behind them, the boiler clunked to a halt, signalling the end of Steph's shower. Wil went up and hurried through his turn, and chirped his way downstairs, hoping to catch Steph before her ride to school. But as he stood at the bottom step, feeling balked by the silence, and after calling for her in the pantry, a disheartening loneliness came over him.

But then, he noticed something. There beside the kettle. A warm cup of tea had been left with little clumps of powdered milk in, and beside it, a banana peel draped in the shape of a heart.

Good-bye. And, *I love you.*

Grinning, Wil thought back to last week... running to catch the Bodhan's car on the drive to pass Steph her dance kit. He got a sheepish *thanks*, maybe because Annie was there in the backseat too... but when the car moved on, leaving him in the middle of the dusty drive, without so much as a glance from the back window....

He suddenly welcomed the wave of memories he was reluctant to let flood his mind last night and thought of those times when Steph would drive off in the back of Granny Lynn's car for a sleepover.... She might have been four then. Or five. Nearly every time, he'd run down the road of the old house, keeping up with the car for as long as he could, curling his fingers and joining his thumbs together while she cheered him through the window. When he couldn't keep up and his heart pounded so hard he thought it had split in half and floated up into his ears, he waited there beside the road, hands on knees, catching his breath as her happy little face beamed out of sight around the corner. How he missed her already.

Staring at the peel, Wil's grin faded. There was that time Steph had to go to hospital to have her tonsils out. The car was by the curb with the engine running, warming up in the frosty spring morning. Mum and Dad gathered last-minute things for her stay as Steph sat in the chair by the door, overly-bundled, pinching her fingertips apprehensively. The commotion carried on around her and Wil remembered Granny Lynn, Mum's mum, sending him upstairs to get his school jumper. When she asked him to go up, he didn't want to. Not just yet. Not until Mum and Dad had left with Steph. But it wasn't the time to make a fuss. Grudgingly, he went up and sifted through the pile of clothes on his floor, and the second he snapped up that jumper, the sound of the car engine gently revved and idled down, sending his heart racing.

Even now, as the banana sat before Wil, that resentment of not being able to say good-bye unfastened inside him. He remembered dashing to his bedroom window, seeing if Steph was already in the car. The backseat windows were still defrosting but he could just make out a dark shape filling the space behind the driver's side. Suddenly, Steph's face peered through a little patch. She was wiping the condensation away—she was looking for him. *Up here! Look up here....!* He shouted at her over and over... knocking frantically on the glass, and when Granny waved from the path and Dad rolled up his window, he knew there was no time to get down there. Despite her little swipe fogging up again, he made their sign, pressing his hands hard against the glass. *Bye Stephie...! Bye...!* At that moment, he felt certain she was about to pull away from the curb without seeing his good-bye, but then she suddenly wiped her window afresh and her pale little face filled the clear patch. She was looking upwards in his direction! His heart leapt, for she smiled wide at him, and maybe she was even saying something. Shouting. Her mittens then filled the space, covering her face as she tried mimicking him: *Good-bye... I love you....*

And then she was gone.

Wil remembered spending the whole day expecting Granny to tell him Steph was never going to come home…that something horrible had happened, as it so often did in Dad's cryptic hospital stories over dinner.

Steph was four when she had her tonsils out, the same age she was in that photo Wil saw last night. Why that memory caught him off guard when she showed it to him, he didn't know, but it gave him such contentment to know that while they made their heart-shaped hands for years… and stopped for reasons he couldn't put a finger on… here they were again, using the gesture to rekindle their friendship. Ironically, it seemed more like a *hello* than a *good-bye*, after so many years of nothing.

Wil microwaved his tea and sent Steph a heart-hands emoji. He then texted Ben, who replied,

Going in for Planetarium Training. Let's meet at 11.

Wil had his tea, and rinsing the powdery clumps out of his mug remembered to get more milk. Half an hour later, he found himself in the large supermarket on the edge of town.

Bargain announcements played over the loud speakers as he headed for the electronics section at the back, however, the 9am crowd could not be inspired, ambling along with their baskets in a trance state, letting their trollies lead them like some sort of divining stick. It was a sight to watch compared to the frantic after-work crowd he found himself caught up with every now and again. From the look of it, this lot were too tired to be in a hurry. Bedraggled night-shift staff, just off from work at the hospital and still wearing their uniforms, seemed to go adrift. Even the mum with a baby and two toddlers that screeched in the snack aisle louder than the deal-of-the-day announcements had come unmoored, drifting with a blank expression down the aisle towards Wil. He wished for a moment that he could tune out the noises as easily as she could.

Ten minutes into perusing headphones and cameras, the monotone voice from a female store clerk interrupted a prerecorded advertisement on the audio system. Her lips, too close to the microphone, rendered her sentences unintelligible and shoulder-rollingly loud. Thankfully, whatever she had to say, it was brief, and the speakers reverted back to pacifying elevator music.

And there she goes again…!

Irritated, Wil moved from the phone accessories section and on towards the laptops where a speaker wasn't right above him. He tried blocking out the now urgent, grating voice, but....

This... this is torturous.

Abandoning all desire to hang about in the shop for longer than necessary, he headed for the milk aisle as the same voice went on a third time, however, with less abuse of the audio system.

'This is a customer announcement...' she enunciated, her lips clearly away from the mic, 'if anyone knows a Sadie, please come to the Service Desk. Sadie is waiting at the kiosk... please come and find her. Again, come to the Service Desk kiosk at the front of the store, Sadie is waiting. '

Sadie? Wil stood there stupidly. *Did she actually say Sadie?* He cocked his head sceptically there in the meat aisle, uncertain as to what he actually heard, but at that precise moment... a most vivid image of Sadie appeared in his mind—Sadie under a tree, imploring. *She did say Sadie,* he was convinced, *she did.* Why it was of any concern to him, he couldn't be sure, but replaying the clerk's words in his head... seeing Sadie... he started walking slowly to the front of the store.

'What am I doing?' he realised halfway down the aisle. '*Milk—I need milk.*'

The involuntary move towards Customer Service unnerved him as he turned around and headed for the dairy section, and while the words from the announcement played over in his mind, that image of Sadie was what really had his attention. What was she doing—saying?

Without warning, the two thoughts meshed and that imploring Sadie began mimicking the announcement running in the background of his head—and it hit him—in one step-stopping instant, it hit him hard.

This morning's dream....

Just as he remembered something of the nap yesterday hours later when he again thought of Steph, positioned away from him and Annie like the bull's-eye on the dartboard... (*...We're on the same side...*) ...this morning's connection suddenly came to him in one unexpected, vivid and bursting moment. *Find me.* That's what Sadie said under the tree. *Find me....* Wil carried on towards the milk aisle, trying hard not to turn towards the front of the store, but the further he went, the more he remembered dream-Sadie pleading,

...You're dreaming now. When you wake up... that's when you need to find me. And you mustn't forget this time....

But the PA—the dream—they weren't connected, surely....

...This is a customer announcement... if anyone knows a Sadie, please come to the Service Desk. Sadie is waiting at the kiosk... please come and find her. Again, come to the Service Desk kiosk at the front of the store, Sadie is waiting...

Standing there in front of the milk, Wil couldn't help but find the timing, the wording... coincidental. Part of him wanted to run to the front of the store, part of him wanted to stand right where he was for as long as possible, because really... would Sadie be waiting there—waiting for him to go down that aisle to find her?

Of course she wouldn't. He was almost certain of it.

Almost.

At that moment, when logic and absurdity seemed one and the same, Wil felt the great weight of some vague thing clambering over him. Whatever it was, it had the power to undermine any thought he had, any choice he felt himself about to make. This great thing, it seemed to hold his feet in place, keeping him from doing anything, thinking anything— anything accept *milk*.

'Milk,' he managed to say to himself feebly, contending with this thing that now rendered him immobile. 'Milk....' Why couldn't he think of anything else? *This* began to occupy his thoughts.

For a split second, the weight of this thing shifted and it was like Wil had snapped out of a trance. Decisively, he grabbed two jugs of semi-skimmed and hustled towards the front of the store, zipping past a dazed old woman scrutinising the label on the back of a tin. Whatever that something was that snagged him back there, it seemed to hang on his heels by its fingernails as he dragged it with him down the aisle on the way to Customer Service. The only way he felt certain to get away from it... was to see if Sadie was there at the kiosk. Lengthening his stride, he couldn't help himself. Nothing else was as important. Nearing the end of the aisle, his heart raced, his breath became slight. Any second now....

He rounded the corner and stalled.

The hanging Customer Service sign swayed under the air-conditioning vent above the desk, its inane movement harassing him as much as the something he couldn't shake off his heels. *Where is she...?*

No one was there—aside from two teenage store clerks who eyed him oddly, like he disappointed them somehow.

Just then, a frantic voice came from his left, 'Sadie...?' It was the mother with the toddlers and baby, and as Wil stood between the desk and the woman hurrying towards him with one child missing from her trolley, he began to feel deeply disgusted with himself. *Of course. A lost child. Named Sadie.*

The taller clerk came from behind the desk, holding the hand of a little girl who promptly yelled 'Mummy...!' and broke free with a wild stomping run towards her horrified, though relieved, mother.

'I was just trying something on...' she began to explain, as though the store clerks had just revealed themselves to be social workers. But Wil didn't bother to stay and listen to how she lost track of her child because all he could hear were Sadie's pointless words going through his head, over and over as he went through the self-checkout. *When you wake up, find me... find me, Wilden... find me....*

But by the time he dropped the milk off at home and dashed across campus to meet Ben in the planetarium, he dismissed the supermarket experience as nothing but coincidence. That, and wishful thinking.

'*Finally*...' Ben huffed, standing outside the planetarium staff door, 'I said *11am*—I've got to take the keys back in 20 minutes....'

'Sorry,' Wil breathed, seeing it was already ten past on his watch, 'the carpark was a nightmare.' Ben got over his annoyance and gave Wil a wicked grin as he opened the door wide, welcoming his friend down the dark hallway.

Wil looked cautiously into the blackness. 'What are you up to in there?'

'Just come in,' Ben urged with a hurrying movement of his upper body that looked like he was mime-heaving some heavy thing out of the way so Wil could pass. 'You won't believe this place. C'mon—it's absolutely *amazing*—we haven't got much time....'

Wil stepped enough inside that Ben could close the door behind them. 'What have you been doing in here?' he felt the need to whisper all of a sudden.

'Learning the technical stuff,' Ben said obviously. 'But other stuff too. You've gotta see this... don't worry, no one's here....'

Ben led them down the narrow hall, lit like a movie theatre with dim uplighters along the floor, and as Wil's eyes adjusted to the dark, they entered the small control room where screens and indicators glowed above dials and sliding switches across a console desk. Wil noticed too, now that he could see better, that the shape of the desk was that of a crescent moon, and that the lunar workstation purred quietly while various parts made self-regulating noises.

'So they let you loose in here after just a few hours?' Wil asked doubtfully.

'Of course,' Ben said, taking a seat in the swivel chair and pulling himself into the sweeping arc of the moon as he repositioned one of the wiry fibre-optic lights that grew out of the control panel like a coarse hair. 'Now, watch this.'

An almost undetectable glow of morning twilight crept above the artificial horizon in the main room. The simulation was so faint that Wil wasn't sure if his eyes were playing tricks on him, but as he watched Ben looking from the controls to the darkness outside their little room, comparing the effect with whatever he was doing through the laptop and dials, a beautiful, gradual change was indeed happening around them.

Wil found himself moving to the doorway, a step into the projection dome. This was his first experience in a planetarium and he couldn't help but notice the eerie dampening of sound, like being in a closet full of coats, contradicted by the appearance of an open expanse above him. As the shift from night to day hastened, the idea that the entire simulated universe could be compressed into such a small space... felt like quite an amazing accomplishment for whoever invented planetariums. And just as Wil started wondering how Ben could get himself into a Wednesday activity that was this cool, something ridiculous spoiled the morning sky. The words *SHELLIE, KISS ME* appeared on the dome surface and their uncomfortably bright font seemed to offend more than just Wil's eyes.

'*Seriously?*' Wil mumbled, realising this was what Ben had been all keyed up to show him. He turned to Ben. '*What is that?*' he demanded dully.

'What do you mean, *what is that?*' Ben challenged, eyeing the words as though they couldn't be clearer. 'What does it *look like?*'

Wil rolled his eyes. 'Please tell me you're not planning to actually do this when Shellie's *in here*. Please tell me this isn't the next step in your big plan.'

'No...' Ben answered defensively, then perked up with 'but it's *one* of them' like he had a dozen other ideas he wanted to try first. 'Seriously? Do you not see the potential here? Personally, I think it's ingenious.'

'It's definitely to the point,' Wil noted, squinting up at the audacious words. 'I'll give you that.'

Ben fiddled with something on the console, removed the words, and morning became night with bright stars fixed in the distance. That deep darkness and those sparse points of light spoke volumes about the universe, Wil thought as Ben left the desk to stand beside him.

'When you look at this stuff, doesn't it make you feel so small, like a grain of sand on the beach...' Ben suggested quietly, '...a meaningless bit amid all other meaningless bits? It occurred to me earlier that you can either stand here and see yourself as insignificant or you can try and *do* something, *be* something significant. Listen to me! I'm starting to sound like *you*,' he chuckled and returned to the desk. 'Seriously though, how can I sit here and see all *that* and just *plod on*?' He started typing on the laptop but then paused, fixing on Wil thoughtfully. 'It's either *be nothing*, or *be something... am* nothing... *am* something.... I mean, it's beyond comprehension any way you look at it. And when you think about everything *out there*,' he nodded to the simulated universe beyond, 'it makes you wonder *how* people ever find purpose, happiness, and when they do... it seems meaningless to have looked for it in the first place— look for anything, pursue that *something*... and well, basically... *die*.'

'Geez Ben, where did all *that* come from? You've obviously spent too much time in here!'

'I'm just saying... it's all mind-blowing, don't you think? Whether you choose to *be something* or not, it's all pointless in the end... in *all this*....' His mouth gaped momentarily towards the constellation Cygnus, to which Wil declared flatly,

'Yeah well, don't look at *all that!* C'mon Ben, you can't possibly think life is *that* meaningless if you're sitting there contemplating your existence *all for the sake of a girl?* I mean, that *is* why you're sitting here in the first place, is it not? So are you trying to tell me you've already given up on Shellie then?'

'Are you kidding? I'm still a *man* Wilden—I have needs,' he beamed, coming fully out of his existential lament. 'Speaking of, so are you. And seeing as we are men of the something-not-nothing kind, have you thought about the possibilities?'

'Possibilities?'

'You know, the ones I was telling you about yesterday.'

Wil had no idea what he was talking about.

'*The earplugs!*' Ben exclaimed, prompting Wil to throw back his head in recollection. 'I'm sure you thought I'd just forget all about it...be too consumed with Shellie. The thing is, I can't let you waste an opportunity, mate.' Again, Ben briefly did something on the laptop. 'Do you know how easy she's making it for you? I mean, if Shellie gave me something…. Seriously, there's a way in *right there*. You just need to talk to her.'

'We'll see.' The incident in the supermarket quite honestly made any talk of Sadie feel weird. And as far as Wil was concerned, having seen Ben's track record, and experiencing the folly of wishful thinking only hours ago, it was yet again apparent that grand ideas about romance never amounted to more than disappointment.

'*We'll see?* What does *that* mean?' Ben recoiled, irritated.

'It means I don't have to do anything about it right now. Just wait til next week. I don't know… just wait and see.'

Ben slid forward in his swivel chair, wearing his confrontational face. In the darkness, it looked particularly intimidating. 'Do you actually think you'll feel any differently by then—if you just *wait and see*?' His sneering tone annoyed Wil now. 'You're the one who wants to be the Behavioural Psychologist, Wil, and if you think *doing* something is *waiting* until next week when you'll end up sitting behind her, daydreaming about saying something, but doing absolutely nothing, then *nothing* is going to happen between the two of you.'

His convincing authority on the matter caught Wil off guard. In fact, Ben's impassioned words got Wil feeling slightly insecure, because he was right. Ben was right. Ben was never right.

Noticing how uncomfortable Wil was just then, Ben rolled back in his chair and softened his tone slightly, 'You know she has a class in the Sedgemoor Building that gets out in ten minutes. Why don't you conveniently…' he shrugged menacingly like a mafia boss '…cross paths?'

'I don't think so,' Wil decided swiftly, feeling physically unwell at the thought of such spontaneity. 'Besides, she'll think I'm stalking her or something. And just out of curiosity, how do you know where her class is?'

'Doesn't matter,' Ben did that shrug again. 'Now c'mon,' he urged, having none of it, 'if anything, she'll think you've gone out of your way to see her, and girls love that kind of stuff.'

'That's your tactic, Ben. Not mine.'

'No, *yours* is let's wait and see what happens. And what happens? *Absolutely nothing.*'

He was absolutely serious. Maybe even angry. It made no sense.

'Why are you *bothered* about this? Why do you even *care*?'

'Because *you* never take your own advice, Wilden. I do, and where has it left me? You're too cautious and you won't even admit it… I mean, seriously, how many girlfriends have you had?'

There was an awkward silence between them because the answer was an embarrassing *none*. And Wil couldn't even keep count how many Ben had, there had been so many. As much as Wil wanted to avoid thinking about it right at this very moment, Ben had a point. His advice *was* cautious. And where did that get him, them?

'Just take my advice for a change,' Ben soothed. 'What's the worst that can happen?' He slid into to the curve of the desk, apparently indifferent now to what Wil might decide, and it was here that Wil realised his friend was making considerable effort to do right by him. This conversation wasn't about *Ben's* love interests, what *Ben* could gain… it was about what Wil had often wanted, but never had. 'I'm telling you though,' he added with mock-heaviness, 'what's the point of anything if you don't put yourself out there and fight for it a little? Otherwise, you're only fighting yourself… your fear….'

'Where are you getting this stuff?' Wil retorted, amused slightly. 'And where's my friend Ben?'

'Everyone knows the truth hurts sometimes,' Ben acknowledged, enjoying his elevated position in the conversation, 'but you can't just expect the girl of your dreams to fall into your arms, now can you? You've got to go and get her.' He nonchalantly pressed a button on the laptop so that something appeared on the surface of the dome. The sudden bright light grabbed Wil's attention, and glancing up to the dome, still confused by Ben's new approach to relationship advice, Wil saw words stretched across the night sky. Only, they weren't *SHELLIE, KISS ME.* Instead, they were *Go Find Sadie.*

'I dare say, it's written in the stars,' Ben declared, making light of the now stunned look on Wil's face. 'Now go and ask her out….'

But as soon as the words up there passed in front of Wil's eyes, Sadie's voice began sounding in his mind, like a train far off. He could hear it gaining momentum, volume, force, and as he blinked hard at those unlikely words, her voice suddenly clacketed through him, whooshing past, pushing him back with such power that he slumped against the wall of the control room.

'No need to be dramatic,' Ben sniffed.

But Wil couldn't answer. Sadie's pointed voice roared inside him: *What's it going to take to get you to find me, Wilden? Neon signs don't work. What about a megaphone? Writing in the sky? Would you find me then? What's it going to take to get you to find me Wilden—neon signs don't work—what about a megaphone—writing in the sky—would you find me then?* They went over and over again, almost rhythmic the fourth time around, forcing him to listen... forcing him to understand.

And then suddenly, he did.

Like that moment in the supermarket when he actually thought Sadie might be waiting for him at the service desk, he believed again that he was supposed to go and find her. *The writing in the sky....* It was right there in front of him, written across the galaxies—it couldn't have been plainer. *And the megaphone...* he only just realised, but the PA system in the store... it was the megaphone. *And the neon sign...* he had to think for a minute. In the dream she said it hadn't worked, as if he had overlooked it already, before his dream with her this morning....

Of course! The neon pencil pouch! She spent the entire class writing out the words *FIND ME* on it in huge letters last week.

But how can it be...?

The instant Wil questioned the illuminating connections he had made with his dream and the events of his day, a turbulent spin of memories seemed to override Sadie's voice, making her silent, reeling his mind into places beyond comprehension. Dreams and half-dreams suddenly defied logic, and yet they made perfect sense. His unconscious and conscious worlds collided fantastically with Sadie somehow at their centre... and finding her suddenly seemed the most important thing he could do.

Only, Wil couldn't move. Like that moment in the supermarket, when he stood in the milk aisle and that thing clambered over him, it was doing it now, locking his feet in place as it seemed to suck all the inspiration out of him. He wanted to run from it, but couldn't. *Run where?* he felt like he was being forced to think. *To Sadie?* The voice inside his head was snide, as though any thought of running to her would be preposterous.

Wil looked over at Ben hopelessly confused, immobile, but his best friend just sat there, grinning at his handy work gleaming down from the dome.

You mustn't go to her... she'll only laugh at you... don't listen to Ben... when it all plays out, he won't actually be right about any of this....

He closed his eyes, desperate to hush the loudening voice in his head.

Go to her. Find her, something whispered. Something easier, something familiar to hear.

Wil lifted his head to the words shining down on him.

That's what he really wanted to do. Since the first time he saw her. He wanted to find Sadie.

Just then, the horrible thing clinging to him seemed to suddenly slide right out of his head and down his back, lifeless.

Go! Go now!

'I need to find her!' Wil declared, and he left that horrible thing there in the dark and ran down the dimly lit hall to Sedgemoor Building.

'You're welcome...!' Ben hollered.

Chapter Thirteen

Found

The Sedgemoor Building, with its modern, open-plan, transparent features, loomed in front of Wil.

There's no way I'm going in there, he thought to himself as he stood at the bottom of the granite steps and peered into the glass façade, moving his eyes up the first and second floors, searching for Sadie like she was some fish in a teeming fish tank. With classes clearly ending and starting again in ten minutes, bodies began to move purposefully in and out of the building, along the landings, up and down the transparent staircases. If Ben was right, and Sadie was in there, due to come out any minute, she would end up only these ten steps away.

Nervous, Wil began pacing the base of the steps. He shifted his glance to whoever came out of the double doors and periodically inspected the bodies strewn over brightly coloured bean bags in the stylish student lounge that occupied most of the ground floor. For a heart-stopping instant, he thought he saw Sadie, but then realised it was someone else— some other girl with lovely, silky brown hair. Relived slightly by this, it suddenly occurred to him,

And what am I supposed to say...?

There was no sign of that strange thing holding onto him that he encountered in the supermarket and planetarium, however something else was stopping him from wanting to stand there a moment longer. It felt like levelheadedness. Sound judgement. Pure and simple reason, tamping down hard on him, because he was about to tell a complete stranger that he believed... *they shared a dream together.* How was he supposed to do that without sounding like a lunatic? He'd most certainly ruin any chance of speaking to her again, and all for an epiphany he just had in the dark?

But it was more than that, he tried arguing with himself, *wasn't it?*

He stopped pacing and pinched his lower lip, thinking back to last week, right back to where all this began... right back to when he watched Sadie write *FIND ME* on her pencil pouch in huge black letters. It seemed now that she had done it in such a way that she *wanted* him to see what she was doing. There was no denying it. Instead of sitting upright and still, observant and intent like she always did in class, she was languid over the top of the desk, purposefully shielding her scribbling from the Professor with extra books around the edge, catching Wil's attention in the process. And all throughout, she seemed to brandish her secret creation carefully to him from behind the books. *If only you'd let me...* he remembered thinking at the time, on first seeing what she had written.

Yesterday's nap and this morning's dream seemed to be born out of all that, that desire to communicate with her, wishing she had been silently communicating with him. So then how could he explain what had happened in the shop? And the planetarium? Those were *after* the dream, as if pointing to it. Legitimising the instructions his dream Sadie had given him.

Wil inhaled deeply, overwhelmed.

It was one thing to take an event from real life and wield it about in the unconscious mind where all hope and expectation might be satisfied, but it was completely another to then let those contrivances loose in the real world. To *expect* them to be there… to even *hope* they were, and act on them as such. *That* could only be foolishness. *Nonsense.*

Wil glanced apprehensively up at the next little group coming out of the doors and found himself backing away from that bottom step. But at that precise moment, a contrary thought came to him,

Hope isn't nonsense.

If the strange dreams—strange events in the shop and planetarium afterwards—got him standing here outside the Sedgemoor Building, ready to speak to Sadie face-to-face, when in his very daydreams he couldn't even muster the courage to allow himself to be seen, then Wil was determined to have a *little* hope. Enough to find out if there was anything in those dreams after all. And what better excuse to justify a determined encounter with the cleverest, loveliest girl he had ever seen than to negate essentially the supernatural?

He inhaled deeply, pursing his lip out of the pinch and paced slowly again, searching the crowds that moved within the building.

There she was.

The entire world felt as though it were slowing as Wil watched her walk up to the glass doors from the inside with another girl, making her way towards him, though not seeing him just yet. He took a few steps up as a little crowd dispersed ahead of her out of the building. Then she too came out, lingering behind the bodies.

Suddenly, time seemed to catch up with itself, almost in fast motion, and when there seemed to be a straggling barrier of people between them a second ago, Wil realised now that no one stood between him and Sadie and the girl next to her. He took a few more uneasy steps, feeling adrenaline impair him like rust coating mechanical parts, and he watched as she continued slowly in his direction, though still unaware of his presence.

She saw him.

Quickly, he tried saying something, but didn't know where to start.

Are you okay?' she asked finally, wary.

'Yeah, yes.'

'Did you want to say something?'

'Uh, yeah…I-uh…I came to find you,' he puffed, 'I needed to find you.'

She looked at her friend amusedly, but her friend only mumbled something and sauntered off down the steps.

'You needed to find me?' she asked doubtfully.

'Yes. Yes, I needed to find you.' But Sadie glanced around apprehensively, as if unsure to be alone with him. Taking his chance, Wil suddenly blurted, 'I had this—' but a voice in his head screamed, *don't say it—don't say DREAM!* 'I mean, I was given a message,' he retracted carefully.

Sadie's interest seemed to peak. 'A message?'

'Yes. A message. It started off with a neon sign… then a megaphone…' he watched her for any sign of fear or worry, 'and finally…' she listened eagerly, 'it was written in the sky.' He waited for her to furrow a brow, or cringe, knowing how absolutely ridiculous all that sounded. But it was strange, it was like none of it seemed to register with her and none of it seemed to scare her off either, yet she definitely heard it. Wil wanted her to do something, say something. The suspense was almost crippling. 'Have you any idea what I'm talking about?'

Sadie's absorbing pause grew into a faint smirk and Wil couldn't tell if she was sympathetic or amused or what. Leaning forward, ever so slightly, so that she kept her distance but created a speculative air of friendliness, she whispered, 'I see you finally got my message then.'

Wil cocked his head, certain he heard her wrong, but in a faintly mocking voice, she added clearly, 'What's it going to take to get you to find me, Wilden? Neon signs don't work... what about a megaphone, writing in the sky?' And then, as though there could be nothing odd about what she had just said, she digressed into her normal voice, 'For a second there, I thought you were about to run out on me.' She smiled though, obviously a little relieved that he hadn't. 'I mean, I made it quite clear with the Sharpie, but sometimes these things take a while. Unfortunately. Or fortunately, depending on how you look at it.'

He took a step down away from her, utterly astonished. She had *actually* repeated what she said to him in his dream.

Suddenly, everything Wil thought and remembered about Sadie became jumbled. Time and events, dreams and daydreams, and even all those times he ever saw her in passing or in class last year... it all became... unbelievable. All of it. Because anything with her... in his journal the year before... in his head, it all somehow led to this, right here on the steps where an impossible thing was happening. And whatever happened around even the fringes of her—waking early to get the seat in the back of class each new term... the longing to say something day after day, night after night, then into the daydreams and dreams that followed... it was beginning to feel unreal. Like it had never even happened. Even meeting up with Ben when class let out... or going off to meet the Rugby rats... or whatever he chose to do after having been in the same room with her... it needed to be unthreaded back to a beginning—a time before her. That would be where his reality was... because this... *this*....

He eyed her doubtfully, only to get an encouraging smile back.

'You should see your face right now,' she teased.

'This isn't happening... or it's a wind-up...' he reasoned.

'Wil,' she said gently, 'I asked you to find me. And you *have*.'

He nodded, still trying to make sense of it all, and it suddenly occurred to him that maybe *this* was another dream. Another one like the Mulbryn ones that seemed so real, until he experienced the contrast of real life, real waking. It had happened before.... He ran his hands through his hair and turned around to the vivid fullness of the campus and the tree-lined green that sprawled away to buildings in every direction. None of it looked like a dream.

'You're not dreaming, Wil. You are awake,' she insisted.

All Wil could think was that if this *wasn't* a dream, then how did Sadie get him to dream about her—to dream about specific things… and then get the clerks to make an announcement? And Ben to do his thing in the planetarium? *He must be in on it too! He found out about Sadie when we were in Exeter on Wednesday… that gave him two days to work together and produce the connections with the dome… and this craziness…. That must have been how he knew where she'd be,* Wil realised—*in Sedgemoor Building.*

'You're trying to make sense of it Wil, but I promise, whatever you come up with, it's just as impossible,' Sadie cautioned. 'Let me guess, you think I was behind whatever happened to you today that made you come and find me. So, tell me. What was it? What was the megaphone and the writing in the sky that tipped you to believe what I said in the dream?'

He turned back to her there on the step, incredulous. 'You already know.'

'No. I don't.'

'The store…' he accused, 'the announcement from the Service Desk… the lost little girl named Sadie….' She might not have been involved in the details, but she had to at least know it had something to do with the store—and the woman with the little girl. Unless that little girl was just anyone, pretending to be named Sadie. The look on her face though, when she saw her mother coming to the Service Desk, *that* didn't seem like acting, acting from a two-year-old. 'She was fine though, safe, but properly lost for a little while there.' Wil had to admit, some serious engineering had to take place for Ben to pull that one off.

'A store announcement. And a lost little girl. Clever…' Sadie said appreciatively, so much so that Wil almost thought she was genuine. 'And the writing in the sky? Let me guess, a smoke plane—no,' her eyes shrank to another possibility, 'that's too obvious. Something else. Tell me then.'

'The planetarium,' Wil admitted reluctantly, feeling like maybe Sadie wasn't in on this as much as he thought. 'Ben wrote something on a slide and put it up in the dome between classes.'

She shook her head in disbelief. 'Ingenious. I forgot about the planetarium.'

'And you had *nothing* to do with it—Ben didn't put you up to *any* of this?' He didn't know her well enough to know if she was telling the truth or was just a good liar.

'I told you I didn't,' she insisted, exasperated now. 'If this is just a wind-up, why would I team up with someone I don't even know and convince some parent that it would be a great idea to let their little girl think she was lost?' She rolled her eyes as if that were beside the point. 'And how do you explain how I just *quoted* from our dream?'

'I can't,' he answered feebly.

'No, you can't. Because I actually *did* speak to you in your dream. You just don't understand how it happened. Just like you don't understand how forces were working with us and against us all day, creating and destroying the path that would lead to this moment. Forces you have no idea about Wil—forces that are trying to keep you from remembering anything we ever said to each other, anything we ever did that would bring you here. The last thing on my mind is to carry out some prank for your friend.' She waited a beat and exhaled deeply. 'I mean how much of the dream did you even tell him?' She searched him for an answer.

'None of it.'

'Good. Well that simplifies things then. If *you* didn't say anything to him, and *I* surely didn't, I think you're safe to assume he had nothing to do with this.' She looked at him hard, giving him no indication of what *this* really was.

The sleep experiment!

Wil cupped his hand to his forehead, completely stumped as to how he hadn't seen it earlier. And of all the people to overlook the power of suggestion. Those prompts... *FIND ME*... featuring into his week since he first saw the writing on the banana case.... Again and again they popped up in some shape or form, wheedling their way into dominating his subconscious thought with earplugs and such, to the point that even his dreams were marked by them. And to think, this innocent-looking girl, pulling off such an elaborate Psychology project, Derren Brown-style....

'This is all about that sleep experiment!' he exclaimed, pleased with himself for having figured it out.

'Sorry, what?'

'The sleep experiment. The one with the earplugs.'

But Sadie's harassed slump of her shoulders made him regret his triumphant discovery immediately.

'No, Sherlock,' she wound up, incensed. Checking for bystanders, she hunched down towards him those two steps away. 'There is no *experiment!*'

And just like that, the tidy little bridge Wil spent a moment triumphantly building, linking Sadie's incomprehensible claims over the dreams with his reason for how he managed to end up here... it crumbled rapidly, leaving him searching for some other bypass over the illogical, because he wasn't ready for how she could claim to be in his head when he slept. Desperately, he picked through his day, his week, the months even, back to some point in time that made sense.

'I saw you nearly every day,' he mumbled. 'We were in the same class.... *Classes*,' he corrected, deep in thought.

'And I couldn't say anything then,' Sadie interrupted him sharply, setting her jaw, 'because this is about the *dreams*, Wilden. About trying to get *you* to remember them. About trying to get you to *act* on what you remember. What good would it have been me telling you about a dream we *might* have until you had it already? And until I knew it was actually *you* in the dream, how could I just talk to you outside of it. I mean, I took a huge risk writing *FIND ME* in plain sight,' she rolled her eyes as if the act had been ridiculously foolish, 'but that was out of sheer desperation… because I haven't much time—*we* haven't much time... I could've botched the whole thing writing what I did.' Her eyes flitted about, clearly antagonised by such thoughts. 'There was no other way of confirming you heard me in the dream,' she said firmly, 'no other way. And it can't have been for nothing, not *now*...'

'Okay...' he accepted vaguely, not wanting to frustrate her further. 'So now what do we do?'

At that moment, Sadie began scanning the shrubs and campus furniture nearby as though trying to spot someone spying on them. 'Now… we need to find a place to talk,' she answered distractedly, her eyes darting around, 'because like I told you before, we can't just trust anyone.' She arched an eyebrow at him, pressing the point. 'One wrong move and all the progress we've made could be undone by morning.'

Remarkably, he remembered her saying those very words all of a sudden. *Don't trust anyone*, she said in the dream from the nap, *we're on the same side.*

Just then, a dramatic gust of wind picked up around them, drawing both their attention as it whooshed through nearby shrubbery and trees and wildly peeled leaves and debris off the cobbled pattern on the ground outside the library foyer. It lasted only a few seconds, but as soon as the stones leading to the sliding glass doors had been exposed from their seasonal litter, Wil found himself momentarily distracted by the design there on the ground, for he was certain he hadn't noticed it before. In fact, looking at it from this angle on the steps, the two-tone pattern of circles-within-circles reminded him of something rather important. Of course, he dismissed the thought altogether in light of why he was standing there in the first place. But the image was tenacious. Provocative. Inspiring, even.

Involuntarily, Wil cocked his head slightly and peered there, intrigued.

'Do you want to go in there?' Sadie asked pointedly, appraising him and the building as though suspecting collusion.

'The library? No,' he said innocently, shaking the idea of familiar circles well off him. 'I mean, we can if you want to.'

'You know, Wil, there are discreet ways of getting people to do things without them even realising it,' she heeded, glancing away from the library as if ignoring the insolence of a child. 'The same discreet methods are used to keep everything you hold dear for ransom. So you never really know what's required, or how much.' She glanced at the cobbled entrance outside the library once again, causing Wil to do the same as he considered these curious heavy words, this curious, heavy situation.

The wind there was minimal now, curling and spiralling as a weak whirlwind around the smooth stones.

'I'm sorry you had to find me, Wil.' The tone of regret in her voice was ominous. And he could feel her watching him now as he stared at the little leaf tornado roughly making its way around the innermost dark circle. 'I'm glad, but I'm sorry. I wish it was the other way round.'

The sentiment had a complicated effect on Wil. On the one hand, he was briefly smitten by the notion that she may have overcome obstacles to get him here, for he was aware of doing nothing but following blind intuition, and hope. But now that he had finally connected with her, such words had a foreboding gleam coming from this complete stranger. And he was pretty sure he didn't like the idea of some supernatural force binding them together anymore.

'I just want to know what's going on,' he confessed.

'C'mon then,' she said with a nod, indicating that he should follow her down the steps.

Chapter Fourteen

Keyholes

Sadie dumped her bag against the trunk of a tree in an isolated corner of the green and sat down, patting the ground so that Wil would join her, just like she did in the dream from the nap. He recoiled mentally at the similarity and gingerly sat down adjacent to her.

'Now, Wil,' she leaned left and right around the base of the tree, checking for bystanders, 'I did actually speak to you through a dream, and I know how it sounds, but if getting you to finally sit right here with me hasn't proven something, then maybe you'll believe me by morning.' A student walked along the nearby path and Sadie waited, looking over her shoulder until they were out of earshot. 'What I end up telling you today,' she continued eagerly, 'go away and test it. Challenge it. Don't just walk away in disbelief, *prove me wrong*. It's the only way either of us can be certain we're not being taken advantage of.

'I mean,' she cast forbidding eyes to the sky and smiled, 'I wouldn't want you going away thinking I'm crazy or something.' A hard expression quickly took over her face, intimating that she knew exactly what he was thinking. 'Which I'm not,' she asserted.

'Of course you aren't,' he acknowledged expediently, not sure what precisely he thought of her anymore, because the girl from his daydreams and the one who sat near him in the back of class, neither seemed to be this Sadie. This Sadie, he conceded, disenchanted him with her incessant attention to nearby strangers and their whereabouts from the second she led him away from those steps. 'Are you waiting for someone,' he asked curiously, watching her do a surreptitious 360° of the green, 'or avoiding someone?'

She didn't answer.

Instead, her eyes focused on loiterers, individuals enrapt on gadgets perched here and there, those purposefully heading in the direction of buildings. Everyone received her scrutiny. Wil found himself following her trail to a distant couple pawing at one another, shuffling across the grass in their direction. As it became clear the two were unaware of where they were going (or maybe didn't care), an almost predatory patience took over Sadie as she honed in on them, suspicious.

'Everything around you isn't as it seems, Wil,' she warned, shaking her head slightly at the couple, 'only you can't see that yet.' She then squinted at the lovebirds, confrontational, as if daring them to come closer.

'You can't see that the mundane and trivial is a disguise for the profoundly significant,' she continued, fixated, 'and that years of work have been put into you sitting here with me.'

Years? Wil tried not to frown, for she stiffened all of a sudden, apparently anticipating the bloke would look their way, but he only threw his eyes to the sky in a rapturous laugh.

Annoyed, Sadie set her jaw to the pair then carried on to Wil's fascination. 'Those things that dominate your thoughts… the dilemma that captures your mind while the trivial and mundane get away with everything…' the bloke finally caught her eye and veered left, taking the quickest route off the grass with his fawning partner, 'you might just start to see them for what they are. *Distractions.*' She snuffed at the pair and turned to Wil with a resolute expression. 'Simple diversions.' Spying the couple over her shoulder now ambling down a narrow path between the buildings, curling into one another from the wind, she spoke barely loud enough for him to hear, 'Just something to try and stop you from doing what you really should have been doing in the first place.'

Forgetting them, she turned to him, resolute.

'It's all about influence. Take the externals, for instance, like work or school. External influences are obvious. They're like a fixed framework. Essentially, they create the part of our day that is out of our direct control, carrying on whether we take part in them.' She leaned towards him, 'But the *internal* influences,' she said, lowering her voice, glancing around for ears passing by, 'you must tune your mind to those. Basically, think about what you do, when you decide to do it and why you're doing it in the first place. I know it's a lot of work,' she relaxed again, leaning back, 'another way of thinking, but you'll see them more clearly. Internal influences motivate and inspire us, they take over off the back of externals and get under our skin using things like social norms, the law... tradition. Equally, they can deter us. Squelch us. If we aren't aware of them, they can get inside us and provoke a feeling, then eventually an action—or inaction. And like Pavlov's dog, we respond to them over and over again.'

She stopped herself and straightened up, looking thoughtfully at him.

'Internals can go on for a long time, Wil,' she said regretfully. 'Even when we're searching for them we don't always notice them, they can be so ingrained. Sometimes we think they're a part of who we are. That we can't change that particular thing about ourselves.'

She indiscriminately plucked a blade of grass and started splitting it with her fingernail.

'The last one I noticed was a sound,' she admitted. 'A song. Prepping me. Reinforcing a mood. Eventually, it reached out to me like a handshake. It didn't cross my mind for a second that I should slap it away. So I made a decision based on what it provoked inside me, without even thinking. Like a dog,' she said matter-of-factly, lingering only for a second on the incident. 'I tell you this because this is where you have to start filtering, Wil. Gauge your sensory response to things that would otherwise go unnoticed. Whatever an internal influence may be for you, it always gets you to do what you're supposed to. And if you figure it out, beware, a new one will come along and it'll start all over again. I imagine some carefully timed ones will have happened this week for you,' she insisted, 'and more to come.'

As Sadie studied the green briefly again, enrapturing Wil as she scanned the bodies around them, he realised everything she had just said mirrored the material in their Psychology syllabus from the last month. In fact, they were on hypnosis now and all that stuff about recognising stimuli and learned responses, association and conditioning... it was exactly what the module quiz was to cover on Tuesday.

'Maybe I'm stating the obvious here,' he began tentatively, 'but these *internals*... isn't that just another name for a learned response?'

'If we were talking about people controlling animals, maybe, or people controlling people, but we're not talking about either of those things.'

He gauged her, intrigued.

'What are we talking about then?'

'We're talking about something that hides behind the coincidental.

Hides inside the insignificant, Wil, like camouflage. Do you really think the most significant things in your week were the dreams you and I shared—or that it was really the messages you had from them that got you sitting here?' Smiling doubtfully, she then glowered hard at him. 'You don't want to see what I'm talking about. No one does. But why is that? Is it our own fault? Or is the only reason you and I can see anything right now because they finally want to be seen?'

'Who wants to be seen, Sadie,' Wil asked delicately as the grip her eyes had over him loosened, because whatever *they* were that she spoke of, whether *they* were real or not—whether she was crazy or not—he was desperate now to hear everything she had to say about *them*.

'The Tret and Tare.'

Perhaps he would go cautiously.

'The Tret and Tare?' He tried sounding pleased. Glad to hear these strange and foreign words.

'Do you remember seeing something in your dream Wil—something you wouldn't describe as human, and yet—'

'The light creature,' he admitted, stalled at the thought of that tanned pixie.

'That's him. He's not just an idea in your head. He's the real thing. A real...' she momentarily searched the treetops for a better word, '...entity,' to which Wil's eyes widened.

'Entity?'

'I know how it sounds,' she assured with a smile, only to grimace helplessly, 'but these things—the Tret and Tare—are in our dreams. Are in our heads.'

There was no doubt, she did sound crazy. 'And how do they get there?' He smiled and grimaced too, mirroring her, for he was determined to keep the boat level.

'They're so small—quantum small—they can interact with anything, penetrate any object. The nearest thing they can be compared to is light. Obviously we see them as these flashy, bright things in our dreams, but being like light, they have the potential to create energy. Put simply, they warm neurons inside our heads, like voltage along cables, and mess with our wiring. Getting us to feel and imagine as they please. And they pass right through us undetected, unless, of course, they reveal themselves to one of us through the dreams.'

You are not dreaming... whispered faintly in the deepest part of

Wil's left ear. 'Okay...' he tried not to sound too sceptical.

'The one from our dream is Aeolus. Apparently he was called that because Aeolus is the ruler of wind in Greek mythology. You know, because of the hair,' she said, briefly whirling her fingertips around her ears.

'No... entirely fitting,' Wil assured, smiling faintly, for the name sounded a little like the exposed, stinking end of a cat. 'God of *Wind*, very appropriate.'

'You're unlikely to see him outside your Initial. Unless something's very wrong.'

'My Initial?'

'It's the starting point of the dreams, when you first fall asleep. Every person has one and each is different, personal, like a name, which is why over the centuries they ended up with the name *Initial*. Generally, it's the place in your mind you feel safe. So my safe place is that field at the moment.' She paused for a second, and looked worriedly at her watch, only to then look back at him with a degree of relief.

'And mine is nothing,' Wil understood vaguely.

'Yours is *fog* because you feel safe in it,' she corrected hastily. 'Now about the Tret and Tare,' she hurried the conversation along, apparently aware of the time, which made Wil realise that he didn't actually want their strange little meeting to come to an end. 'The Tret and Tare are two opposing forces that use dreams to work people against one another,' she said plainly. 'They're in our dreams, but they're around us all the time too—not just when we sleep. They're what brought us together today, and tried stopping us all the same. In fact, the entire week, some of them would have been working hard to keep *this* from happening.' She indicated their meeting in the grass with a back-and-forth gesture of the hand. 'Their most effective work is by keeping some dreams hidden from you, while others, they resurge to make them seem more significant, or simply to drown certain ones out. The whole reason they do this, use the dreams, is so that when you wake up and have to make a real decision, a rich base of influence is already there, right inside you, making you feel certain about something, or creating doubt... cancelling out logic. Or sometimes they use it...' her shoulders fell a little, regretful '...to make you feel indifferent towards something you'd otherwise have an incredible emotional response to.'

She paused here, checking him, roving those lovely green eyes from beneath her brow all over his face.

Nodding most comprehensibly, he assured her that he was in fact getting all this, to which she gave him a vaguely regretful smile and carried on.

'Both forces are trying to be one step ahead of the other. One step ahead in making you do what they want you to do.'

'So Tret and Tare...' he tried absorbing, not sure if he was indulging her anymore. 'Does that mean something too, like Aeolus?'

'*Tare* is a shipping term; we still use it today,' she said without even a hint of insanity. 'It's the weight of an empty vessel when you're trying to weigh only its contents. You subtract the tare. The Tare are like that, empty vessels, constants, never really making any gains.' She was deep in thought briefly before moving on. 'And their opposition is the Tret. It's a term that isn't used so much these days, but it was an allowance taken off the weight of goods like wool, to account for impurities. You didn't want to pay for dust, dirt...sand, so merchants had this tret to cover the rubbish really that was no doubt hidden in the goods. Obviously these names go way back, because the Tret and Tare have always been here.'

'And so where does Aeolus fit into all this?'

'The Aeolus in my dream is Tret. But he's had a prominent role in your dreams too lately.'

'And is he on the good side, or bad?'

'It's not about good and bad, Wil. It's about which side you feel naturally drawn to at a given moment. There are little rhymes for either side, depending on your loyalty. *Fret the Tret, share with the Tare. Trust the Tret, and beware of the Tare.*'

She was so serious, dispelling even the notion of fraudulence, that Wil found himself chuckling at their ridiculous conversation. 'I'm so sorry...' he said with a smile, trying to compose himself.

'You wouldn't find any of this amusing if you knew the kind of things they were up to' she heeded, wiping his face straight with her tone. 'Listen,' she checked her watch again, 'I've got to go in a minute.'

'—I'm sorry,' he said, regretting himself thoroughly, '...it's just... this is all so... so involved. And so... *unreal*. I mean, you're asking me to believe there are creatures in our dreams. Controlling us, basically.' His placating shrug at the thought of such nonsense however did not deter her.

'Well then you explain how we shared a dream, Wilden.' She eyed him coolly. 'I didn't think so. So like I said, instead of sitting there thinking I'm crazy, prove me wrong.' After a beat, 'I mean, aren't you even the slightest bit curious as to why the Tret and Tare are inside every human head, yet the only person who has mentioned them to you is me?'

Indeed. 'Okay. So why hasn't anyone else mentioned them then?' he challenged lightly.

'Because we're all made to forget. Only a small percentage of people know who they are, and even *they* know the situation might change, that one day they might know, and the next, all is forgotten.'

Here, her features tightened and vacated slightly, as though she had seen this very thing, the effects of it.

'They use the dreams like keyholes,' she emerged with eyes wide. 'Only, when you peek into that little gap from this side of the door, you think you're looking through one hole, into one mind's dream, your own dream perhaps. But there are many doors, perfectly lined up with yours. So we look through what we already know is there... past what we don't. We sleep, we dream... but we forget.'

She held up her hands so that her palms touched, representing the doors aligned, then peered at Wil's reluctantly absorbed expression through a V in her fingers. 'But when one of these gaps shift,' she let her index fingers fan apart, 'the whole door shifts. And ours have shifted, Wil. Yours and mine.'

She quickly reached out to his knee and took his hand. Then scooting right up beside him, pressing her hip against his leg, she bent and twisted her arms around his, positioning his hand between hers, aligning them all.

'They want us to overlap in the dreams for a reason, Wil,' she said, close enough that he could smell grapefruit... and lily. Close enough that he forgot whatever she was doing with his hand. 'But for some reason, they aren't using the dreamnesia as camouflage. Do you see?' she urged up at him from over her shoulder, prompting him to look as she slowly fanned her hand at the bottom of the pile, working his fingers open. 'Aligning my mind with yours, and you're suddenly aware of them.' She glanced back at him, catching his eye, jettisoning him into some strange intoxicating place he was certain he did not want to go just then. Directing his pained gaze to her fingertips, she slowly fanned her parallel hands in opposite directions either side of his so the dappling light filtered to the fingers of the underneath hand. 'You see me... I see you.... We see them.'

Wil stared as her underneath hand lowered and radiated bright sections of light despite his shadowy likeness cast across it. And just as he was about to silently inhale her fragrance again, she abruptly entwined both sets of fingers around his into a large knot,

'Actually, it's all probably a bit more like this when you think about it,' she sniffed.

'Probably,' he agreed stupidly as she let him go and went and sat opposite him again.

'The way they influence us is ingenious, Wil. Dreams are the perfect shadow to hide in if you want to announce yourself but are afraid what kind of reception you'll get.' She hooked her hair behind her ear. 'I mean, think of those alien invasion movies, where two worlds collide with all guns blazing. The Tret and Tare are nothing like that. We're not even half as intelligent and we've at least figured out that to manipulate and understand something outside us, we have to think like it in some way. Mimic it. Track its development, catalogue how it communicates with its environment and learn how the thing works first, undisturbed. Like a bacterium for instance.'

Here, Wil took a recoiling blink, for the word bent awkwardly in his ear. *Bacterium.*

'We watch it do its thing,' Sadie went on. 'We see what it does in certain situations, and then we use that information to anticipate its behaviour. And if we want to change it, we try to become like it— without it even knowing. Binding receptors... using molecules like words. Communicating chemically. Now, *we're* obviously not bacteria, but if we manipulate *them* enough, mimic them enough... understand them enough... we'll eventually get the results we want. None of this annihilation rubbish. Because we already know how that ends. They just come back stronger, adapt, and the battle carries on. The key is to be *like* them. So they don't see a need to adapt.'

'This Tret and Tare, why are they trying to get inside our heads?' he found himself asking. 'I mean, what's the point if they make us forget anyway?'

'They hide in the dreams so the globe doesn't go into fearful meltdown. And they get inside our heads so we will slowly come to accept them.'

'And if we don't, they just keep us from remembering?'

'It's a bit more complicated than that. More complicated than just getting us to remember a few dreams. I mean, think of what it took for your friend to come to the decisions that got you interpreting my writing in the sky message. The engineering to align all three of our paths today, and in our dreams before, in time... out of time... the reasons become so advanced... beyond our understanding that we can do nothing but reject them if we knew—because our nature is to reject what we don't understand, especially if it means we can't possibly control it. Understanding is control.'

116

Wil thought just then of those bacteria, out of control.

'Listen, if you can appreciate the work that went into you sitting here with me, then turn on the news. There's a reason why war started in this country... or that treaty was signed... why those dictators are finally being overthrown, one right after the other, or why nations have decided to rise up after how many decades? These things in the world happen so quickly. A whisper inside communities. A rumour in the media. Or a suggestion made over the internet. Suddenly crowds become like-minded. People want to blame the media, but the real connection isn't just through the words sitting on a screen... or page... or a rallying shout from the television and public squares. It was the idea sitting in the back of individual minds when they *weren't* united that made people unite. That's when I know where the ideas have come from.' There was that vacancy again. 'But was it Aeolus' allies? Or his opponents?'

'Some things in the world are simply people wanting to come out of their oppression though,' Wil argued innocently, 'that's just a natural human desire, to live peacefully, without dictators.'

She put a cautionary hand on his knee. 'And how do you know that Wil, what *some things* are? How do you know what human desire is? Or preference... or what truly is behind anyone making what they believe is a completely free choice? There will always be influence and suggestion. In our environment, our experiences... our dreams. Every choice is based on it. So how can you differentiate between a free choice the masses make and the influential hand of a subversive, dominating power?' She took her hand off him and stared hard.

He assumed they weren't talking about the likes of Bashar al-Assad or Kim Jong-un anymore. 'I don't know,' he resolved, faintly wishing she'd put her hand back.

'Of course you don't. So it plays with your mind. What are they doing—because they're doing *something*. Why else are *you* now remembering when they went undetected for who knows how long? And of course, they may not profess to be our enemies, but they themselves have enemies and where are we in all that? And I've not even told you the half of it....'

Just then, her phone made a little noise in her bag. She dug for it and stared at the display. 'I need to go...' she said, stuffing her cardigan into a compartment. She zipped it then got up quickly and swatted grass from her backside. 'Now for whatever reason we've been given this little overlap—whatever reason you and I are remembering the same dreams at the same time, we mustn't forget that it serves them. They wouldn't do it otherwise. So we've got to be careful. When you enter your Initial tonight Wil, don't leave it. Don't venture off until I find you.'

'You'll find me?' he asked, losing sight of the seriousness of the conversation momentarily and liking very much the idea that Sadie might pursue him in some way.

'I really have to go,' she insisted, 'but yes, I'll find you.' Lugging the bag's strap over her head and across her chest, she then pulled a small notepad from a side pocket and scribbled something on it.

'This is my mobile.' She ripped the page off and handed it to him. 'Call me in the morning, okay? When are you going to sleep tonight?'

'Uh…well, whenever. What time do you want me to go to sleep?' He felt strange making this arrangement as he got up, like they were *pretending* to meet up.

'Shall we say 10pm?'

'Okay.' He folded the slip of paper, growing almost panicky at the thought of her leaving. 'Great.' But he didn't want her to go. In fact, he felt almost certain that he could believe anything she told him—truly believe it—if she stayed just a bit longer….

'Right, I'll see you then.'

He stood there under the tree and watched her leave as an urgency to stop her grew exponentially inside him with each step she took. The abruptness of her going suddenly troubled him almost more than he could bear.

'Sadie!' he called out.

She turned, looking a little worried. 'What?'

'Just a minute,' he said jogging towards her. Within the small gap of time that she had turned her back and he was meeting her again, he felt certain he didn't want her to leave him ever again. 'What if I don't see you—I mean tonight?'

Her expression eased a bit. 'You will, I promise.'

He wanted to believe her. He was sure he did, but the world suddenly felt surreal as a vague pressure built up around him, like he was sinking in the deep end of a swimming pool.

'I know all this is hard to take in,' she admitted. 'But wait until tonight. So many things will be easier to understand…and then tomorrow we can talk again.'

It was just what he needed. The assurance of seeing her again. The real her. He smiled and nodded, satisfied.

'Use your earplugs,' she urged, hurrying off, leaving him in the middle of the green.

On his way past the Sedgemoor Building, he realised after everything they talked about, she hadn't actually told him how she got into his dream.

Dreamnesia: Retrospect

Chapter Fifteen

Omission

Wil waited for Ben and met him in the carpark.

'So you found Sadie,' he beamed, having had the text. '*And…*'

'And… we're meeting up some time,' Wil shrugged as if it were no big deal. There was no point in mentioning 10pm tonight, dreaming.

'Excellent!' Ben congratulated with a chummy nudge of his elbow as he did his seatbelt. 'So if the cosmos can make a success of *you*,' he declared triumphantly, reclining his seat and looking like he was about to take a little nap, 'it can surely make a success of *me*.'

'About that. How did you come up with the whole writing in the stars thing?' Wil asked.

'You mean your fortune?' Ben amused himself.

'Sure,' Wil indulged, wishing he'd sit up and take this even a little seriously. 'How did you come up with it?'

'I don't know.' Ben's greater concern seemed to be why his ride wasn't moving. 'It just came to me.'

'And Shellie?' Wil couldn't help himself now. All the questions that bombarded him after he left Sadie were waiting to jump off his tongue, one by one. 'How did you know she was in the planetarium on Wednesdays? Did you follow her after class or something?'

'No,' Ben said defensively. He turned his head and cocked a half-open eye at Wil. 'I happened to use the loo there last week and saw her in the foyer,' he said simply, putting his head back. 'And then I saw her go down towards the technician entrance—the one you used this morning, and of course, later, I put two and two together.'

Wil checked his mirrors and wondered why Ben would use loos in the planetarium? It was miles away.

'So it wasn't one of your *accidental* crossing of paths?'

'If it was, do you think I'd have any trouble admitting it?' He scoffed at the mere suggestion and must have sensed the conversation required more of his presence of mind because he put his seat upright and looked intently at Wil. 'Is there a problem if I followed her? *I didn't.* But if I had, what does it matter?' He pursed his lips in a conciliatory expression then asked pointedly, 'Any more questions about Shellie?'

It was a little jibe, but not enough to put Wil off.

'I was just wondering how your great idea came together,' Wil declared innocently, trying for the life of him not to sound sarcastic. 'I mean,' he craned his neck over the seats, preparing to reverse, 'I know I thought your big plan was going to be counterproductive, but so far,' the car rolled back slowly, 'I have to admit, it's obviously working.' He straightened out and started for the exit. 'I mean, when you set out to do an activity that oddly leaves you and Shellie more alone in a room full of fifty people than any other thing you could possibly do on campus, it takes some careful thought. And maybe even a bit of luck.' There was a short queue out of the carpark. 'And to be honest, I wasn't expecting it, but you've even managed to help me out with Sadie. That's quite a plan, wouldn't you say?' He didn't mean to sound patronising either, however Ben seemed glad this wasn't slowly turning into another row about Shellie.

'Honestly?' Ben suddenly puffed with childlike pride. 'I just woke up a few days ago and thought: *Hey, she works in the planetarium, why can't I?* I don't know why it didn't come to me when I saw her before— you know, when I was actually there at the loos, but the minute I woke up, I knew that's what I needed to do.' The blissful admission left him contentedly rubbing his palms over the ends of his knees.

'You just woke up one day?' Wil asked unpalatably, determined not to see this the way Sadie wanted him to. 'Are you saying you had a dream about it?' Wil didn't want to lead him, but he felt the need to be sure.

'Maybe.' The point was obviously not as important to Ben.

They came up first in the queue and Wil waited for a gap in the Friday traffic that surrounded the campus.

'It must have been Wednesday,' Ben scrunched up his forehead, hiding half the freckles above his eyebrows. 'Yeah, Wednesday, because I saw you in the afternoon… and by then I knew what I had to do.'

Had to do. 'So two days,' Wil pretended to be enthusiastic, nodding, noting that was the day the strange thing on the train happened, 'that's impressive. So you just woke up Wednesday with this plan, and…?'

'…I don't know….' Ben was getting a little annoyed now. Hungry, probably. 'I just woke up and had a great idea, I guess. Why all the questions?'

Wil gave a reserved wave to a girl who stopped and let him go ahead of her.

'Well, I just thought if I'm going to take your relationship advice, I need to know where your inspiration comes from. You know, where a great idea comes from and all that.'

'Right here,' Ben tapped his own temple and beamed. '*Envious,* are we?'

'Obviously!'

They both laughed, though there was something hollow about it for Wil. Though Sadie's words were right there in his head, he found it difficult here in the car with Ben to believe her now. And yet, he definitely looked forward to 10pm tonight. It was probably best just not to think about it.

'Lunch at my house?'

'Uh *yes*... obviously!' Ben happily pointed an elbow out the window. 'Now enough about me. So, tell me, what really happened between you and Sadie after you ran out on me?'

As Wil turned towards signs *SOUTH* around town, he realised he was going to have to tell Ben a watered-down version of the conversation. 'We didn't talk long. But the highlights…. She's a nice girl. We're keen to see each other again. But she's quite busy, so it might get a bit complicated. But we'll see.' He turned for the road towards Darlingdon and wondered if omission of information was the same as lying. The motivation to deceive definitely felt wrong.

'So *we'll see?*' Ben gave Wil that quizzical look. 'The way you ran out of that room… I hoped there was more to it than just we'll see. I thought something big was going on in your head when you left. I mean, it's not like you to really go after a girl. Now you just sound like you wished you hadn't done it.'

Wil found himself needing to justify the feigned indifference he now used to hide the craziness he dare not speak of.

'Not at all,' he insisted, glancing over and seeing Ben's apprehension. 'I'm just a bit overwhelmed by it, that's all.'

'All right then, success can be overwhelming,' Ben granted, getting all smug. 'And of course, you have *me* to thank for it. Go on....'

Wil drawled a monotone version of Ben's chipper request, 'Thanks Ben....'

'Well, that was anticlimactic now, wasn't it?'

'What do you want me to say? I already told you your idea was clever, and I've just said thanks.'

'You could at least mean it.'

'I did mean it!'

'No you didn't.'

It was obvious that Ben knew something wasn't right, that he was being fobbed off, even if he couldn't quite articulate why.

'Ben...' Wil pleaded '...seriously, thank you.'

But he was having none of it and instead turned to the open window and sulked.

'Oh Ben, don't do this.... It was really kind of you to try and get me to talk to Sadie today,' Wil said sincerely, keeping one eye on the road and one eye on his best friend. 'You're my best mate! You know I'm always thankful when you look out for me.'

'Justin Salinsky,' Ben mumbled defiantly over his shoulder. 'You seem to forget you have balls because of me. Balls enough to say a proper thank you, that is.'

Wil stole a smile, then composed himself.

'I'm indebted to you,' he said graciously. 'And not just because of that, but for all the times you've been there for me.'

Ben however didn't budge.

Wil frowned hard and took a deep breath as he looked at that loyal, burly... moody mound of a man pretending whatever was going on outside the car was more important than what was going on inside it. 'Listen Ben. This is the first girl I've ever like—I mean like *properly* liked. And I just spoke to her today because of you. I took your advice and walked up to her and said, I needed to find you... as if she were the most important thing in the world. You said girls love that stuff, and it worked. She's willing to meet up with me now. Because of you, it worked.

So seriously,' Wil looked over as they drove along, 'thank you.'

'Now that's more like it,' Ben declared, inflating again as he turned away from the window. 'I wanted you to appreciate me, but that one was... nice.' He beamed and shrugged, gratified. 'And you're welcome!'

They came into Darlingdon and turned for the manor. The dusty lime along the drive dazzled under the blazing sun and billowed behind the car. In the rear-view mirror, it oddly reminded Wil of the dreamy fog as it swirled and blocked all view of the main gates behind them.

Shutting the car door, Ben waved politely at the old woman standing in next door's first floor window, but she gave no notice.

'Maybe she's blind,' he said, squinting up at her stoic glare which seemed to challenge his reasoning.

'Maybe. What do you want for lunch?'

'Have you still got some of that ham...?'

The car cooled and creaked in the sun as they went inside.

After sandwiches and drinks, Mum came home, prompting Ben to swiftly pull his feet off the coffee table when he heard her key in the front door.

'Hey Liz,' he flashed his charming, cheeky grin to her from the couch, 'I've come to eat you out of house and home, but you'll have to blame Wil for inviting me.' He picked up on Wil eyeing him. '*What...?*'

'Don't tell him it's no bother Mum, or we'll never get rid of him' Wil joked as he took a bag of groceries off her. 'And that reminds me, we need to hide the house key somewhere else.'

'Hey! I'm always inviting *you* back to my house, but you always say no. That's not my fault.'

'Does your sister still hate me?'

'Only a little.'

'Well then.'

'You two...' Mum started. 'Ben, you're part of the family. You can come and go as you please just like the rest of us.' She winked at Wil as she passed him on the way to the sink. 'Just so long as you empty the bins, stop drinking out of the milk bottles and be sure to leave a fiver in the pot by the door as often as you leave,' she teased.

'You can always tell me to shove off if I've overstayed my welcome you know,' he said melodramatically, clambering his solid arms over the back of the couch and giving both of them one of his wounded looks.

'No we can't,' Wil exclaimed, 'because you'll just find the key again and make use of it when the house is empty!'

'It's not the food…it's the company,' he protested.

Wil waited a second as Mum disappeared into the pantry. 'And is it the company when I find you raiding the fridge while you think no one's here?' he whispered.

'You know, it's true what they say: *you always treat the ones you love the most… the worst.*'

'Yeah, you just keep telling yourself that,' Wil muttered on his way over to the couch. 'And why is it you put up with this abuse again?'

Ben reached out and threw a playful punch, missing Wil by inches, then flopped back down on the couch. 'I know what you really think of me. You won't believe how apologetic he can be, Liz,' he called out. 'I thought *I* was good at speeches. All that grovelling in the car on the way here….'

'Traitor,' Wil said dryly.

The vindictive smile on Ben's face instantly disappeared as Steph came in the door and dumped her bags in the hall.

'Hey Benny-boy,' she said under the archway, 'Just the man I wanted to speak to. I'm going to the cinema tomorrow night. Do you mind asking Zara if she wants to come?'

'Not if your crazy friend Annie's going to be there,' he answered without hesitation.

'Annie? No, she's not coming. It's just me.'

Wil looked at her with a degree of worry. It was a bold move to exclude Annie, hooking up with her ex-best friend.

'Are you doing anything tomorrow night Wil?' she asked, kicking her shoes off at the foot of the stairs.

'Dunno. Why?'

'Would *you* want to come?'

Wil caught Ben's eyes widening. No, he definitely *did not* want to come.

The last time Zara spoke to him was nearly three years ago. After the unfortunate swimsuit incident. Still believing he did the right thing in urging Ben to get his oblivious sister a towel, Wil however wished he knew what he did that made her avoid him like the plague since. There was no way she'd go to the cinema with Steph if he came.

'Not sure,' Wil tried being diplomatic. 'What are you going to see?'

'That suspense thriller…'

'Oh I know the one.' He didn't, and suddenly pretended to remember something. 'You know what, I can't. I'd love to though, but I might be meeting up with someone.'

'Is it *Sadie*?' Ben guessed.

Wil rebuked him with a hard stare for a second.

'Possibly,' he answered sharply.

'I take it they don't know about her then,' Ben announced without shame.

Wil rolled his eyes. 'They do now....'

'It's not a problem, Wil, you can come another time,' Steph assured, loyally minimising Ben's damage before Mum got too excited.

'Eh-hem,' Ben piped up. '*I'm* not doing anything tomorrow....'

'If Zara comes, then of course you can come too,' Steph agreed. 'Besides, we need a ride.'

'Great,' he said flatly.

'Anytime.' She patted him twice on the shoulder and disappeared into the pantry to Mum.

That evening, as Wil lay in his bed and tried believing the Sadie he encountered on the green was the same in his dreams, he found he much rather preferred the one on the bench in his daydreams. This version of her hadn't told him about Aeolus and Initials. And as the pre-dream substitute wound his mind into stranger, more illusory thoughts, he couldn't help but wonder if any time he imagined her, she could somehow be in his head, experiencing his own thoughts of her. Had she been there all those times on the windy bench, torturing him? Making him invisible?

There was so much he didn't understand, but on the cusp of inevitable sleep, it all seemed possible. Likely, perhaps.

Strange familiarity welcomed Wil to the dreams, like déjà vu, and the urge to find something took hold of him there in the fog.

Suddenly, there was someone a few metres away in the vapour. At first, Wil thought he recognised this person, but as the figure came nearer, he was filled with intense distrust.

'Wilden, don't be afraid. I am Aeolus.'

Chapter Sixteen

Aeolus

Wil wasn't afraid.

'I already know who you are,' he said apprehensively. But whatever familiarity he felt regarding this man-like thing before him, there was an overwhelming sense of knowing nothing at all about him.

'Do you?' Aeolus' voice was deep and kindly. Disarming.

'Yes, I think so,' Wil answered, depending on a frustratingly dilapidated memory of himself doing this very thing: staring at those eyes, noticing that strange waving hair. The impression of having done all this *already* dangled precariously in his mind.

'Why, then, is the fog still here, Wilden?' Aeolus asked like he already knew the answer. He then cast a mildly concerned glance at the vapour wall beside him. 'I imagine this is here for a reason,' he concluded thoughtfully, looking back to Wil. 'Don't you?'

'It was here when I arrived.'

'And when was that?'

'Just now....'

'And do you remember precisely where you were before arriving here… just now?'

Wil tried thinking, but his mind was incapable of going back that far. *But that's impossible.* He tried again, but there was nothing.

'Perhaps this… fog has something to do with that.' Aeolus' manner was so intriguing, persuasive and measured that Wil found himself quite flustered for being shown to have no memory outside of here and now.

'What are you?' Wil asked guardedly.

'I am your friend.'

'You're not my friend. You're not even human.' He stared at the luminous ghost-like skin contrasting with the clothes. It was as if paper doll cut-out clothes—a white T-shirt and linen trousers—had been put over a convincing hologram. And the more Wil tried focusing on Aeolus' strange flesh, the more his eyes seemed to play tricks on him, like colour escaping at twilight. *'What are you?'*

'I am what you see.'

'And what is that?'

'Look.'

The colour in Aeolus' eyes seemed to churn, compelling Wil to do just that: look.

He stared into the face before him, and just as he wished he could remember where he had seen it before, Wil noticed something vast, a fixed point hidden there behind—*inside* the form of Aeolus.

Wil suddenly perceived at that moment that he was looking into a body-shaped window frame, and there behind the flesh-like glass of this creature was a space of complicated, infinite depth. Like the expanding night sky. And with childlike curiosity, he wanted to reach out and dip his finger into the illusion, or maybe swipe his hand through it, through that unfathomable thing before him. Without even thinking, he began to raise his fist slowly from his side, stretching his trembling fingertips towards Aeolus' arm. It was only when he saw his own hand almost directly in front of him that he remembered himself and quickly tucked both hands behind his back, where the urge felt even stronger.

Now he was a little afraid.

'You don't need to be afraid Wilden.'

The calm words had the opposite effect however. All Wil could think was he was beginning to lose his mind. Unable to remember time before now... feeling like he was gradually losing control of his body... talking to a ghost... what he really wanted to do was be somewhere else... out of this fog.

'But where would you go?'

Wil was certain he hadn't said anything. He eyed Aeolus dubiously, not liking that this creature somehow had access to his unspoken thought.

'What do you want with me... and how is it that you know me—is it here?' he asked confusedly, stepping back in frustration. 'Was it here in the fog...?' Imagining such a time here, a time that seemed impossible before here and now, it was beyond Wil's comprehension. 'Just tell me...' he insisted furiously, 'tell me what you want from me!'

'I want all the things you want, Wilden, and if you want to be somewhere else, let's go there.'

'We can't just go. Can't you see...? We're *stuck* here!' Wil threw an arm out to the dense white around them, presenting the obvious. Aeolus stood there impassively, as if being stuck meant nothing, and it suddenly occurred to Wil that he hadn't been in the fog the entire time—that Aeolus had to have come here from somewhere else... to find him.

Wil put his arm down, the realisation all over his face. 'But you're not stuck here, are you?' His eyes narrowed distrustfully. 'You were looking for me.'

'I was.'

'And you know my name.'

'We all know your name, Wilden.'

A search party, Wil imagined. Just what he needed.

'So what then, are you going to help me get out of here?'

'Only you can do that, Wilden.'

What kind of search party is this?

Wil rolled his eyes and sighed, tired of the cryptic conversation. 'Fine then,' he said plainly. 'I will.' He turned his back on Aeolus and started walking blindly into the white. 'This can't go on forever,' he said defiantly over his shoulder, swatting at wisps of vapour. After a dozen or so steps, certain he would have lost Aeolus by now, he looked back to find it was as if neither of them had gone anywhere. 'What are you doing?' he shouted to the calm, unmoving form behind him. 'Why am I not going anywhere?'

'Because you want to be here, Wilden.'

'Don't be ridiculous—I don't *want* to be here.'

'You do. You've just forgotten why.'

'No, *you* want me to be here! You're doing something to keep me from leaving.' Wil scuffed the ground, checking for some strange mechanism that prevented him from moving, but it was just asphalt.

'I'm doing nothing,' Aeolus said placidly. 'We cannot leave until you remember why it is you're here in the first place.'

'Then where did *you* come from,' Wil asked accusingly, 'and how did *you* get here?'

The collected expression Aeolus held throughout their conversation suddenly broke, and an incredible smile bloomed over his face, making even his strange, churning green eyes seem brighter.

'You want to know where I've come from?'

'Please.' Wil rolled his eyes. 'And how did you get here?'

'Now that, I can show you.' Aeolus came round and put his hand on Wil's shoulder and led him forward into the dense fog.

'Where are we going?' Wil asked, worried.

'Absolutely nowhere. And everywhere.'

Suddenly, the fog moved purposefully around them, swirling, condensing, thickening. Where it seemed to permeate everywhere before, now it was creating a distinct wall, making Wil feel as if he had just walked into the eye of a small tornado. The white moved in a continuous slanted direction upwards, creating a black hole directly above, and Wil felt Aeolus take his hand off his shoulder.

'This is where I came from.'

Suddenly, Wil's knees buckled beneath him and like an elevator accelerating at high speed upwards, he ascended towards the hole above. Within seconds he had bulleted through a night time cloud cover and steadily arched up and up, like a rigid arrow to the stars. The town... the county... the whole South West... shrunk behind him, quickly leaving the edges of the entire UK a pronounced shadowy outline. Nuggets of gold light glinted over the large cities and small flecks came off towns until the sun splayed its rays over the horizon. Wil realised he had passed the Armstrong's limit miles ago and that his blood should have been boiling already, and when he started thinking he would soon be in outer space... he was already there. *Breathing.*

'Aaaaaaaaaagh...!' he screamed, unable to flail his arms or kick his legs with the force of his acceleration, unable to even push his tongue forward to pronounce the '*st*' in *STOP!*

The earth shrank steadily beneath him, making his feet appear much larger in comparison. The dark half of the planet, the half sleeping the night time away, hearing nothing of his cosmic cries, disappeared against the blackness of space, and a few seconds later, the earth became a speck. Too tiny to see. He passed the other planets rolling along their invisible paths until the entire solar system too was just a blurry bright spot in space, no different from the other blurry bright spots around him. Faster now, Wil lost track of the sun. Instead, he saw a beautiful gaseous cloud in the distance to his right. It looked both still and yet violently moving as colourful gossamer ribbons of green and purple, pink and red particles froze in a winding and unfurling pose. Then it too… was gone. There were more ahead, like surreal cobwebs hanging on the threshold of deepest space, and Wil sped faster, ascending higher and going further than even the technology from earth had ever photographed. And in this deep dark place, he noticed that supernovae and quasars, stars and galaxies, became fewer in the blackness.

There ahead, Wil saw a dull grey haze, like a thin gauzy veil draped in the dark. It stretched out before him the faster he sped towards it, like a wall expanding in every direction, seemingly having no end or beginning. No edges at all. How he hadn't seen it before, he didn't know, but it had obviously been here all along, hiding behind the black.

He steadily approached the thing before him and realised his smallness in comparison. He was going incredibly fast now. Incomprehensibly, the veil was everywhere, behind, in front, all around, leading Wil to believe he was inside it—inside this dark grey film surrounding the edges of the universe, like the woven lining of a deep and dark pocket. As Wil continued through its gloomy depths, aware that it had to absorb light in order to be concealed so, he realised that whatever light had come to it had to be concentrated ahead, for there was something bright up there. Incredibly bright.

All of a sudden, white was around him, so white… white like the blackness of space, seemingly forever, and there in the distance he noticed black spots. Looking again, it was like *they* were stars, galaxies… quasars and supernovae. Only they were black here. Black this side of the universe. Wil felt the heaviness of acceleration disappear and looked behind to find that mysterious and great divide was now completely white too, totally unseen, like outer space hiding beyond the earth's bright blue sky. Within seconds, he was upon one of the black spots until everything around him became black again. Like a fly caught up in a hurricane, a heaviness descended and he had no control of where he was going.

Just then, Wil landed hard… on asphalt. And there above was the hole he saw before, closing now that he had fallen through it, and he was right back where he started. In the fog. With Aeolus.

'*What the hell was that!*' he demanded furiously, getting up and rubbing his elbow.

'You wanted to know where I came from.' Aeolus' hair seemed

more emphatic than the creature himself.

'That's not what I meant,' Wil spat as he plucked bits of gravel off the graze on his forearm. 'I meant, where were you just before you came here—here in the fog?'

'That, too, I can show you.'

Only Wil didn't like the sound of that.

'There's no need to be afraid, Wilden,' Aeolus assured, taking careful steps in his direction.

'I don't want you to show me,' Wil stepped back, wary, finding himself right up against the turbulent fog wall, 'just *tell* me.'

Aeolus took one more step and suddenly, Wil went over backwards. But instead of tumbling onto his backside, he was falling. Falling as if he had gone over the edge of some tall building.

The thick fog became darker and darker... and finally black, leaving Wil to wonder if he himself had blacked out. But had he been on even the highest building in the world, he surely would have met his end by now. But no, instead, he was still very much awake. The only thing that made sense in his mind was that this was another of Aeolus' strange journeys through space, taking him to vast depths after hurtling him to great heights, because he began to feel light and floaty.

And small.

Very small.

Quantum small.

Gravity had no hold over Wil here. His limbs felt buoyant, his head light. When he flew through outer space to the white side, he was restrained and rigid. Useless. But this journey gave him a sense of being incredibly free. He felt a quickness about his movements. Precision. Like a tiny ant. And he shrank and shrank still. He could no longer recognise the world; his eyes reverted to some sort of tunnel vision. He had to be smaller than the particles found in visible light, for his seemingly miniscule form took on a curious purple glow. But as quickly as the purple covered him, it began to fade, and he descended to greater depths, watching as the purple became like a rippled, dissipating mist away from him.

It took only a few seconds for Wil to realise his senses were ineffectual. His eyes couldn't actually see, yet he perceived an achromatic world of bizarre and massive presences blurring and popping in and out of sight. And his ears *felt*, rather than heard, the vibrations of agitated, unseen projectiles humming in every direction. Fleeting points of energy moved quickly around him, creating fuzzy-looking shells in which they seemed confined. They moved so quickly, they appeared and disappeared, projecting a strange sort of cloud. A blurry illusion.

All of a sudden, Wil zoomed forward, feeling the clouds inflate to something he could no longer distinguish from his surroundings, and the more he seemed to shrink, the more he was reminded of that first time he saw the old footage of Apollo 11's descent to the surface of the moon. That little landing leg was miles away from touching down. And then it landed— much sooner than he was expecting. His brain made a huge shift that instant: the mountain was just a little moon rock, the massive crater a pothole-sized depression. The descent to the surface seemed forever…until there was resistance. That's exactly how he felt now, without some way to measure how far things were, how big or small… he just waited for resistance.

And then it came.

It sounded like a tiny mosquito in his ear but then quickly became a deep drone. And with no notice whatsoever, some dense thing enveloped Wil into its loud, purring belly.

The source of the purring became clear as smaller objects— hundreds it seemed, like marbles—bounced and jittered off one another in peculiar dances of attraction and repulsion. Wil noticed that while some were slow, as though indecisive, a few were quite quick, smacking into an unsuspecting target as if singled out intentionally. Convinced he had just entered the nucleus of an atom, its proton, he was certain these missiles in front of him were quarks and anti-quarks, and the oppressive force around him that felt like he was wearing a wetsuit… were gluons, their field, holding his little experience together. Wil was afraid of becoming smaller, of experiencing the unknown of the world beyond here, for things were appearing and disappearing, annihilating one another. Feeling like that swimsuit was shrinking a size too small, a clack of impact suddenly sent unseen waves around him and forced him into a knees-up spin in the foetal position like a needle on a compass.

Wil slowed to a stop. He couldn't believe his eyes. In the 20 or so rotations he had made, the active little marbles around him had grown to the size of *cars*—fast cars ready to run him over. One pale orb was definitely coming at him, set on a predetermined path, and oddly, Wil felt himself moving towards it too. They were both picking up speed now, undeterred by the calamitous collisions evolving around them, with impact waves rumbling like thunder. Wil hoped that maybe he'd simply go *inside* the ball racing towards him, but seeing what was going on everywhere around him—*CRUNCH!*

Any second and it was going to smack into him!

Wil tightened into a ball and stared in horror between his fingers as the inner workings came into view. That thing was packed inside—there was no way he was going to fit in there!

It was upon him now, imposing. Ballooning. Wil held his breath and scrunched his eyes closed, waiting for impact. *Any second now....*

But nothing happened.

He reluctantly opened an eye.

To his relief, without event, the pale ball had absorbed him, and it was moving him quickly to its centre where a strange and fuzzy mass, like that of a cotton ball, shuddered. What started to appear as tiny fibres in this mass soon became large flattened strips, like pearly elastic bands. Closer still, their fuzziness proved again to be the illusion of movement, constantly changing size, tension, position even, in an ever-morphing unpredictable manner. Wil found himself staring in disbelief as one loop in the mass became four and another bent and curved inside itself in an impossible manoeuvre. The bizarre interacting joins and overlaps defied logic, like an Escher staircase, disappearing into one place and popping out in another.

All those crazy segments interacting with each other... contorting and vibrating in that squirming, writhing mass... they could be heard. Like a thousand spin cycles gone mad they chirped and squeaked, vibrating in a signature chorus. The fuzzy fibres, like those of a giant cosmic cotton ball, had been magnified to at least a few metres across—he had shrunk to such a measure—and they became so loud, Wil covered his ears.

I've done this before... he suddenly realised.

He struggled to think past the incredible discomfort of the noise, against the here and now.

It wasn't exactly like this... but the sound... the vibration....

With elbows pointed outwards from his head, and hands pressed hard to his ears, Wil felt the vibration of the flat strips gliding and sliding against one another beneath his feet.

Wil suddenly pictured the blonde girl... and the man... stoic and crouching... and the flitting lights. Aeolus was there too.

The Tanned Pixie.... The dream!

At that moment, something jerked at Wil's foot. He looked down, but both his legs were gone now, his lower half disappearing into the nacreous surface of those deceptive cotton fibres that had grown to the width of a suburban road! Their shifting planes bent and twisted round and Wil imagined rather logically that his feet would pop out of the other side, for the depth was only a metre or so, but there was nothing. His body had disappeared into the ever-morphing joins! He half expected his legs to show up three loops to his right, sliding away without him, but it all made no sense whatsoever....

And the noise...

It's just a dream, he told himself, closing his eyes, well up to his waist... his chest now, and he was going in quickly, like sinking sand. *It's just a dream... all you have to do... is w—*

The squeaks had stopped.

Wil gingerly took his hands off his ears and opened his eyes. He was there in the fog again, with Aeolus beside him. Oddly, the pulling feeling remained, but after feeling so weightless, Wil realised it was just normal gravity. Like he just got out of a pool after hours of floating.

'And what was that supposed to be?' he asked, partly annoyed, partly perplexed, searching for any change in this hazy place.

'You wanted to know where I was, and am, before I met you here.' Aeolus' Spock-like lack of emotion irked.

'I meant for you *to get us out of here*, but instead you just showed me a load of... *nonsense*.'

'I showed you how I had been here, Wilden, at a single point in space time, *and* elsewhere. All at once.'

Wil glared into those black pupils, feeling like he had been inside them, inside those mysterious places beyond deep space. 'Like I said. *Nonsense.* So now what?' he demanded, irritated. 'Are you going to help me out of here at all?' But he suddenly remembered that this all had to be a dream... that none of it was real, and he felt safe all of a sudden. Maybe even... a bit reckless. Eyeing Aeolus' expressionless face with slight contempt, Wil realised that he didn't actually need the creature's help, because we could just wake up any moment he chose.

'Yes, you do need my help, Wilden,' Aeolus assured, glancing at the graze on Wil's elbow with a hint of concern. 'And this isn't a dream. This moment in time has emerged between us because our existence is entangled. What one of us does... the other suffers the consequences.'

Wil smiled wearily at the thought of Aeolus reading his thoughts again. 'You can do that all you want,' he shrugged, 'but it only proves the fact that you're not real.'

'I'm no less real than you are, Wilden,' Aeolus insisted, prompting Wil to scoff at such a claim.

'So I suppose you expect me to believe you just sent me to the ends of the universe…? Into outer space—where I *can't possibly* survive?'

'Not at all,' Aeolus said meaningfully, staring away any suggestion of ridiculousness Wil clung to. 'It is of no benefit to tell you there's no reason to be afraid and then send you into danger. I was merely showing you where I was—where *I am*—the moment you and I met here. Just as you asked.' Aeolus pursed his lips in a consolatory human-like manner. 'Had I told you, you wouldn't understand. So I sent you there, and kept you here simultaneously, demonstrating how I had been in two places at once. Showing you was a most effective option.'

'Because showing me *out of here* wasn't?' Wil erupted. Bothered, he just wanted to wake up—wake up from this pointless dream, because he knew it was just that. A dream.

'Wilden, you are not dreaming.'

'*Stop saying that*. Why do you keep saying it?'

'I say it because it's true.'

'You know what, I remember you,' Wil accused as he looked down his nose in distrust, 'you were there *before*… before when there was the noise… and you thought I forgot, but I've remembered, and it *was* a dream—*it is* a dream!'

Aeolus stepped towards Wil, but Wil took a step back, keeping his distance.

'Wilden…' Aeolus pleaded, showing his first real sign of emotion as he reached out. However, Wil retreated a few more steps.

'Don't touch me again!'

'Wilden.' Aeolus paused, then said calmly, with more resolve, 'If you know you are dreaming, then why don't you just wake yourself up?'

'I don't know… because I'm awake….'

'Then… this isn't a dream…?'

'No… it is! It *is* a dream…!'

'Then if this is a dream… and you are awake… what shall we do?'

Wil was confused now. He didn't know what to think.

'You are only really dreaming if you are asleep Wilden. Yet, you know this is a dream. Does this mean you are actually awake?' He let Wil think about this for a second. 'But if you are awake, how can you possibly experience all this?' Aeolus brought an index finger to the air and pointed it lazily to the fog, causing it to turn and twist in on itself in obedience. Not for one second did he take his eyes from Wil's. 'Do you have another explanation as to why you can't wake yourself up?'

Wil tried again, fearfully now. He closed his eyes and imagined his bed and his pillow... that he would open his eyes. He opened them in desperation, but was still in the fog. If only he could think *I'm awake* and *be awake*.

'Wilden, you are not dreaming. And what you think is a dream is nothing of the sort.' He took a careful step towards Wil. 'None of this is a figment of the mind... it is a reality across dimensions. Dimensions you have no room for when you wake. So you forget them.' His hands stretched slowly open at his sides, a gesture to the fog around them. 'You forget this... along with everything else I've shown you.'

But Wil didn't care. As far as he was concerned, this was a dream and he didn't want to remember any of it anyway. 'People forget dreams all the time,' he said coldly.

Aeolus stared, as though genuinely disappointed, then looked away to the white still holding its shape around them.

'I dare say the reason any of you forget,' he said heavily, 'is not because you were dreaming.' He returned to Wil, dismayed. 'You forget because you are human.'

There was a short pause as Aeolus impressed his point upon Wil. Then all of a sudden, his persuasive demeanour changed. It was as if he had been trying to coax an obstinate pet from the corner of its cage and now realized it was of no use.

'Whatever you may think of me, Wilden,' he said lightly, staring up into the conical dimensions above, 'the fact is, I know you. I know what you think. I know what you feel.' He fixed his eyes on Wil again. 'I know how you work and why.'

Something caught Wil's eye then. A blot of colour behind Aeolus' shoulder appeared on the surface of the fog. Wil immediately reverted to Aeolus, expecting him to instinctively glance over his shoulder, but the content expression on his face suggested he already knew. Caused it even.

Another shot came.

Then another. Like rotten tomatoes splatting.

Wil was engrossed now.

Reds, yellows and blues peppered the smooth vaporous wall surrounding them, driving Wil to look in every direction as each appeared. Bursting, one after the other, like fireworks in a cloud... and they then diluted elegantly like droplets of dye in water. The effect left a lovely faint watercolour stain. But the superficial spattering on the surface of the wall soon culminated into a barrage of shades deep within, overlapping, stunting the beautiful show of dilution. Faster and faster, shades pelted the bleak space until nearly every inch of the fog had been filled at varying depths with explosions of radiant, dynamic colour. All Wil could see now was the initial pulse of red, green, purple.... Soon it began to look like some three dimensional pixelating canvas... a mural of impressionist art.

A large section to Wil's left had no activity for a while. It looked like a blurred background maybe, with a pale colour dominating. The spots became finer, tailoring something familiar. But it was too soon to tell what. There were blurred, dark images in the foreground.

Within seconds, the entire space went from dotty abstract shapes to the crisp fullness of reality. Objects appeared that Wil began to recognise. It was like turning on his old television... watching and waiting for the picture to become something you knew. And it *was* becoming something he knew! *His room.* And everything in it.

Wil was suddenly there, in his room, as if he were standing in it. He looked around at the four corners in amazement, inspecting their realness. Then strangely, as he turned, the parts of the room falling out of the periphery of his vision... they began to change into someplace else. He looked behind at his bedroom door and back to his bed which was now the sprawling green on campus!

Wil surveyed the buildings around him as everything transformed again. The astonishing changes left him shuffling stupidly in a circle. He couldn't help himself. The more he saw, the more he couldn't stop seeing. Quickly, he became dizzy, standing still in complete exasperation.

All Wil needed to do was recognise where he was and it began to change again. He simply remained in one place, flitting his eyes here and there...and everywhere he had ever been flashed before him. The places changed from recent locations, to where he had been in the past and on to places in his childhood, places he had forgotten. Even the smell of familiar things momentarily filled his senses: cigar smoke in Uncle Louis' house, oil and cider in that pub, the dank smell in the neighbour's cellar he went down into as a dare; it didn't seem so big and dark now.

And sounds....

He could tell an indoor place he surveyed to the left was becoming an outdoor place already on his right. The openness of outside—of sound waves flying through the air without banging into walls and objects—was distinct enough that he found it odd to experience both, inside and out, completely and at the same time.

Wil carried on through places which made him smile. That creaky gate from the neighbour's garden. Whatever happened to the little boy he used to play with there? Lawn mowers putted away outside the caravan in Polzeath... there was that constant drip he heard outside the window on rainy days when he sat in Reception class... that diligent blow of the wind at the end of the garden in the Autumn, rustling up the birches and taking away with it dead leaves and sunshine. Wil remembered how it made him a little sad, but the novelty of it now didn't bother him. It was absolutely amazing... to experience these places once again. To have the same thoughts about them, once again.

They were slowing now. The change from one place to another became more gradual. He was able to look over his shoulder and see the colours refining into the likeness of a place, where before, the change almost got ahead of him. As the room transformed, Wil couldn't figure where it could be. He couldn't think of any place that he hadn't already seen. A small room took shape and finally a cot appeared against the wall in the corner. He hadn't remembered it from this perspective. Not from the middle of the room with it over there and the door behind him. This room was from a photo in the baby album, redecorated before his arrival. That was his memory... adopted from a photo.... The room slowly changed to an adult's bedroom. Wedding photos of his parents were on the chest of drawers. The bed was unmade with a large wet patch on the sheet. Quiet voices in the adjoining bathroom caught his attention. It sounded like a woman in distress. Wil heard a man's familiar voice soothing and comforting her. 'It's all right, Liz... they're on their way....'

The amazement of Wil's journey—of seeing all these places—instantly left him as he realised his parents were behind that door, helpless to his dangerously early arrival.

Another moan came from within.

What was he to do? The fear of someone seeing him and his worry for his mother forced him to stand petrified and listen.

She cried out again. This time, she was desperate.

141

Wil moved to the door. Gingerly, he looked over his shoulder to see if Aeolus would permit him to go in. But Aeolus was gone. Wil turned to the bathroom. And so were the desperate voices.

He wrapped his fingers around the door handle and hesitated, listening for the sound of his parents. There was only silence. Then in one decisive moment, he pushed.

It was his bedroom. Right where he started.

Wil stood in the doorway, overwhelmed, wondering what he had just experienced. As he stepped inside, he half-expected the room to disappear the minute he interacted with it, but it didn't. Cautiously, he sat down on the end of his bed and sensed someone in the room with him. Aeolus was there beside the dart board with the door now shut.

'It is as I said, Wilden. Whatever you believe about me, the fact is, I know you. I know what you think. I know what you feel. I know where you have been, where you are and where you will end up. And I know why.'

He inclined his head towards Wil's as though trying to hear him better, only Wil had nothing at all to say, for he was completely dumbstruck.

'The significance of any of those places comes from how you remember them,' Aeolus went on, pulling a blue dart from the bull's eye and rolling the tip between his fingers, twirling the feathered end. 'Built and stored in your memory. However, those places you have been that you are incapable of remembering... they're no less significant. Their effect has not diminished. You simply become unaware of it.' He pulled open the door halfway like he was going to leave. 'In such circumstances, you must simply rely on those you trust, those who do remember, to tell you how it was... and why it's worth remembering.' He blindly pushed the dart back into the centre of the board, went out and closed the door behind him.

Wil shut his eyes with all the confusion and frustration of such an encounter, and fell back flat onto the duvet. It was at that moment that he heard three gentle taps at the door.

He opened his eyes, but it was dark, too dark to see his room anymore. There they were again.

'Wil...' came a whisper from the other side. '*Wil....*'

'Who is it?'

'Are you awake...?' He recognised the voice as Steph's.

Sitting up, he expected his legs to be off the end of his bed, just as they were when he sat down only seconds ago, but instead, he was under the duvet, in his flannel pyjama shorts and T-shirt, in a state that suggested more like he had just woken from a dream than was still inside it.

'Wil, are you awake?' Steph whispered.

He rolled over groggily and tossed the duvet back.

The clock glowed a pathetic *9:38pm* as he reached for the lamp.

Steph stood there in the hall with her favourite rainbow pyjama shorts and vest on, apparently distressed.

'I thought you might still be awake,' she said apologetically, pulling the frayed ends of her long plait between her fingers, making him forget instantly all that he had dreamed.

'Yes, of course. You all right?'

'I was hoping the invitation to come and visit anytime might go both ways.' Her brow took on that hopeful-worried shape that made it difficult for him to say no. It was the exact same look that swindled him out of lolly licks and sizeable Curly Wurly chunks when they were small.

'Of course,' he said, hiding his delight as he let her in. 'Any time.'

Chapter Seventeen

Blind Spot

Steph closed the door and sat on the desk chair as Wil jumped back into bed. She was itching to say something, yet she was doing what he did in her bedroom on his recent visit: taking in the atmosphere. Her eyes went round the room and stopped briefly over things like shelves and table tops, picture frames and posters.

'It's incredibly tidy in here,' she noted, fixing her attention to the chest of drawers over by the door where a small collection of knick-knacks congregated. Wil felt certain she wouldn't have thought it tidy after his hunt for the journal. '*Oh my gosh...! I totally forgot about that....*'

She was looking at the clay dish he made in Reception, where they did a hand impression and glazed it as a Christmas present for Mum and Dad. Despite it being theirs Wil held onto it. Presently, it stored the odd euro, an old bike lock key and a thick layer of dust.

As Steph went over to have a closer look, Wil felt there was something odd about this visit. Like his sister was forcing herself to be distracted until she knew how to say what she really wanted, or was waiting for the perfect moment to say it.

'I did one of these too,' she said nostalgically, pressing her fingers into the little depressions from his hand.

Cutting through the pretence, 'Steph, are you all right?' he asked, concerned, sounding just like Dad.

'You don't remember, do you?' she implicated.

'Remember what?'

'You broke mine.'

There was a brief pause. Was he to apologise for breaking it, or for forgetting he had done so? Both probably, by the expectant look on her face.

'I'm really sorry,' he said, hoping to appease her. This certainly wasn't the reason she had been out in the hallway obviously distressed. 'I'm sure I didn't mean to break it,' he added sincerely.

'No, you did,' she insisted, 'but it doesn't matter anymore. You were only six. And besides, Mum asked if I could do another one and they let me.' Carefully, she blew off the dust, put the bits back into the plate then re-arranged its position. 'But I have to say, the first one was better,' she turned around, 'it looked just like yours there. They made me do the second one too quickly and it turned out rubbish.'

'You haven't come here to take my plate, have you?' he teased.

'Of course not,' she assured, taking the chair instead. 'I thought you'd forgotten,' she picked up a pen and started clicking the end of it, 'so of course, it's my duty to remind you.' Her smile was weak, but genuine. 'There's got to be some psychology thing you've studied to account for that, how you don't even remember something you did, and I can remember like it was yesterday....'

Wil's faint smile slipped.

'What did you say?'

'Don't worry,' she dismissed, twisting in the chair like Ben did when he sat there, clicking away on the pen at an annoying rate now, 'I'll only mention it every time I see it.'

'No, what did you just say?'

'Nothing.' She indiscriminately threw the pen onto the desk. 'Seriously, I was just joking....'

'Please, Steph,' he tried containing himself, 'say what you said again—about remembering....'

Her eyes darted to the left, perturbed, recalling. 'I just thought it was funny... how you don't even remember...' she shrugged self-consciously, 'and I remember like it was yesterday.'

Wil immediately looked over to the bull's eye on the back of his door, right where Aeolus stood in the dream, its nonsensical fullness coming to him completely.

In such circumstances, you must simply rely on those you trust, those who do remember, to tell you how it was... and why it's worth remembering.

To dream about that, then seconds later have Steph walk through that door and say something along those lines... it was like so much of his day: the shop, the dome... Sadie.

'Are you okay?'

'I'm fine,' he lied. 'What made you think of saying that,' he asked distractedly. 'Why would you point out something I've got no recollection of...?'

'I don't know, Wil,' she confessed, stiffening, emboldened, 'I was just making small talk.'

The same look she had in the hall was on her face now and remembering himself, Wil realised his sister looked like she was about to get up and leave.

'I'm so sorry Steph... I'm sorry, I had this weird dream when you knocked...' he pretended it was all a bit of a muddle, 'and you know when you wake up and it seemed like it was important... like you shouldn't forget about it when you wake?' He had no intention of telling her about Aeolus and the coincidence of her words reiterating a creature's from his dreams. 'It's like I was in two minds of a sort just then, like you reminded me of something I thought I forgot... but actually, it was just a dream. Nothing really.' His forced smile felt like it was splitting his face open. 'Bad timing,' he said lightly, 'that's all. I'm properly awake now.' He wafted the duvet absentmindedly and took in a deep I-don't-know-what-came-over-me breath and tried desperately not to think about what Aeolus said there by the door.

'Now,' he digressed amicably, eager to keep this rare occasion from going sour, 'I know you didn't come in here to tell me what a mean big brother I am to you. So why did you look so upset?' He gave an offhanded nod to the door. 'It's about Annie, isn't it?' *Again.*

'What could possibly give you that idea?' Steph said sarcastically, relieving them both of any awkwardness. 'I want to tell you about it—I need to talk to someone, but you mustn't mention a thing to Mum....'

'Hey, I've never told any of your secrets,' he pointed out, pretending to be wounded.

'Not even what I did to Mum's quilt?'

'Never.'

Steph looked thoughtfully up to her left and said, 'Well, she found out about it *somehow*. I always thought it was you.'

'Well, if remember correctly, you did write your own name, right along with all the other things you scribbled.'

'Oh yeah… I forgot about that bit.'

'So do I meet your standard then?'

Eyeing him sideways, she however pretended to be extremely dubious. 'For now.'

'She hasn't gone off and gotten herself actually pregnant then, has she?'

'Be serious.'

'I am.'

Steph sighed and rolled her eyes very much like her best friend, but with a little more yielding. 'No, she's not pregnant, Wil.'

'Well, it's the worst-case scenario as far as I'm concerned….'

A regretful look shot across his sister's face, making Wil realise this was maybe more serious.

'What would you say to mental illness then?' she asked pointedly.

His eyes widened.

'And what makes you think that?'

'Everything.'

Wil figured Steph wasn't prone to overreacting, not with a more scientific mind than he was capable of.

'In what way?'

'In every way,' she declared. She scooted her chair a bit closer to the bed and spoke more quietly. 'I'm sure you've noticed she's been acting strangely this last year….'

Wil raised an eyebrow, withholding comment.

'Listen, I know she's been controlling and everything since we got back,' Steph conceded, 'but Annie's life isn't easy. She's maybe a bit insecure… and some of those insecurities aren't unlike my own, but I'm not a complete doormat. I always kept it in the back of my mind that if she stepped over the line, I'd have to back off. And even though I was never quite sure what that line would be… because I always felt I was becoming more and more tolerant of whatever she was capable of… I've had to actually think about what it is… because recently…' she paused and drew a proper breath, prompting Wil to shift a bit further up against his pillows, '…recently….' The word just hung there, leaving its unpalatable aftertaste all over Steph's face.

'Recently what?' He hated it when she did this. Like a firework, she'd burst then peter out.

'Well, you know how she does things to get attention...?' He nodded impatiently, wishing she'd just spit it out. 'Well, most of the time she gives me some sort of idea that she's in control of her stunts... that she means for things to happen as they do—even when they might make her look bad. She just lines another one up quickly if she wants people to forget the rubbish one before and it's like her way of still being in control.' She took a deep breath. 'I know you'll find it difficult to believe... but she doesn't actually take herself all that seriously. She just wants everyone to think she does. It's part of the drama. And that's the bit she likes to control. Making people think something that's not.'

Wil felt his expression straining slightly with disbelief in Steph's version of Annie. He didn't want to seem judgemental and quickly flashed his concerned look as soon as he realised he didn't appear sympathetic.

'The thing is, Wil, things are getting to the point now that I can't actually tell if she believes herself or not. It's not about the drama anymore. And whatever she tried to convince others about herself, that's all gone now. She's not interested in annoying her mum anymore, or being the odd one out. In fact, she's trying to keep a low profile.'

Wil's immediate thought was that all Annie's antics were just catching up with her.

'I thought at first she was maybe exploiting another avenue to get people talking about her...but then I wasn't so sure....' She gave an exaggerated shrug of perplexity then continued. 'This time though, things are making me properly uncomfortable.' Steph narrowed in on Wil after a brief glance at the door. 'She's trying to get me *involved*,' she whispered.

Her expression suddenly went blank and it was like she was imagining herself in that situation again, where being *involved* was stored up in her mind. But she quickly seemed to reject whatever it was, shook her head and leaned back as though replaying some sort of repulsion. 'I just can't...I don't want to...'

'Involved? What do you mean she's trying to get you *involved*?'

'I don't know. Sometimes it comes across as... a conspiracy theory or something.... I even thought it was the occult, but I'm sure that's not it,' she said thoughtfully. 'Then I imagined she had some sort of identity disorder. I know she has issues, but I didn't think she has those.... And now I'm not so sure. Not with all the other stuff....'

'What other stuff?' he asked eagerly. He was struggling to be patient. For a scientific mind, Steph was terrible at relaying the important details first. For as long as he could remember, she'd leave out a vital piece of information and tell her stories as if she hadn't. And of course, when clarification was required, she'd throw the missing bits in haphazardly, as if they had no real significance, changing the entire scenario completely. He was starting to feel like it was one of those conversations.

Steph hesitated, embarrassed for her friend.

'Like yawns,' she said quietly.

'Like what?'

'Like yawns.'

'Like *yawns?* What does *that* mean?' Wil leaned forward, intrigued.

Glancing at the door again, she started off even quieter.

'Annie believes yawns are a sign of being influenced.' She did the quotes in the air thing.

'Influenced?' Wil forgot to be quiet. 'Influenced by what?'

Steph bugged her eyes and put her finger to her lips, reminding him to control his volume. 'If I knew, I'd tell you,' she whispered, 'but that's where I thought you could come in.' The idea of helping Annie while she was getting on with what was likely to be one of her little sideshows did not appeal to him one bit. 'You're the one who knows psychology,' Steph argued, 'and you'd know best if she's off the wall and if I need to be telling her mum some of this...'

Wil sighed, reluctant. 'Listen, Steph, you can't expect me to speak to her, and I'm definitely in no position to start making assess—'

'—It's not like I'm asking you to *diagnose* her,' she retorted. 'I just want to know if the stuff I'm hearing is worth taking seriously. Just let me tell you what happens when she is in one of her moods and be my better judgement.' She leaned onto her elbows and clasped her hands together in earnest. 'Listen, I haven't even told you half of it yet and I'm starting to wonder if I'm not taking it seriously enough. I'm the only one who really knows her... and if she needs help.... I don't want to do it on my own.'

There was that Curly Wurly look again.

'Fine,' he couldn't believe he was saying it, 'but you already know I think she's a bit crazy anyway, don't you?'

'Yes. But this is different.'

'Well, if she puts you in danger—or puts herself in danger, it's a no-brainer.'

'So far, that's not been an issue.'

'So what then?' he asked heavily, preparing himself. 'What's the other half you haven't told me?'

'Well, there's chills... cramps... forgetfulness... déjà vu....' Her incredulity seemed to increase with each item, '...headaches, fever, nausea... seizures....'

'What does all that have to do with anything?'

'Well it's all a sign of this influence, this influence that's all around us. We can't avoid it... and she thinks she's the only one who can see it... that the rest of us are oblivious, basically. And she keeps wanting to prove it to me... that she's not crazy....'

'You said she wanted you to get involved?'

'I think she just wants me to adopt her ideas because if I ignore her or *carry on in the ignorant way that I do*—that's how *she* puts it—then I will just be a pawn... a puppet for these influencers.' She took her plait and started playing with the end again. 'You know, I can't even have a normal conversation with her now, so I've backed off, which she says is exactly what they want.' Rolling her eyes, she sighed. 'Whoever *they* are.'

'Is that why you're trying to meet up with Zara?'

'Partly.'

'So that's been what, in the last week? When did she start talking like this?' He was beginning to wonder if the intensity of things, especially since Steph was making moves to actually try on new friendships, had anything to do with him reclaiming his relationship with her. It wouldn't take much to tip Annie sideways if she saw that photo Steph had hidden down behind the pillows.

'Well, she mentioned odd little things before we went up to Mulbryn...'

'But that was *years* ago,' he said in disbelief. 'Are you saying she's been talking about this influence stuff since then?'

'Well, mostly it's been just the odd remark, but the last month.... Actually, it's been the last week that's been the worst. Before, it was like it was some inside joke, like something she knew about and kind of relished that I was oblivious to.... But now, it's like it's the breaking point of our friendship if I don't start listening to her and believing this stuff.'

'So, years,' he confirmed flatly, still a bit shocked that his sister never said anything before. 'And you put up with all that weird stuff about yawns this long?'

'Now that, that's been recent.'

Wil couldn't help notice how the burden of this knowledge seemed to pull at Steph's shoulders and spine as she recounted Annie's deterioration, for she was most definitely curling into herself as she sat there opposite him. Again, he was so glad he knocked on her door....

'So what now? How have you left things with her?'

'Well we sort of had an exchange,' Steph confessed, avoiding his eyes. 'I was angry... she had embarrassed me again in front of people I respect and I had had enough. I told her she's manipulative,' she admitted sheepishly, looking at the ends of her hair, 'and that she doesn't actually care what I think about anything, unless of course, it benefits her.' Catching Wil's eye for a second, she then added, 'And I told her the only influence I was worried about... was the effect of hers over me.'

'You said that?'

'Yes. And I meant it.'

'When did you tell her that?'

'Yesterday morning. Talking to you the night before about the Steph-Annie thing helped me to figure out what to do: just be her puppet, or my own person. I just hope she doesn't go and do something stupid now.'

Wil felt physically ill at the thought.

'Just to clarify, what do you mean by stupid?' he asked warily.

'I don't mean *that*. Good grief not *that*.'

Relieved, 'Well, you never know,' he said sarcastically, 'is she hearing voices?'

'This is Annie,' Steph pointed out with a little laugh. 'Of course she is.' Instantly though, she seemed to regret any amusement in her answer and her expression now teetered uncomfortably between seriousness and humour. 'You think I'm joking.'

'Are you?' She clearly wasn't.

Steph shook her head slowly, ominously. There was nothing humorous there now.

'First, she heard it in her dreams. Then in her daydreams, when she was so tired she fell asleep anywhere. And now, she avoids sleep, but still says they come even when she's awake. I'm sure it's like micro sleeps or something....'

A sickening, worrying feeling came over Wil just then. He couldn't put his finger on the exact thing that alarmed him, for it was just out of his comprehension, like an incredibly huge, significant thing there in his blind spot. Only a small portion poked out to warn him something was there. Not enough to see it for what it really was.

'Maybe,' he agreed distractedly, thinking back on everything Steph had told him in a desperate attempt to identify this unknown, daunting thing. And like a reflex, his mind replayed his sister's words: *yawns... chills... cramps... forgetfulness... déjà vu... headaches, fever, nausea... seizures... influence... dreams... voices....*

Whoever they are.

The significant thing gradually moved into view. At the same time, an incredible feeling of nausea undermined Wil's focus.

'You don't think she would do something stupid, do you?' Steph asked, sounding worried.

'No, no.... I don't think she'll.... No.'

He didn't want that thing to be what it was.

'Are you okay?'

'I'm fine,' he lied again. 'I just remembered something, I think.'

Pulling a tight-lipped smile, Steph glared at him suspiciously.

'Not another thing from that dream, I hope. You're starting to sound like Annie.'

That thing in his blind spot suddenly stood there in full view.

'I just started feeling a bit sick, that's all.'

'Ugh, don't say that. Annie says they use it as a deterrent.'

All of a sudden, he couldn't bear hearing any more. The thought of Annie experiencing anything similar to what Sadie had told him under the tree on campus earlier—about forces working and influencing people... nations....

'Listen,' Steph said gently, 'I know this is a real gear shift, burdening you with her mental health when she's been so... well, so horrible. But if there was anyone else I could speak to....'

The last thing he wanted was for her to speak to someone else about this.

'—I wouldn't mention anything to her mum yet,' he blurted, desperate to contain this unsettling feeling burgeoning inside him, for it carried with it an unexpected empathy for Annie's predicament, the effect of which seemed to numb his brain. Nothing should be done until all felt back to normal and he could think properly.

'No, I wouldn't dare say anything to Selena on my own, I'd get

Mum to do it if it got to that point,' Steph admitted as an aside. 'I think what I'm trying to say is that I'm not running to you just because Annie's being weird. Annie's always been weird. I've come to you because I knew I could trust you, that's all.'

'I hope you'd always feel you can come to me, Steph,' he said assuredly, though was quite aware of his inner distraction.

She flicked her plait over her shoulder and smiled resolutely at him. 'I do.' Then slowly creeping her feet across the carpet, she rolled herself back towards the desk, got up and sat on the end of the bed. 'You know, when I was standing out there hearing you snore away, deciding whether to bother you,' she amused herself at the thought as she fiddled with the ends of her drawstring, 'I really just wanted to come in here and not mention anything about Annie at all. Because I didn't want you to think she was yet again dominating our relationship. But now that I have mentioned her,' she stopped fiddling and looked at him directly, 'it's like she's not the real reason we're sitting here talking like this. Because we had something all along that's allowing this to happen the way it is. I couldn't have gone to anyone else because you'd always be the one I'd choose first.'

She pursed a smile and got up, leaving Wil to feel as if he hadn't properly appreciated what she had just said.

'You don't have to go...' he fretted, bewildered slightly, wanting very much to shake his apprehension and embrace his sister.

'It's okay,' she assured, 'I know I woke you.' She started to leave then added, 'By the way, you've got an earplug stuck in your hair. I meant to mention it before.'

She left as he patted his head for the little lump.

Teasing it out, he suddenly remembered... *Sadie.*

The clock glowed *10:10pm.*

But how could he think of Sadie when Annie had yet again managed to assault her way to the front of his mind? And this time, spectacularly. As Wil leaned into his pile of pillows, his mind felt like a deflating balloon, fizzling in all sorts of directions, and losing momentum quickly.

Whatever Steph could have meant by it all, whatever Annie meant... he hoped there was just some simple misunderstanding. But something inside him told him otherwise. Something inside him was forcing him to accept that thing he didn't want to see before, that thing he imagined was hiding in his blind spot. Annie was experiencing the same thing he was. Aeolus. *And* the Tret and Tare, just as Sadie said.

He didn't want to believe it, but he couldn't understand why else Annie would use some insanity stunt that clearly jeopardised her most valuable friendship. And while it would have been all too convenient to conclude that it was mere coincidence Annie and Sadie suffered the same mental illness—the same delusional disruptions even, Wil couldn't dismiss any of it because of course, he saw the same Aeolus Sadie spoke of. *Heard* him, and not just in his sleep. It was no crazier than hearing Aeolus' voice on the train. Or hoping to dream with Sadie.

Stubbornly, Wil closed his eyes and heard her words again there under the tree at campus, pleading for him to believe, but as he tried to find fault with them, he quickly found himself in the fog again.

Chapter Eighteen

Here

White clambered over Wil, making him wary, claustrophobic. Yet he remembered being here before. He remembered Aeolus and the journey high and low and the pixelated presentation of all the places he had ever been. They were there on the surface of his memory as if they had only just happened. He even remembered Aeolus' parting words at the threshold of his bedroom door:

In such circumstances, you must simply rely on those you trust, those who do remember, to tell you how it was... and why it's worth remembering.

They were much more meaningful now, prodding at parts of his brain in some free-associative manner that made him feel he was seeing them in a new light. A more relevant light, here in the strange fog.

'Are you all right?' Sadie asked, appearing out of nowhere and approaching him with an apprehensive smile.

'Yes,' he answered, surprised to see her as she came quite close to his face. Close enough that he thought at first she was stretching up to kiss him. But she merely peered quizzically at his eyes. 'Why?' he asked, recoiling slightly at her proximity, avoiding any appearance that he might have misunderstood her. 'Why wouldn't I be all right?' He did have the feeling he was forgetting something. Something that had to do with her.

'I thought you weren't going to make it, that's all,' she said, lowering from tiptoes. However, he had no idea what she meant. 'Don't worry,' her smile became more genuine, 'it's not seamless right away. You'll remember bits as we go.'

Then taking his hand, she led him through the fog, where after a few steps, he began to feel a slight heaviness around his legs, a heaviness that moved up his thighs and around his waist as he kept up with her.

'What's happening? Where are we going?'

'You'll see…' she said coyly over her shoulder. 'Just don't let go.'

'But something's—' He tried looking down at the thing clinging to him, for his legs felt encased, elongated, but the white was too dense.

'Just ignore the lower half,' she urged gripping his hand tighter. 'It only lasts a few seconds.'

Wil did as she said and padded along blindly through the fog until the pulling sensation disappeared completely and the asphalt under his feet began to feel spongy like grass. And after a few more clumsy steps over the uneven ground, a bright sunny clearing opened out in front of them.

'It was that easy?' he exclaimed, looking behind in amazement, imagining they merely walked across a grassy verge beside some country road to finally get out of that seemingly endless, horrid fog.

'No,' Sadie said flatly, 'it wasn't that easy.'

'I've been here before…' he remembered vaguely, certain he had seen that old oak opposite in this very field not long ago. This time though, it had a simple swing, two ropes knotted through a broad plank, hanging from a horizontally reaching arm. 'We've been here before, haven't we?' Beautiful patches of yellow covered the rolling hills surrounding them, and as the fragrance of rapeseed filled Wil, there was no doubt he had experienced all this before. 'But the swing wasn't there,' he noted, contending with his piecemeal memory.

'It wasn't,' Sadie said rather cheerfully as she pulled him beside her then let his hand go as if to free him out into the open like some unbridled pony. 'Now why don't you tell me everything else you can remember.'

As Wil took an unsure step away from her, clearly pleasing her as he did so, he looked around, doubtful there could be anything else he knew about this place. However, the pond at the bottom, with its vaporous blanket, obliged him to reconsider.

'There…' he said hazily, sensing some negative association with it now, 'you… you didn't want me to go there,' he felt certain. 'You were standing just there when you said it.' He pointed behind her, not far from where she already stood. That, he remembered.

'Good. Anything else?'

Surveying his surrounds, he struggled. The hedges were no help. Neither was the bright blue sky above. But the shady patch under the tree… and the pond… there seemed to be something in those two places, a hike of evasive emotion as his eye passed superficially over them. A breeze built up just then and rolled down the field, bending the scraggly-tall buttercups so that they pointed towards the pond, and Wil was suddenly curious as to why the wisp down over the water remained. Under the intensity of the sun, he was certain it should have burned off by now.

As he considered that even the wind should be blowing it away, two images of Sadie flashed in Wil's mind, forcing his eyes to draw steadily away from the peculiar mist and rest halfway to the tree. In one, she stood in front of him, then ran off, and was gone. In fact, it was *right here* in front of him, on the slope. In the other, he remembered sitting beside her, looking at her; one minute she was there, the next, gone. Unexpectedly—inexplicably, she had disappeared. Twice. Only it all seemed to be the same time and place, that familiarity pointing to the same occasion.

Again, images flashed, like strobe lights now, but this time, words filled the spaces between them. Sadie's words.

'You told me to find you,' he mumbled, concentrating now as *find me* seemed most significant all of a sudden. Instinctively, his eyes roved slowly up the field to the shadow under the tree.

'And…?'

'And…you asked what it would take to get me to find you…a neon sign. A Megaphone. Writing in the sky….'

Wil's eyes darted to a spot in front of him. *Right there.* That's where she said those things.

'Yes, and what else? What else did I tell you when we were here once before?'

He squinted at the pond, convinced something important went on there, but his mind drew a blank.

'Don't think about it too hard Wil, or you'll block it.'

But something was coming to him. He had spoken to Sadie here—here where he stood—*and* there. Sitting under the tree.

'Wait,' he said decisively, cocking his head to the side, 'I've been here *twice* before….' But it seemed impossible, because while this place was familiar, he couldn't remember when he came and left even the once, much less twice.

Like a game show host pressing him for a final answer, Sadie asked,

'Are you certain…?'

'I'm sure of it.'

She appeared as pleased as she was relieved, despite the confused look on his face.

Suddenly, more detail of the two visits ricocheted inside Wil's head like steel balls inside a pinball machine, striking with multiple contexts almost simultaneously, making him believe they were one and the same, but no sooner did he think he had something—knew exactly *what* happened *where*—the image… words… feelings… they shot away.

It was happening faster now.

Impressions launched through Wil's mind, but now there was so much zipping around it seemed almost easier to actually apprehend something.

'You told me that we're on the same side…' he said carefully, seeing Sadie's lips move—the Sadie in his head—as if she were sitting in the shade—the shade of the oak, 'and…' this part was the most fleeting, 'and you said… if any of them are on our side, I'll remember.'

'Absolutely perfect,' she beamed, coming around to him.

'That's not all. You said…' *that can't be right*, 'you said… I was dreaming?' The gleam in her eye told him it was exactly what she hoped he'd say. 'You wanted me to find you when I woke up.' *But why would she say such a thing?*

She looked at him, incredulous. 'Do you know how long it took me to start matching the seams?' She left him no time to even make sense of the question. '*Months*,' she insisted. 'Months.'

Laughing a little, her reaction unnerved Wil because he wasn't sure what he had done that astonished her so.

'I didn't believe him…' she mumbled. 'I didn't think it was possible….'

But after a moment, Sadie's look of amazement faded and a more sobered realisation came over her, as if the thing she had been encouraging him to do had an unexpected downside, because already he could feel her regarding him with caution now.

'Do you remember anything else?'

Fixed on her slightly hopeful expression, Wil didn't want to disappoint her. But he didn't want to lie either. 'Like what,' he said delicately, grimacing.

Taking him abruptly by the hands, she met him squarely and

suggested, 'Like… anything.'

Unfortunately, he stared into those lovely green eyes and could think of nothing else.

'I'm sorry.'

'Maybe next time,' she said easily, letting him go. 'Seeing as you forget the things I've told you,' a coldness was there in her voice as she stepped away from him and turned to the hills, 'I want to remind you again that nothing is coincidence. Not here, not anywhere. And the fact that you remember anything is for one reason only. Because it suits them.' She turned back to him. 'I'm speaking of the Tret and Tare of course.' (He knew that. As soon as she said the names, he didn't know how, but he knew who she meant.) 'Shall we see what it is they'd *rather* you remember?' she suggested almost defiantly, giving him little room to object. 'What about a time not here? Do you have a memory concerning another time we've spoken?'

'No…' he said uncertainly.

'Well, we have. We had a long chat somewhere else. But because you're *here*,' she put a hand to his elbow, 'you block whatever's *there*. The trick is to make a little shift in your mind. Like touch typing.'

'Touch typing?'

'Precisely. To engage with me fully here and now, you have to become aware of every extension of yourself. So like your fingers typing away on a keyboard,' she took his hands again, knitting her fingers between his, compelling him to make note of his metaphorical appendages while ignoring the exhilarating zap in the middle of his stomach, 'your mind is suddenly in two places at once: here with me on the computer screen,' she fluttered her eyes at him, divesting him of any urge to look down, 'and there where the keys are.' She squeezed his fingers and chased his eyes simultaneously, making every effort to keep his attention to her face. 'You see one thing… and feel another,' she maintained, inducing a soporific effect over him. 'Do you understand now?'

'Yes, I think so,' he admitted, swallowing hard.

Detangling her fingers, 'We spoke another time too,' she said. 'Under a tree. At college.'

All of a sudden, the idea of college brought on a storm of disconnected images: the noticeboard and *Who's got Gonorrhoea*, Sadie handing him the earplugs, talking to her on the steps… and under the tree. Wil immediately tried putting them into some chronological order that led to here. The more he thought about college, the more he seemed to remember, and it was like a key slid into his mind, and was lifting tumblers one after the other, for he was suddenly aware of every word Sadie said to him on campus today. He recalled perfectly the events that pointed to them needing to meet… him needing to find her. He remembered too that unfortunate scepticism of the Tret and Tare…. Aeolus….

That name suddenly brought the pixelated rooms and his ride through the universe into a dramatic context, because he hadn't first heard that name *here*. It had been *there*, there where Sadie promised they'd meet again. Yet, she promised to meet him here too. Here in a dream…. Here where Aeolus had taken him to those impossible places.

Wil's two worlds began to collide.

Whatever residual scepticism he felt from the college green… it was gone, because here, he could accept more easily that all those things Sadie told him were real. That they were possible. Likely, even. Because this… *this* was actually happening.

'We're dreaming together…' he concluded in astonishment '…just like you said.'

With the line between awake and asleep disintegrating, Wil's memories gave him an incredible sense of clarity. So seamless was the divide now, he began to feel as if he could do anything, say anything, *be* anything. It was, after all, a dream, and nothing like those crushing daydreams that left him feeling so invisible.

'It all *feels* so real' he declared, watching her turn from him to the pond.

'That's because everything here *is* real,' she corrected firmly. 'Everything you see *here* has to do with something *there*. That's why it's here. *What* we dream here is *why* we dream.' She stared at him hard from over her shoulder, making him digest her words. 'It's easy to forget about the other side, because here, you're more aware—you feel more awake. But you're not,' she said plainly, 'you're not awake.'

'But if I'm not dreaming…' he remembered Aeolus telling him this on the train and in the dream '… and I'm not awake as you say… and all this is real, then what is this?' he asked with a castaway shrug towards the field and hills beyond. 'What's any of this?'

'It's not about awake or asleep, Wil,' she turned to him fully. 'That's where everyone gets it wrong. It's about remembering and forgetting.' Sadie focused back towards the pond, then turned her head slowly in his direction, surprising him with an unexpected smirk.

'Shall we see what happens *there* when we investigate *here*?' Her smirk stretched into a wide, wicked smile. 'Shall we?'

'Okay…' Wil agreed, hesitant.

With that, Sadie suddenly grabbed his hand and pulled him at a clumsy run down the field towards the pond, laughing a little as she did so.

'Don't be afraid!' she called out as their legs cut a wide trail through the tall grass and buttercups. 'Just don't let go!'

The turbulent mist ahead responded to their coming by quickly moving over the water, curling and spinning its vapour so that the pond surface couldn't be seen.

'Ignore the fog,' Sadie shouted. 'And don't stop!'

At just over halfway, Wil imagined that she might slow down, but she didn't. Instead, she grabbed his wrist with her other hand, forcing him to steadily run alongside her even faster, committing them both to run with unrestrained exhilaration as their feet pounded the earth determinedly. Neither could stop now even if they wanted to.

As they approached the bank, it became clear what Sadie wanted them both to do.

Right in the middle, Wil thought, *just like Ben would do.*

Suddenly, they both leapt.

His limbs mid-air, Wil closed his eyes. Already falling, he waited for the splash of scummy pond water to cover them, but there was no splash. Just that strange pulling sensation around his legs he felt before, before when they had moved from the fog to the field.

He opened his eyes and found that they were floating in the sky, slowly drifting downwards, still holding hands. Above was the shrinking, pond-shaped hole showing the murky water he thought would drench them. Somehow they had *come through* it, perfectly dry, leaving the field behind.

'Don't let go of me,' Sadie told him, grabbing his forearm with what looked like genuine fear. 'You'll feel the drag like before for a few more seconds,' she assured, confirming the elongating feeling in his lower half, 'but otherwise, are you okay?'

'Fine!' he shouted, only to realise immediately that there was no loud wind rushing past at incredible speed. If anything, there was a soft breeze that could oddly facilitate even the quietest of conversations. 'No need to scream then,' he said sheepishly, looking around with a faintly confused look on his face, and feeling the heaviness around his knees easing.

The blue sky appeared endless in all directions and fluffy opaque clouds slid slowly around them like gigantic snails.

'And this isn't a dream?' he asked incredulously, perplexed as the underside of one cloud moved directly overhead.

'No Wil, this isn't a dream.' Again, the quietness of her voice seemed to contradict the fact that they were essentially skydiving.

'Aeolus told me that on more than one occasion,' he admitted wryly. 'Whether I was awake or asleep, dreaming or not, I wouldn't believe him.'

'When you experience all this, the word dreams begins to lose all meaning,' she explained uneasily as her hair gently flicked into her face. 'When we're made to remember them properly, like this...' she looked directly up to a wisp cloud dissipating to nothing '...it's not the ramblings of the imagination we can just dismiss anymore, or some disconnection from reality as one thinks of dreams. And it most certainly isn't unconscious consolidation to help with learning and memory recall,' she hauffed[1], hooking strands away from her lips as her grip around his fingers tightened. 'Dreams are where the Tret and Tare hide so we don't reject them.'

Here Sadie adjusted her grip and pulled him slightly closer.

'When you take into account what we talked about before... about the global population experiencing things like this, yet not remembering for a reason... well you can see then how dangerous it is to assume this is all just harmless, can't you?'

'Can I?' Wil asked, seeing nothing so threatening in sleep such as this that anyone should be prevented from remembering it. And seeing too that consciously dreaming was beginning to feel like an evolutionary milestone. 'This is amazing.... Dangerous...? I mean, it's not like you'll literally die from falling through these clouds, because it's more or less a dream, isn't it?' he reasoned boldly. 'I had to fall asleep to get here. Certainly there isn't any danger in that—and I've never heard of anyone having *a sleep-overdose...* in fact, *without* sleep, we'd surely die.'

'If overdosing on sleep is what you want to call it, then yes, plenty of people die in their sleep. It's not the actual sleep they're overdosing on though Wil, rather what's happening inside it. This basically,' she

---

1 **hauff**: to exhale a short audible breath, often through the nose. Often used to regard something in a contemptuous, disbelieving or frustrated manner. A combination of *huff*, and *laugh*.

maintained, sweeping her eyes to the blue and white around them, making him consider for a moment that maybe she was clinging to him because she had a fear of heights. 'But of course, we're trained to believe it's the ideal way to go, the least traumatic.' She shook her head, evidently hostile to such an idea. 'It's only the least traumatic for those who aren't here,' she said. 'I can think of no worse way for my life to end. This side. In what the world knows as *dreams*.'

The suggestion of death in this place prompted Wil to look down at the endless blue beneath them. A small panicky feeling brewed inside him, for he could see something dark down there. A spot. And it was getting bigger. It occurred to him that while they seemed to be floating all the way up here... *down there* was coming at a splatting pace!

Instinctively, Wil reached for the nearest passing cloud and grabbed hold, hoping to slow their descent, dragging Sadie with him.

'What are you doing?' she demanded.

'Slowing us down!' His motive though somehow confused her. 'What, well we can't just die here...!'

All of a sudden, they found themselves suspended in their reclined falling positions as if time had stopped. The clouds paused and even the little spot below them had become a fixed point from where Wil observed it, to his relief.

'Ugh, thank God...' he exhaled, only to find Sadie staring at him in utter shock.

Then remembering herself, she quickly yanked her hand from his and began flapping her arms out to the side like she was trying to fly away.

'What?'

'Just keep away from me!' she shouted. 'Just get away!'

'Why? What is it? Don't let go,' he begged, reaching for her while clinging to the cool clumpy cloud beside him.

'You're not Wilden,' she sneered, 'and I knew it! These clouds aren't fog...!'

'*What?*' She was talking nonsense. 'Of course I'm Wilden! *Sadie...*' he pleaded, glancing at the poised white giant she was now looking enraged by and was steadily backstroking downwards from. 'What are you doing—hold onto me!'

Shaking his hand in her direction, he reached as far as he could, and all of a sudden it was like a gust of wind blew her towards him.

'Stop it—don't touch me!' she screamed, flailing furiously.

'I'm trying to *help* you Sadie…' he insisted, reaching for the hem of her trousers, '…just stop kicking…!'

But it was no use. She wouldn't be still long enough for him to grab hold, and after a few minutes of struggling, they both created a gap between them that allowed each to observe the other in isolated bewilderment.

'So what now?' he panted, certain they couldn't just stay like this forever. 'How do we get down without injury?'

'Don't toy with me,' she puffed, looking hurt. 'Just get on and do what you always do. *Shadow or shame?* I choose shame.'

What was she on about? 'Listen Sadie. I don't know who you're confusing me with, but I'm *Wilden*—Wil from Psychology. I don't really know what's happening here, but I was just worried we'd fall…' He wondered if holding onto the cloud was what prompted her fear of him. And as neither were obviously going anywhere now, he let go. 'Was it that?' he asked, already spurning the white fluff beside him. 'If I shouldn't have grabbed it I had no idea…. I didn't realise everything would stop, that it would cause this.' His eyes fell to the gap between them. 'I'm sorry,' he said, faintly indignant.

Sadie glared at him in silence for a minute or so. And as Wil watched her with a degree of suspicion, he noticed her expression soften.

'Give me your hand then' she said finally, reaching out to him. Glad, he put his hand out and felt such relief that he was not prepared when her weightless body suddenly shot decisively towards him, forcing him to catch her sideways in his arms.

'Whoa! Did *you* do that?' he marvelled, holding her awkwardly.

'No. *You* did.'

'Did I?'

Pushing herself away a bit, she seemed a little annoyed with him for not knowing this.

'Yes. You did.'

'Well, I didn't mean to,' he insisted, feeling the need to apologise again.

'You did mean to, Wil, which is why it happened,' she said plainly. 'And those clouds are obviously fog,' she determined, looking up and prompting him to do the same. However, nothing there seemed like fog to him. 'Perhaps I shouldn't have mentioned people dying in their sleep at this particular point,' she admitted, rolling her eyes to the stifled sky around them, somehow taking responsibility for what just happened and reminding him again of what she had said, that dying in the dreams was the worse way to go.

'You thought I was someone else,' he recalled matter-of-factly. 'Who?' But she rolled her eyes, avoiding the question. 'Why won't you tell me?'

'I thought you were an imposter,' she said curtly. 'But you obviously are not.'

'Obviously? Is there anything *else* you want to tell me about that?' Catching her eye, he forced an inviting smile, from which she simply turned. Then as he pushed her torso away, startling her slightly as he did so, he repositioned his hand around her wrist, instead of allowing her to be the one holding onto him, for as much as he wanted to trust her, he didn't just now. 'Anything else at all…?'

Eyeing him briefly over her shoulder, 'If you can't remember anything from the dreams beyond a week ago, then no.'

That settled, Wil stared, despondent, at the endless sky. 'So now what? How do we get out of here?'

'Well, you could hold onto that cloud, think about squeezing your pillow and all this will end relatively quickly,' she suggested lightly, sarcastically maybe. 'Or we can go down there.'

He peered between their suspended bodies at the dark spot far beneath them.

'What we dream is why we dream,' she reminded. 'It should only take you a second.'

'Me?'

'C'mon Wil. You just stopped this entire show.' She gestured with her free hand to the clouds that still loomed motionless everywhere. 'You can get us down there if you really wanted to.'

He wanted to believe her, and very nearly thought he did, when all of a sudden, it was as if they had plummeted the entire distance in an instant. The whoosh downwards was a mere puff in the ears, and the minimal lurch in their stomachs was all that accounted for the descent as they stood in this new dark place.

Whatever that brown spot was, it became the inside of a house. A hallway.

'This is Ben's house,' Wil realised as Sadie's wrist slipped from his hand, 'but it's different….' Everything seemed a little skewed: too long or

167

narrow, unnecessarily wide or high, like the deceptive photos on property websites where living rooms and kitchens squeezed and lengthened, suggesting unlikely dimensions.

'It's like that here,' Sadie whispered, hunching a little as they both noticed a strange scraunching, slopping sound down the hall.

'Let me go,' Wil mouthed, creeping towards the diningroom entrance. He pushed the door slowly then straightened his form at the sight, prompting Sadie to sneak behind him and see for herself.

There inside Ben's tiny dining room was an enormous table— maybe thirty feet long—the kind that adorned the great dining halls of National Trust properties, and it was punctuated with candelabras between dessert platters, elaborate jelly mounds, ice cream statuettes and various three-tier stands of every meaty delicacy one might think to enjoy. Wil expected the white laminate table from the 70's that seated six, but this… *this was weird.*

He and Sadie stepped tentatively inside the strangely expanded room and heard the noise again, this time louder. Halfway down the table, they saw Ben's head poking above the feast like an animated centrepiece stuffing his face. Every few seconds or so an arm reached out and grabbed a bit of this or that and that slopping noise was played all over again. Clearly unaware of his audience, Ben piled up slices of meat in his hand, without plate or bread, and savagely bit through 10-15 slices like some bunless burger, chewing and cramming until it looked like he'd bite his fingers off for pressing it all into his mouth so heartily.

'I'll have a word,' Wil whispered back.

'Be careful. We don't know who that is.'

Wil threw her a frown, for this was most obviously Ben, Ben she had seen before at college, seen in the class they all shared.

Cringing at another round of chewing and smacking echoing throughout the room, she poked him forward.

'Hey Ben…' Wil called out, passing impressive cakes and beautifully wrought pastries as he strode towards the middle section of the table.

'Wil…!' Ben's surprise was suppressed slightly by a mouth full of masticated meat. He chewed frantically and swallowed hard a few times, then grabbed a plate and started filling it.

'Ben, why aren't you wearing a shirt?' Wil asked curiously, seeing between the large stand of fruit and sky-scraping chocolate cake that his best friend was in fact naked!

Shamelessly, Ben continued reaching far to the left… far to the right… exposing his hairy backside in the process as if he hadn't heard his best mate at all.

'*Ben…*' Wil rasped, checking Sadie's proximity, 'what are you *doing*? You're *starkers!*'

'Am I?' he said rather casually, looking down at himself. And though he seemed a bit surprised, it didn't seem to bother him one bit. 'The more meat the merrier!' he chuckled. With that, he shrugged and held out the dinner plate of ham slices stuffed with cream cheese, a modest selection from the nearby cheeseboards, pastrami-wrapped gherkins and salami slices pinched to form dainty little rosettes. But Wil shook his head, refusing.

'You're all right' he said, disgusted.

'You sure?' Ben eyed him sideways, already lifting an indiscriminate handful of the contents to his mouth as if he were preventing the waste of such an offering. 'They're really nice….' With the plate nearly half-empty, he began refilling it, reaching faster, piling higher, until suddenly, it slipped from his hand and onto the floor with a *crash*.

'Ooop,' he tried to say, only his lips couldn't touch for all the food that was between them. But it didn't matter because it seemed all of a sudden that Ben didn't care whether his friend was there as he started poking food into the recesses of his cheeks faster than he could chew. He worked in such a frenzied manner that the abandoned plate now allowed him to carry on straight from the platters as before, slowing only to stop them from sliding and toppling as he reached around the various ones on stands and tiers.

It became too much though. Drunk on meat and having been so gluttonous that his reflexes were impaired, Ben knocked one apple on the massive fruit pyramid and, too slow to catch it, Pink Ladies, Granny Smiths and Red Delicious tumbled across the table in all directions, knocking and toppling everything within arm's reach that rested on a stand. When all stopped rolling, sliding, a jumbled pile of food and dishes rested reverently at the feet of the large melting ice cream rabbit up on its hind quarters, as though begging for more.

'Ooops,' Ben said quietly, chewing little and looking a bit sorry for the mountains of delicacies tipped out all over the place. He then grabbed a chintz saucer full of meaty balls impaled by toothpicks further down the table where things appeared untouched and brought it back to his friend. He offered it as consolation.

'You've got to be kidding!' Wil hauffed, snatching the plate off him, chucking it to the pile.

'Shoot yurshef!' Ben said snidely, swiping his hand across the top of another dish and grabbing whatever. But before he could plug the hole in his face with anything else, it became clear that something wasn't right, and lowering his little bouquet of meat creations, he started wallowing his tongue around in his mouth like he was trying to isolate a nasty bit.

'I've wost my cheef!' he announced.

'You've what?' Wil recoiled.

'Wook!'

Sure enough, Ben opened his mouth and revealed a gob free of teeth. He then pulled his lips in and, amused, smacked them together like a fish. Oddly, without them, he looked at least ten years older and most certainly a bit on the rough side.

'Dat's dis—' Wil started to say... only to find his *own* front teeth pushing forward as his tongue formed the words behind them. Involuntarily, he pressed his lips together to keep them from falling out, but they were easing inwards from the pressure of his cheeks and lips working to contain them! As Wil poked his tongue along the gum line, he felt molars popping right out from their spaces and rolling around at the slightest movement.

'Ugh!' he heaved, spitting them out, fearful of choking on them while Ben seemed to find the whole thing hilarious.

'I mushta ate mine!' the naked lion roared.

Wil loosened and spat out another.

All of a sudden, Sadie came up from behind and was doing the same thing, discreetly spitting her teeth out into her hands! She looked even more scandalized at the grotesque absurdity of the event now that Ben's bits were within everyone's view.

'Dis is your *Initial*?' she directed to Ben, wiping spit from her chin with the back of her hand. Horrified, she suddenly cupped her fingers to her mouth and produced another pile of teeth. It was like she was some shark or something, growing them back as soon as she was losing them. 'Jusht dop it Wil—make it all dop!'

But he couldn't. He didn't know how.

'Whuh do I do...?' he pleaded with her, unable to stop his teeth from falling out of his face as he spoke… unable to help either of them…. 'Tell me!' He even looked to his best friend for help, only to find the freckly beast standing there with that blank hole under his nose spreading wide, cackling away.

Stooping again with her hand over her mouth, Sadie expelled yet another collection of teeth, shaking them out of her hand and scattering them everywhere across the floor like little pearls. When she was finished, she glared at Wil and stood up, literally spitting blood.

'Itsh not me…' he defended, 'I'm not doing dish!'

At that moment, Sadie did something odd. She stiffened, narrowed her eyes at Wil, then moved her hands—a sort of fanning thing, one over the other—and was gone. Just like that.

Wil suddenly remembered that she had done that in the field. He originally thought she had clapped and disappeared, but no, she must have done that.

'Now wook what you've done!' he turned on Ben who was still laughing so hard he actually looked like he might pass out. 'What da hell is dish anyway?' Wil demanded, surveying the entire length of the table and its contents disgustedly. 'And what is *dat*?' he finally pointed at Ben's nakedness like he was swiping a mosquito out of his face. 'I've had enough….'

Annoyed, he headed for the door. At the hall, he pushed his thumb and forefinger into his eyes as he heard Ben cackle one more time. It was enough to make him want to burst. And just like that, the sickening sound stopped, the lights were all out, and he found himself back in his room.

The clocked glowed *6:42am*.

His phone suddenly chimed:

Meet me at Vivary Park. 10am. At the enclosed play area. S

Chapter Nineteen

There

There was a chill in the air, manifest in the steam trails behind both the postman and a boy from the village shop delivering the Saturday newspaper on his bike. Along the nearby lanes, the odd drainpipe could be heard sloshing and spluttering from bathroom ablutions and kitchens topping up their kettles. Curtains and windows eased open here and there. Cars stood silent along the curbs and drives. All of it, proof the village wasn't deserted.

Wil leaned against the cool alcove wall and lifted the sash a few inches further, as high as it would go, disturbing the ratchety call of a crow on the wall outside. He had been sitting here in his pyjamas for an hour, watching, unaware of how swiftly the time had passed, and only now had convinced himself he was actually awake, for the transition this morning from dream to wakefulness... it had been seamless. Unsettlingly so. As if sleep never even happened last night. As if waking never really happened this morning.

Suddenly, the very thing he hoped to see all hour finally came into view: pipe smoke curling above the hedge line along the footpath off Wide Way. It was Llewellyn, the old widower in his brown flat cap and green tweed jacket, doing his rounds, just as he did every day, trolling the village for a bit of human contact before hitting the chatty newsagents and post office staff up the road.

Like clockwork, the old man used the concealed path and it had become a satisfying habit to spot him exactly where Wil expected him to be. But this morning, it was more than that. Knowing Llewellyn's whereabouts meant not only that Wil was awake, but that he could be sure the world hadn't changed beyond recognition. It was still right where he left it. Despite what he had come to terms with over the last hour, the last 24 even.

Llewellyn's slightly hunched form stepped uncertainly onto the street. He then crossed to the corner opposite, having spotted a neighbour gathering milk bottles from her porch a short distance away, and stopped at the low stone wall just outside the cottage. He was obviously speaking to her, precariously gyrating his balance over the end of his cane as he did so, but the woman looked uncomfortable, adjusting her dressing gown tightly, avoiding eye contact or any gesture of friendliness. And a few seconds later, she dashed inside, sparing only a few inches courtesy through a small gap in the door (a smile while nominally waving him off), before abruptly closing it.

Seemingly unfazed, Llewellyn shuffled to the curb and looked up one end of the lane and down the other as if deciding whether to go directly to the shop or potter around the village on the off-chance he might see another soul to connect with. Wil saw how the poor chap did this every day, becoming a minor neighbourhood nuisance, hastening the villagers ahead of him by his mere arrival on the street, provoking smirks and muttering, rolled eyes and childish retreating. For who could endure the loneliness of an old man for five minutes?

'No wonder the world was oblivious,' Wil muttered under his breath.

This elevated view over the lanes and rooftops, where he had spent hours in the past harvesting epiphanies on the habits of individuals, the rhythm of a community, existence… it served as Wil's metaphorical pinch this morning, that he was in fact awake. And that he wasn't deluded. He had meticulously set out absorbing, *sensing* the reality before him, over and over again, looking for signs of life that shared *his* understanding of the world now. Life that had become so determined as to take its existence to the extreme in some way. But nature and inanimate objects revealed no fantastical agenda. The setting of his awake world was as expected. Consequences, fairly predictable. Unlike the dreams.

Of course, Wil's difficulty in the window hadn't been to simply figure whether he was awake or mentally off-balance, because nearly every conclusion he sought to determine his state of mind—his awake state—was met with a counter. *And what if that's what they want me to think?* It was

174

there in the back of his mind no matter which direction his thoughts turned, playing dead, but then as he rationalised his situation it would twitch and flinch, forcing him to hesitate, doubt any sense he made of a world where *they* couldn't exist. No. He was here at the window, clinging onto what was left of his life from before, because nothing could keep him from believing *they* were real now. Overnight, the idea had become indestructible. And as much as he preferred collective evidence to determine fact, he knew the existence of the Tret and Tare was bound up in his personal experience, his belief that he had dreamed with another person last night, but that in a short while, he would go and meet Sadie at Vivary, and she would tell him what they did together in the dreams… proving to him that he wasn't crazy believing what he did, that none of it had been a prank… that it was all as real as the world outside this window here.

With his breath steaming up the lower corner of a pane, Wil thought of Sadie and began to feel foolish for running to those steps uncharacteristically, to meet her, allowing himself to be swept away by the idea that they were being drawn together beyond will or reason. He had been so ignorant. Even remembering the exhilarating rush to the pond, hand-in-hand, stirred only a residual fluttering in his stomach, for the loveliness now was smothered by those ideas of influence and manipulation Sadie had been so keen to impress upon him from the start. Of course the last thing she would have been thinking was whether he cared for her or not.

Wil closed his eyes and sighed, ashamed to have been so selfish, so… unlike himself, hoping something might happen between them, hoping some supernatural thing had been drawing them together. The best thing for all that now was to forget it.

Opening his eyes, he wiped the white patch on the glass clean away, making Darlingdon much easier to see now. And there, further into the village centre, he spotted Llewellyn again. As Wil watched him find a detour and amble down a side lane towards the church, he felt a small loss at the thought of nothing ever happening now with Sadie. Nothing great. But it was there. However, he wouldn't allow himself to be drawn to it and instead became marginally interested in what Llewellyn was doing disappearing behind the vestry.

It seemed surreal now, that the old man down there, right along with the rest of the world, had no awareness of those like Aeolus. All Wil could glean from the general population (including himself until last night) was that the absence of literal dreams was nothing significant. No one seemed to worry it was the sign of some dream-dredging thing working the human mind. Scanning the churchyard for the lonely villager, Wil saw how the lives around him had become a sort of lie, for that inability to comprehend such a force as the Tret and Tare suggested reality was more elusive than he ever thought possible. It wasn't just truth based on the perspective of the observer anymore. It was complex. Incorporating time and space, dimensions even, considering how unseen things motivated one to move from point A to B, or prevented them from such destinations all the same. And not just one person, but all of them.

Squinting towards the vestry now, waiting for some sign of Llewellyn, Wil found himself entrenched in this idea of awareness. Humanity's lack of it. And it began to trouble him that more often than not, even the vastness of the globe escaped the thoughts of those inhabiting it, for people had a tendency to confine their existence to their awareness of the immediate world around them. Not the greater world, but the very personal one. The one they knew so well. He was just as guilty of it until today. Of course, with each individual's perception of that world then, *their* world, the size of it could subjectively expand beyond comprehension... or reduce just the same... without actually being greater or lesser in any case. Admittedly, some versions had to be hideous, Wil thought, some divine. Others no doubt were mundane or tragic. But even the most impacting on history, such as Aristotle... Einstein or Hitler, they were surely inimitable examples, suggesting the constant of reality wasn't as compelling as Wil thought.

'But the fact that the world *is* doesn't change,' he concluded aloud, under his breath, 'despite the varied perception of it by its inhabitants.'

Giving up on the old man now, Wil looked out over the stirring village and wondered where he fit in with the masses now. What was his life now that the idea of motives... *inspiration* had become so muddied? It suddenly felt pointless to see the constancy of the greater world outside him, yet defy it with sentimental interpretation... *meaning*... significance. But this was the default manner of all mankind: dreaming of more. He was almost certain that if humanity could not impress itself with some sort of ambition, some sort of distortion of the world, then what really would be its point? *Survival?* For what? *Life would surely be meaningless.* There had to be more to existing than mere existence.

The sun broke through a cloud just above the hills and Wil closed his eyes, imagining a world irrespective of the observer, that wayward inhabitant. The world he considered was a place where humanity couldn't corrupt with its flawed interpretation. It was a serene place. What came to mind behind blazing eyelids was the earth in its simplicity, tilted and spinning counter clock-wise, like a beach ball suspended in a darkened room. It was beautiful and quiet in Wil's imagination. Like the world he used to know, comprehensible. Yet, it was profoundly complex in all that it contained. Spinning. Seemingly doing nothing but that.

The longitudinal point, where half of the earth lit by the sun met the half in darkness became a beautiful marvel as land and sea rolled along from the threshold of day to night. Wil's mind focused there for a moment.

Remarkably, that humble spin had a way of penetrating even the most disillusioned, stripping back human expectation to a 24-hour cycle, forcing everyone to wake and sleep, or suffer if they didn't. And whether it was the extraordinary ponderings on a window seat or a momentous coming-to-terms in that final moment with death… there came a time when *every* person put down their banal delusions and noticed the cruel manner in which the world continued to spin. With, or without them.

Beautifully cruel.

It was no wonder such a formidable glance at the simplicity of reality often forced an individual back to their trappings of ambition and disillusionment. Their grandiose version of the world. And if the old ones weren't suitable, new ones would suffice. Reality was cruel that way, Wil started to believe. Catching your attention… enlightening you… knowing you'd fritter it away for a lie. But despite all this, he saw that it didn't really matter what people did with their understanding of the world. Their days were limited and the earth would continue to hang and spin regardless. So complex… and yet so simple, existence.

Wil suddenly realised his pensive journey made reality seem an almost tragic alternative to the dreams of mankind. But how much more amazing was the *real* world that relentlessly made itself known to its blind inhabitants? Its persuasive case, the case for reality, diminished hopes and dreams to a daily desire for sleep. That physical and mental pause. That silencing of man… to listen to the case of the real world's spin… to show him he cannot forget himself within it so easily… so completely… to suppress his actual place in the universe, no matter how many fanciful entanglements he indulged in. So what of ambition, hope… virtue… when the earth so effortlessly invaded all pretence with its mere arrangement in the sky?

Of course, man in his defiance had a way of squandering truth with dreams. But the opportunity would come again tomorrow. Every mind would unknowingly prepare itself to listen. All of humanity would lie down, close its eyes and sleep.

A dog suddenly barked, drawing Wil's eyes open from the rolling earth. A world within a world. He had to take a second and remind himself that the village before him was real, that he hadn't fallen asleep and that the Tret and Tare were also very real. His thoughts now came full circle to those first few moments in the alcove where the idea of sleep seemed a necessary evil and he yielded to it, finding it gave a familiar feeling of completion he was eager now to embrace.

Llewellyn's brown cap suddenly poked over the top of a headstone in the churchyard and as Wil realised the old man was standing at his wife's grave, sleep did indeed seem a necessary evil.

Staring compassionately at the old gent in the distance, Wil was suddenly startled by a wood pigeon that slipped off the guttering above the window and flapped haphazardly onto the ledge in front of him. The jaunty creature seemed to take no notice of the person sitting only inches away and decided to shoot a hefty pile of poo from its backside onto the paint-crackled ledge. It then darted its head around, taking in the view as if nothing had happened.

Wil's first thought was to wonder if there was something in this gluttonous bird coming to his window at this particular moment. Of course, such a thought, he could already see, would be the trap of the Tret and Tare, finding them in everything, bringing significance to even the most trivial of circumstances. And it went against everything he thought about the beautifully cruel world that didn't care what man imagined. Reluctantly though, Wil backed away from the compelling idea, unwilling to search for meaning in some pooping bird, as tempting as it was. And with a quick swipe, he knocked it off the ledge into the crisp morning air, watching as it flapped haphazardly and landed on the high stone wall where the crow had called earlier.

Click.

Steph slid the latch in the bathroom, prompting Wil to think just then on their conversation about Annie last night, but that too was like peeling back the covering over some foul thing which seemed better left alone. Having woken to find his entire world transformed, Wil decided his sister's best friend was the least of his concerns.

No. Annie will have to wait.

Chapter Twenty

Vivary

The play area was busy for 10am compared to the rest of the park, attracting mostly parents with toddlers. It had doubled in size since Wil could remember trips here when he was a child and he couldn't help take in the changes as he looked for Sadie. A raised terrain topped with sand sprawled along like some decomposing beached beast. Climbing frames impaled it along with clever contraptions for water-play, delighting children as they scrambled up the poles and beams or frantically twisted and pulled mechanical parts full of sand and water under the semi-watchful eye of phone-tapping parents. The last time he was here, half a dozen sad structures were fixed amid marshy grass patches and black rubber matrix tiles that burped mud all over his shoes.

'Wil!'

His stomach contracted. Sadie was there to the right sitting on a blanket under the shade of a tree, waving. She wore oversized sunglasses and a white hat with her hair tied back, making her unrecognisable.

Dropping his chin to his chest, he hurried to meet her, but before he got too close, she halted him with her hand.

'Now before you say anything...' she opened her mouth wide, brandishing a full set of teeth, 'they're all there.'

'Really, that's not necessary,' he assured, slipping his hands into his jacket pockets. 'I have no doubt now' he self-consciously lowered his voice 'we did exactly what you said we'd do.'

'Well, just to be sure there's no misunderstanding,' she eagerly patted the blanket beside her and got him to sit, 'you and I went to my Initial, we went into the pond, came out of the sky and ended up in some place with your friend making a pig of himself. You're hairy *naked* friend.' Her jaw jutted to the left a little as she clearly pressed her tongue against a molar. And there was a hint of that incredible disgust tainting her face again as well. 'I don't think Tret or Tare could ever make me forget that one, no matter how hard they try,' she said wryly.

'No,' Wil twisted his head and grimaced at the thought of toothless Ben cackling away with no shame, his bits hanging out amid platters of rolled ham and cocktail sausages, 'it's all very much stuck there, isn't it?'

Sadie suddenly peeled off her glasses and put them in the jute bag beside her. Now that he could see her face properly, Wil thought she looked even lovelier than yesterday. Lovelier than in the shade on the green... or under the oak in the field. (*But she isn't here because she's enamoured,* he reminded himself harshly.)

'I take it you didn't stay long after I left then,' Sadie guessed.

'Only seconds. He just kept cackling.... It was infuriating. By the way, what was that thing you did, the thing that made you disappear?' He mimicked the movement with his hands there in the shade.

'You don't know?' she asked curiously. 'So how did you leave then?'

'I don't know, I just woke up I guess.'

Here, Sadie forced a rather confused-looking smile.

'It was your first go,' she seemed to reason. 'We can't just assume things are intuitive now, can we? Anything else you didn't quite understand happening last night?'

'Well, yes, actually. I couldn't help wonder this morning if that was really Ben. I mean, did we actually go to *his* dream—his Initial-thing, or were we just making him up in our own heads?' But before Sadie had the chance to answer any of that, a few more things came to mind that he didn't quite understand in the window this morning. 'And you said last night it took you months to do what I had done... and that you didn't believe him.' He distinctly recalled her astonishment. '*Him*, you said. Him who? Aeolus?'

He looked at her expectantly.

'Anything else?' she said with amusement.

'Well I still don't understand why you thought I was someone else when everything stopped in the clouds. You seemed quite fearful.'

The way she let go of him... when she had obviously been afraid of such heights... scrambling away like he was trying to kill her.... 'And that stuff about shadow or shame—that you'd choose shame... I couldn't help wonder this morning what all that was about. Seriously, I have a ton of questions.' He wasn't interested in answers anymore and instead wanted to shed a bit of weight from nearly three hours' of this morning's mind-bending revelations. 'Shall I carry on?'

'Please.' However, she was less amused.

'That fog over the pond... you avoided it the other time I was in the field. Why is that, when this time we jumped right through it? And you said the clouds were fog... I didn't really get that.... And you've never really said how it is that you and I managed to dream together.... And the biggest question really... is why me—why am I remembering—why are they keeping me from forgetting, and why not someone else?

'After last night, I accepted that the Tret and Tare were some alien things like you said, but then I wondered how they could actually influence us—like from a scientific point of view.' He started talking faster to keep up with his thoughts. 'I mean, do they use waves of a sort that penetrate our brains? And if not, how else do they get inside our heads and change how we think and do things? They're so quick, but how quick? Quick enough to whisper something inside our ears and be gone so fast that we don't even know they've said anything? And does that become like our own thought—that voice in our head? Then I wondered from the sleep and dream perspective if maybe they whispered all night long, influencing us through like... osmosis or something.' He paused for a second, thinking. 'But then I toyed with the idea that maybe they influence on the quantum scale, like disrupting a thought process using synaptic junctions—so like literally stopping brain activity on a minute level, an undetectable level... preventing thoughts... creating inhibition, inspiration. Like how you said, that they warm neurons in our heads, like voltage along cables, messing with our wiring. Basically, precise thought selection.' The satisfaction of saying these things aloud brought little relieving embellishments into Wil's body language. And pausing long enough to realise his questions were revolving around how the Tret and Tare got into someone's head, it occurred to Wil that he hadn't even touched on *why*.

'Do you want me to carry on?' he asked innocently.

Oddly, an oh-bless expression shot across Sadie's face. Pity really.

'No Wil, you don't need to carry on. Everything you've just asked... the answers are already there in your head.'

Her remark was obviously not registering.

Bracing herself, 'First-timers reject or run, but you... you're trying to understand again,' she explained. 'Don't you see? That's why you've asked those questions, Wil. Because you *know* the answers behind them. Because somewhere in there...' she peered into his eyes as though looking through peepholes at the real him '...you know you've done this all before.'

'All... of what?'

'You've had contact with Aeolus before in the dreams. Thousands of times' she said flatly.

He tried rationalising that statement, that figure even.

'Yes, but they make you forget,' he recalled her saying, 'they keep you from remembering....'

'Wil, you're not understanding me,' she said sharply, bending her knees towards him, squaring with him. 'There was a time when you *couldn't* forget. You've dreamed with others... you've realised the Tret and Tare were real *already* once before, long before you and I ever crossed paths.' She turned away and looked over at the slide. 'You had a life that side... bigger than any awake life could ever imagine.' Turning back to him, 'Yes, you were made you forget, but it's more than that. It's *why*, and *how* and everything else that's brought you here with me now.'

Disbelieving, Wil half-smiled. It was one thing to talk about the strange things that had happened in the last week—all of which managed to stick in his memory... but it felt quite another to try and believe it had been a regular occurrence when he could find no proof of it.

'I know it's hard to take this all in, but think about it,' she urged. 'Dreams have been a feature in your life before this week, haven't they?'

Her desperation was distracting, bringing the familiar vision of them standing in the field together and him receiving earnest instruction to find her.

'I don't know,' he tried focusing, 'I don't know....' As he pushed his hair out of his face he was certain he should have remembered other encounters with Aeolus if he had had them.

The Mulbryn dreams did come to mind, reluctantly so.

'I had recurrent dreams when I was at school in London,' he said, off-handed, 'but they weren't anything like what you and I did last night. They were just the same thing over and over.' Over and over for about six months, he wasn't in a hurry to point out. But Aeolus was definitely absent during all that.

Sadie bit her lip, thinking.

'Any dreams you can remember before this week are important, Wil. These recurrent ones, how would you say they were significant?'

'I don't know.' Seeing that Roops had disappeared finally from the library with a more satisfying existence, and that it was a complete stranger who took his place there in the tent on the shore made Wil reconsider his answer. 'They changed a friend,' he retracted.

'Ben?'

'No. Someone I don't even know anymore.'

'Of course.'

'Why of course?'

'Because it's tidy, Wil,' she said plainly. 'It suits them. Just like it suited them that you had to forget in the first place—just like it suits them that any of us do.'

Just then, a little girl ran towards them.

'I need a drink!' she announced out-of-breath, going straight for the jute bag beside Sadie.

'Mine's the blue one,' Sadie reminded, digging around in the bag too.

The situation threw Wil suddenly as he wondered who this young person was. She looked just like Sadie, with high cheekbones and thick lashes, though with a silky brown bob cut high up her neck that poked out from under her yellow sunhat. From her age, (he guessed maybe five) she looked more likely to be a little sister.

'This is Lily, Wil. Lil, say hello.'

There wasn't a mother's pride in the introduction. But there was the familiarity, the caring. *Definitely sisters.*

'Hel... lo...' she breathed between long swigs off a pink drink bottle, catching Wil slightly, for he felt incredibly fond of her all of a sudden, as though familiar. 'Can... I... still... play...?'

'Go on then.'

Lily flounced off in her frilly sundress having made it obvious why Sadie chose the play area to meet.

'My sister. She's five.'

Sadie watched her run up to a slide and begin climbing it as two bigger girls waited their turn at the top.

'Lily...' Sadie chided in a low stern voice, '*up* the ladder, *down* the slide.'

Immediately, Lily let herself slip nonchalantly back down on her knees, her yellow dress puffing around her like an unfurling spring flower. She then ran around to the ladder, checking for her sister's approval.

'Well done.... What was I just saying?'

'It suits them that we forget.'

'Yes,' she carried on as before, 'and it can happen to any one of us at any moment. Entire conversations... *gone*, relationships... *dropped*. Events are forgotten like you wouldn't believe. Those of us who remember, we have to tread carefully if we want to keep it that way. And we have to have a plan for when it all falls apart. Anyone who remembers long enough to start thinking it would be a detriment to forget... well, they start putting things in place. Just in case.' She glanced at him before looking back to Lily at the slide. 'Which is why I need your help, Wil.'

'Help? Help you how?'

'Lily's been having night terrors,' she said apprehensively.

'Night terrors?' He was incapable of re-framing the context of such a statement. 'What does that mean—I mean I know what night terrors are... but what does it mean with the Tret and Tare and everything?'

'It means my sister falls asleep and is being terrorized by something I can't stop.' She took her sunglasses from her bag and put them on, then hugged her knees to her chest. 'She's five, Wil. *Five.*'

He turned to the little girl in the bright yellow dress now making a cake-shaped mound in the sand. Her little lips moved like she was singing, or running a quiet commentary while patting and decorating her sand creation with twig and leaf toppings. He saw too, from the corner of his eye, that Sadie was wiping tears away from behind her sunglasses.

'Could you not have woken her?' he asked, realising as soon as he said it that the simplicity of such a suggestion sounded insulting considering the circumstances. 'I mean, can you not wake her and stop it from carrying on?'

'Of course I can, and I have, but when I'm asleep at the same time, it's not that easy. And there are consequences to waking her. It's not as simple as that. You remember when I had to leave you at campus yesterday? I had to get Lily home from school to have a nap. She's been sleeping so poorly, waking up at all hours that she can't even get through a day, so the school's been letting me take her. We basically nap at the same time and I've been bringing her to my Initial the last few sleeps because it seems safer....'

It suddenly occurred to Wil why he saw the swing hanging from the oak last night.

'But last night, I left her in her own Initial. I checked on her, and she was fine… then I met up with you… and when I left you and Ben, I went back to see how she was, but all I could hear was her screaming. She wasn't there… but I could hear … her….'

Her last few words sort of squeaked out as she wept quietly.

'That's awful, Sadie,' he breathed, trying to see her sad eyes. There was nothing but his own concerned expression looking back at him.

'There was a fog, Wil… and it was so thick…. I feel guilty for not bringing her to the field, but I needed to meet you… and I didn't want her there…. She would have complicated things….' Sadie sniffed and wiped her eyes discreetly again. 'All I could hear was screaming. She was screaming and saying no. Over and over again…. I tried to get through the fog,' Sadie's words sounded like they were forming in the back of her mouth, 'and I walked for hours following her screams… but I still couldn't reach her….'

Hours? That amount of time didn't seem possible after she left Ben's dining room, then texted shortly afterwards, as he woke, for them to meet here. 'It'll be okay,' he soothed helplessly, imagining some distortion of time in the dreams accounting for Sadie's version of events, 'we'll figure this out….'

He wanted to put his arms around her and show some level of compassion, but seeing that she was going through considerable lengths to hide her tears without using the small packet of tissues sitting there in the top of her bag, he imagined hugging her now would attract unwanted attention from Lily.

Sleeveless arms worked frantically to clear a moat around a mound and Lily beamed their way as she sent sand flying.

Sadie forced a smile and nodded encouragingly at her little sister, her chest quivering as she stifled an all-out sob.

'I won't give you a hug because I know you don't want to alarm Lily… but I can see that you're so much trying to be strong for her while she looks this way….' He began to feel his own eyes welling up. 'Whatever I can do to help, please, just tell me….'

They were quiet for awhile after that, watching Lily and the other children unaware of the world as it really was.

'I just didn't expect them to do this kind of thing. And *here*….'

'Here?'

'Her Initial is here, Wil. The park.'

'Good grief,' he whispered, imagining Sadie walking around this place in the fog, trying to find her screaming sister... to then come here now and pretend like it never even happened. 'And she remembers *nothing?*'

Sadie shook her head.

'It's probably best that way,' she admitted. 'She never remembers... and we keep coming back.... I want to know what they do to her... and how she can forget if it's so horrible.... I mean, she *screamed*, Wil. She really screamed.'

Sadie pressed her sunglasses snugly to the bridge of her nose and sniffed.

'When you say *they*, do you have any idea who it is?'

'There's only the one I can think of.'

The thought of that Aeolus, calm, collected, tormenting a five-year-old....

Just then, a streak of yellow caught both their eyes as Lily ran to a fibreglass pelican mounted on a spring and then climbed on top of it, wobbling as she went. 'Listen Wil, I know this thing with Lily's only been a week, but the dreams make it feel like months. And the closer you are to someone... well, then it may as well be *years*, the suffering is so intense.' She took her sunglasses off just then and turned to him, eyeing him fiercely. '*Years* since Lily's been in such a horrible situation.'

Just as Wil found her words a little odd, the tense awkward or something, her phone chimed. It was the same noise he heard on the green yesterday.

'Perfect timing,' she muttered. 'We need to go,' she said in annoyance, looking at the screen. 'I need to get Lily back for her nap.'

And like yesterday, he felt again like she was slipping away.

'Listen, Wil. I don't know how many opportunities we'll have here, but I didn't just pursue you in the dreams on a whim. Aeolus said you would remember again, that you could help me. Of course, coming from him, I was sceptical.'

'He told you to find me?' Wil wanted to be clear. 'But you think he's the one behind Lily's night terrors.'

'I know,' she shook her head a little, confused. 'But it was do nothing, or do something. And knowing it was you...' her phone went off again, but she pursed her lips and ignored it '...a human... well, it seemed better than just staying in my little world with Aeolus, didn't it?'

'I guess...' Wil accepted, now worrying what his own role would be in all this with Lily. 'I can't imagine what he thinks I can do though. It's not like I even know what's going on.'

'Listen, Wil, you don't need to worry about that. *I* have no idea what's going on. But what other options do we have? I mean, what would you do in my shoes? What would you do if there's this rumour about a person who was going to remember again, who could control their dreams… and then that turns out being exactly what you need to help your five-year-old little sister? Now, I obviously don't know if Aeolus was trying to help or not. And I don't know if he's been the one behind Lily's dreams or not, but either way, I haven't got many options. And to be honest, I'd much rather turn to flesh and blood than any of that smooth-talking lot right now.'

As Sadie looked towards the sand for her sister, Wil began to feel the wrong man for the job. Not only did he have no memory of whatever he got up to before, but he couldn't understand what was happening with his present foggy dreams, much less control them. And something here didn't seem quite right about Sadie's version of Aeolus.

'Seeing as Aeolus was so kind to bring us together,' Wil started unpalatably, 'why then doesn't he do more to help Lily? I mean, I've seen it myself. If anyone can control dreams….'

Sadie's shoulders fell at this question.

'Because he knows I won't trust him about anything to do with Lily. He knows I already assume it's him. His solution to that was to suggest someone help who's not, well, who's not one of them.'

Yet you just trusted him suggesting me…? Wil's growing disappointment with the situation was beginning to feel very much like role-play, for any negative feelings he had towards Sadie on account of her interaction with the Tret and Tare leaned towards the absurd, because they didn't seem real now—not like her, sitting here so worried for her sister over there.

Again, that blasted phone went off.

'Shall we see if any of them can keep their word?' she said rather defiantly, causing him to eye her uncertainly as she dropped the mobile into her bag. 'Did you drive here?'

'Yes.'

'Good. Why don't you give us a ride home, and you can stay for lunch. There's something I meant to bring I'd like you to have. Besides, it might serve us both if you know where I live.'

'All right then.'

Chapter Twenty-One

Eat

'Just there.'

Sadie pointed to a gap along the curb off Staplegrove Road where ornate Victorian homes towered over the tree-shaded street with their five bedrooms and three stories.

Wil slid in and turned off the engine. 'Which is yours?'

She indicated directly outside his window with a little nod, prompting him to appreciate the exterior of the Bowen family home as Lily escaped from the back seat. A black-and-white tiled path led to the glossy black front door, which was flanked by two large bay windows. The manicured hedge was hemmed in with cast iron railings and gate pillars. It was the picture-perfect family town dwelling.

As they got out, the faint rhythmic squeak of Lily already around the side jumping on the trampoline in the back could be heard.

'We're home!' Sadie hollered as she put her bag down in the hallway. Then urging Wil to follow she took his hand, just like she did in the field.

The room to their right had colourful wooden artefacts mounted on the walls. Over the chimney breast was a large batik fabric of fishermen catching gilded fish, and around it, box frames containing insects of all sorts. An assembly of beetles caught Wil's eye, with some shining like oil on water, and others like emeralds, sapphires and rubies. A light source from behind the door, a mirror maybe, sent them brilliantly alight as Sadie led him deeper into the house.

'You'd think we've lived here decades with that lot,' she said dismissively, catching him eyeing the décor. 'But Mum put it all up the first day. Before her bed was even assembled.'

Taking that to mean these were essentially her mother's treasures, Wil asked curiously, 'So how long have you been here then?'

'We moved to the area two summers ago.' Wil took note that was the same summer he and his family moved back to Taunton and into the manor. 'We rented first then moved to this place last month.'

The next room was too dark, a dining room perhaps, while the third room was most obviously Mrs Bowen's office. Stacks of paperwork cluttered the desk by the window, books were open and piled high on another side table in the corner, and the laptop was in suspend mode on a pedestal that looked like a prop out of a Roman theatre production.

Mrs Bowen wandered around the kitchen with her phone pressed to her ear looking like she couldn't get a word in edgeways. Straightaway, Wil saw the resemblance.

Sadie's mother was tall, sinewy, with long, dark brown hair pulled back in a sleek French plait. There was a Mediterranean look about her: olive skin, blue-green eyes set above freckled crags of cheekbone and shaded by a thick canopy of lashes that had obviously been passed on to Sadie and Lily. Her black tailored trousers and grey silk blouse seemed over-dressed for a Saturday.

'Sorry, Honey,' Mrs Bowen whispered in what sounded like a Spanish accent, covering one end of the phone, 'I'll be done in a minute. Conference call.' Her r's rolled like the purr of a cat, and every word seemed indulgently fervent. Noting Wil's presence, she looked at him delicious-like but then plucked her eyes impatiently to the ceiling. All of a sudden, she turned to the sink and exclaimed into the phone, 'What dealer is going to pay that kind of price?' Then agitatedly excusing herself, she went to her office, closed the door and promptly broke into terse instruction on the insurance liability in transporting items over surface versus air.

'You know, I could come back another time, when it's more convenient,' Wil suggested, hearing Mrs Bowen exude flamboyant temper. 'Oh don't mind her,' Sadie said dismissively, poking through the contents of the fridge. 'She's always like that. Mum transports artefacts to museums from abroad, and it's all deadlines and insurance and whatever. I'm starving.... Ham sandwiches?'

'Sounds great,' he said distractedly, listening to the commotion down the hall while Sadie got plates and packets out.

Just then, Wil's pocket chimed:

Cinema with Steph and Zara tonight. U coming?

He texted back:

No. Ask Shellie?

'Sorry. It's Ben.'

Sadie peeled off slices of ham from a packet and stopped herself. 'I'll never think of him the same. Or this.' She wiggled the pinched wafer in front of her. '*Ugh.*'

Just then, phones rang throughout the house.

'You!' Mrs Bowen erupted in her office. She then ranted quickly in mixed English and Spanish, leaving Wil bemused as to whether she was angry or happy.

'That's Dad she's talking to' Sadie explained, cutting a sandwich into quarters. 'She thinks he's forgotten her birthday so he's out getting her a mobile, which she needs, but what she really wants is some watch.' They listened for a few seconds to Mrs Bowen refusing to choose a colour. 'He's just winding her up,' Sadie said, amused. 'He got the watch for her last week. Besides, her birthday's tomorrow.'

'Seriously?'

'Yep.'

'I take it she doesn't know anything about the dreams then, about…?' he nodded towards Lily out in the garden.

Sadie just looked at him like he was crazy and returned to rinsing grapes.

Mrs Bowen was laughing now, and as Wil watched Sadie stoically carry on making lunch, he couldn't help but ask,

'Doesn't it seem trivial sometimes?'

'My mum's rant?'

'Not just that.' He went over and watched her pack things back into the fridge. 'But everything.'

'Don't let them do that to you, Wil.' Sadie eyed him severely as she held up the bag of bread and twisted it closed. 'They'll have you starving yourself and believing a few crumbs at your most desperate hour can't be trusted. Seriously. I mean, what's the point of me standing here making sandwiches when all I can think about,' she glanced at the office door and lowered her voice, 'is Lily? *Because we're hungry,*' she said after a beat, '*that's why.* And being hungry is a fact, not some philosophical question.

So when you're hungry,' she shrugged the obviousness of the answer, 'eat.' Stuffing the loaf into an overhead cupboard already full of bready things, she added, 'Besides, it suits them if you're desperate for something, so don't let it get to that point.'

Maybe making sandwiches wasn't as pointless as Wil dared to suggest, but since his think on the window seat this morning, the timing of everything seemed significant, if not the events themselves. For instance, at which point did a person decide they were hungry enough to go and do something about it? What of those few minutes' delay? And was eating an activity the Tret and Tare relied on everyone taking part in numerous times a day to their advantage? ...And what about those times when a meal had been inadvertently or unavoidably skipped?

'It doesn't take much to see them behind everything,' he confessed, thinking of the pigeon pooing on his ledge.

'You've got to maintain some sort of normal and not be afraid to meet your basic needs,' Sadie insisted. 'Speaking of, I'm going to take these out to the girls.' She carried two loaded plastic plates to the back door. 'Back in a minute.'

The voices of two girls squealing in the back garden made Wil realise he hadn't heard Lily on the trampoline anymore. But now, through the window, he could see her, along with a similarly-aged child, scrambling onto its creaky frame, laughing and pushing as each tried to be the first to get bouncing. Sadie heeded something and they both stood upright on the uneven surface with less scuffle and began bouncing, their springy rhythm gaining height and giggles.

Lily's happy face gleamed in the sun as she came to the top of a bounce, frozen for a second with legs bent, haphazard. Her dress then billowed and straightened, pulsing with the force of another elbow-swinging jump.

Seeing such innocence there, something stirred inside Wil just then and he found himself wanting desperately to protect her. But not like a stranger as he was. As a brother. Someone familiar. He began to deplore deeply whatever made her scream in the dreams, that place where all this, sunshine and giggles, were exchanged for some horrible, mysterious thing. It was a hideous trade-off he thought, ignorance for normality.

Hearing Sadie mention the word *nap* to the neighbour at the gate as she passed over the plates, and seeing Lily's brown bob splay outwards as she twirled mid-jump but then landed awkwardly on her knees, Wil no longer felt this was role-play like he did at the park. In fact, the *normal* he saw Sadie wrestling with in her own life highlighted how his own had changed overnight. Finding her… dreaming with her… and waking to spend an extended period at the windowsill in order to make sense of it all… this was the new normal now. The new normal he had to hide from the other normal. Just like Sadie was managing to do.

Checking the office door was still closed, 'Why do we have to pretend everything's normal when it isn't?' he asked when she came back.

'Pardon?' She brushed past him to the sink, swiping paw marks off the lower half of her white top.

'Well they obviously want us to know they exist,' Wil accepted, 'are *allowing* us to know, but what do they expect us to do with this knowledge?' He watched her pump the soap and wash her hands. 'I mean, why are we even pretending they're not there? I couldn't find a thing on the internet about them this morning, so why isn't anyone blogging them, telling others—why aren't we pooling experiences?'

Sadie grabbed a hand towel and kneaded it.

'Because a realistic response to their presence might fast-track us to the psych ward,' she warned heavily. 'That's why.'

'Of course, that's one reason,' Wil admitted, seeing her answer as beside the point.

'Just a minute,' she held up a hand. 'You *are* taking that into consideration I hope, Wil.' Throwing the towel to the side, she narrowed in on him. 'If we don't *pretend* as you say, people who have no idea what we're talking about will simply think we're crazy. And have you even thought about what might happen if we were made to forget everything off the back of that—after we're already diagnosed and labelled? Where would we be then?' She shook her head fearfully, pressing the point.

'Neither of us can underestimate the threat of forgetting, Wil. I don't want *you* forgetting our dreams together, and *I* certainly don't want to end up oblivious to what's happening to Lily because one of us has made the wrong move.' She indicated *one of us* with a wavering finger. 'And even if it doesn't come to that—to us forgetting, those who remember their dreams… they won't hesitate disassociating with us if we're not discreet.' Her eyes widened, 'Putting *anything* on the internet is not discreet.' Here, she disengaged slightly, for there was no doubt he was beginning to appreciate the threat of forgetting. 'Besides,' she gave a fake smile, 'don't you think others have tried? You hear about these kamikaze attempts, but nothing comes of them' she sniffed, *'for a reason*. And just so we're clear, *I'm* not keen on accepting everything as normal any more than you are. And I certainly don't want to accept what's happening to Lily as normal. But what is the alternative? Forgetting and complete ignorance?' She cast a disgusted glance at her mother's office. 'The problem is still there.'

She handed him his lunch.

'Going rogue never works,' she said plainly, walking into the room with the framed beetles and taking the futon behind the door. Wil took the black chair in front of the shelves and balanced his plate on his knees as Sadie did. She took a few ravenous bites out of her sandwich and chewed quickly. 'If you think you're going to get away with something, they make a spectacle of you. So if the threat of forgetting is nothing, you can be sure it does the job for the rest of us who'll have no choice but to watch you crash and burn, maybe even clean up after you.'

The thought was alarming. 'Spectacle? What do they do?'

'All sorts. I'm not going to go into detail. But I have been full circle with them. Loving the dreams, wanting to be only in them, then hating them. But once you realise reality consists of the Tret and Tare at all times, no matter what state of mind you're in, well then they become the constant then, don't they? They're the constant that constantly influences, awake or asleep. Rogue or representative.'

'Surely they're less effective when we're awake though,' Wil reasoned, imagining that wakefulness gave people a cognitive edge over the Tret and Tare. 'Surely we can recognise what they're doing, what they're suggesting, especially those of us who remember, and override what they get us thinking.'

'Override?' Sadie hauffed wearily. 'Wil, if Aeolus gives you an instruction, you'll have no idea that's what it is. You'll carry on with your day, but it's like a little seed planted inside you. And it can be there waiting for months, years even. All of a sudden, at that crucial moment, you'll find yourself doing something completely out of character, exactly as they planned.' Her eyes were wide again, chiding. 'Of course, you had no idea it was there, that it was them, because they planted it where you'd least expect it. Like, Wil, don't look at my feet.'

She watched as he inadvertently did just that, glanced at her feet.

'Don't you see?' she beamed, catching him out. 'You can't ignore the seed of suggestion. No matter how hard you try. I wanted you to look at my feet, to prove my point, and that's exactly what they do. If you think you're doing what *you* want—maybe even defying them in the process—you're actually doing exactly *what* they told you to do, *when* they told you to do it.'

Wil realised the implications of the Tret and Tare influence knew no bounds. This seemingly omnipresent force suddenly reminded him of those mind-boggling revelations in Religious Education at primary school, where the idea of free will was always so difficult to get his head round. How did his eleven-year-old mind go out at playtime and make a decision after finding that an almighty Someone knew everything he was going to choose in the first place? Did that mean he made choices to begin with? Or was he simply accepting the choices already made for him?

'You know,' he broke their silence, 'all this really puts the human condition into new light.'

'I've often wondered if depression is actually people becoming overwhelmed by the Tret and Tare,' Sadie said thoughtfully, popping grapes into her mouth. 'I'm not saying I think the depressed are remembering their dreams, but complete paralysis of life… maybe it's a consequence of the can't-remember-your-dreams block. I've certainly seen them immobilise people with discouragement.'

Wil considered a few times that he himself had been discouraged in life. When he lost out on things.

'You said you wanted to give me something,' he remembered, clearing his plate of crisp fragments, to which Sadie covered her mouth and nodded vigorously, chewing.

'First, I need to tell you about objects,' she said, clearing her throat. 'They're how I got into your dream.' He was clearly puzzled. 'Basically, if you were the last to touch something and I hold it while I dream, I can get into your Initial. And vice versa. We already do this instinctively from an early age with babies holding transitional objects… children cuddling loveys before they go off to sleep. Then later, wearing keepsakes… lockets, rings….'

'So how did you get into *my* Initial?' he asked, unaware of ever giving her anything. Maybe it was what she had given him. 'Was that the earplugs then?'

'Nope.'

Her huge smile dared him to guess again, and he considered what she might have taken off him.

'Did you pinch a pencil off me?' But she was still smiling. 'A hair…? …DNA…?'

'I took the tack!'

'The tack?' he frowned. 'What tack?'

'The one you picked up off the floor outside class and pushed back into the notice board.'

He vaguely remembered the tack, the lame motive for standing out in the corridor avoiding Ben. 'Here I was worrying that you thought I had gonorrhoea,' he laughed slightly.

'Gonorrhoea?'

'I don't, by the way,' he assured, seeing now that she would have had her eyes on the tack, not the leaflets.

Dismissing him, 'You know we don't always need objects though,' she said. 'If we're not strangers, we can be in each other's Initials if we're trying to be at the same time. So like, if I'm about to go to sleep and so are you, and we're thinking about being there with the other person, we will be.'

'And what happens if I fall asleep before you?'

'You wait in your Initial and when I eventually fall asleep, I end up with you, bypassing my Initial altogether.'

'You said it can't happen if we're strangers….'

'Yeah. So think of the Initial connection like a social networking site. You can easily get into the lives of others by association. But if you don't know someone, they don't just open their door to you. You need a key. The object.'

'So if I wanted to get into anyone's Initial, I just need them to touch something?'

She hesitated for a second, apparently considering an exception, but dismissing it, 'And you need to be touching that object when you go to sleep.'

'Presumably, that can work both ways though,' he realised. 'Can someone I *don't know* come into my dream using an object I touched?'

'I'm afraid so.'

Wil imagined how that might be to his own benefit, and work against him.

Just then, her phone went off in the hall.

Coming back into the room with it in her hands, she appeared to send a brief text and sat down, unsettled slightly.

'You all right?'

'Fine.' She forced a smile. 'Now, Lily. I'd like you to take her, basically.'

'*Take* her?'

Sadie went out and then came back in with a small grey envelope.

'There are some hair clips in here she's touched last,' she said, handing them over. 'What I'd like you to do is wear them tonight,' she explained, sitting back down. 'If I stay with her until you arrive, you can get her out of there the second someone comes for her.'

He didn't even know how to do that. 'And then what?'

'I'll try and catch him. Or her.'

But Wil didn't like the thought of Sadie potentially dealing single-handedly with Lily's abductors. 'Surely you shouldn't be there on your own. What if *you* take Lily and *I* deal with whoever comes? Presumably they want nothing to do with me....'

She appeared to think about this alternative.

'The Initial shuts down when the dreamer leaves it. So Lily needs to be there somewhere. I just want one of us with her at all times, keeping her as unaware as possible. If you could be a ways off from us...' she said thoughtfully, persuading herself. 'It's just, if I don't end up seeing who it is and you do, you won't know who we're dealing with.'

'Listen, I know what Aeolus looks like, he's been in both our dreams. And isn't that who you think is doing this?'

'Yes, of course,' she said with slight distraction.

'So I just go to sleep like normal...'

'With a few of those in your hair...'

'With a few of these in my hair...' he smiled and lifted the envelope, 'then I'll be in Lily's Initial.'

'I'll be there ahead of you.'

But as he considered what might happen if things didn't go to plan, Wil couldn't help remember everything Sadie told him, how thought and action were pretty much under the direction of the Tret and Tare. That maybe this was exactly what Aeolus *wanted* them to do.

'If you get chucked out, Wil, you'll end up in your own Initial, probably because she's woken. Initials shut down not just when the dreamer leaves, but of course when they wake.'

It all seemed so simple. Maybe too simple. And just when Wil was about to clarify that he was only there confirming an identity, not there to confront or engage with anyone, Sadie said all of a sudden,

'You need to keep Ben close. You can't afford to have him on the wrong side. Aeolus hasn't anything to do with him so tell your best friend what's going on.'

Immediately, Lily's voice could be heard calling from the back garden.

'There it is. I've said too much,' Sadie said wryly. 'Well,I guess we know now where the line is. And since I've already stepped over it, don't let them convince you the human mind is *un*predictable. You'll believe anything they say if they've convinced you of that.'

There was Lily again, running into the kitchen.

'Don't lose that,' Sadie urged, watching Wil tuck the envelope into his jacket pocket.

The little girl they made such preparations for stood there in the doorway breathing hard. Her little dress was thoroughly soiled now with two green and brown bands where she had crawled around in the grass.

'Lauren's mum said I have to come home now. She said it was my naptime.'

Sadie flashed Wil an anxious look just before beaming at her little sister. 'Indeed it is, my Dearie,' she said cheerfully, checking her watch. 'We need to say good-bye to Wil here and head upstairs. And you need to change out of that filthy dress.'

Her little feet procrastinated up the steps even as Wil stood outside the front door, prompting Sadie to slip outside with him and close it slightly behind her.

'I'll see you tonight,' she promised.

'And what about now?' He indicated Lily's nap with a nod to the upper floors.

'They've not bothered with them yet. Not that I'm going to get lazy about that fact.' She seemed to be thinking of something to say, or was perhaps making sure she hadn't forgotten anything. 'Thank you so much, Wil.'

Lily called out suddenly from upstairs. 'Sadie... I need help with my zip!'

'Use the clips, okay? Ten o'clock.'

It crossed Wil's mind that that would be much too late for a five-year-old, but ignoring the thought,

'Will do,' he promised.

Chapter Twenty-Two

Charcoal

As Wil parked in front of the house, he saw the neighbour in her window, but Mum and Dad's cars were gone. Dropping his keys into the chamber pot in the hall, he received a perturbing text from Steph:

Spoke with Annie. She's worse. We need to talk.

He immediately texted back:

How worse?

He stored Lily's clips into his side table upstairs and waited for Steph's reply on the window seat. Having entertained a few unlikely scenarios, he sent another message.

Where are you btw?

Eventually,

Everything I said last night, voices, dreams, vandalism. I'm at Ben's.

Vandalism? he wrote back. *You didn't mention that.*

Before she could possibly have read his message though, she sent another text,

Can't text now. Talk later. xx

Wil chucked the phone on the bed, certain she hadn't mentioned anything about vandalism last night.

Scowling thoughtfully over his shoulder at the village, he didn't want to think that maybe Aeolus or the Tret and Tare had something to do with Annie's behaviour. He certainly didn't want to think it last night or this morning. But now, something inside him was prepared to believe it. In fact, the more insane Annie sounded, the more reasonable it seemed there could be no other explanation, especially when only days ago he himself believed he had been suffering from some sort of perception disorder, what with weird dreams and voices on the train. None of it was a hallucination now, because he knew... thanks to Sadie he now knew about Aeolus and the Tret and Tare. Of course, Annie didn't have anyone to tell her about the creatures, or whatever they were. The only person she had was Steph, who obviously had no idea what was going on.

I should tell her, he thought, not sure if he meant Annie or Steph as his eyes now fixed on the grey clay-like swirl of pigeon waste on the ledge. However, his mind stirred immediately against the idea, because there was too much at stake in assuming the Tret and Tare were the reason behind Annie's outrageous behaviour. This was, after all, Annie. This was normal-for-her behaviour. Not everything was about Tret and Tare....
But as Wil sat there, drawing his eyes from the pigeon pile to Wide Way, where he often looked for Llewellyn shuffling about, a very small, niggling thought prodded him.

Isn't that what they want you to think?

And just like that, all uses of logic Wil employed to justify his idleness suddenly worked against him, grinding his arguments to a halt. How could he possibly think the Tret and Tare had nothing to do with Annie, considering what he knew about them? And what of his sister being prepared to ditch her for Zara? It was unlike his sister as much as it was unlike Annie to carry on pushing her so. It indicated how desperate Annie was and what capacity Steph had to deal with her. And with it all coming to a head, how then could he see nothing of the Tret and Tare in it? The voices... the dreams Steph dared to mention last night... he was an idiot to try and put such things out of his mind, especially when his own sister couldn't.

Appreciating how the Tret and Tare could use indecision to prevent action, Wil became that much more determined to help Annie. But he couldn't escape that idea Sadie left with him: that no matter how many times he went back and forth with what his fiddled conscience was telling him, it would serve *them* in the end. No matter how he decided to help Annie, it suited them that he was drawn in. And made to help her.

A sad emptiness came over Wil as his focus left Wide Way and moved to the rolling fields of Darlingdon. Never again would he see this place like before, where the villagers had their comforting routine, their rhythm.

Their oblivious rhythm.

This vista now seemed to overlook a beautiful battlefield, designed to induce surrender.

Feeling already a casualty, Wil closed his eyes and turned away from the window, opening them in the general direction of the floor down by his feet. He inadvertently focused on the sketchpad sticking out there from under his bed, and he had an idea. It was ridiculous, he thought, but no worse than deciding to sit here and do nothing. If he was going to be a casualty, he certainly wasn't going to surrender.

'Not without a fight,' he said under his breath, reaching for the pad. And before he could change his mind, he ran downstairs and out to the car where he smiled and waved euphorically at the indifferent neighbour in the window again, then sped off to Bradfidd Close.

Selena's car wasn't there, which suited Wil fine in the event Annie decided to make a scene. In fact, he was glad she was out, because her embarrassment always seemed to feed Annie's drama the more she tried acting like the in-control mother. It was always too much, too late.

With his pad under his arm, he pressed the button, certain Annie saw him through the patio doors adjacent. A distorted image moved behind the textured glass, jingling keys, causing Wil's heart to race. Annie pulled the door open and looked at him, rather displeased.

'Steph's not here,' she said, insolent.

She was almost unrecognisable without makeup. Her too-short fringe was greasy and pressed to her forehead and her bob was tangled and matted, sticking out a bit at the back. The horrible dark circles under her eyes, pyjama pull-ons and hoody gave the impression she had a bad night, especially as it was well after midday.

'I've not come for Steph.'

Annie tilted her head to the other side as though he couldn't possibly have a better reason to be standing at her door.

'I've got a project,' he lied, 'and I need a drawing.' He held up the pad as proof. 'I'll pay you.'

'Pay me?' she crossed her arms, eyeing him doubtfully. 'What makes you think I'll do something for you for money?'

'Listen, Annie. You know I wouldn't come here unless I was desperate,' he tried looking like he didn't want to be in this position. 'I don't need a Picasso, just a rough sketch. And I mean it, I'll pay you.'

It seemed a long moment that she stood there, narrowing her eyes as if it might provoke him to spontaneously spout out the truth. And just when Wil thought she saw right through him and might suggest a dark crevice to stuff his notepad, she said distrustfully:

'How much?'

'Ten pounds?'

'Twenty.'

'Deal.'

A triumphant rush filled him as he tried thinking what she should draw.

'What is it then,' she asked apathetically, 'this drawing?'

'Um—a face—a scary face.'

'Fine.'

She stepped back and started closing the door.

'*Wait*... what are you doing—where are you going?'

'I'll send you your picture,' she assured, indifferent as to when.

'But you can't go' he said fretfully, through the narrowing gap. 'I need it now' he insisted, stopping the door with his hand. 'I need it *today*.'

'It's Saturday, Wilden,' she gauged him through ten inches' leeway, 'you don't need anything today.'

'But I do,' he pleaded, thrusting the spiral end of the notepad in her direction. 'Seriously, I've got the money here....'

Without thinking, he fumbled for his wallet, and whether he thought Annie had taken the pad as he haphazardly pushed it into the gap of the door or he let it go by accident, it slipped from his hand and laid open at his feet. There was an awkward moment as he watched her do a double-take of his amateurish interpretation of Aeolus, but he quickly picked it up and stuffed it under his arm.

'Just come in,' Annie said impatiently, to which Wil froze, his fingers still poking into his gaping wallet. 'Are you coming in or what?' she demanded, throwing an agitated hand to the air.

Annie led him into the room that looked out through the sliding glass doors and pointed at the small dining table the other end, outside the galley kitchen.

'You can sit there.'

Dutifully, he took a seat while she looked out the window. With her back towards him, he noticed the huge flat screen telly in the corner, but no photos of Selena or her daughter. No knick-knacks or anything personal. It was like a hotel room.

'What do you need the picture for, Wilden?' she asked, throwing him a suspicious look over her shoulder.

'Psychology.'

'Why?' She came as far as the fake fireplace, midway in the long room, and appeared to inspect something on the empty mantle.

'To um... illustrate... fear.' He was a little disappointed with his answer, but there was no taking it back now.

'You think I know how to draw fear?' she asked, turning and measuring him precisely. 'What makes you think I can do that?'

While her intonation was full of typical Annie venom, Wil thought her stale face, without the dramatic eye make-up somehow made her more human and less threatening. But before he could answer, she came and took the chair opposite him.

'Well...?' she pressed.

Whatever he said, he didn't want to appear insincere, nor did he want to provoke her anger.

'You can draw anything,' he said plainly, trying not to sound too flattering, however, her unfamiliar, unpencilled eyebrows lifted, haughty.

'That won't work on me, Wilden. Why are you here?'

'Seriously, I just needed you to draw something for me.'

But she was obviously not buying it.

'I'm not new to this you know,' she informed him wearily, forcing a sickly smile behind slow blinks that made her appear intoxicated. 'You have two options: you can either tell me the truth... or you can get out.'

Wil didn't take the ultimatum lightly, for this was an Annie he had never seen. Whenever she had the upper hand, she mauled and pounced like a cat over a mouse, methodically and brutally. But now, she was intent on *not* playing games. She had clearly invited him in knowing a drawing wasn't the real reason he had come, and if he carried on with the excuse, he was convinced she'd turn him out in no time. He had to be slightly truthful.

'Okay,' he said resolutely, patting the air between them, halting her from acting rashly, 'I'll tell you the truth... but...' he couldn't possibly mention Aeolus or ask about her dreams directly, 'the truth is a little difficult,' he admitted, running a hand through his hair and then rubbing his forehead, delaying.

'Then let's make it easier for you,' she proposed, idly taking his book from the middle of the table and flicking through the pictures. 'Have you come here to tell me off about something?' she asked with disinterest.

'No....'

She turned the notepad a little and tilted her head to make out one of his images, and Wil began to question what he hoped to accomplish in coming here, after feeling so certain that it was of the utmost importance.

'Have you come here to tell me that you fancy me...?'

'*No!* I mean... no.'

For a second, he was sure he had offended her, but his emphatic answer now had her looking at him hopefully, as if he had just crudely simplified things.

'Have you come here to tell me something about this?' With only a hint of interest, she pushed the notepad towards him. Aeolus' roughly drawn face innocently stared out from the page.

Wil searched her for a clue. Was she giving him an opportunity to mention the creature—the dreams? Whatever he said, he couldn't afford to mess it up.

'Actually,' he proffered carefully, 'I was hoping you'd tell me.'

Her intent expression weakened. She sighed slightly, making him realise she had been holding her breath.

'Then forget it,' she snapped. And like that, the moment was lost, her hopeful expression with it. Pushing the notebook away, she added coldly, 'And you can keep your twenty pounds.'

'Annie...' he pleaded, utterly confused, 'I was just—'

'What do you want from me, Wil—why are you even here? Because of a stupid picture?' she regarded the image of Aeolus with contempt. 'You can draw your own rubbish... so don't insult me with this... this I-need-an-angry-face rot!' Seething, she folded her arms and glared. 'If the real reason you're here is because someone sent you, then at least have the courage to say it.'

She had to mean Steph, he was certain. Believing the picture wasn't as meaningful to her as he thought, he shifted gears immediately.

'Listen, Steph's been worried about you... she said you've been hearing voices... and she said—'

'—Do you think I'm hearing voices, Wil? Do you think something's wrong with me?'

'I don't know,' he said frankly, 'I don't know what's going on with you. But....'

'But what?'

'But… whatever it is… you're isolating yourself, and you shouldn't deal with this alone.'

She scoffed and rolled her eyes towards the glass doors. 'Have you any idea how long I've dealt with things *alone*, Wil? *Have you?*'

'All I'm saying is people are worried about you,' he backed off slightly. 'Steph doesn't want to—'

'—Steph isn't the reason you came, Wil,' she accused, meeting him squarely.

'Maybe I should go,' he said sheepishly, taking his notebook.

'Actually Wil, I want to show you something in my room. Now that we're clear you don't fancy me,' her tone pre-empted his objection, 'I can trust you won't get any ideas.'

Wil met her fatigued seriousness with compelling curiosity and, against his better judgement, cautiously followed her up the narrow staircase to the room at the end of the hall.

There was a latch on the outside of her bedroom door he couldn't help notice.

'What's that for?' he asked, dubious as to whether she was trying to get him in there so she could lock him in.

'Oh, that? I started sleepwalking.' She said it like it was a new hobby she found herself surprisingly good at. 'Mum locks me in each night. Just in case I get up to mischief,' she added lightly. 'Now, can I ask just one more time,' she said to him over her shoulder, her hand on the door knob, 'why you really came to see me?'

There was that vaguely hopeful look again.

'We're worried about you, Annie,' he maintained, guarded, wondering now what might be behind that door. Wondering now where her mother was.

'That's fine,' she pursed a disappointed smile and turned the knob, then pushed the door open an inch or so. 'You can go ahead.'

Gingerly, he stepped passed her, gauging from her face that this was no joke, and as he pushed the door open into the bright bedroom, he saw nothing untoward but an obsession of charcoal sketches plastered ceiling-to-floor over the bed, around the windows and behind him on the wall. Looking back to her, he realised this was what she wanted him to see.

Relieved, Wil took in the sheer volume of black and white images, only to notice a familiar feature amid them that unexpectedly took his breath away.

The faces, they were obviously Tret and Tare faces. Tret and Tare he had never seen before. Some were feminine-looking, powerful. Some were in steely prominence while others passive. There were repeated scenes of crowds to his left, and while the faces in them all looked generally alike, there seemed to be a depiction of sides. Like a stand-off. His attention was then held by a collection of overlapping pages, at odd angles, creating a large image over the bed. Everything seemed to centre around this scene opposite him. It was mostly blackness, pages and pages of it, with the vague profiles of several individuals standing as a group. None he recognised, for the detail was less in this coagulated image than in the others, but their presence loomed, confrontational.

Wil drew his attention away from the individual scenes and looked at the mass. Annie had cleverly used the sprawling collage of pages like a collective canvas to draw a sweeping fog that wrapped around her entire room. It infiltrated each textured sheet as a background shadow, swirling and moving along the corners of some pages and filling the blank spots of others. In the blackened scenes, it appeared as white curling waves.

Wil turned to Annie, speechless.

'Steph didn't send you, did she?' Annie asked bitterly.

It suddenly occurred to him that even with his partially-true excuse, his sister wasn't the reason behind him coming.

'No,' he answered, admitting it ultimately had to be Aeolus.

It suddenly made sense to him why Annie didn't believe the picture explanation and what she meant when she urged him to at least have the courage to say who had sent him. Conveniently, he thought she meant Steph.... But having seen his own picture of the creature, it was no wonder she kept asking for the truth.

'So... I'm not going crazy then?' She set her jaw.

'No, Annie,' Wil said soberly, 'you're not crazy.'

She looked so relieved she began to sob, convulsing her shoulders, becoming more and more emotional.

After seeing her be so dramatic over the years, Wil realised he had never actually seen Annie cry. All her dramas had been built around shock, anger and confusion, but never such vulnerability. In fact, there were times he thought she ought to have cried, and because she hadn't, it had a way of fuelling his scepticism. But here, now, there was no pretence, and in an awkward quasi-compassionate effort to comfort her,

Wil reached out and put his hand on her quivering shoulder.

'It's okay,' he soothed from a distance, inadvertently prompting her to lean against his chest as she heavily sobbed. His natural reaction was to reject her, to stiffen and snuff at her closeness, but she was so inconsolable that he ended up patting her shoulder uncomfortably, never seeing this moment coming. Ever.

Then without warning, she drew back a fist and hit him hard on the chest. Again, sniffing and weeping, she tried hitting him with the other hand, but he caught her wrist, forcing her to weakly make contact with the first hand again.

'Annie...' he made sure to grab both wrists '...stop this...!'

His first thought was that she was trying to back him into her room, to lock him in, but her feeble swipes and near-punches clearly had a different motive.

'What are you *doing?*' he demanded, managing her pathetic little arms easily. 'Just... stop...!'

They scuffled there in the doorway in front of the myriads of Tret and Tare faces until she finally relented and pulled away, retreating against the wall in the hall.

'Why didn't you say?' she blubbed angrily, shoving her fists into her hoody pocket and avoiding eye contact with him. 'Why didn't you say you knew?'

'How could I?' he reproved. 'Why didn't *you* say something...? You saw the picture....'

But instead of answering, Annie resentfully sniffed back the tears and wiped her cheeks against her shoulders.

'You were willing to walk out of here...' she shook her head, wounded, incredulous.

Wil now appreciated that her questions at the table had been tests, tests he had utterly failed. But her reticent stance from the moment he walked in gave little margin for anything else.

'How long have you known, then?' she said eventually, hardening herself from another wave of tears.

'A few days.'

'A few *days?*' This seemed to upset her again, and she swallowed hard and blinked upwards towards the ceiling with a strange contortion of her lips that got her chin quivering.

'It's been strange for a week,' he explained, 'but I've only known what's been going on since yesterday.' He hoped this absolved him of any perceived wrongdoing despite Annie's guilt of the same thing. 'What about you?'

From the work on the wall, he imagined months.

Annie rolled her eyes and smiled weakly, insinuating his ignorance was offensive.

'What if I told you' her pathetic smile faded 'that it's been years? That I can't remember when I *didn't* know about them?'

'*Years?*'

'Yeah.' Grudgingly she looked at him. 'Do you remember Charlie?'

The name didn't ring a bell.

'My imaginary friend?'

'When you were little?' *You aren't suggesting....*

'Yes. And Murphy?'

That was the teenage boyfriend no one ever saw, the one who got her pregnant. Only, she hadn't been pregnant at all, leading everyone to believe it was an attention-seeking don't-leave-me stunt.

'I remember you *talking* about them...' Wil admitted, for he wouldn't go so far as to say he *remembered* them.

'That's how long,' Annie said quietly as her eyes fell to the floor. Wil didn't want to believe it. That was... most of her life. With Charlie... she had to be like... *five.*

Sadie's voice suddenly shot through his head, (*She's five, Wil. Five...*) and just like that, he believed the Tret and Tare could have taken hold of Annie years ago just as they were invading Lily's little life now.

'I believe you,' he made clear. 'Annie, I believe you.'

'Would you believe me too if I said you have a history with them? That you've known them for more than just a few days?'

'Yes, I'd believe you,' he shrugged. 'I've been convinced of a lot of things I didn't think I'd believe the last few days.'

'Did you recognise anything in there?' She glanced hopefully passed him to the far wall in her bedroom, to which he looked over his shoulder and went in.

'Just that these are Tret and Tare,' he said, scanning the scenes again.

Annie came in alongside him and walked up to the wall behind the bed.

'Tret and Tare. No one uses that anymore. We called them Friends and Enemies.'

'We?'

'Even talking like this,' she said in disbelief, 'you really don't remember?'

'Remember what?'

'We were a team, Wil,' she explained over her shoulder, rubbing the dark chalk of fog curling up a corner. 'You... me... Steph... Ben and Zara... and Murphy.'

Her fingers then touched a page with an attractive male face, a face without strange hair around it like the other Tret and Tare faces. Wil took this to be her Murphy.

'These were our battles,' a more pensive tone came out of her as she attentively blew charcoal dust from Murphy's narrowed gaze. 'It's a visual record, in case they made me forget. Do you not recognise your own face?'

Annie was an excellent artist, but he could see nothing of himself in the pages sprawled here.

'What about there?' she pointed to the wall the other side of the bed. 'Something rather significant happened to you there.'

Intrigued, he went over and inspected the images. They were so small he hadn't seen himself before, but close up, there he was. In fact, the lengthy zig-zag of overlapping A-4's coming from the ceiling showed a sequence of events in such detail, it was clear to him now that he was the prominent character.

'What is this?' he asked, seeing a Steph likeness along with an Annie there in the smudged lines. It looked to be a hostile situation. Annie was being held back, as if for her own protection. She was angry, shouting, reaching out from the arms and bodies that prevented her from running with the large mob on the left. Aeolus was there too. Behind her, saying something in her ear amid the chaos. Wil saw himself in the background being taken away into a cloud. He then realised it was merely a wisp of the fog that permeated her massive collage.

'Start from the top,' she instructed. 'It'll make more sense.'

Wil did so, and after twenty minutes of reading captions and interpreting the execution of emotion behind frozen facial expressions and body gestures, he began to appreciate how strange it was for Annie to have experienced all this with him, yet without him having any memory of it at all.

'*Code…?*' he questioned, looking at an image of Annie's distraught face screaming the word to a downcast Steph. 'What does that mean?'

'Keep looking, Wil.'

After another ten minutes, he finally came to the end of the sequence and felt these things couldn't have been his life. Even his dreaming half, for they were too far removed from him… too significant for him to be standing here feeling nothing. The emptiness towards such profound actions… it began to trouble him deeply.

'How could I sacrifice my memory…' he hated the thought '…to protect Aeolus?'

'Damned if I know,' Annie drawled in a fake southern accent. 'But you did,' she said plainly, pointedly. 'And you weren't the only one. Steph and the others did the same.' She sat on the bed and squinted at the blu-tacked events in question. 'They followed your lead,' she said with a hint of disapproval.

'And is that why you hate me?' he asked, still unable to imagine himself making such a decision.

'I don't hate you Wil. I was hurt. And I can't blame you for what you don't remember. Just like I don't blame Steph for making the same decision.' He turned from the image to her sitting there on the bed. 'But you all left me, and everything we did… it was like I had imagined it, that none of it ever happened. And the end came so quickly… we didn't even have time to code it.'

She caught his quizzical look and clearly realised he didn't know what that meant.

'We regularly used a word, or a phrase' she explained 'that was agreed upon in the dream—often related to what had just happened, then when we woke up, we'd know it was actually *us* who had been there.' She began plucking fuzz off the duvet. 'There were times we thought maybe an imposter or someone posing as one of us infiltrated the ranks, so we used codes for all sorts. Even before we got into a dream, we agreed on one, so that when we got there, from the start, we knew who we were dealing with.'

It suddenly made sense to Wil why Annie was shouting the word *code* to Steph in the image behind him. He had a look at it again and began appreciating the subtle detail, for the strained lines in Annie's face, the grief in the shape of her eyes, conveyed an Annie desperate to know something. Not an Annie impatient for some new code to tag the horrendous event for when they woke later, but an Annie who was prompting her best friend to declare her identity.

'I desperately wanted that Steph to be an imposter,' she verified his interpretation. 'I thought she would have at least shouted out what we agreed before we entered the dream... so I knew it was her....'

Annie shook her head faintly, clearly recalling the events in more disturbing detail than was plastered around her.

'But she must have known,' she continued soberly, 'she must have known I was hoping... and that if she answered, I'd have gone crazy.... It was better she didn't say anything. A mercy, really. By the time I woke up, I knew it had happened.' Annie made a little snuffing noise as though pretending to be amused. 'Everything was gone. She couldn't even remember the word we all agreed before the dream. None of you could.'

'What was it?' Wil asked as a definite heaviness filled the room, like they were speaking of a deceased loved one.

'We had been watching The Sound of Music earlier that day,' she said reminiscently, 'but with them...' disgust instantly filled her face, 'everything's significant.' After a beat, '*Adieu*. Steph suggested it without even thinking. Of course, I thought nothing of it at the time. We knew we'd both remember it easily, having sung it all day.' Annie then hauffed, indignant. '*Adieu*... the whole day,' she said, shaking her head with a wide-eyed vacant expression. 'We had no idea what was coming.' Then as if changing the scene in her head like a slide show, she blinked and was back to the present. 'I guess we had already said our good-byes.'

To think of Steph saying that word... right then.... Annie was right, his sister wouldn't have. It was a mercy. And not just for Annie, but for him too. The anger Annie must have been feeling at that moment in their past, towards him... presumably having left her out of their decision....

'Why didn't they make *you* forget?' he asked curiously.

'I don't know,' she answered readily, understandably annoyed. 'I didn't even know until Aeolus told me, *as* it was happening. And a second later, they were carting you off to do whatever they do to the rest of the world every night.'

Wil looked to the wall, to the angry mob... holding her back... ending it all in front of her before she had the chance to do anything... the chance even to understand why. Wil wished he could have remembered himself saying those words Annie had placed neatly over his charcoaled head, understood why he publicly agreed to give up his memory for Aeolus.

And as he tried imagining the aftermath of Steph and her best friend in such circumstances—of himself putting them there... and *why*... he found his thoughts pushing up against some familiar but elusive barrier. This obstruction, whatever it was, attracted his mind, but then cut him off, like a tiny insect bumping hopelessly against a sun-filled window. He had hit it before, many times in fact, searching for answers he felt were within reach. But now... here in Annie's room... seeing the person he had been, he was beginning to believe that if only he tried harder—beat against this wall with more force—he might break it down and be reunited with his past.

Determinedly, Wil looked at the disturbing image beside him where he made his deal with Aeolus and mentally adopted it, filling in pertinent, but imaginary detail until he could almost see himself there, as if he remembered. He felt the desperation of having to make such a decision. The powerlessness of losing so much... of wishing there was something else he could do or say that might change everything.... He saw himself in front of the mob, telling them what they wanted to hear. But he felt something else too... that he was taking himself out of the equation so that Aeolus might be spared, so the creature might bring them all back together... at a later date... it was the only way.... He could hear himself saying the words... consoling the others with them.... *It's the only way....*

(The rigid glass began to yield a little, like a polyethylene film.)

But of course, his friends wouldn't let him do it alone... they carried the burden with him. They would all forget and trust it wasn't all in vain.... In his mind's eye, Wil saw himself speaking to Ben and Steph... saying something to them that meant they couldn't misunderstand him... or doubt who he was.... It was a code... his *own* code... because they all had one... for emergencies such as these... only this time... the first time he really needed it... they didn't laugh....

Just then.

'No way...' he mumbled in disbelief. '*No way....*'

'What?' Annie sounded worried.

Wil turned to her, unable to believe what he was about to say, for he wasn't sure if he had invented the importance behind such words, but he said them anyway:

'I fancy you....' They came out almost like a question, he was so unsure of them.

Annie stiffened cautiously there on the bed.

212

'What do you mean by that, Wil?' she eyed him warily.

'It's code!' he declared, realising. '*My* code!'

The joy in her face looked like sadness at first, because she stood up and cried, but she was happy. Very happy.

'I never did actually fancy you though, did I?' he asked, slightly confused as to where events from his imagination and reality separated.

'No...!' she laughed and cried at the same time. '*Never...!*'

'My God... *that's* why you kept asking,' it suddenly occurred to him. '*That's* why all the digs about me fancying you...' all those occasions when they were alone... those hints... those suggestions, what he thought were innuendos and her trying to come onto him, or make him uncomfortable in his own home... 'and the question downstairs just now... you were trying to see if I remembered.'

They both began laughing either side of her bed with such confusion and relief that neither really knew what to make of what was happening. Eventually, they stopped and stood there looking at one another curiously.

'What does this mean?' he asked, feeling exhilaration leave him as something more important, something heavy and indeterminable, took its place.

'I don't know what it means for you...' she shook her head, smiling, 'but for me...' her amazement was directed at the ceiling now, 'it means I'm not alone anymore.'

No. She wasn't, he felt certain. And as he looked around at the thousands of faces staring back at him in her bedroom, he could see how everyone here had made her feel incredibly isolated. All those stunts she pulled.... They had to be some sort of outlet, some coping mechanism. Briefly, Wil's mind flitted over the incidents that had made their biggest impression on him: the flash mobs... Murphy... the fake pregnancy.....

Suddenly.

It was like he again made connections that were illogical, impossible. But they popped into his head with such inspiration, such cohesion, he couldn't ignore them.

'Annie... I think I remember *your* code,' he said uncertainly, cocking his head to the side like some psychic receiving supernatural messages. 'And Ben's. *And* Steph's.'

'Go on then,' she urged.

'*I'm pregnant,*' he blurted, surprising her. 'And Ben's,' he continued, 'who would have guessed: *I detest food...* and Steph's: *I hate you.*'

Annie sat, flabbergasted on the end of her bed and stared at Wil. There was less enthusiasm in her expression and more caution now.

'We chose something we were likely to never say,' she explained guardedly, clearly finding the barrage of connections he had made somewhat worrying.

'Somehow... I *know* that,' he admitted, 'but I don't know *how* I know it. I mean, *I'm pregnant*... I didn't just make that up.'

It suddenly hit him: the going away party.

'Good grief, Annie....'

She looked up at him sadly, apparently aware of his thought precisely, 'I was trying to get you to remember. It had only been days before that you all forgot....'

'You insisted for weeks,' he remembered. He remembered too how pathetic he believed her to be for such a claim, a claim that everyone knew was false.

'It seemed pointless only when I realised the situation wasn't temporary. That's when I gave up.' That's when her mother got the confession it was all a ruse, Wil realised.

The present deserted Annie, filling her eyes with a blankness that prompted Wil to revisit the party in his own mind with this new context. He couldn't believe the embarrassment, the humiliation she had been willing to go through to try and twang some numbed nerve that might get them to remember what they were all able to do in their dreams together.

'What about after, though,' he asked curiously, 'with the flash mobs and everything... all the stunts....?'

'I didn't give up for long,' her vacancy continued. 'They were our experiments... so I just carried on on my own.'

'Experiments?'

Snapping back, she blinked rapidly and met him squarely. 'It was our way of trying to get people to remember their dreams. We thought that if we tried handing out flyers in a public place, then used them to meet those individuals in the dreams... well, then maybe we could trigger some kind of awareness of what we had experienced together.' She shook her head faintly. 'We were constantly trying to find who was on the cusp of Transition, but then you all forgot... Murphy disappeared... so I carried on alone. I thought it must have been important if that's why you all were taken out of the equation. Why else would they have done such a thing?'

'But you've been doing that sort of thing for years,' he couldn't help put out there, seeing no difference in those public dramas from what she did all her life. 'Since I can remember.'

'No, Wil. I'm sorry,' she corrected, 'but you and I had been dreaming together with Steph and Ben for at least five years before you all forgot,' she insisted, shocking him with this fact. 'Yes, so I wasn't doing any of those ridiculous things without your help,' she said indignantly. 'Anything from primary school... that was Charlie and me, before I realised it was all real and not just my imagination. But everything else... it was *us*.

'That's what happens in all this,' she said, rolling her eyes in frustration. 'They take away everything you remember that might relate to them. They've taken away memories of our meetings... our dreams... our before and during codes.... We were obsessive about those codes. We may not have hung out all day long because we did actually have lives outside one another, but whatever was related to them awake or asleep—all that planning... it's clearly disappeared. So now, when you look back, I was just this weird idiot. An attention-seeking freak working on my own. But actually, we did those things *together*. Things I was sure even members of the public would remember—maybe even post on the internet or print in the media. We hoped, but there was nothing. We searched, but no one made reference to them, or dreams. No matter how hard we tried.' She looked at him hopelessly, mirroring the defeat behind such realisations at the time. 'It was obviously pointless, but we all took part, Wil. I'll admit happily that I did most of the public things, because I didn't mind being in front of people, but now, without any memory of dream Friends or Enemies—any memory of motive—everyone just sees me as this... this....'

She gave up finding a word.

'I don't see you like that anymore,' he insisted. 'I don't see you as attention-seeking or weird.' In fact, he saw her now as brave. Courageous. Able to do what he never could. It crossed his mind that perhaps this was the reason she was left to remember. 'I don't see you as a freak either, Annie.'

'I appreciate that. But it doesn't take away the fact that Steph sees me as this strange person. I hadn't realised until this week how I must have appeared to everyone. All I kept thinking was *you've got to remember...* and that whatever we were onto, it was worth continuing.

So many times, I wanted to be in your shoes... to have life be so simple....
But now, my closest friend is on the verge of leaving me. *For Zara.*' There
was the venom, the bitterness that now seemed wholly appropriate, for
Wil suddenly wished too that his sister wasn't trying to replace Annie.

'What is it with Zara?' he dared to ask. 'Ben said you've got this
thing against her?'

'It doesn't matter,' Annie shook off. 'She's a back-stabber. And
you can trust me on that one,' she said pointedly. 'Don't trust her with
anything, especially your sister. You've got to think: this is a battle.
Friends... enemies.... You're remembering for a reason. Because it suits
some of them. And it surely won't suit others. So we're in the line of fire
right now, Wil. Right this very minute.'

Wil was aware again of the thousands of Tret and Tare faces
around him, captured behind charcoal dust and staring. It occurred to
him that he should mention Sadie and after briefly explaining how he
came to know what he did the last few days, Annie cautioned him further,

'Just be careful, Wil. You don't know who's working her.'

'It's Aeolus,' he was certain.

'*Our* Aeolus?' She seemed to think that odd. 'You still need to be
careful.' She got up from the bed and lingered by the door, thinking. 'You
should start coding.'

'About that,' he said, coming round to her side of the room and
looking at the pictures as he went, 'aren't codes pointless if they can all
get in our heads anyway? I mean, won't they know what it is, or tell their
friends?' Murphy's face, as Wil took one last look, did seem vaguely
familiar just then.

'It doesn't work like that, Wil. Think of it more like... we're
assigned to different ones.'

'Aeolus is clearly in your dreams too then,' he nodded to the
sketches.

'No, I know Aeolus because he was there in your dreams when
we met with you. I had my own Friend. Hyosha. You knew her.' Annie
directed him to look at the bold female face near the lamp. 'Of course,
Hyosha and Aeolus are both Tare, so when they prompt us to come up
with a code, that information is essentially kept in-house.'

'Tare?' Wil said, remembering Sadie telling him that Aeolus was
actually Tret. *...Fret the Tret, share with the Tare...* and *...Trust the Tret,
beware of the Tare...* her rhymes came to him from the green. 'And the fact

that Aeolus is in both Sadie's and my dreams...?' he tried to figure.

'They look after loads of people, Wil. In most cases we never know who those individuals are. But things are obviously changing. And you still need to be careful who you trust. Especially as you've only just started remembering more than your Initial.' She shook her head, still amazed by it. 'Listen, my mum will be home soon. We should probably go downstairs. I don't want her seeing you and getting any ideas. Or talking to Liz.'

'Sure.' But just as he was about to leave the room, he noticed a pattern in one picture on the small margin of wall beside the doorframe. It immediately pricked his interest, and for a second he felt certain it was more meaningful to him than he was consciously aware. 'What's this?' he stooped and squinted at the rings within rings, like the sunken steps in a circular amphitheatre.

'That's where we used to meet. Where you and Aeolus figured out a way to get our dreams to converge at the start.'

'Huh.' He stood up with no memory of it, not even that bit of subconscious affinity that stopped him in the first place. 'Do you mind if I take a few pictures before I go,' he put a hand on his breast pocket, over his phone, 'in case it helps my memory later?'

'By all means.'

He snapped away at the prominent images, and anything with Steph and Ben, Annie and him. The four faces—some wrought with jagged, distressed lines that seemed to mirror its content, right next to simple, sweeping creations—all portrayed a group of people fastened together by something profound. Something impossible. The Annie behind him was closer than he could ever imagine, yet the Annie there on the wall had been closer still. And the Ben... Annie conveyed the bond in his frozen poses with Wil that was nothing short of a Justin Salinsky moment: complete devotion and sacrifice. But the most striking of all, now that Wil was looking closely, was Steph. She was portrayed as wise, beautiful and strong, always to his right, and close beside him in every picture.

Downstairs at the table, Annie explained how desperate she was for Steph to remember while she sketched away in Wil's pad, and how fruitless her recent efforts had been. She explained too the vandalism Steph mentioned.

'Basically, sleepwalking, spray paint and CCTV are my enemies at the moment. So how's this for an angry face?' She signed and dated her sketch then presented it to him.

He studied the perfect image of Aeolus apparently roaring like a lion. His flicking mane, equally enraged. 'Better than I can even recall in my head,' he said with amazement. 'I've never seen him like this though. He's always been calm. Collected.'

'That's the last time I saw him, any of them actually,' Annie said, staring at it meaningfully. 'He was trying to tell me it would be okay. Smiling. Keeping me calm. But then he erupted. Not at me, but right after they took you. Of course, I knew none of it was okay at that point. We all knew it wasn't okay.' She closed the notebook and pushed it in his direction. 'I'd offer to meet up in the dreams, but I can't tonight.'

'Because of the sleepwalking? Annie you need your sleep.'

'It'll be fine in a few days,' she dismissed. 'Until you get your memory back completely, you should be okay in there on your own. Anyway, here, take my number. If you have any trouble, or questions, text. Any time.'

After exchanging numbers, Wil left her there by the front door, his sketchbook under arm, feeling the Annie he thought he knew had merely been some foul fictitious character, made up by someone equally as foul.

Chapter Twenty-Three

Opposed

Wil didn't mention he saw Annie when he dropped Steph off at Ben's later that afternoon. Or that she accused Zara of being a back-stabber. But after hearing his sister's version of Annie's recent eccentricities, realising it was Annie simply not coping well with Steph's inability to remember their past dreams, he did his best to dissuade his sister from finding a replacement friend in Zara.

'You know she hates me for some reason,' he reminded, watching Zara line herself directly behind Ben there in the doorway as Steph got out of the car, wondering if Zara herself remembered something of their past he couldn't. 'Just don't go making besties overnight, all right?'

On the way back home, he replayed the scene outside Annie's bedroom over in his head… her punching him there in the hallway, after he let on that he knew something of the dreams, of Aeolus… and he couldn't help think of all those times she asked if he fancied her…. She had clearly been trying to see if he remembered something. But of course, his reaction told her plenty when he hatefully answered no, or got up and left the room in disgust. Over and over again. He was certain he deserved more than a punch.

'I had been so cruel,' he admitted to Sadie over the phone upstairs in his room, having told her nearly everything, 'but she carried on. Over three years. Since we left for Mulbryn.'

'Good grief, Wil. *Years?*'

Well how was I supposed to know these emergency codes were things we thought we'd *never* say?'

Sadie let out a thoughtful *humph* then urged,

'Can we go back to the creature bit again? You said you had some kind of understanding with him?' she tried clarifying.

Only, Wil intentionally skimmed over that bit, because the plan he extrapolated from Annie's sketches, precisely before he comprehended the codes, made him see why he had to face that stark mob, and why he had to tell them what they wanted to hear. It had all been so Aeolus could be spared. And once he appreciated the codes, it became clear that sparing Aeolus meant the creature could bring them all back together in the dreams at a later date, remembering again. *That*, he didn't tell Annie as he snapped away at her wall with his phone. And of course, telling Sadie was going to be tricky too, because the Aeolus Wil believed he protected in the past to restore his memories in the future—the present as it now happened to be—was the very Aeolus Sadie believed tormented Lily.

'About that,' he turned the chair back to the desk, bracing himself, 'is there any possibility someone else could be behind Lily's night terrors? Someone other than the Aeolus in our dreams?'

Sadie hesitated to answer. 'Why…?'

'Because the creature in Annie's pictures,' he grimaced and closed his eyes, not wanting to say it '…was Aeolus. And Annie said he was Tare.' He opened his eyes and squinted, waiting for her to respond, hearing only a controlled exhalation like she was annoyed slightly. 'Sadie?'

'Well this Annie is obviously mistaken,' she concluded flatly.

'But… the face on her walls is the same one I've been talking to in my dreams,' he insisted, getting up and taking the pad from under his bed. He wedged the phone between his ear and shoulder and studied the pencilled image there by the window. 'She did a sketch of him in my book before I left,' he said, flipping back to his own lame attempt. 'It's a good thing she draws so well, seeing as we can't take photos in the dreams. I mean, I tried to draw Aeolus last week, but it was rubbish. Obviously it was good enough that she realised who I was trying to draw… but what she's done here,' he flicked back to roaring Aeolus and sniffed down the phone, impressed at the simple accurate lines on the page, 'it's perfect. The square jaw… pointy cheeks… that long nose… everything is spot on. And that hair…' he couldn't create angry in hair if his life depended on it. Wil suddenly became aware that Sadie had been much too quiet. Lowering the notebook from his face, he put the phone to his other ear.

'Is it possible for him to have been Tare then and Tret now?'

'No, Wil,' she said sharply. 'So this vague plan you thought you made with him, this understanding—'

'—He was going to help me—and Annie and Ben and Steph—help us remember the dreams again.' Wil was in no doubt as to how Sadie felt about him making any agreement with the creature, past or present. 'Listen I'm not trying to defend him here in asking these questions. I'm just trying to figure out what's going on. Is he Tare or is he Tret? Is he the one behind Lily's night terrors or not?' Despite his expectant pause, Sadie didn't answer. 'Is there something you're not telling me here? Do you know something about hi—'

'—Aeolus doesn't have a square jaw and pointy cheeks, Wil,' she said finally. 'And his nose isn't long. He's not the Aeolus in my dreams.'

'*Our* dreams,' Wil insisted, correcting. *But it is. It is the same Aeolus*, he was certain. 'Listen, I've just not explained him well, that's all,' he tried assuring, feeling the urge to prove this to her, prove the roaring creature in front of him was the same as in their dreams. 'Let me text you a photo.'

'Go on, then,' she sighed, sounding like it would be a pointless exercise. 'It's not him, Wil,' she declared a minute later.

'But Sadie,' he slumped onto the end of the bed, bewildered, 'how can you say that when he's been in *both* our dreams?'

'Because he clearly hasn't.' The weariness in her tone suggested she was beginning to realise something he hadn't yet. 'Think of one dream where the three of us were in the same place *at the same time*, Wil,' she challenged, 'seeing each other face-to-face.'

One dream sprang to mind immediately.

'Okay. Well there was the one where he walked past me and said *look*, then the two of you were talking like I wasn't there. You were sad or worried or something. It was like he was prepping you for something you didn't want to do, and he wanted me to see you in distress. You disappeared after that,' he remembered clearly, 'the pair of you. But then I called out for you and suddenly you were there again. You, on your own, smiling like nothing even happened.' The threat of imposters now settled lightly into his mind as a possibility. 'That *was* you, wasn't it?'

'Yes. That was me.'

'Well?'

'I didn't see you when I was with him.'

'We were too far away from one another, that's all....'

'I'm sorry, Wil, but think about it. If I didn't see you, but you saw me... and I know what dream you're talking about....' She stopped herself and exhaled loudly. 'Did you *see* his face—the face of who I was talking to—did you *actually* see his face... *as* I was standing with him?'

Wil thought back, realising that no, he didn't. In fact, it was Aeolus' positioning, keeping his back to Wil, that made Sadie's pained expression so obvious. And as he recalled this just now, he became aware that it was this precisely what made him feel so slighted, so unwelcome at the time.

'But I *saw* him... he was right there....'

'You saw *one* of them' Sadie acknowledged, flustered, 'because there are two, Wil. *Two* Aeoluses—one Tret and one Tare.'

'Two? So one's an imposter?'

'No, Wil. They're nothing alike,' she said irritably, prompting him to frown wildly across the room, for the hair and that strange skin—and clothes—were certainly consistent. 'They're opposed,' she explained. 'And they're constantly undermining one another. In fact, the dream you saw us in, it wasn't really your dream—I mean it was, and I did have that experience, but in my own Initial, before I came to you in your fog—it was your Aeolus showing you what mine was doing. Like a vision. So you weren't there,' she determined, 'because had you been, you'd have known something wasn't right—that there were two opposing figures working us separately.'

Why it never occurred to him that there could be two creatures annoyed Wil slightly, especially as Annie told him only hours ago that they were assigned to different people.

'Okay... so one is Tret and the other is Tare,' he said as though it was of little consequence. 'Does it really make a difference which one's influencing us when we have to guard our thoughts against all of them?'

However, a little part of Wil divided at these words, for he was quite aware that the only way he remembered the codes—remembered the vague plan with Aeolus—was because he had trusted the creature at some point. Trusted him to provide the memories Wil now struggled to convince Sadie wouldn't undermine Lily's safety. But as he tried to dismiss Aeolus' importance, he couldn't help wonder what the creature was trying to accomplish when he instructed him to *look* in that dream. Was he trying to reveal the hand of an enemy? Reveal that such an enemy had influence over Sadie—influence enough to cause her significant distress? 'What was he saying to you anyway,' Wil asked, 'in that dream? What did Aeolus, your Aeolus, say to upset you?'

'It doesn't matter.' Her dismissive tone however told him otherwise.

A moment later,

'You know what, they knew it would turn out this way,' she determined, sounding vindictive now, rather than hurt, 'they *knew* it—they planned it!' She sniffed like she was crying, and a crackling noise came over the phone like she was wiping her face. 'And not once did I think it would end up like this,' she said regretfully. 'Not once. I should have known though. I should have seen this coming.' Neglected suspicion seemed to amplify her resentment. 'I just followed their lead. Well not anymore. *Not* anymore.'

'Sadie...' he warned, fearing what she might do.

'Did you know, Wil, there's a reason your Initial is fogged?' she offered defiantly. 'To put off Aeolus—*your* Aeolus. To keep him guessing. A lot of good it does though if he uses it to his own advantage—uses it to show you what the Aeolus in *my* dreams is doing!' She hauffed at the thought, then divulged in all seriousness, 'It's being used to hide something from you.'

'Hide what?' It occurred to him that she trudged him off away from that fog every chance she had in the dreams. 'What are they hiding from me with the fog, Sadie?'

'Aeolus—my Aeolus—told me that when you were ready, you would clear the fog and find it was an air field. A landing strip or something.'

That deep droning that brought him to his knees.... *Of course... jet engines.*

'A landing strip,' he appreciated.

'But don't put too much stock into it, Wil. Aeolus told me to keep it a secret only to oblige me as his ally. He said it to give me a false sense of security, didn't he?' she derided. 'Like he owes me something for me not telling you. Well, he can't give me anything I want. And do you want to know what I really want? To have *nothing to do with him!*' she spat.

'Seriously, Sadie, be careful.' He couldn't bear the thought of her Aeolus doing anything worse than what he was doing already. 'Think of Lily....'

'Lily's *fine*, Wil,' she pronounced, sounding drunk now with anger, 'she's fine and I *don't* actually need you.... You know what, it's exactly as you said, if Aeolus wanted to help me with *Lily*, he would have!' Wil couldn't help notice the way Sadie said her sister's name. She sounded sarcastic, mocking. 'But he didn't,' she continued, 'and I keep forgetting that. So I'm not going to do his bidding anymore. If they need someone to anchor you... to build your strength or confidence or whatever, they can do it themselves, *without* me!'

Wil pinched the bridge of his nose, perplexed now as to why

Sadie contacted him in the first place, for there was obviously more to her persistence in the dreams than she had initially let on. And there was more to what was going on with Lily he now felt certain. But whatever the reason, he didn't want Sadie to cut ties with him now. No matter which creature was behind either of them.

'Sadie, what if this is exactly what they want? What if they want you to isolate yourself? Didn't you say it, that there were forces working to prevent what's happening between us as much as there were forces trying to make it succeed? ...It doesn't matter what *they* want—what do *you* want...?'

'I'm sorry, Wil, but you haven't got a clue as to how any of this works yet if you're asking me that. You think it doesn't matter who's working my mind as long as we band together? But that's what this is all about. *Sides.* Opposition. Who's working whom? The Aeolus in my dreams will do anything he can to undermine the one in yours—they're opposed! Have I not made that clear?' She waited a beat, re-loading. 'We can't be friends. We can't be anything,' she maintained, her voice cracking. 'It's happened before, and it will only happen again. So I'm doing us a favour, Wil. A *favour.*'

She was now properly crying, unable to speak, and Wil felt certain she was about to hang up. And the more desperate he felt at the thought of not seeing her again as he saw her in that glowing room of dazzling insects... sitting comfortably on the futon, putting her trust in him, her hope... the more he felt he could no longer put away those amorous feelings he managed to so easily at the window this morning.

'Please Sadie...' he pleaded '...you and I aren't enemies.... It doesn't matter which of them is influen—'

'—It *does* matter, Wil,' she interrupted sharply, her voice trembling. 'It's *always* mattered. Don't you *see?*'

All Wil could see as he clenched his jaw tightly was that creature in her dreams... that Tret Aeolus, with his vile tugging of threads, tied deep inside her mind, jerking and swaying her away like some marionette being carried off by its manipulator.

'You don't have to do this,' he said firmly, but she was already weeping and apologising for what she was about to do.

'Don't come near me, Wil,' she croaked, 'or Lily.'

Feeling his eyes stinging now, 'Don't do this,' he told her.

'The choice isn't mine.'

'It is... *please,*' his voice cracked as he held back the tears, 'please don't.'

But she had hung up.

Chapter Twenty-Four

Smoke

Wil sat for a long time at the window, disquieted, contemplating the grim and glorious views that met him from this space in recent days. And as the lowering sun moved westwards, dragging its autumnal light through the atmosphere, that awareness of shortened days galvanised a loneliness within him, for everywhere his eyes fell, the world seemed to be rotting away, withering. Perishing. Gilded, fiery death was there in the bronzed thinning treetops, the scorched crimson-patched hedgerows and gold-stubbled fields.

Swallowing hard, and wiping the tears away with the back of his hand, Wil resolutely decided that he hated Autumn. He hated both Aeoluses for being opposed somehow and he hated too how Sadie could just hang up on him like that, after what they had been through, what they were a part of. It wasn't actually his fault that there were two creatures… that Lily was having night terrors… or that the Tret and Tare chose to manipulate the three of them. All he ever wanted to do was help—help Lily, and now… now he was seen as the enemy…. He now hated his Aeolus all the more, for if Sadie's wouldn't do anything, then why wouldn't his?

It suddenly seemed a pointless exercise to have sat here earlier, convincing himself that he had successfully put his feelings away for Sadie as a sacrifice to the greater good, when the last half hour all he could do was quietly cry for her and wonder hopelessly how she could allow herself to play such a fleeting role in his life. But what was he to do? Everything seemed beyond his control now, at a point of no return.

Angrily though, Wil's mind moved from Sadie and surged like a rousing squall to the creature he now felt had taken her from him: that second Aeolus. If there was anything to be found out about this individual, he wanted to know it. So great was this desire, this impulse to lay blame to anyone but Sadie, that with eyes glazing furiously over the line of hills to the south, Wil's memory consumed him, sending him back to the fog where Sadie and the creature stood together in the distance, both obviously unaware he was watching them.

That originally vague shoulder profile Wil saw in his mind's eye revealed a much thinner Aeolus than his own this time. Incredibly thinner. How he had not seen this before in the dream, or on recalling it when he spoke to Sadie on the phone, disturbed him a little, for it seemed so obvious now. And the hair.... The colour was similar to the Aeolus he knew, but Wil now realised a striking difference in how it moved. The Aeolus he knew had tresses that curled and flicked at the lengths like tongues of fire, but this creature's prodded the air like feelers. Their pattern was uncertain, cautious. Perhaps, like moods, it wasn't a feature he could rely on heavily to distinguish one head from another in future dreams, but how he hadn't picked up on the more obvious difference in body shape earlier was still particularly annoying. And to top it all off, he even started seeing the distance between him and that second Aeolus in the dream as determinable, despite the fog.

After having assumed Aeolus to be a single individual, to then see the dream with this layered acuity, Wil recognised that it was not his own attention to detail or incredible memory power that now brought the significant dream into better focus. It had to be Aeolus. His Aeolus. Ratting out the Anti-Aeolus, just as he tried doing in the dream originally. *...Look...* At least, that's what it felt like.

Wil cocked his head to the side and wondered what else this peculiar clarity he imagined Aeolus giving him might bring to light if he thought back to a different dream. Like last night, when his Aeolus stood just over there by the dart board... or on the train to Exeter when he heard his voice... or in those early hours Tuesday when the foggy dreams started and he made eye contact with the creature for the first time, the first time that he could remember, that is. But that effortless comprehension that allowed Wil to see the Anti-Aeolus so clearly now prevented him from delving into any of these other memories, and instead swept his attention from that lanky creature in the fog to a more intriguing space inside Wil's head, where something of even greater significance seemed hidden.

The vaguely contemplative expression he wore now stirred into wary fascination, for something—some*one*—was obviously steering his thoughts. Conspicuously so. And sensing somehow that it would be to his advantage, Wil braced himself, realising that in doing so he gave permission for this thing to move more freely inside his head.

Just then, Wil felt a jolt in his middle, like that hideous drop onto the asphalt after his jet through the cosmos. The world beyond the window disappeared and he was transported to what looked like… a Midwestern plain.

Tempestuous black clouds overshadowed the barren landscape, their achromatic blooms advancing across nearly every inch of the sky. A sepia hue gave the scene that eerie, ominous feel as splayed rays of sun perforated the gloom maybe ten miles or so to the west like spotlights on a stage, and for all the drama in the sky, there was no breeze. No wind at all. Not one grass-shivering, hair-moving sigh of it.

This place, Wil felt certain, was neither dream nor real, but somewhere halfway between. An elaborate daydream perhaps, for he knew he was still sitting at the window and that his mind had simply been caught up elsewhere. But as he tried turning around, as one might easily do in a daydream, to survey the vast expanse of land behind him, he found he could not move from the shoulders down. It was as if he had been swallowed up to the neck in quicksand. Of course, the effort of moving and not being able to provoked a momentary claustrophobic panic, prompting Wil to look down at his chest to see if he was even breathing. He gave his stiffened frame a proper inspection, quashing his irrational fear.

Of course I'm breathing! But this was no daydream, he became certain, not when that indulgent control daydreams afforded had become completely absent as it was now.

Unexpectedly, as he pointlessly tried shifting his weight from one foot to another, Wil understood why he couldn't move. He was being forced to wait for something, something that might otherwise prompt him to flee. How he knew such a thing, he could not quite explain. But sensing moments ago that his thoughts were being managed by someone outside himself—and most importantly, that it would be in some way to his advantage—Wil felt obliged to accept what was happening around him in the same way he accepted that peculiar clarity with which he perceived the second Aeolus, the Anti-Aeolus, a moment ago.

Wil twisted his head round, ready to see what he feared might make him want to run. In the distance over his left shoulder, a few miles to the southwest, a curled white ribbon dangled down from the darkened sky. However, it quickly became apparent the unusual sight wasn't a ribbon, but the beginning of a tornado, snaking frailly across the barren soil and kicking up a faint bowl of debris around its base as it moved towards a chink of sunlight streaming down near where Wil stood.

He couldn't take his eyes off it.

Within seconds, the unassuming, winding form grew from tentative dust devil to menacing burgeoning twister, gaining breadth and rigidity, accumulating dust and soil, moving almost imperceptibly closer to where Wil stood immobilised. Remarkably though, the rotating column did not frighten him, for he knew none of this was real. He knew he wasn't on a Midwestern plain, and that that wasn't actually a tornado. And he knew too that there was nothing here that could possibly be of any danger to him whatsoever, for all this… *all* this… was just some sort of an illusion. A dream.

However, the funnel seemed to grow against such liberating thoughts, grow against this idea that Wil was not really there. Its roar suddenly filled the air just as a wind sprang from nowhere. It thrashed his hair into his eyes, and though Wil couldn't move from the neck down, he felt as if a veil had been lifted off of his body, exposing him to the humid temperature of the troubled atmosphere surrounding him. What had been eerily still about this place now could be heard—could be seen moving and shuddering impatiently as though eager to feed the stirring column in the distance. Such an instantaneous realness of this place felt as if it had transcended the stuff of dreams and daydreams… and for a brief moment, Wil was afraid.

Just then, as fear segued into confusion, everything suddenly became clear, and in one inexplicable, amplified, abstract mentation that often only dreams can afford, Wil understood precisely why he was there: *I'm here… because that thing needs to destroy something… and I… I must watch.*

The tornado grew in size and strength the instant Wil perceived its purpose, but instead of simply seeing it there in front of him, coming at him, it was as if that massive column of air and debris had leapt from the terrain into his head, for he couldn't tell the two places apart anymore—

his mind… or the plain. The spinning roar was *in* him now… the wind… swept *through* him. The plain regained a calm he himself did not feel, and it was then that everything seemed to become a synaesthetic jumble, for Wil began to perceive sound... as *objects*.

Voices, one by one, *appeared* there on the plain… as buildings.

A familiar garage, a flimsy shed, a dilapidated Wendy house… bungalows and cottages…. they came up out of the dust like inflatable props filling with air, hissing, then, whispering, until finally, they stood upright and talked. Only, it wasn't as if doors flapped about like lips in that animated way one might imagine a house talking, for they didn't move once they were in position and solid as the material they were apparently made of. They talked like those concealed looping systems at amusement park rides, installed to heighten anticipation while you queued. Each sounded as if they had their own recording, and together, the lot emitted a clamour like a crowded public place.

Wil suddenly heard an exclamation from a building to his right, but when he looked in that direction, what caught his eye was an old stone pigsty oddly on its own that must have appeared just seconds ago. All the other structures promptly quieted into background noise as the voice from this sturdy little building became clear, distinct over the rest, having drowned out even the exclamation Wil had initially looked for.

'People forget dreams all the time' came from somewhere inside the dark, low doorway, and Wil recognised it as his *own* defiant tone. The words repeated until he could no longer tolerate their angry discharge and was forced to look in the opposite direction where a cottage piped up with the sound of Sadie's voice. She spoke of writing in the sky, megaphones, but before Wil heard it all a second time, he tore his eyes away to another place, then another, shifting his focus from structure to structure, finding Steph, Sadie… Ben… speaking to him from one recent memory or another. It seemed that every instance—every subject these houses spoke of—had either directly or indirectly formed his understanding of the Tret and Tare. And Aeolus.

It became apparent too, as brick, wood and metal rose up from the soil, that there was a correlation between the durability and size of a building to that of the impact of the words coming out of it.

Soon, a proper neighbourhood had emerged, only it bore the unfortunate resemblance of the empty buildings on a nuclear test site: disused, made of various everyday materials… and waiting to be engulfed. The ominous observation suddenly catapulted Wil's thoughts regarding the Tret and Tare to the forefront of his mind, temporarily blocking out the audible buzz still going on around him, and in that strange, inexplicable manner in which his head and this place were one, whatever he thought about Aeolus and those like him began to feature in the landscape as well. Not as buildings, but as smoke. Foul-smelling smoke.

The fumes appeared from nowhere and permeated the air around his legs, just below the knees. They then billowed with dark and light concentrations and spread away from him like prodding fingers towards the buildings ahead, spilling into their deserted alleyways, winding their rotten way from one conversation to another like toxic vapour until its white and dark puffs homogenised into dull grey.

Wil recognised those internalised mutterings accompanying the great swathes of smoke as his own, whooshing along the unpaved streets, changing topic seamlessly between those conversations that he had had… those garrulous buildings that stood unmoving. Eventually, the grey slipped from behind the most westerly ones and converged in a steady stream towards the heated updraft maintaining the vortex. It was then, as Wil saw his vaporous thoughts—saw the tangible constructions surrounding them—and beheld that monstrous column of cloud and debris, that he finally understood the fullness of what was happening:
These remote houses… this rancid smoke… they harboured his assumptions regarding the Tret and Tare.

All this had been flushed out of his head to welcome that great invading twister, that great undoer of everything he used to justify his fear of the Aeoluses.

Understanding this, his eyes moved from the tornado to the neighbourhood, and then to a greenhouse directly in its path there on the outskirts. The fragile building was heard clearly saying amid the smoke streamlining around it, 'No, *you* want me to be here! You're doing something to keep me from leaving.' As the dream popped to mind, where Aeolus insisted he had been a friend… had claimed to want the same things as Wil… the glass frame lifted and was completely obliterated in one merciless instant. Not even its pieces could be seen circling the insatiable funnel. However, in the structure's sudden absence, Wil felt certain of one thing he had not been certain of before: when he was in the milk aisle on Friday, and he perceived that strange unseen thing grabbing his heels on his way to the service desk… that was Aeolus. *His* Aeolus.

Convinced of this, he suddenly wondered why the creature tried stopping him, why it was so important that he not go to the front of the shop, but as he speculated, the dense column inched ever eastwards, heading with mesmerising force for the rest of the ghost town, where one conversation after another went up with a pop and a crack into the grey.

Magnificently, every assumption Wil ever made about Aeolus and the others began to disappear as that funnel churned fiercely, powerfully, battering conclusions, premises, displacing their foundations, bending their supportive framework with such torsion that there was hardly anything left.

The destruction was happening so fast now that Wil's head felt aloft, having produced a hyperventilating lightness he thought both pleasant and impairing. Its most marked effect was how everything he had been uncertain of regarding the Tret and Tare felt as if it had been freed of him. And as he perceived the chaos flying above, taken from him, unpinned from his own incomprehensive mind, there was a great sense of relief and comfort in mentally detaching from it all, even as he saw odd familiar bits whizzing round. Whatever vague association they conjured, it was negligible now.

With mindless satisfaction Wil watched the steady tornado pass in front of him. It swallowed everything in its path, clearing the vicinity with its shocking diameter in a matter of seconds until, unexpectedly, it stopped travelling northeast and just stayed in one place.

The gratitude reflected in Wil's expression disappeared, for debris began emerging from deep within the whirlwind and started flying in a peculiar manner along the funnel's outermost layer. The great stones of the pigsty swept along up there as easily as roof tiles and timbers, and they moved with what seemed intent. Alarmed now, Wil saw stone and brick, wood and metal, reshuffling in unison before him, lifting high and low, reconfiguring. And as it did so, a remarkable, massive shift began to take place somewhere inside his turbulent brain. Synaptic signals bombarded him. Familiar pathways redirected. Impulses honed. The old way of thinking had been taken up and was being replaced with the new. All those ideas about the Tret and Tare were no longer negligible, whooshing separately from him—beyond him—but instead, they were being transformed and reinstated *within* him.

Extraordinarily, it was all done as quickly as it had been undone, leaving no sign there on the plain of the resurrected buildings or the devastating cloud, for all that Wil could see of the destruction was a subdued greyness in the east. Then, as he spun around, having no hindrance over his body whatsoever, it occurred to him that where this place seemed to be as one with his mind, the two now were separating. And the place where all those buildings originally sprang from—where he had not realised they existed to begin with—that's where they stood. Remodelled. Somewhere inside him.

Wil's vacant eyes widened over the barren prairie, unafraid now of the creature Aeolus, because somewhere inside his brain, where the chemicals of thought begin as jolted molecules, that hefty, compelling idea of the Tret and Tare setting out to dupe all of humanity no longer seemed likely. In fact, with the dramatic demolition that had just taken place, Wil saw how the premises he used over the last week to make sense of his world—of Aeolus and his kind—had all been erroneous. Ignorant. A desperate, stubborn attempt really to justify his fears.

This epiphany pulsed from axon to axon, dramatically redefining Wil's plight in a matter of nanoseconds, working deeper into his mind like nutrients down the roots of a tree while he sat there in the window seat, stuporous. Physically, he felt a light heaviness he had never felt before, like lead-filled threads were being gently pulled from his extremities. His fingers and toes tingled with the sensation. His mind felt pleasantly relieved by it.

Then, as if awakening, he blinked rapidly towards the stippled silhouette of evergreens outlining the Blackdowns and felt a marvellous, elevated sense of understanding. And like an object from its shadow, he was able to determine this new way of thinking from the old, for the new had not done away with the old completely, but rather, stood in stark contrast to it.

The dramatic transformation of his mind pushed that veiled idea of death, of autumn closing in, of things coming to an end deeper into Wil's psyche as his gaze fell from a green wooded ridge in the distance to the flaxen-patched foothills below, just outside his window. And as the rusty colours of a ripened hedgerow miles away inverted onto his retina, he had the strange but reassuring feeling that Aeolus was simply protecting him from that blind humanness that refused to observe and intelligently understand. That humanness determined to discredit and condemn anything it felt threatened by. And he was glad for it.

Feeling somehow indebted to the creature now, Wil was suddenly ashamed of how he had treated Aeolus. Something dark flooded him and he felt immersed in deep regret. Deep regret for hating Aeolus earlier, despising him for being so opposed to Sadie's creature. Deep regret too at all the horrible things he remembered with incapacitating efficiency that he had said to such a patient, gleaming face in the dreams:

You're not my friend…. You're not real…. You just showed me a load of nonsense….

As that amazement Wil held over the creature's measures to secure his memory shrivelled under the engulfing shame, Wil felt the ingratitude, the anger. How obstinate he had been. And it deepened, because the whole while, Aeolus had just stood there, taking it all. Proving himself. Showing Wil he had been present with him even before birth in the pixellated wall… taking him to the far reaches of the universe… demonstrating how one could be in two places at once. Though Wil still didn't even know what Aeolus meant by that just now, instead of marvelling at the time, ignorance and fear spurred him to say something so cruel, so shameful…

People forget dreams all the time.

The shame felt as though a clean cut now. Right beneath a rib. Wil had no idea how poignant such words had been considering that sacrifice he believed he made in the past for the creature in giving up his memory—considering Aeolus' diligent attempts at restoring it through Annie… through the sketches she chronicled in her bedroom. Not only did Aeolus go through such lengths to reveal a remarkable past that did exist, he did it kindly, proving to Annie that her work, her patience, had not been in vain. As Wil recalled that look on her face, the pained joy, he couldn't help wonder why Aeolus would have anything to do with him when he had been so cruel. Why would the creature even try to get him remembering when he squandered what had been handed to him left and right the last week?

Overwhelmed, Wil closed his eyes and felt something recede inside him just then. Like the changing of tides. Shame pulled away and he began to see that despite such horrid pronouncements, maybe even because of them, the creature carried on patiently, purposefully, so that this moment might not be undermined. This moment where Wil believed anything he remembered from before was because Aeolus *needed* him to, and not to undo Wil, but to show him the path back to himself. Back to the person who relied on such an unlikely confidant as the creature.

How Wil knew such a thing, he wasn't certain, but he could *feel* it, just as he felt his way back to remembering the codes, for feelings, Wil was beginning to see, weren't always his adversary.

Resurfacing from these thoughtful depths, Wil drew in a disengaging, bolstering breath, sitting up straighter as he did so. He shifted his shoulder up the wall of the alcove and noticed with amusement the little pile of pigeon poo, now dried and brittle, on the ledge outside the window. Then turning indifferently from it to his bedroom, he was immediately unsettled, for everything looked different, as if every item had been set askew by a few degrees, moved a few centimetres.

As Wil glanced at the furniture and objects lying around, absolutely certain nothing had been changed, it all continued to demand his attention, as if requiring a nudge here, sliding there, to put it back into place. But as his eyes fell to the dartboard, he saw Aeolus' form there from last night overlapping the present perfectly, and with no effort at all, he understood what the bronze, opalescent figure meant before closing the door there in the dream. It wasn't just Steph he needed to trust, or Annie even, he now realised. No. The one he needed to rely on, who remembered his past, who could tell him how it was and why it's worth remembering... was Aeolus. His Aeolus.

Wil scanned the seemingly disturbed space again and realised the change hadn't actually been with the room, rather, himself.

Quickly, he texted Annie about the two Aeoluses, Sadie wanting to have nothing to do with him and that the fog was hiding an airstrip. She asked a few odd questions about the fog and less than a minute later, she was ringing.

Chapter Twenty-Five

Hits

Wil thought he heard someone call his name from downstairs but pressed *ANSWER* anyway.

'Why didn't you mention anything about fog in your Initial earlier Wil?' Annie demanded down the phone.

Surprised and confused, 'I... I don't know...' he spluttered. 'I guess it didn't seem important.'

And there it was again. His name. It sounded like Mum calling. Shouting actually, from the pantry.

'Just a second, Annie,' he interrupted, poking his head out into the hall, wondering if everything was okay down there. But all he heard was Mum clinking dishes, unloading the dishwasher. 'Sorry.'

'Listen, Wil,' Annie said sharply, obviously irritated now, 'you can't just expect me to figure things out for you. Everything in the dreams is significant. There may come a time when I can't answer your questions or spot the things you've overlooked—because whatever gaps in your understanding you hope I can help with, *I've* got the same. Aeolus hasn't told me *anything*... he hasn't *been* in my dreams.... I have *no idea* what's going on. Remember?' Her voice wavered. 'You never told me what was going on....'

Recoiling slightly, Wil realised her reprimand wasn't just about what he failed to mention at her house this afternoon, but what he didn't tell her three years ago. Of course, in her mind, that point in time was where many things had been left unfinished. It was understandable then that the resentment she inevitably harboured over his voluntary amnesia all this time—resentment there was no benefit in airing until now—had finally found its place.

Annie suddenly let out a deep, long breath, like that of someone at an utter loss, and Wil was almost certain she should have detonated by now, sending him reeling in the opposite direction. However, he got the distinct impression this wounded girl was trying hard not to default into the character she had been in recent years and was perhaps trying desperately to go back to the person she had been before. Before they were all separated from the dreams. Just as he was.

'Annie, I'm really sorry I didn't mention the fog. And I'm sorry I didn't tell you why we decided to forget without you. I can't defend it because I don't even know why we did it.' Not completely at least. All he knew was that it meant they'd all be remembering again. Why it had to happen in the first place, why Aeolus needed to be spared to begin with, was still a blank.

All of a sudden, Mum's muffled voice startled Wil from the other side of the door. Forgetting completely at that moment his conversation with Annie, or that the phone was still in his hand, he opened it to find her standing there with a neat pile of laundry in her arms and a surprised look on her face.

'You all right?' he asked, concerned, remembering the odd shouting he thought he heard.

'I'm fine, Love,' she said casually. 'I thought I heard a voice, but I didn't hear you get back.' She then stared at him, absent-minded, as if recalling another reason as to why she sought him out, but it seemed to escape her because she shook her head and said dismissively, 'I guess I could have checked to see if your car was on the drive....'

'Well, I'm here,' he assured, shrugging and giving himself a once-over glance. It was at this point that he saw her eyes sharpen to the illuminated display on the phone at his side, where the name Annie glowed brightly in huge letters.

Annie!

'Sorry, Mum,' he hastened, remembering, 'I was on a call. Are those mine?'

'Oh, yes.' She promptly slid a hand up her arm and passed him the pile.

Thanking her, he buried the phone under the clothes as they balanced on his forearm. The last thing Mum needed to know was that he and Annie were on talking terms—bedroom chat terms, even. Something short of a miracle would have had to orchestrate such a truce as that in her eyes, and a miracle, at this point, seemed easier to explain.

'Well,' she pulled a broad tactful smile, relinquishing any other reason to stay, 'I'll be downstairs.'

'Sorry for that...' he breathed down the line after closing the door. 'I'm pretty sure she saw it was you on the phone,' he mentioned as an aside, trying to think back to where they left off, for the interruption had derailed his thoughts completely.

'Listen, Wil—you have got to get rid of that fog,' Annie blurted.

'Well I would if I knew *how*' he insisted, dropping the clothes onto the bed.

'You really have no idea, do you?' she remarked. 'Wil, real fog is used by the Tret and Tare as an isolation technique. The side that creates it is the only side that can access the isolated individual. We used it to protect vulnerable dreamers, like a safe house.'

'A safe house. That doesn't sound so bad,' he said innocently, flinching a shrug.

'So three years in Tret fog—*Enemy* fog—wasn't so bad, was it?' she asked snidely, prompting him to re-think the cloud he saw himself taken off to in her sketch, the cloud that was actually a wisp of that fog which featured in every section of her massive collage. 'No, I didn't think so,' she sniffed. 'Safe house... *prison*.... Either way, a true fog keeps the isolated dreamer from navigating their dreams or from remembering them. Yet you remember yours, Wil. For the last week you've remembered. So this fog you're in... it *can't* be real.'

'Okay...' he accepted, wondering why she wasn't enthused about this. 'So why is it so important that I get rid of it then?'

'Because it's your *Initial,* Wil,' she declared. 'Initials project what the mind perceives as safe. And at the moment, yours is mirroring precisely the protective fog you've been in the last three years. *Under* an Enemy.' She hauffed. 'And what do you think Aeolus is making of it?' she posed. '*Your* Aeolus. I imagine he's not impressed seeing you reproduce the very thing that kept you two apart all this time, and watching you have no problem with it,' she determined pointedly.

Roaring Aeolus popped to mind. If the creature had been

infuriated by a fake fog this last week, he certainly didn't show it. Not like in Annie's sketch.

Just then, Wil's phone alerted. 'My battery's low,' he told Annie. 'Just a sec.'

Plugging his mobile into the charger, he remembered just then that Aeolus mentioned the fog. In the dream with the search party. In fact, Wil recalled precisely that Aeolus told him he should just get rid of it, like it was no big deal, that he was only stuck in it... *because he wanted to be.* The words provoked Wil's frustration even now.

'Annie, if I'm not in isolation anymore, in Enemy-Tret fog or whatever, then why doesn't Aeolus just clear what's in my Initial?' He couldn't help think of all the incredible things the creature did with the offending mist, controlling it to show him his past. 'I mean, if he knows *I* want it gone... and *he* wants it gone... and he can control my mind anyway, then why not just get rid of it himself?'

'Aeolus can't just hijack your Initial like that, Wil. The dreams don't work that way. You play a role whether the Tret or Tare want you to. If an Initial doesn't feel safe, you won't be able to return to it. But if there are elements from it you believe are still safe, well you'll only reproduce them in the next Initial your mind fabricates. So Aeolus won't have gotten rid of the fog. If anything, he'll have ensured it returns. *You* have to be the one to do it.'

'Yes, but *how*?'

'You've got to think outside the fog, Wil. Anywhere else but there.'

As Wil thought of Aeolus, envying how he managed to use the vapour to show him all those places, he asked Annie what the motive could have been behind such a dramatic display. 'Going to the stars and all that, I still don't know what that was about.'

'It's exactly what *I'm* trying to tell you,' Annie said obviously. 'He was trying to inspire you to think outside of what you've known the last three years in there. Not only did he use the very personal, but he used our entire spectrum of existence,' she said, sounding impressed. 'Too bad it's not worked though. Wil, that's why—'

'—Just a sec, Annie,' he interrupted, hearing Mum yell frantically up the stairs. 'I think something's wrong.'

'Mum...?' he quickly unplugged his phone and went out into the hall. 'Mum, you okay?'

'Yes, fine, Love,' she hollered from the bottom of the stairs, clearly straining her voice to be heard. 'Are you here tonight, or meeting the others later?'

Perplexed, though relieved, he stopped short of the landing, unwilling to go any further if there was no actual crisis. 'I'm staying home,' he called back, dropping his shoulders. 'Why...?'

'We're doing take-out!' she exclaimed with a manic shriek that was wholly unlike her. 'Is Chinese okay? And if so,' she cleared her throat and enunciated loudly, 'what-do-you-want-us-to-order?'

'Chinese is great,' he shouted back, rolling incredulous eyes. 'Just order whatever... and I'll be down in a bit.' Surely takeout wasn't *that* pressing, he thought, returning to his room.

'Shall we get the same as before?' she went on, stopping him from closing the door, 'You know... the lemon chicken and duck...?'

'Yes I know,' he said impatiently, wondering why she didn't just text him like she usually did in the house when they weren't on the same floor. 'Yes that's great, Mum. I don't mind whatever. I'll come down after I'm done on the phone....'

'Oh, sorry Love,' she said sheepishly, obviously moving away from the bottom of the stairs. 'I didn't know you and Annie were still talking....'

Again, he rolled his eyes. *That* would have to be dealt with at some point.

'Sorry,' he said agitatedly into the phone. 'That was weird....'

'I heard. And she'll do it again, Wil,' Annie assured. 'Only next time, it *will* be urgent.'

'What do you mean?' It was a stupid question, because he knew exactly what she meant. '*How* urgent?'

'Urgent enough to get you off the phone with me. But if you go outside where you won't hear her calling, I can assure you, whatever is being cooked up this very minute will not happen.'

'You mean, like... just leave?'

'I mean, like *get out now*, Wil.'

Unsure as to whether getting out of the house might actually prevent Mum from chopping off a finger or falling and banging her head, Wil decided he didn't want to take the chance and followed Annie's instruction. He tiptoed to the top of the stairs, bent down and watched the lower half of Mum's body as she went about the kitchen. The second she was out of sight and he heard the sound of cupboard doors opening in the pantry, he made a light-footed dash down the steps, out to the terrace and around the back of the house to the common garden.

'Done!' he breathed into the phone, passing the stagnated fountain where all the garden paths converged. He strode along the gravel towards the gumdrop-shaped shrub down by the far corner near the folly, checking over a shoulder every few yards, then sliding into its shade, concealed from onlookers, he sat and caught his breath. 'That was weird...' he exhaled, checking the path once more. 'I've never heard Mum be like that. Her voice was actually like cracking with craziness.' No one was coming. 'You'd of thought she'd just won the lottery or something.' But of course, knowing that wasn't the case, he blurted disdainfully, 'She sounded manic.' The thought of which disturbed him deeply, for not once did he ever see his mother lose her self-possession in such a way. And what was beginning to disturb him further was how he could just run away and leave her, while whatever had its hold on her back at the house.

'Where are you now, Wil?'

'The garden. Near the folly. Behind one of those shrubs.' He had just about regained his breath.

'Good. If she comes into the garden, take the gate nearby.' He glanced at the carved door half-hidden by the overgrowth of wisteria, pained further at the thought of having to run away from his mother yet again. 'Have the phone to your ear so she can see it and don't look back if she calls out to you,' Annie instructed, displaying an expedience Wil found disconcerting.

'She's not coming,' he assured, glancing back at the house. The thought of his mother innocently rummaging around in the pantry, unaware of what had momentarily possessed her mind, or worse, unaware of what stroked and nudged it routinely, disheartened Wil, for he could see her doomed to these uninhibited episodes of the creatures' insatiable rousings and suppressings the second he strayed from their mysterious purposes. No doubt it wouldn't just be his mother, but anyone. Family and friends... strangers. A ravenous despair seemed to devour whatever innocence Wil perceived about the relationships around him, for any of them, at any moment, could be used to control him. It was Mum this time, but who would be next? Who would be used to control him in say... an hour? And what measures would be required if he put up a bit of a fight?

'I feel horrible running from her like that,' he said despondently, eyes wide and vacant. 'I mean, just running away like that, like she was bad or something….'

'Don't worry about your Mum,' Annie insisted too lightly. 'She's not on the dark side or anything. She just did what sprang to mind.'

'The dark side?' He couldn't help take offense at such an insensitive correlation to Star Wars, for that was fiction. His mother unwittingly harassed to act outside of herself by the Tret and Tare was fact. 'And sprang to mind?' He could barely say the words, recoiling as he did so, for Annie made it sound as if Mum had had a momentary impulsive lapse of her own accord, which they both knew couldn't be further from the truth.

'She was under a lot of pressure, Wil,' Annie reminded innocently.

A constricting gloom filled him just then.

'Pressure?' he retorted, finding her choice of words, again, a far cry from the truth. If anyone saw the bigger picture—the greater implications of being so embroiled with these creatures—it was her, Annie. How then could she be so aloof? *'Pressure?'* he found himself saying rather belligerently as a tingling sensation prickled across his face: preparedness for confrontation. 'Is that what we're calling being influenced by one of them then? Just say it Annie—say what's actually going on with my mother. Say something's inside her head,' he demanded, pressing the corner of the mobile into his own temple, depraved-like, unaware that he was doing so, 'say it's taking her mind over to do who-knows-what. Don't sugar-coat it,' he insisted angrily, 'just say it!'

But instead of saying anything, Annie just waited, silent, compounding in Wil's view this message of cold-heartedness towards the one person who ever looked after her properly—the one person who actually treated her like a beloved daughter.

'Say it, Annie!' he shouted, his chest now heaving with outrage.

But Annie remained unprovoked. To the point that Wil equated her prevaricating silence as justification for his outburst, justification for his anger. And allowing that dark to drown him, he became convinced she had been manipulating him somehow.

Anger-driven adrenaline chilled Wil's hands as he leered out into the untidy corner of the garden, withering one into a fist while the other tightened around the phone until his knuckles turned white. But just before he managed another outburst, Annie finally spoke.

'We all take hits off the Enemy when we're awake, Wil,' she said calmly, resolutely. 'So before you get too upset there, remember that not only is your mother taking a hit right now but so are you. So am I,' she maintained, then paused for a second. An amused sniff then came down the phone that caused Wil's adamance to falter. 'Do you think it's easy for me to sit here and talk to you like this after the last few years? That I'm in one single mind about everything you tell me... and that you're the only one agonising over whose side your thoughts and actions benefit? If you had any idea what was going on in *my* head right now...' a tone of disgust tainted her words, 'you'd at least *try* a little harder, Wilden.'

The remark cut through every ounce of that determined irritation... that anger he clung to, making him wonder what, in fact, was going through Annie's head just now. *Who* was going through her head.

'So now, you've got two options,' she said matter-of-factly. 'You can take the path of least resistance and close your mind further to anything I say—just pretend like what they're doing to you right now isn't happening at all, because something tells me you're not in your right mind at the moment—or... you can acknowledge the fact that they're using your fear... your anger... your shame against you, and instead, turn it around on them. *Listen to me...* and frustrate their efforts, Wilden,' she said firmly, as though instructing him. 'Keep them from sabotaging this conversation,' she continued, compelling him to see that's exactly what was happening, 'because that's what they want. To make you so angry you'll have no choice but to reject me, reject everything I say... and what we're doing here now.'

She was right, he realised, blinking and darting his eyes around the lawn with a renewed awareness of himself. His anger felt so justified. So unyielding. Like he *wanted* to hate her. Yet he didn't know why.

'They're trying to knock you off course, Wilden. And you're letting them. Right now. Right this very minute.'

No, I'm not, he decided, narrowing and fixing his gaze to the garden wall in front of him. Already, he could see that semantics in conversation scarcely riled him so. *The dark side... pressure...* to take such offence was out of character. And while his anger seemed justified, tangled up with concern for his mother, was it really? Was it as simple and honourable as that? Wil loosened his grip around the phone and felt the actual warmth of blood flowing back into his fingertips. The ache in his temple subsided too. With his fist loosened, he patted the grass there beside him and became suddenly aware that he had always been fiercely protective of his mother, so much so that such a devotion, he now saw, would inevitably be used against him. And when a most pressing conversation needed to be had such as this, how then could he possibly blame Annie for the inevitable, much less her tactful description of it?

Wil pulled up a knee and rested his elbow atop it, bracing his forehead with his hand. The relief of his anger abating now, just lifting out of him with a strange heavy lightness, felt as though a leaden thread pulled from every sinew. It was the same physical sensation he had at the window earlier, and he accepted quite readily, *they were all taking hits.*

'I'm sorry,' he said as he closed his eyes for a second and amended his thoughts. 'I'm not angry at you,' he exhaled dismally, shaking his head, for sneaking past his mother's shadowy figure poking around in the pantry still irked him. 'Just Mum obviously has no idea… and I can't bear the thought of her being like a pawn….'

'You can bear it,' Annie said confidently. 'We have each other, and we have the likes of Aeolus. The way I see it, his lot keeps the Enemy from being successful with the big stuff, while *we* make sure the little things don't add up. But in order to do that—in order to keep on top of the little things—we've got to trust each other now, Wil. We've got to trust and rely on the other's judgement, especially when we're not in our right minds.'

'You know I trust you, Annie,' he said pointedly, certain that he trusted her more than she could possibly trust him. He did after all give her reason to be cautious. 'I wouldn't be sitting here if that weren't the case. But whether I'm in my right mind, how do I know it's *you* I'm trusting and not *someone else* when every single mind around us is being fiddled with?'

'You don't need to worry about who's working in my head,' Annie heeded. 'That's for me to worry about. What you have to trust is the fact that I know you, and that I know you *well*. So when your baseline behaviour suddenly changes, and I draw your attention to it, I can point out the obvious, but it's you who has to figure out whose side you're acting on behalf of. Not me. You have to be clear in your own head whether your actions are born out of your identity as Wilden, or someone else.'

'And by someone else,' he clarified, 'do you mean Aeolus, or' he couldn't help but sound sarcastic 'his evil counterpart?'

'Aeolus won't sabotage you, Wil,' Annie corrected firmly. 'What I mean is, you have to figure out whether it's him, prompting you to act on your own behalf, or whether it's someone else neither of you want controlling your thoughts and actions.

'Now sometimes it's not so clear, but thankfully, Friends have an affinity with us—each one of us. Probably in the same way Enemies have the same connection to those averse to us, but it's that connection, that natural inclination that makes it easier to figure out who's behind our thoughts. And for someone like me, watching from the outside, even I can see evidence of it. A perfect example is how you stopped yourself from being angry with me a minute ago when you could have easily put the phone down. So while you may not have been assured of who was behind your thoughts just then, I certainly was, because I know you aren't the type of person who is so easily angered.'

Wil couldn't help recoil with a frown at those words. Of course he was easily angered. Surely she had forgotten that his incidental desire to explode at her two minutes ago had actually been a habitual occurrence over the last few years. However, he forgot only momentarily that it was all probably one of her tests. Not just the strained banter, but the big blow-ups too. To see if he'd for once not get angry, see who was working his thoughts.

'And when the two of you overcome one of these little battles of the mind,' she went on, 'that affinity you preserve in doing so, that connection... it's rewarded with an incredible feeling of relief. And I don't just mean wipe-of-the-forehead-phew relief,' she assured.

No, the feeling he had had the second his unfounded anger towards her finally left him a few moments ago *was* different. Like something deeply imbedded had escaped far outwards. Leaden threads, pulling right out of him.

'Consider it a reward for making the right choice,' Annie said, 'because you'll never get that with an Enemy. Trust me on that one. And don't get the idea that you can wait for the feeling to come, and then when it doesn't, you can change your mind,' she warned, 'because sometimes, it's too late to go back and make the right decision.' Her pause emphasised the point. 'Like I said, think of it like a reward. For making the right decision in the first place.'

Just then, his phone alerted.

Staring at the message on the screen, Wil moaned. 'Annie, I've only got 20% on my phone. And it's a rubbish battery.'

'What a coincidence,' she said wryly. 'Listen Wil, you obviously don't remember the dreams properly right now, and this Sadie friend of yours is clearly taking advantage of that. And it's clear to me that a Tret is targeting you quite specifically, using someone who has a connection with your real world *and* your dreams, and that alone makes this Sadie and whatever she says to drop your guard dangerous. I mean, have you any idea how much damage she can cause in your life? She's flesh and blood and already *in* your head.' Annie sighed then added delicately, 'And I know there's a romantic interest there you've conveniently not mentioned, but that makes her an unfathomable weapon for anyone who's got it in for you, Wil. Do you hear what I'm saying?'

'I do,' he admitted, having never realised, having never really appreciated the potential of Sadie's role as a possible adversary.

'Now, I want you to tell me everything she's told you, and I want to know everything the two of you have done together. And don't forget, we've only got 20%.'

'All right,' he said, raking his fingernails over the grass.

Chapter Twenty-Six

Dream-Drag

'How much have you got now, Wil?'

'14%.'

'Right. You need to know a few things here before we even think about what Sadie *hasn't* mentioned to you,' Annie declared, sounding displeased with everything he just told her.

Wil stopped patting the pile of grass accumulated there beside him. 'Okay....'

'First, there are *three states* in the dreams: the fog, the Initial, and the open dreamscape. You listening?'

'Yes of course.' He patted his pile of grass three times, reiterating as he did so, 'The fog, the Initial and the open dreamscape.'

'Good. Now like I said before, the fog is like a safe house, reserved for those of us who remember our dreams, but temporarily shouldn't for reasons we can't get into now. But don't confuse a fogged dreamer with the rest of the world who can't remember their dreams, because they're *not* the same,' she warned. 'Fogged dreamers switch loyalties on a whim, moving from Tret to Tare thousands of times in the day. They never cultivate an affinity with either long enough to enable them to remember their dreams in the first place, *so there's no need to make them forget,*' she said as though it were obvious. 'So keep it clear in your head Wil: *the fog is for us.* Those who remember. It merely enforces a period of forgetting as protection. Awake or asleep, you won't remember the dreams.'

It suddenly occurred to him,

'So that's how we know mine is fake.'

Annie gave a *humph* down the phone. 'We're only just getting started my dear! Now's a good time to mention that the one you have an affinity with is the same one who puts you in the fog. The only exception I know is when you were taken in the real Tret fog. Aeolus had just cut every Tare connection in you—your affinity with him was severed—but the Tret took you straight there, without even making the effort to turn you.' Wil saw himself beyond the mob, looking impassively over his shoulder as charcoal arms pulled at him. He had gone off with someone there in the background. Presumably a Tret. 'In fact, you didn't even have the chance to wake and prove to everyone it had happened, that you weren't Tare anymore,' Annie added. 'When affinities are severed, waking is like the reboot on a software update.'

'Maybe they thought they could sort the affinity out when they had me,' he determined, feeling like they weren't actually talking about him anymore, for the speculation of such events, with no memory of them at all, began to feel surreal now.

'There were enough Tare around at the time, my only guess is that they didn't want you thinking another Tare-thought even for a second and just thought *stuff it, get him in there* and worked out the details later.'

With his mind roving the sequence on her wall again, his voice was barely a whisper, 'Yes. Maybe.'

'Right. That's fog, Wil,' Annie said abruptly. 'Now the Initial,' she hastened. 'It's the first place you dream, and relatively safe. The minute it doesn't feel safe though, it starts to break down and becomes something different the next time you dream. Most people don't remember their dreams, but if they remember anything, it's the Initial. Usually the breaking down of it. Once you leave it when you're dreaming, you can't go back unless you wake up and fall asleep again.'

'Wait a minute. So if it breaks down, I have no safe place until I wake up—is that what you're saying?'

'*You* don't. But you can join up with other dreamers—those who have Tare affinity like you—and use *their* Initial until it breaks down. Of course this works both ways. Anyone with Tare affinity can do the same with you. Think of Initials like hiding places, hiding places that constantly change to protect Tare dreamers from Tret dreamers.'

He nodded faintly there in the shadow, absorbing this.

'Now the Initial protects you from Tret *dreamers*, but not the Tret themselves,' she however stressed. 'Both Tret and Tare can come into anyone's Initial, no matter *who* you are or *where* you are. The fog is their only limitation.'

Wil quickly imagined a scenario. 'So is that what makes it break down then, those like Aeolus from the other side coming in and, I don't know, causing chaos?'

'Exactly. It gives you an edge over dreamers from the other side, but that's about it,' she said plainly.

Wil's mind snagged on this last statement and at that moment received a text:

Where are you?????

'What was that?' Annie asked sharply.

'Mum. She's asking where I am, with a lot of question marks.'

'Don't answer it. And don't let it show *Read*. Now have you understood what I said about Initials, Wil?'

'Yes, I think so,' he assured, trying to ignore his phone and focus instead on the fact that Sadie had been there in the fog with him—*in his Initial*—despite insisting they were on opposing sides. 'I think I understand.'

'The third state of the dreams is the dreamscape. Basically,' she sounded thoroughly disgusted, 'it's a free-for-all. No place is safe there. Every dreamer in the world sleeping at that moment contributes to the dreamscape you experience, even those in their protective Initials. I like to think of it like the web, without firewalls to filter out the scary stuff. Now if your Initial breaks down, you can either shadow off to someone else's, or join the dreamscape. Either way, the best thing to do is *just keep moving*,' she stressed. 'Take shadows til you wake, basically.'

'And how do I do that?' he asked. 'How do I *take* a shadow?'

'By putting one hand over the other, focusing on the blackness and imagining yourself somewhere else, Wil. It's usually where you'll end up. There are limitations however, but generally, that's how it works. It's the way all dreamers travel and whenever Sadie left you in the dreams, that'll be how she did it. You mentioned how she left Ben's, well that's what she was doing.'

Bewildered as to why Sadie never mentioned this, Wil apprehensively put a hand on top of his head and stared vacantly through a little swarm of midges hovering in the sunlight halfway between him and the garden wall. He had asked her directly about it he now recalled, at the park, but she somehow managed to avoid the question.

249

'Maybe she just didn't realise how ignorant I am about some of this stuff....' he rationalised aloud, prompting Annie to hauff down the phone.

'No, Wil,' she insisted, sounding belligerent. 'Sadie *knows* you had no idea. I'm sorry, but taking shadows has been done for as long as people have been *dreaming*. From slipping into shafts of blackness, to realising over the ages all it took was a finger poked into a darkened crevice. She knows *all this*. She'll know too that people use their hands to create shadows. It all started during the Enlightenment, when they realised the fog's ability to diffuse light could prevent shadows from appearing in the first place. But fogged dreamers still tried leaving, using the only thing they did have in there to create a shadow. *Their hands!* These are historical facts everyone knows, Wil—everyone who remembers for more than just a week. So I'm sure if you think long and hard, you'll find a few other examples of Sadie moving her hands in some curious manner before disappearing, because she was trying to *hide it* from you.'

Admittedly, a memory came to, Wil, causing his hand to drop from his head. Sadie was running off towards the pond... she then put her hands together and was gone.

'I have no idea why she's not told me any of this,' he said, perplexed under the little swarm of midges, for they had moved directly over his head now.

'To keep you from *going* anywhere else,' Annie declared. 'And I'm sure she hasn't told you your fog could be harbouring Imposters *and* that you'd have incredible difficulty spotting them because of it. I mean, if she can accuse *you* of being an imposter Wil, I think you ought to be checking *she* isn't one,' Annie warned. 'She's obviously expecting them to be there.'

'I asked her about the whole Imposter thing,' he admitted, shrinking from the insect cloud now darting at his forehead like some weird single-minded entity, 'but no, she wouldn't tell me.'

'They're Tret and Tare,' Annie explained, 'the same entity as Aeolus and the others, only they don't represent opposing sides that Tret and Tare do. In fact, their interaction with you isn't about loyalty at all. It's about gaining your trust only so they can exploit it. Their whole purpose is to cause confusion and fear and ultimately break down Initials to force dreamers through the dreamscape.'

'And what do they gain in that?' he asked, grimacing, for he found the cloud of bugs now growing denser around him.

'I don't know, Wil. Everyone's afraid in the dreamscape. Maybe they feed off fear more easily there. What I *do* know though is they target all three dream states, can get into your Initial like any other Tret and Tare, but that they can't actually get *inside* fog—*real* fog.'

Here, Annie paused for a moment, and Wil had the urge to check over his shoulder back towards the house. No one was coming.

'Imposters fill that ambiguous gap between Tret and Tare,' she went on, 'being a strange mix of Aeolus and the others, and *something else*. They have the same need to gain our trust, yet they don't want our loyalty and instead want our fear. They're a horrible lot. You want to avoid them at all costs.'

The creature Gollum from Lord of the Rings came to mind, making Wil think of that perversely mesmerising coaxing, the childishness set precariously atop the psychotic.

'Annie, what exactly do these Imposters look like,' he asked warily.

'Exactly what they sound like, Wil. They're imposters! So they never manifest as the individuals they are,' she said obviously. 'Instead, they are always someone else, and that someone else is always human.'

'So they wouldn't try and be someone like Aeolus?'

'No. And you can tell them from their eyes,' she advised. 'With normal Tret and Tare, their eyes make you feel like you're moving *towards* something. Spinning nearer. Sucking you in.'

Wil understood this very effect, having felt that endless space in the first dream with Aeolus... the spiralling effect he tried creating in his sketchpad.

'But with Imposters, you're spinning away. Never getting near enough. You'll have to experience it to know what I mean, Wil. Obviously, we looked into a lot of eyes in the past and could spot the difference easily, because both sides use Imposters.'

'Which is why we used the codes,' he suddenly appreciated, 'in case we couldn't see the eyes.'

'Every time, Wil. And really, we should still use them with whoever we plan to meet in the dreams. Establish a keyword or phrase before going in without exception, and right as we leave, where possible. It confirms identities at any point. Awake or aslee—'

'Sorry to be so focused on these Imposters,' he interrupted, slightly fearful at the thought still, 'but how often do you think I'll come into contact with them then?'

'I couldn't say, Wil,' she said honestly. 'I mean, whenever *we*

251

came across them before, it was when we were settling fogged dreamers. Always the fog...' she insisted in annoyance, 'like sharks to blood. Because Imposters can't get into fog like normal Tret or Tare, they would try and pose as friends and relatives outside in some sort of peril. Essentially, they tried undermining the effect of the fog by panicking the isolated dreamer. It was awful, hearing them pretend to be injured children—children the isolated dreamer would recognise—basically the dreamer's worst fear, and I mean worst' she made clear, 'or they would be babies screaming... spouses yelling in fear.... Just awful,' Annie breathed. 'That's where the droning came in. We figured that as long as the dreamer couldn't *hear* Imposters, all would be fine. They wouldn't be so afraid. So we created a noise so strong it disrupts message and receiver all at once.'

'The droning,' Wil realised unpalatably.

'Precisely. Check if your mum's coming, would you?' Annie urged.

'You're fine,' he said over his shoulder, peering, for he too felt like Mum might appear there on the path at any second.

'Listen Wil, I'm sorry to have to tell you this, but that noise you mentioned was in your Initial, your fake-fog Initial... it's the same droning you would have experienced in *real* Tret fog every time someone tried contacting you there but was being blocked. You're without a doubt reproducing what you experienced.'

He swatted at the swarm around him and got up from the grass, frustrated.

'So it's not aircraft engines then,' he asked sourly.

'I know what Sadie told you, but no, it's not aircraft engines.'

He kicked at the swarm, dispersing it.

'I know it's tempting to think about Sadie's loyalties,' Annie acknowledged, 'but trust me, that's the last thing you should be thinking about right now. We've got to think about the bigger picture here. So listen, Wil, there's another aspect to this I need you to think about. *I* know you want to get rid of the fog because you associate it with the Tret, and I know Sadie said you would be able to lift it when you were strong enough, but *Imposters will know that too*. They will take your desires, your hopes and wishes, and they will come to you offering help. They often come as a form of help,' she said heavily as an aside, 'but if you accept it—if you take anything from them that helps you to get rid of the fog, you *won't* actually get rid of it in the end. In fact, the moment you realise it was an Imposter you aligned yourself with, your mind will hold onto it that much more. Are you hearing what I'm saying, Wil?'

'Annie, I'm in no hurry to get rid of the fog,' he made clear, feeling that doing nothing was best at this point. It was his default stance with most things he found dreadful. 'And the noise....' He didn't know what to make of that, whether it was still coming from his old Tret-fog experiences. However, it did make him think immediately of the couple earlier in the week. The bloke especially. There had been nothing unusual about those eyes: no weird spinning. Realising he hadn't mentioned the girl standing there as though asleep, or the bloke forced to the ground, Wil quickly confessed, 'I wasn't the only one overcome by the noise in my Initial,' and told her everything.

'You clearly felt safer subjecting this guy to the noise,' Annie said frankly, 'which reinforces the Initial state, doesn't it?' Only, Wil knew for certain he himself had experienced the droning too. In that first dream. The one that sent him to the loo vomiting, his body found the sound so offensive. 'Residual probably, that one,' Annie reckoned. 'Leftovers from the actual protective fog before you returned to normal Initials, I would have thought. I mean, you were in there for *three years* Wil,' she reminded.

'So you don't think they're Imposters?' he wanted to be sure.

'They could be,' Annie conceded, 'especially the girl, if she's not showing her eyes.' Then reconsidering, 'But your Initial would have deteriorated if you felt a direct threat.'

'I did feel threatened though, didn't I?' he argued. 'That's why I inflicted the noise on that bloke.'

'You were *alarmed*, Wil,' Annie granted, 'not afraid. Trust me. All hell breaks loose when you're properly afraid. Fear isn't taken lightly in Initials. Your mind wants to resist being chucked out into the dreamscape for as long as possible.' Trusting Annie that it wasn't a pleasant place, he reckoned that no, he wasn't truly afraid of the bloke. If anything, he wanted to help him. And the girl, well he was intrigued by her. By both of them, actually. 'If they show up again, keep your cool' Annie instructed 'because that's what's instigating the noise you've obviously got the knack of. You're trying to block them from contacting you. But it's worth having a conversation to find out what they want.'

Just then, another text arrived.

'Your Mum again?'

'Yes. Same as before. And I've only got 10% charge.'

'We need to talk fast then,' she insisted. 'I'm really sorry here, Wil, but I've got to be cruel to be kind. Sadie's obviously not been as honest as she could be.' Wil moaned, affirming. 'So now you need to put what she's said and done into the context of everything I just told you. For instance, how is her little sister remaining in the same Initial every night if she's so terrified? If Lily was afraid, she'd have a new one every time she fell asleep.' It didn't even occur to Wil to realise this when Annie told him what breaks down Initials. 'So the tears at Vivary... I think Sadie must have been crying about something else,' Annie determined blandly, causing Wil to feel utterly foolish at Sadie's profound, emotional display.

'And the airstrip claim,' Annie wasted no time pointing out, 'well I can't tell you what's behind your fog, Wil—you're the one who decides that. But if you start believing what Sadie's telling you, then you'll create it eventually, in this Initial or the next. And whatever she's said about you being strong enough to lift it—that *her* Aeolus said this—the one you don't trust, well all I can say about that is *be careful*. You don't know if she's using your ability to get rid of it as an indication of your readiness for something else. *Something else* you may want delayed for as long as possible,' she warned.

'What about Aeolus—*my* Aeolus—suggesting I get rid of it,' he however remembered from the dream in which he thought Aeolus was part of a search party. 'He was telling me then that I could do it, *should* do it, even. And *you* said before that it offends him,' he pointed out. 'So if *he* wants it gone, but removal of it might set off some weird thing with Sadie's—'

'—Sorry, Wil,' Annie cut him short, 'one more thing,' she blurted, completely ignoring him and sounding incredibly distracted. 'The most significant thing she's done with you in the dreams is dream-dragged your dream to Ben's.'

'*What?*'

'Dream-drag. It's where one Initial is compressed and dragged into someone else's by a skilled third person. It was common practise for a while there. In fact, *we* used to do it. All of us did. You, me, Ben, Steph. When someone became too distressed in protective fog, like with the Imposters I was telling you about, we'd bring loved ones in with them to prove that family members weren't being harmed.' She was talking faster now, and there was an unevenness in her voice, like she was getting up and moving, going up stairs. 'We'd just pull someone in, Initial and all, creating a dream inside the fog. It seemed the best thing to undermine

Imposters' claims from the outside, and for a while there, it was an incredibly relieving measure for everyone involved in tending the fog, so we ramped up our activity like never before, across the globe. But it quickly started backfiring.'

'Backfiring how?'

'First, fogged dreamers started sleepwalking, but then it got worse. We quickly realised that when the mind doesn't want to be dragged—or dragged *to*—it walks. *Sleepwalks.* Basically the dreamer feels trapped, and in our case, the fog made it worse and their mind just devised the only way out it could think of. Now, obviously we couldn't have a global increase of sleepwalking recognised, so we tried finding a more aggressive alternative. But until we started using the droning, we realised another side-effect of dream-dragging.' She paused long enough that Wil checked his phone still had battery.

'Go on,' he said eagerly, seeing 6% and wondering what was going on on her end.

'Sleepwalking was just the physical manifestation of a more underlying problem,' she went on a bit less distractedly now. 'The real devastating and unintended consequence of dream-dragging was that it put the two dreamers brought together at odds with one another. In fact, the more often they were dragged together, the deeper a distrust emerged between them. You can imagine that in our ignorance we ended up making the problem worse, until eventually, the dreamers who were dragged to the fog ended up completely changing sides—going from Tare to Tret in a matter of days. Of course, that meant they weren't even viable candidates to help calm their fogged partners anymore, and *we* couldn't access them in their Initial at that point. With affinities changing, friends in the dreams became enemies in real life, making it evident that this was the outcome the Imposters intended all along. It was awful, Wil. It took less than a month for our intensified use of dream-dragging—a practice which has been used for millennia... before fog was even *invented*—to finally be officially recognised as archaic. *Harmful,* even. So after that whole fiasco, dreamers across the board decided to stop using it. The noise was much better practice. It was automatic and instant. Efficient.'

Annie inhaled sharply, catching her breath, then let it out loud and slow. 'Dream-dragging is harmful to anyone. *Anytime,*' she said with what sounded great relief to finally tell him. 'Which brings me to the obvious question, Wil. If it puts the dreamers' relationship at odds... then why would Sadie work as the middle person and drag you to Ben's Initial?'

Flabbergasted, he couldn't answer.

'Did you feel the drag, Wil? That's why it's called dream-dragging. Because when you're being pulled through, your legs feel heavy. Elongated.'

The words caused Wil's heart to sink. Without a doubt, he felt the strange sensation when he jumped through the pond to the sky beneath with Sadie. Her insistence that he not let go of her hand now made him feel sick.

'Can I take your silence as a yes?' Annie waited only a moment then added, 'I'm afraid that explains why a prominent feature of your dream followed into hers: the fog. It was the wisp over the pond that clearly tried pulling you back to your own Initial, because she also dragged you to hers.'

The feeling of asphalt turning spongy under his feet as he entered the field—*twice*—and that weight around his legs as he followed Sadie's lead... it shallowed Wil's breath with utter regret.

'When elements from our Initials appear as your fog did in those dragged dreams, it's no different from the sleepwalker's desire to flee. They want to get you out of there. And the same fog featured later in Ben's as the clouds; the constant projection of what you still deemed as safe. In all that blue, the white was *determined* to be seen. You even *grabbed* it,' she laughed slightly, making him feel mocked, summoning the old Annie that made his insides turn with hate. (*That's not the real Annie*, Wil however reminded himself, believing that whatever was forcing Annie to callously hurry their conversation, it was probably the same thing that left them stuck with a low battery and him being attacked by mosquitos.) 'Your Initial, Wil, was dragged to *both* their dreams. From yours to hers, then hers to Ben's. Come to think of it,' Annie hesitated, 'she would have needed help in order to keep *her* Initial open,' she contemplated aloud, '...when she was off fetching *you*.... So she probably used the other Aeolus as her third person, the middle man, to get you to hers.'

Look....

Wil couldn't help think again that his own Aeolus must have been pointing this very thing out—showing him what the other was doing. It was here that he began to wonder if that was why Sadie looked so distressed. *Because she knew what effect it would have on both of us,* Wil wanted to believe. *That it would eventually divide us.*

'Wil, what I really don't understand is why Ben had to be involved in the first place. Does she even *know* him?'

'We're all in a class together,' Wil explained, wondering himself, and suddenly appreciating what dream-dragging might mean for him and his mate.

Another text came.

'Listen Annie, I've got 4%,' he said despondently, glancing at the screen, 'and Mum's texted again.'

'Have you been coming up with reasons to avoid contact with him?' There was a sting in Annie's directness, a sudden change of tack.

'Sorry?'

'*With Ben.* Have you felt the need to avoid him since your little dream together?'

'I'm not rejecting him,' Wil insisted emphatically.

'Maybe not outright, but the effect of dragged dreams causes insecurity, shame, jealousy, all of which distort and fester indefinitely, inside and outside the dreams until you change sides.'

Wil twisted his neck uncomfortably. 'Nothing's festering,' he said sharply.

'Then you need to tell him about the dreams, Wil—about everything that's happened over the last week,' Annie instructed.

'I'll tell him tomorrow, then. First thing,' Wil decided, and at that precise moment, a wasp flew momentarily into his face, causing him to throw his head backwards into the prickly yew behind. 'I'll tell him,' he promised, stiffening his back away from the deceptively smooth shrub, 'Seriously, I will. Anything else before my phone runs out?' he asked trying to rub the itchy spot between his shoulder blades.

'You're too measured,' Annie pointed out, her tone now softening, for it seemed whatever she felt pressured to tell him, she finally got it all out. 'It's like everything you are this side of the dreams, is to make up for how you were there. I know you won't remember, but you were the bull in a china shop… Steph did her quantum thing… Ben was the mnemonics freak….'

Wil was suddenly distracted by the thought of his oblivious friend remembering anything important aside from his own birthday and the agreed time for meals.

'Ben and mnemonics?' he said doubtfully, smiling. 'And what were you, then?'

'Your strategy girl. Right alongside Murphy.'

'And Zara?' he slipped in.

'The double agent, of course. The Dual.' Annie suddenly snuffed down the phone. 'Actually, a double agent at least has a loyalty to *someone*. Zara was just out for herself. I mean it when I say don't trust her. Now about tonight,' she quickly digressed, leaving him no room to ask anything more of Zara. 'I take it you no longer have plans with Sadie?'

'Shall *we* meet up then?'

'We can certainly try. Now don't worry if I'm late—'

Her silence after a few seconds felt odd.

'Annie?'

His phone was dead.

Chapter Twenty-Seven

Appreciation

To Wil's relief, Mum was poking chicken with a spatula on the hob when he returned through the terrace doors.

'*There* you are,' she announced over her shoulder, annoyed slightly. 'Did you not get any of my texts?'

'Sorry. Dead battery.' Wil held up the lifeless screen of his phone as he kicked off his shoes. 'You're cooking? I thought we were having take-away?'

'Well we were... but then I thought it would be more sensible to use up the chicken in the fridge.'

Hearing her use the word *sensible* made him feel like he had his mother back. At least for the moment. 'Using up the chicken *is* more sensible,' he agreed, taking a stool at the island.

'And thanks for getting the milk.'

'Not a problem.'

Annie's reminder that they were all taking hits settled lightly into Wil's head. It made him wonder just how many glugs Ben had to take off the milk to require that journey to the shop yesterday, where his megaphone moment occurred. A journey, Wil now realised after his mother explained about the pointless service to the car, that required some strange fault to the electrics in her dash. Yet it was now all working fine.

'I wasted my time, basically,' she moaned. 'And all that dragging your Dad along to give me a lift....'

'Nevermind. At least you got it checked out,' he soothed. 'You can have peace of mind now.'

Peace of mind. He hauffed quietly at the thought. And as he watched his mum carry on cooking and serve up just as Dad was due home, Wil began to see how complex his relationship with his mother over the years had been. With all his family, actually. All those times he fell out with one of them... craved to be nearer... or couldn't care either way, it made him wonder just how much was made up of his own desire, and how much if it had been motivated by the hits Annie talked about. Wil suddenly felt a greater appreciation for his family as he sat there on the stool in the kitchen, certain the smallest thing, after a thousand small things, could leave him bereft of any one of them; the wrong manoeuvre on the motorway—or the right one... the right place, but the wrong time.... It prompted his quietness throughout dinner after Dad came home, and even throughout the funny parts of the comedy Dad and Mum started on Sonya. In the end, for their benefit, Wil told them he was just tired and went up to his room.

Fully charged, Wil's phone displayed the last text he got from Sadie, just below Mum's. However much he had secretly adored the girl in his Psychology class, there was no denying it now, she had been out to get him. The lies, the deception and half-truths... the scene at the park... he now felt a fool.

Yet.

Yet.

Something inside him was prepared to accept that Sadie had been driven to behave this way. That she wouldn't just do it unless she felt she had to. Or was made to. Maybe like Mum's moment over take-away at the bottom of the stairs, Sadie was being hit left and right. Bombarded. To the point that her real motivations had become obliterated.

Wil texted Annie that he was nearly ready, but received no text back.

At 11pm, when he still couldn't get to sleep, he texted her again and heard Steph come in from the cinema. Again, no reply.

By midnight, Mum and Dad came up and the house became strangely silent.

Chapter Twenty-Eight

Insomnia

It was 2am and lying in the dark felt pointless. A detached strangeness made Wil hyper-aware of where his thoughts deviated. As trivial as they were, it unnerved him as to whether they were in fact *his* thoughts.

'You cannot sleep, Wilden.'

Wil sat up immediately and turned on the lamp. But there was no one. Then with no warning whatsoever Aeolus appeared, pearlescent and tanned, there in the middle of the room. That waving hair and those bright, mesmerising eyes, it was just as Wil remembered. He couldn't help but wonder if the bed he had been sitting up in was like the bedroom from the pixellated wall. Dubiously, he scanned the corners, the desk, the floor, searching for evidence of a dream.

'You are not dreaming, Wilden, nor am I a hallucination.'

From the side, Aeolus' linen trousers and white T-shirt made him look no more than an actual person in the room, perusing items around the desk like museum artefacts. But the arms... the bronze sheen of those deep-looking arms... there was nothing human there.

'It is unwise to dream tonight,' Aeolus remarked over his shoulder.

'Just as well,' Wil hauffed faintly, 'I was dreading it.'

'You dread it because you have seen what they can do.'

But having no memory of what exactly that was, Wil was convinced his dread stemmed more from having no idea *who* or *what* would be waiting for him on the other side. 'Yes, well I'm afraid I don't remember any of that,' he admitted, watching as the creature touched the cover of the journal there on the desk.

'Don't you?' Aeolus asked, turning to him. 'You don't remember seeing the numbers coming at you from every side, appealing to every desire and ambition you held? All at once? Challenging all decency and appropriateness... every truth you ever tried preserving, in one compressed, prolonged moment in time—when such a thing should never happen?'

But before Wil could even answer, sooty faces—those of Steph, Annie, Ben... Murphy... Friends and Enemies—pelted through his mind like buckshot, confabulated from Annie's bedroom drawings like some glitchy animated short film.

'Another second and you would have gone mad,' Aeolus attested, abruptly ending the reel in Wil's mind.

'But I didn't.'

'No. You didn't.'

Wil pictured his charcoal self again, confident. An uncomfortable itch crept across his shoulders at the thought of Annie there too, distraught.

'Because there was a plan,' Wil proffered. 'A plan that I'd forget everything, knowing you'd help me to remember again.'

Aeolus pursed a tired smile in Wil's direction. 'It won't be long before you establish the difference between intuition and the lengthening roots of your rejuvenating memories,' he declared, moving to the far corner of the room where the chest of drawers stood. Then picking up the hand-mould plate from Reception, he pressed his impossible pale, bronze-toned fingers into the depressions just as Steph had done a few nights ago. 'You cannot dream tonight, Wilden,' he said firmly, setting the mould down, 'even for one second. So, let us use this time to prepare.'

'Prepare for what?'

'Annie told you about the three states within the dreams,' Aeolus moved to the dartboard and started rearranging the darts, 'two of which you have experienced recently. *The fog*, she elucidated adequately. *The Initial*... and the open dreamscape. You have not been there yet, as a shadow is the way out from the Initial into this space. You are familiar with these things now, are you not?' With red dart poised, the creature turned his head to the side, revealing a facial profile for Wil to answer to.

'Yes. But why are you telling me this when Annie's already told me? Why don't you tell me about how things were before—before when

I remembered?'

'You will learn about before soon enough,' the creature assured, leaving the dartboard. He scanned the shelves and surfaces in the room with a preoccupied curiosity. 'There is no point mentioning that which will only be used against you at present. Instead, we must consider our friends.' A family holiday photo mounted on the wall attracted Aeolus' eye in particular just then. 'They are of utmost importance in the dreams.' After a lingering few seconds, Aeolus ran an almost glowing finger along a stack of old CDs, pulled one out half-way then twisted his head round to read the cover, pointing and poking those tentacle-like clumps of hair in Wil's direction.

'In most instances, Initials are useful for only a brief time. You quickly find this to be the case when forced to move on from your own, and exhaust those of every close friend and family you can think of until finally you enter the dreamscape.' Aeolus was now looking up to a frame holding a collage of Roops and a few of the Mulbryn bunch. 'However, it's worth pointing out,' he said in a strained-neck voice, picking up the frame and bringing it closely to his face 'that in order to make any voluntary advances in the dreams, a level of insight is required to meet someone else, somewhere else. Therefore, those who cannot remember anything about what happens in the dreams are left completely incapable of navigating them. They become as clouds passing overhead. Sometimes you notice them amid the dreamscape, most often, you don't.' Putting the frame back, 'Any interaction you hope to have with such a torpid mind really must be initiated by you,' he said.

Wil considered this, that anyone he knew outside the dreams was basically useless inside them if they couldn't remember. That included Ben, which was evident in the tooth-spitting feast... and it included Steph too, possibly Zara. He still knew nothing of Murphy. However, Annie remembered the dreams.

Aeolus tentatively pinched the spine of the Final Year propped open at eye level. 'May I?'

Wil gave a permissive grimace and nodded, watching with intrigue as the creature interacted with something physical, sentimental. It hadn't crossed his mind when the darts were being rearranged, (he glanced at the back of the door to find Aeolus left a single blue amid all the reds), but now, he suddenly wondered how something that seemed to exist only in his head—his dreams—could be in his room, lifting things off the shelf.

Aeolus paused for a moment, stared intently into the book, drawing Wil's attention as he did so, then quickly closed the glossy cover as though indifferent and put it back on the shelf. Then with eyes that worked like hands, holding and leading, he drew Wil's attention to the dart board again.

'Wilden, it is essential that you leave the Initial before it breaks down completely.' He began pushing in the limp darts crowded into the bull's eye. 'Any unsettling emotion triggered by the loss of your Initial will follow you into the dreamscape and effect your judgement there.'

Aeolus put the single blue dart just outside the centre, on a white radial section, leaving the reds. It seemed that this was to represent him— Wil—leaving the thronged middle of the Initial.

'Ideally, you should move from one Initial to the next, keeping in mind that those you travel with may have bypassed their own Initial altogether to join you. For instance, if they joined you from the moment they fell asleep. Now should an Initial suffer severely, before you have a chance to escape it, those comrades risk being forced back to their own Initials, instead of the dreamscape, leaving you alone and vulnerable. Therefore, timing here is essential. While some rely on this process as a protective measure when they are caught out unexpectedly, jettisoning back to their scrap of safety, it no doubt wrong-foots them the rest of the night. It would be wise in such circumstances then to avoid these friends until you all wake.'

'Okay....' Wil tried imagining himself with no Initial to run to, or those of friends for that matter.

'If others are automatically disappearing to safety, you must decide whether you can leave with them or if you must enter straight into the dreamscape. Choose another Initial and the decision will inevitably need to be made again. You have only a second or two to decide while the dreamer holds their degrading Initial open.'

'And if I don't—if we don't? Decide, that is.'

'If you and the other dreamer purposely resist the thrust into the dreamscape as everything breaks down, then I'm afraid neither of you will wake,' Aeolus said rather plainly, shocking Wil slightly with this information.

'So, are you saying we *die*?' Sadie's fear of such a thing came to mind.

'I'm afraid so, Wilden. A successful night will have seen you move

264

from Initial to Initial, together, gaining in numbers, eventually increasing in strength until you are able to control the dream around you easily. When you get this far, the running can stop.'

Running? Wil found it difficult to imagine himself in such a fast-paced environment after this last week. All he could see himself making was mistakes.

'Mistakes are unlikely,' Aeolus assured. 'It is all intuitive. You've been dreaming for most of your life. It is not foreign. Only your awareness of it is. And you will never be alone because ultimately my affinity with you is like that of your friends'. It is this which manifests as intuition and guides you. And if you find yourself in doubt, those select few friends you keep with you will be experiencing the same thing. You can rely on their judgement, their intuition if necessary.'

But Wil had no friends, none at least who remembered. Anguish, miserable anguish filled his exhausted frame as it slowly slumped there on the bed.

'Now listen to me,' Aeolus said sharply as he went over and squatted down to meet Wil's face. 'You have done all this before, with admirable finesse. You just don't remember. *Wilden*, I need you to listen to me.'

'I *am* ....'

'The second you find yourself in the dreamscape,' the creature said earnestly, 'it's up to *how* you dream, with *whom* and what you *decide to dream about* that becomes a form of protection.'

Overwhelmed by the thought of even getting that far—to the point of making clever decisions in the dreams, or coordinating with dream-savvy dreamers—Wil closed his eyes wearily, feeling how incredibly tired he was. He so wanted to fall asleep, but not into the world Aeolus had just described. Fighting the urge, he stretched his eyes open and forced himself to sit stiffly upright where he met that dazzling, anxious face in front of him. Minimally revived, he summarised,

'Don't wait for chaos. Right. So now what?'

Aeolus gave him a dispirited smile.

'Now, we try and keep you awake.'

The creature squeezed Wil's shoulder encouragingly, stood up then looked him over questionably from the middle of the room.

'And where will *you* be in all this?' it occurred to Wil to ask. 'And I don't just mean that affinity-connection thing. Where will you be *like this?*' He wagged a finger at Aeolus' pearlescent form as it turned away to the shelves of photos and knick-knacks again.

'I will be there with you. Just not every second. Many need my help. All at once.'

A glazed expression came over Wil at the thought of being in a dream without Aeolus. Of going from place to place with the fear of never waking when he didn't even know how to really do any of the things the creature had asked of him.

'I am no different from my counterparts, Wilden. Just as you are bombarded most nights by them, I too must drop in on dreamers I have no affinity with… and nudge them out into the dreamscape.' Here, Aeolus threw a passive glance in Wil's direction, to which Wil frowned, disconcerted.

Of course, Annie made it clear both the Tret and Tare could enter anyone's Initial, but the thought of Aeolus jettisoning vulnerable dreamers most nights out from a place of even minimal safety put the creature in a contrary, albeit slightly beastly light all of a sudden. And as Wil watched him stoop in front of those shelves, he couldn't help but see him as a kind of predator, no different from the others who took advantage of dreamers in their Initials.

'And there it is,' Aeolus said with a wearied satisfaction, apparently spotting something significant in the old school pictures, disengaging from them and standing upright as if he had been waiting for this very moment precisely.

'Wilden,' Aeolus sighed, dismayed, 'I am no predator.'

The words fell on Wil like an icy splash of water, all he could do was hold his breath.

'Right now, that is what they want you to believe,' Aeolus turned his back on the shelves. 'They are taking your fatigue, even as I stand here before you, and are trying to turn you against me.' He took a step closer, stopping in front of the old blocked-up fireplace. 'They are disguised as your own thoughts Wilden, but it's you who has to determine if they are. It is you who has to determine whether I am a predator.'

The sudden silence compelled Wil to blurt an answer. 'Of course I don't think you're a predator.' Then blinking and shaking his head, he said more confidently, 'I *know* you're not a predator….'

'But you thought it,' Aeolus pointed out, bending his neck to catch Wil's ashamed, lowering face. 'You thought it because someone else was at the right place, the right time, and looking the part. You entertained their whisper as if it were your own and saw our situation here differently as a result. Only for a brief moment,' he said to Wil's credit, catching his eye, 'but it happened.'

Their eye contact broke as Wil began sheepishly rubbing a thumb into his palm.

'The dreamscape is the thoroughfare to past, present and future,' Aeolus explained. 'Fear is what constricts the mind there. Without such fear, the mind expands and is freed. But only if it knows what to look for.' Here, the creature sighed. 'Unfortunately, nothing is as it seems in the dreamscape. That is where I come in.

'Perhaps I am a predator,' he accepted, shrugging half-heartedly, 'lying in wait to exploit a vulnerability. But then,' the blasé disappeared from his expression, 'you must ask yourself who is making such an accusation?'

'I'm sorry,' Wil mumbled, overwhelmed with shame now for having thought of the creature as such, after all that they had been through. 'I'm sorry...' he said again, fiddling with his fingers, looking in the direction of his toes. 'I don't know why I ever thought it.' Then as he closed his eyes and ran a hand through his hair.

'Open your eyes, Wilden,' Aeolus said sharply, '*open your eyes now*' to which Wil did so obediently, to the creature's satisfaction. 'Good. You don't need to apologise,' he assured, softening, 'you were not making the accusation. And you don not need to feel ashamed for the things that have entered your mind—the things you have fought and overcome—because you are part of a battle right now. A battle, even as you sit there on that bed. A battle you *are* winning.'

Winning? Wil didn't see how he could be winning anything.

'I don't even know *who* I'm battling anymore,' he said, bewildered.

'That doesn't matter for now. What matters is that you recognise when it's going on. *Timing is everything*.' Aeolus insisted. 'One second their efforts will be futile, the next, they'll have you. I'm afraid, from now on, you must distinguish when such activity is happening. You must trust yourself to know instinctively when they are present, and when they are not. From moment to moment.'

Wil feared such an expectation, second-guessing every thought he was ever to have, was impossible.

'But even if I could...' he considered weakly, tipping his head back, perplexed and exhausted, '...even if I could figure out *when* they're in my head...' his eyes were rolling wearily about their sockets, distracted by another thought '…but *you're* in my head…' he remembered conveniently '*…you* could tell me who… I mean you could tell me *when* they're in….' But it was no use. Wil blinked lazily and sighed, too tired to even try and argue his point. 'Why don't you just tell me what I need to know,' he suggested apathetically, 'say why they want to get inside my head… say what this whole thing... all this is about….' The fatigue was beginning to produce a drunken, impatient disconnectedness. 'Just *tell* me what I need to do… and I'll just go along…' Wil reasoned happily '…because I trust you… I'll do whatever… because I trust you….'

Wil's inebriated grin failed to convince the creature, no matter how long he tried holding it there.

'You wouldn't, Wilden.'

'I would….'

'You wouldn't.'

'I'm telling you, *I would*….'

Aeolus stepped away from the fireplace's mantle and stood in front of Wil, lifting that angular ghostlike chin as though measuring up the flagging heap before him. 'We have only an hour. Shall we not waste time, then?' He strolled over to the desk and put his hands on the back of the chair, positioning himself directly behind it. 'This thing we do, dispersing dreamers out into the dreamscape, is all done to try and disrupt a set pattern of thought. So when you sit here writing in your journal,' Wil pricked an ear and eye in the creature's direction, 'you've just shown me where I've failed you. Where someone got there ahead of me and undid something significant, without me even realising it until the deed is already done. Because this is what we do, Wilden. We undermine one another to undermine the past, and in doing so, secure our future. You see, the past is maintained in the present until we change both simultaneously—all three in some cases.'

Wil grimaced, lost.

'We find fear, Wilden. Trauma. I go and search for it in minds hopelessly locked into a labyrinth of thinking. I show them how that removal of fear might allow their behaviour to change. They may forget in an instant that I have done this, but I must do it regardless. I do not do it out of vengeance,' he insisted plainly, 'in an effort to undo the Tret. Instead, I do it to prevent that individual mind from being taken over so completely that it falls into the same trap as its ancestors. You see, when a person, no different from yourself, is obliged to see their world only one way—*is destined to* because of the decisions and experiences that have been directly passed onto them through the womb... well, my unlikely detour might just for one second offer a view of something else possible. The trauma might stop perpetuating and allow not just *the one* to see their past and present differently... but many. The future.' He seemed to ponder this for a second, then said earnestly, 'Think about it Wilden. If you had the chance to do the same... to show anyone their situation in a new light, a hopeful light...' (Wil's mind involuntarily saw a vivid image of Sadie... almost audibly heard her despairing voice, so bent on assuming the path of doom with the Anti-Aeolus) '...would you not do the same? Would you not try and disrupt her chaotic world in order to help her see a way out?'

'Of course I would,' Wil admitted faintly, finding himself unsure of what he was really condoning, while wishing simultaneously that Sadie could have been less adamant about turning her back on him. It was then that he realised Aeolus said *her*—that the creature *knew* he had pictured Sadie...

...*Or made me picture her....*

Slowly, apprehensively, Wil faced the silent form standing over his desk, over his journals, feeling much less tired now.

'I know what you just did,' he accused. 'You *made* me think of Sadie. Was that to wake me up—to get me to listen?' Such a move made Wil feel manipulated, for the creature knew how he felt about her, *must* have known. It crossed his mind too that a perfectly timed thought of Sadie might have been used in other ways, not just on this occasion, but on many others. 'What are you doing?' Wil demanded, hating the thought. 'Why did you put her in my head?'

Aeolus turned brusquely from the desk and stood by the foot of the bed. That innocuous expression was replaced by a knowing, pleased look.

'I am trying to demonstrate how easy it is to turn you against me.'

Wil recoiled, confused.

'You *won't* just go along with what I say because you trust me,' Aeolus said firmly. 'You won't just *do whatever*, because you trust me.' The mocking tone cut through any indignant thought Wil had, for it occurred to him this was no longer about Sadie's image or voice being used to sway him. 'That is what you said, Wilden, isn't it?'

'Yes,' he answered dismissively, unwilling to let the point be proven so easily, 'but why didn't you just say—make your point some other way... instead of...?'

'I did say. I said you wouldn't just do what I wanted, simply because you trusted me. But you insisted otherwise.' Wil now resented the words being thrown at him like this. 'I'm not trying to catch you out here, Wilden,' Aeolus assured. 'I'm trying to show you how you can be certain one moment that nothing could possibly turn your mind against me, only to find in the next, that certainty never really existed.'

But Wil *was* certain he trusted the creature. Despite his present annoyance. How else could he have gotten this far? That trust... he felt it... *believed* it. Unless it was all just induced... that feeling of assurance... the demolished doubt. To what then was he actually connecting with in his past?

A strained, confused desperation now took hold of Wil's face.

'Right now, you are trying to preserve what you *know* versus what you *feel*. Am I correct?' Aeolus asked all too simply, the effect of which was as if a trigger had been pulled.

'Why are you doing this to me?' Wil demanded distrustfully, rubbing his brow, confused. 'What is this...? You show yourself here without telling me a single thing from my past... and instead you hound me with instructions and put things—*images*—in my head?' he said angrily, for a sharp pain began to shoot behind his eyes. 'How is that any different from what the others do? How is that not just taking control of my mind? And how is that not making me do what you want anyway? Why pretend to give me a choice over the last week... when you'll only steer me back to where you want me the second I go astray? *You've just done it now—twice!* ...Made me feel so ashamed for falling into these traps... but they're traps *you keep setting up.*' An uncontrollable urge was working its way through Wil, dispelling all those distrustful thoughts with which he battled earlier in the week and came out the other side feeling liberated from. Because now... now... he could put all that away for good, and hear from Aeolus straight that all those impressions in the window weren't just delusional musings. That all those encounters with Sadie weren't just the contrived means to an abysmal end. That the friends and family he loved weren't just fair game—fodder in some inexplicable dual existence. Because he wanted it all, that resolve—that hope of being involved in something so much bigger than him—something that was more than anyone could have ever imagined, to be true now. *Real.* *Worth* the agony.

Wil stood up with a great sigh and walked over to the fireplace, conflicted.

'I didn't mean it like that,' he retracted in frustration, laboriously propping an elbow onto the mantle and tiredly sinking a temple into his hand.

'I know you didn't,' Aeolus accepted calmly, as though pleased for the accusations to have finally come out. 'Just like I know you don't think I'm a predator. But this is what we are up against. This is what I mean when I say you need to recognise when the battle is going on. Who you're up against becomes evident in the timing.' He paused, then said abruptly, 'Wilden, would you mind coming away from there?'

For a second, Wil hadn't even realised his eyes were closed, but then he mumbled something affirming, stepped off the hearth and went and leaned his backside against the chest of drawers by the door.

'Wilden, I don't want to dismiss any concern you have regarding my influence over your mind. And I am particularly aware that the very nature of our communication suggests I do just that, control you. However, there is no manner of control at all. In fact, it is the complete opposite. For a prompt, suggestion or any other involvement otherwise to be effective, my motive must become completely sympathetic to those of the person I have any influence over. It is accurate even to say,' he chose his words carefully, pursing his lips in thought, 'I have no influence unless our thoughts are first aligned. This essentially is the affinity I spoke of. Without it, our interaction is like that with most of the world; my influence becomes minimally opportunistic. So, take for instance our past,' he went back to the fireplace again and turned to Wil. 'I could easily tell you about it... in full detail... filling in all your gaps with my own perspective, maybe even allowing you the pleasure of reinterpreting it yourself, to give you that sense of ownership. But then, even those thoughts wouldn't actually be yours. They would be mine inside you. Borrowed.'

Aeolus shook the dissatisfying idea away with a little movement of the head, flaked off peeling paint from the corner of the mantel with fascinating humanness and carried on.

'And I know that telling you everything from our past would provide my counterparts with the ammunition to *completely* destroy you.' *Completely.* The word seemed to hang in the air, leading Wil to believe that the need to lose his memory had been the result of a mere attempt at greater damage. 'They would use such information to nudge you into doubt, prod you into indecision, ultimately driving you to accept nothing I've said as truth. It's unthinkable to imagine where we would be then. You, having no trust in any of us. I'm afraid the only tonic for such a feral mind is forgetting altogether.'

Aeolus stopped picking at the mantle and looked at Wil rather apprehensively.

'Wilden. I'm not in control of your mind. My counterparts *control*. If *I* had control of you, you would be confused. Lost. Profoundly numb. But you are none of those things. So, I can assure you, if you end up doing what I want, it's not because *I* make you. You do what I want because, in your liberty, you make the same choices I would.' His gaze was firmly fixed now. 'We... are like-minded. On the same side.' Wil believed, deep down, this was the case. He was certain of it. 'I have shown myself to you because of this. Because our minds are alike. Had I not,' Aeolus said with a shrug, 'you would never have known I was here. You would have mistaken me for that gut feeling or voice in your head. Or something less profound. And this,' he gestured with his hand between them, 'would never have happened.' A desperate, regretful expression took hold of the creature's face. 'This... I don't want you forgetting again.'

Wil nodded faintly, feeling reassured. He didn't want to forget his connection to the creature either. But then, worryingly, it occurred to him, '*You* made me forget last time, but what if *they* make me forget next?'

'They won't. Not unless you are in danger of switching from one side to another. Which is why I had to make you forget in the first place.'

The expression on Wil's face showed him struggling to understand. While it made sense that the amnesia plan he and the creature had worked out over three years ago was for protection, it had suddenly become unclear as to how and when someone could be made to forget in the first place.

'So, are you saying they *can't* make me forget... because I'm not on their side?'

The question provoked an unexpected reaction, for Aeolus withdrew his engaging stare and let his eyes flit about either side of Wil, as though in avoidance. He then took in a contemplative deep breath through his nostrils, puffing up his broad chest as he did so, unmistakably apprehensive. Just as Wil began to wonder why his question brought on such an unsettled response, the creature slid his hands tentatively into those white linen pockets and walked to the middle of the room, apparently resigned to give an answer.

'Wilden,' he readied himself, 'those who can make you forget... are those you have an affinity with.' However definitive or simple the answer sounded, it was clear to Wil by the creature's conflicted demeanour there was more to it than that; there was more to breaking connections than simply undoing what one had put in place. 'It is a protection the affinity affords,' Aeolus insisted delicately. 'A form of defence and safekeeping. Unfortunately, there are... situations...' he shrugged, evasive-like, '... when it becomes unclear as to which side a person actually has an affinity. With whom they become like-minded... becomes impossible to tell.

'Such circumstances come about when the mind is... shall we say, riding on the fence,' Aeolus continued more easily. 'The ability to make one forget then—when one is on the fence—becomes immediately indeterminable. Therefore, it is unwise... to wait until that point—the Verge of Transition—to try and remove all that could be used against such a person as they move from one affinity to another. Move from Tare to Tret.'

Here, Aeolus stared expectantly at Wil, giving him the impression this was why their plan to forget had been worked out in advance. But Wil could only frown awkwardly in response, for he already knew this; he already knew he had been made to forget so that he would be protected—so that the others would be too—because he would soon be in the hands of an enemy. Why it was the case that he would end up in such a predicament, he still did not understand, but that was beginning to feel beside the point just now.

Anticipating further explanation, Wil gave the creature a perplexed sideways glare.

'None of us want those who remember their dreams to face Transition,' Aeolus went on. 'None of us want them to be forced to forget. I can assure you, that when a mind is on the fence, an abundance of hopeful strategies will have been employed to prevent such a loss. However, I cannot say whether waiting until each one has been tried is worth the risk. Making one forget so close to the line most certainly propels them over it, for there is nothing then to restrain them. No memories to draw them back. But to prevent them from going over, one can wait too long, be too hopeful, and not just lose a wavering mind completely, but squander that last moment in which to hide every positive connection they've cultivated within it.' The creature lifted his chin and looked down his nose, hardened slightly. 'Making one forget severs and seals the affinity,' he said plainly. 'Leaving it open, on the other hand, throughout Transition, means it would surely be exploited once the other side has the advantage.'

For a second, Wil thought that maybe Aeolus was trying to tell him that he hadn't *actually* made him forget. But Wil was certain that he had. He had forgotten. In fact, he had a reliable witness. Annie. She saw it. She saw the moment… and it was there, captured on her wall—the moment when the mob held her back and Aeolus whispered into her ear, *as* Wil was forgetting, *while* it was being done. This was that great bombardment Aeolus spoke of earlier, where the numbers came from every side… appealing to every desire and ambition.

Wil eyed the creature apprehensively. 'You're trying to tell me something here without telling me,' he accused. 'Are you saying you *didn't* make me forget—that you left it too last-minute?'

'No. I'm certain I made you forget, Wilden.' Aeolus' fixed stare began to feel gouging. 'I shall never forget the ignorant relief on your face the moment I did. The way in which you walked so willingly along with them.'

Wil frowned, not understanding then.

'Then what? What are you saying?' As far as he was concerned, he forgot as planned, ended up in enemy hands, *as planned*, and now they were reunited, as planned.

Aeolus looked at him in dismay.

'Wilden. You've been in the fog all that time….'

'Yes….'

It occurred to him just then that perhaps that wasn't part of the plan.

'Instead of taunting us with you in the dreams, in the way they have previously done once a significant affinity falls into their hands, they chose not to. For a reason.'

'Well, I don't know why that is,' Wil defended.

All he could think, having no memory whatsoever of what had happened, was that maybe it took the last three years to ensure all associations he had with Aeolus were non-existent, that the other side had worked incredibly hard to make sure that old affinity had been sealed off… and total forgetting had been done properly.

'My thoughts exactly,' Aeolus said with a heeding sideways glare, reminding Wil that his thoughts weren't private. 'But you haven't come out advocating them now, have you? So did they fail? Or did they do something else,' he posed, shrugging a little. 'And is *that* likely to succeed?'

Wil felt uncomfortable. Aeolus' questioning stare made him realise that the creature didn't, in fact, know every thought inside his head. Especially those from the last three years. But while neither of them did, it occurred to him that because of this, Aeolus now actually viewed him as a threat. Hiding something for the Tret. Something that would no doubt discharge when least expected. Like a Trojan horse.

Winded by the realisation, Wil had to look away from that stony face opposite him, for he felt angry that Aeolus could even insinuate inevitable betrayal. With all that talk about being like-minded... being on the same side, and not wanting to give away too much detail about the past because the enemy would use it to destroy—

'—Is that why you won't tell me everything from before?' Wil asked pointedly. 'Because you're afraid of what I'd do with it?'

'The affinity we have can never be undone, Wilden. I can make you forget about it, but it can never disappear, no matter what they do to you.'

'Yeah, but basically, *I'm one of them now*—that's what you're really saying, isn't it?' Wil regretted immediately the volume of his outburst, but not its content. 'Basically, they could have done who-knows-what' he whispered loudly, glancing at the door beside him, '...so that now... you'll always be waiting for that moment of betrayal—while I sit in the middle, unable to figure out *who's* actually on my side.'

'No. No, Wilden. That is *not* how it is,' Aeolus insisted through gritted teeth, shaking his head as he did so. 'This is exactly what they want you to think, but it is not the case. *As we speak* they are using a three-fold argument against you, and you, on your own, cannot win. They are trying to convince you that *I* am against you, but really that's to turn *you* against *me*. Do you not see this?' the creature pleaded. 'This is what they do... they are trying to stimulate two affinities at once, to weaken you, to flush out anything prominent between the two opposing sides within you.... The fact that we found one another again goes against everything they know, and so they are trying to undo it—to take anything you trust about me—*us*—and destroy it with doubt.'

As Wil leaned sullenly against the chest of drawers, believing everything Aeolus was saying about the Tret, it didn't seem to help that neither of them knew what went on in the fog. Like an undetectable cancer, Wil could already feel something hideous growing inside him. Something indistinct but fixed, waiting to undo the imploring creature before him.

Aeolus relented with a sigh, took a seat in the desk chair then swivelled it a few feet closer to Wil.

'Wilden,' he said calmly, 'I told you about the Point of Transition because those who face it don't remember it. If they remember anything at all, they remember from the moment they've already crossed. But what I didn't tell you, is that most of humanity is hopelessly stuck inside Transition already. Having no real affinity with Tret or Tare to battle the daily influences... they simply change sides as the wind changes. It is this, this opportunistic, ever-rationalising mind that keeps them from ever reaching outside the belly of Transition, *and keeps them from remembering.* If only they would make one decision to protect an affinity, they would quickly find themselves polarised outside of that place, and remembering.' Aeolus paused momentarily, making Wil appreciate that this was what ultimately kept people from remembering their dreams—their own unwillingness to see outside themselves. '*But even the most devout, Wil,*' Aeolus continued, '*especially the most devout, with all their good intentions,* find themselves repenting for what they do not know, yet somehow perceive. The good... know they are bad.' A prickly warmth made Wil uncomfortable under his arms and down the sides of his torso just then. 'With such toing and froing, hundreds of times in the day, one ends up no more good than bad in that place of forgetting. Just as I am no more good than bad here with you, in this place of remembering.'

Wil shifted his weight from one foot to the other, stealing a glance at the creature, then finally looked at him, wanting to understand.

'Wilden, I will always be bad to someone.' His fixed stare pressed the point. 'To those holding your mind these last three years, I was the opposition. To them, I was the enemy. To them... you needed protection, from me. So, in the same way that I am good and bad, so too are you. Whatever your mind is harbouring against us—against both you and me... we are not powerless against it.... And the fact that we are like-minded means you have nothing to prove.' That intent look, the faint, indifferent shrug, left Wil in no doubt. 'You must simply be.'

Just then, it was as if something had broken inside Wil, something he didn't even know was there. The fact that Aeolus knew him... trusted him... despite whatever was inside him....

'But you don't know what they've done to me,' Wil argued, his voice cracking.

'I don't,' Aeolus accepted. 'But neither do you.'

'What if I do something they want me to do?'

'Then it's no different from any other moment in the day, now isn't it?'

Wil resigned himself to this, but felt slightly relieved the battle hadn't changed from three years ago. 'But what if it's big...?' he sniffed, wiping tears from his eyes.

'There's no doubt that it is, Wilden. But do you think I would have done all the things I have in the last week to get your attention if I thought for one second you were not, or could not be, the person of three years ago?'

It was as if a huge weight had lifted from Wil's shoulders... *lead-filled threads* slipping right out of him again.

There was noise down the hall just then. The metallic squeak of a doorknob turning.

As Wil instinctively went and put an ear to the door, keeping his feet away from the gap underneath, he pressed a quietening finger to his mouth and stared with wide, anxious eyes at the creature, who was putting the darts back as they had been.

'Shhh....'

'Listen, Wilden,' the creature said boldly, suggesting he couldn't be heard by whoever was out in the hall, 'it is starting' he warned, prompting Wil to eye him warily. 'There is a flurry of activity preparing for you. Your Initial is changing, and I can't have you there for any length of time until everything is in order. You will want to sleep, but you cannot.'

'I can't sleep?' Wil whispered in exasperation. 'For how long?'

'Just today.'

'And if I accidentally—'

'It won't be an accident,' Aeolus said ominously, stepping back from the dart board.

Wil pressed his ear back to the door, hearing someone go downstairs.

'Steph can explain what I have failed to.'

But just as Wil turned confusedly to the creature, he had gone.

Again, footsteps were heard at the bottom half of the stairs.

Silently, Wil pocketed his phone then switched off his lamp, revealing the bright shaft of light coming through the gap under the door from the other side. Slinking out into the hall, he saw his sister's bedroom door ajar with the light on. As the dull heaviness of fatigue clung to the back of his head like an enormous limpet, Wil went in and turned it off, closing the door behind him, determined not to wake Mum and Dad. He then crept silently to the stairs.

Just then.

A strange sound came from the pantry. It was a faint whimpering sort of noise, one that made Wil hurry silently down the steps. It was definitely Steph. In the pantry loo. She was sniffling and weeping, taking in sharp breaths while yanking frantically on the roll of toilet paper. He had heard these same sounds at least a hundred times before, late into the night as she purged her Annie-troubles. With a concerned boldness, Wil went and gently tapped on an obscured pane of the door.

'Steph?' he whispered. 'Are you okay? It's me, Wil.'

Audibly distraught, she inhaled a sob with a staccato breath and said with forced composure, 'You can come in.'

'Are you sure?'

The door opened from the other side.

His sister sat on the lid of the toilet, legs crossed, with a wad of tissue on her lap and another in her hand.

'What's wrong…?' he asked worriedly, filling the narrow doorway with his frame, remembering that only hours ago she was out enjoying an evening with Ben and Zara. *Zara.* He squatted down. 'Did you have a bad night out?' She shook her head. 'Is it Annie?' He regretted the question immediately, for he now knew Annie would never truly intend to hurt his sister.

Steph nodded as another wave of what seemed happy-sad sobs took over. Then producing her phone from beneath the wad of tissues, she gave it to him as if to offer an explanation for the state she was in.

Ask Wil who Aeolus is. Ax

'I can't tell you what I dreamed just now…' his sister croaked '…but do you know who she's talking about? Does this—does she—make any sense?'

Wil stared wearily at her, his darkened eye-sockets glowing.

'I do know who she's talking about, Steph… and she's never made more sense.'

Chapter Twenty-Nine

Particles

'Then I remember, Wil. I remember.' Her eyes widened with the weight of it all, then shrivelled. 'So what exactly was my life before all this—when I had no memory of any of it at all?'

Wil's lips turned downwards as he remembered thinking this very thing in the last week. The bliss of such ignorance. The tragedy of it.

'I guess,' he hesitated, not absolutely certain himself, 'it was a preservation in a sense. We can obviously know too much for our own good, Steph. Or at least enough to make forgetting the only way back to knowing anything again.'

Steph looked him up and down. 'And how much do you know?'

'Enough to be certain that I'm not going crazy... and that neither are you. Enough to believe Annie's trying to help us and that what seems to be happening... is.'

He hesitated, then confessed, 'But not enough to know really who that person I was.'

'Because you've been in a fog the last three years.' Steph shot him a self-conscious glance from behind her puffy red eyes, making him wonder what precisely a night's Annie-intervention had actually allowed his sister to remember.

'Did Annie tell you that, that I've been in a fog, or do you remember it?'

Clearing her throat, Steph said flatly, 'Annie had me recreate the events. Dream them. In full. From my own perspective.' The annoyed manner in which his sister suddenly hooked a lock of hair behind her ear indicated to Wil that the experience was not a pleasant one. 'Annie said it had to be that way, so she could prove to me she wasn't just putting thoughts inside my head… and so that I could prove to her the memories were still there without distortion—that the two of us did in fact experience such things together.' Looking at her phone, she added, 'Annie showed me things first, basically what was really going on all those times she seemed so cruel, and it may very well have been therapeutic for her to finally get it all out, ' Steph granted, 'but I could see that her keenness pointed to something else. Not just the need for a clear conscience.' Steph threw an I-should've-known look up in the air. 'I hadn't figured it out until halfway through… and it was just like you said—when I finally remembered you'd said it—what she was really trying to get me to show her….'

Wil wasn't quite following. 'What?' he asked, squinting and shaking his head a little. 'What was she trying to get you to show her?'

'Why we made the difficult decision we did. *Without* her,' Steph said, as though it were obvious. 'Perhaps she thought my version of the same events would reveal something. But I was careful. Intuitively careful, actually,' she assured, tearing a crinkled square of loo roll into thin strips. 'Before I even remembered our plan, about how you said it might play out like this… and that she might use me to undo it all, but only because she wouldn't have understood yet… *before all that even came as a memory*, I knew not to give any of it away. Not yet, at least.' She caught his eye, then went back to tearing what was left of her little square of tissue. 'So to answer your question, Annie didn't tell me where you've been all this time. I know. And I know why.'

There was that glance again.

'Why then, Steph? Why did we forget—what's the actual reason? What's the *real* reason behind me being fogged all this time?'

Somehow his earnest was throwing her.

'Is this a test?' She sat up straight and eyed him, apprehensive.

'Why would this be a test?'

'Because you said this might happen.' Wary confusion filled her eyes. 'You said you might try to find out from me how much you really remembered. You said you might even try to force it out of me.' From where Wil was standing there in the doorway, he thought his sister actually looked a little scared at the possibility. 'You said I couldn't tell you anything because if the fog ended up changing you... it might undermine our affinities. Or worse.' She looked him over, uneasy, as though confirming his identity, then added, 'Wil, you said I couldn't tell you anything until you remembered yourself.'

'I said that, did I?'

'Yes. And for good reason. Wil, I've not said too much already, have I?'

'No,' he answered, a little distracted, not liking one bit that such measures had to be taken. Or that his sister looked afraid of him. 'No Steph, you haven't said too much. And I won't try and force anything out of you, okay? I just want to make that clear.'

She nodded, though didn't appear completely convinced. It gave Wil the vague impression that perhaps she knew he might say that too. He didn't want to talk about himself anymore and gave a reassuring smile.

'Can you at least tell me about you,' he asked innocently, 'about where you've been all this time... or what it feels like to remember?'

Visibly relieved, Steph inhaled deeply then declared rather plainly, 'It's as if I'm waking from a coma. Like no time has passed. Everything I used to know and think before... is there suddenly, as if it's always been.'

She blinked hard and shook her head in astonishment, sliding the loose bun sagging at the back of her neck side-to-side a little, and Wil found himself staring at his sister quizzically, for her ability to reconcile herself to their situation, something that took him nearly a week to do, perplexed him incredibly. Not only that, but his sister seemed different all of a sudden. More... familiar.

'And you don't feel confused, or conflicted about what's happened?'

'Wil, we had no choice,' she hauffed. 'And no, I'm not conflicted. It's happening like you said.' She looked apprehensive again.

'You asked where I've been all this time,' she quickly changed the subject. 'Drifting, basically. Annie said that when you were fogged, I was of no use to anyone, and with no memory, I was just left to dream on my own. But I wasn't totally alone. Annie checked on me. Every night apparently. Righting all her wrongs from the day. Undoing whatever she could from having to cover things up.' Steph's less-puffy, less-red face produced a pitying smile. 'I think the measures she's taken to try and get us remembering the last few years have been pretty punishing for her. And looking back at some of the things she's done, well I think there were foolish attempts along the way at hoping I could remember without you. Despite you, even.' Wincing thoughtfully, 'But it was never going to be that way, Wil,' she insisted, accepting an apparently lucid outlook on Annie's futile undertakings. 'We're nothing without each other.' She fixed her eyes up at him again. 'None of us are.   You. Me... Ben, Annie. She just can't see it yet.'

Then without warning she blurted, 'Oh my God—*Murphy!*' to which Wil involuntarily recoiled at the outburst.

'Murphy?' His expression was blank, expectant.

'*Murphy*, Wil. The Elusive Murphy! I can't believe you don't remember him.'

She then gasped, remembering something else.

'*What?*' He was becoming annoyed now.

'Annie's *boyfriend*...!' Her wide eyes begged him to realise this too. 'Good grief, Wil, *Murphy*...! How can you not remember?'

There was a calculation going on there. It was as if Wil could see her back-tracking over their conversation, appreciating his questions had been a harmless plea to fill in the gaps Aeolus decided should be left blank for whatever reason, and something in her relented,

'All those times Annie said she had this boyfriend Murphy, we made out like he was an imaginary person, because of course we'd forgotten who he actually was... *but he was as real as you and me,*' she declared. 'Of course he wasn't ever her boyfriend. Not actually. *Ugh.* We were so cruel.... How could any of us have forgotten him?'

'Maybe we can still find him,' Wil suggested.

'He was *The Elusive Murphy,*' she however enunciated. 'We'll never find him. He was always disappearing off. None of us knew his backstory. I mean, I'm trying to think where we first met him even.... Nope. Nothing. But maybe it's because not everything has come back to me all at once after one night. I might remember tomorrow though,' she said hopefully, cringing.

All of a sudden, the weirdness of this conversation hit Wil with debilitating apprehension. He ran his hands through his hair, overwhelmed and exhausted. What did it matter about one mysterious person when his own sister had actually come to know even greater things in what seemed a few hours? And why hadn't any of this information come to *him*? What was it that Annie did to fill all those gaps? And how could Steph be so calm, so almost self-assured about knowing what she knew when the consequences of having such knowledge should have turned her world upside down?

'So what did Annie do that you remember all this?' Wil asked in frustration, decisively changing the subject from Murphy.

'Seriously? I have no idea.'

'Did you have any indication in the week that something was going to happen—any dreams?'

'Nope.'

After a moment,

'I miss him, Wil. I miss Murphy.'

'I'm sure I'd miss him too,' he said flatly, 'if I could remember anything.' The odd but incredible ease with which his sister seemed to be accepting their situation made him feel further removed from it. As though she were the only one taking part in this mind-bending transformation. And it seemed to be happening as they spoke, for finding her down here in such distress, only to see her quickly embrace some sort of comforting nostalgia… it was a metamorphosis Wil could only liken to his experience at the window earlier in the week. But even they hadn't been this effective.

'Annie said you were having trouble. Don't worry, Wil, it will come. It's *already* coming.'

Wil let his shoulder slump against the wall and watched his sister give him a well-meaning grin.

'You know what I really miss?'

'No. What's that, Steph?' He folded his arms and smiled wryly.

'Ben. Being clever. Really clever. And to think, all this time I thought he was just an idiot' she rolled her eyes 'when not even half the stuff I ever said would have stuck if it weren't for him. It was Ben that got our minds working as one when we least expected. He isn't just a thick cuddly bear, you know. He really is properly clever.'

'He is,' Wil acknowledged without hesitation, now curious as to the Ben Steph knew from the dreams compared to real life. 'Ugh, *I wish I could remember….*'

'You remembered our codes.' Steph's hopeful expression did little to encourage him though. 'Annie said that Sadie did quite a bit to get you interacting with the dreams.'

'Yes, but I can't really trust *her* now can I?'

'Sadie? Maybe not,' Steph accepted with a cringe.

'There was something though' he however explained 'that didn't involve her. When I was sitting at the window in my bedroom, I had this like daydream thing, but more real. It was like the whole thing happened to strip back my assumptions about Aeolus. So I could finally see our plan.' Wil found himself explaining to Steph in detail his experience on the plain, to which they both agreed the ironically destructive little twister might actually have been Aeolus' first attempt at unblocking Wil's obstructed memory.

'Perhaps appreciating who Aeolus *is* is the beginning of remembering, Wil… of destroying everything in the way of restoring your affinity with him, so you can pick it up right where it had been left off.' She gave him her encouraging smile again. 'You've been in enemy fog. Who knows what he's got to try and undo,' she said honestly. 'Or what he simply can't. Either way, it's not going to be straightforward now, is it?'

'No,' Wil accepted vaguely, warily, aware of that thing in him again that made him feel as a shell. A Trojan horse.

'Annie said you should look through some of your old journals. Your diaries. You've always kept one. She said maybe one of them will spark a memory before we went off to London. Who knows, maybe you even wrote yourself a note.'

'Unlikely,' he sniffed. 'I can't even find—' But it occurred to Wil just then that maybe that's why it had gone missing. Because it held old messages. Old conversations. Ones obliterated from his memory, for he only started writing the more ambiguous poetry entries… *after the going-away party.* The entries before were in his narrative style. Wil suddenly saw a correlation. Saw how conversations were no longer recounted. The ambiguous entries of his poetry left a huge margin for their detail to become obscure at a later date. And what of those inconvenient little elements that managed to remain… well they would be confabulated into something new, filling in those disconcerting gaps with something less true, but more comforting somehow. This was how the mind reconciled proof of the inaccessible past. Wil recognised his own intense hate for Annie had been one such filler he hoped never to indulge in again. How he suddenly wished he knew where that diary was. 'I can't even find the journal from the year before Mulbryn,' he realised. 'I have been looking.'

'Well, it's somewhere,' Steph determined. 'Or someone has it. And if it's not you… and it's not me….'

'I thought maybe Annie,' he confessed 'but only because she's here on her own sometimes.'

'Yeah, well so is Ben....'

'I'll ask him,' Wil decided, stepping out of the doorway and into the pantry as his sister made for the edge of the toilet lid as though readying to get up.

She dropped her tissues into the bin in the corner and turn out the light.

Just then, Wil caught his breath, for it was beautifully, painlessly pitch black all of a sudden.

'Sorry... I'll get the other light on,' Steph muttered as she brushed by. 'Just a second...' she grunted from the other side of the pantry, clearly fumbling behind the chair with something. 'I'm trying... to....'

The standing lamp over by the armchair came on suddenly.

'Good grief!' he cried out, squinting and turning his head.

'Keep your voice down,' Steph whispered sharply. 'Now come and take a seat.' She took the armchair and nodded for him to pull up a stool. 'Now seeing as you can't be left alone and' she strained her neck, peering up at the clock over the doorway 'it's pretty much morning... I thought I could tell you where our little Friends come from.' That thing she did with a single eyebrow just then, arching it so, both amused and intrigued Wil.

'Go on, then,' he said, straddling a stool.

Taking precautions, she swept her eyes to the rooms above, and to the darkness beyond the doorway into the kitchen. 'You know someone would love for us *not* to have this conversation, Wil. So listen to what I *do* have a chance to say about our lovely Aeolus as much as what I don't.'

Within five minutes, Wil heard how the creatures were actually particles, present long before the Earth and sun. And that when the universe came to be, they were attracted to the small places that harboured electrical charge. In the same way the loose matter and energy came together from space to produce an earth—*a human*—these tiny packets of energy evolved into something that coalesced with human thought.

Steph then explained with increasing pace (or simply highlighted Wil's waning difficulty in keeping up) how the creatures worked as quantum objects, appearing in and out of time, and saw themselves as saving humanity, something that hadn't even occurred to him. Basically, they were slowly evolving the human conscience to think as one balanced mind, to ensure survival of the race. To prevent human extinction. That mental, daily conflict born out of this symbiotic, evolutionary process therefore, was a weeding out of a sort.

'Survival of the fittest,' Steph went on, rubbing her shins as though a little cold. 'Unfortunately, neither can dominate the other because they are two opposing forces themselves. And I don't mean like Conservative and Labour or Republican and Democrat, but more like the two poles of a magnet. They're made up of the same thing, but with intrinsically opposing, separate characteristics. You'd think this should prevent them from interacting and yet they do. In fact, they manage to maintain completely complimentary ranges and strengths, are incapable of dominating one another... yet they are also entangled.'

She let the word hang there as she pulled her sleeves into her fists.

'Entangled?' Wil scratched the back of his head.

'Entangled with each other,' Steph said coyly, 'and entangled with us.' She watched his expression change from intrigue to a frown. 'I know. They now rely on *us* to maintain their state—their ideal, balanced state. And we can't be taken out of their equation until we all balance one another out equally.' Here, Steph opened her eyes wide and leaned forward over her knees. 'And that balance, Wil, the balance that can extract us effortlessly from their busy little dance… that's *the single mind* they've wanted us to achieve all along.'

Wil sat there for a moment and thought about this. 'So this single mind,' he tried understanding, 'is that basically us losing our autonomy? That the individual makes decisions for the benefit of the group?'

'Exactly. Basically, until we give up our autonomy, everything we do in the name of it drives them closer to us. Entangles them that much more.'

'And if we don't?' he posed.

'Don't give up our autonomy? Then we make decisions that inevitably conflict with human survival and at some point we all die.'

He sniffed at the conclusion, for his fatigue was beginning to make everything feel far-fetched. 'And what happens to them, then?'

'They move on. But they can't until one or the other happens. Until we achieve a single mind, or become extinct. Whatever we do, they'll get their result in the end regardless of how we do or don't respond,' Steph maintained. 'One day, they will leave us,' she said firmly. 'And it's probably worth mentioning that they can last infinitely longer compared to us.' She stared at him, pressing the point. 'Infinitely.'

'Are you saying that whatever this thing is they're trying to do is going to destroy us, despite their efforts to save us, because they outlive us no matter?'

'I'm just saying...' she clarified, 'we might destroy ourselves thinking we're getting rid of them. That's all.'

Wil let out a tired sigh and briefly rubbed his eyes with his thumb and finger.

'There's another element to all this,' she went on. 'And that is that they have the ability to affect change throughout generations. One little tweak in my head can be genetically passed onto my children.'

Here, Wil ran a hand through his hair and dipped his chin to his chest. 'I'm sorry,' he said with a sigh, rubbing his lids closed, 'I don't have the brain power to hear any more.'

The dark backdrop soothed like a balm.

'Open your eyes *now*, Wil!' she shouted, to which he did just that. 'They're *open*...'

'They are *now*....' She rolled her eyes, annoyed. 'Why don't you get up and walk around or something?'

'I'm fine.'

'I'm carrying on then, because you need to hear this stuff. Yes, they can control our genes,' she wasted no time explaining. 'They can influence our biochemical response to a situation which then influences whether a gene is expressed in one human body. And of course, that one body might pass the same influenced material onto their offspring.'

'Okay, I get it,' he said wearily, throwing his head back. 'They affect gene expression.'

'*They make our children inherit our fear*,' Steph corrected sharply, drawing his attention back. He brought his head level and gave her an odd look.

'*Inherit our fear?* How's that?'

'Experience trauma or severe abuse and the chemical structure in your body changes,' she said simply, shrugging. 'Molecules increase or decrease in number, blocking or freeing the function of others. An emotion becomes a physical process in your body. Ultimately, this determines whether one gene is turned on or off. ...Whether you have Mum's phobia of clowns or Gran's fear of dogs.'

Wil blinked slowly, his mouth agape slightly.

Just then, the toilet flushed upstairs in Mum and Dad's room, causing Wil and his sister to freeze. Their eyes fixed to the corner of the ceiling behind the armchair, listening as faint creaks moved overhead from the en-suite… towards the bed… then across the large bedroom to the hall door almost directly above Wil.

'Turn out the light,' Wil whispered, waving a hand to hurry her.

Without hesitation, Steph dove for the switch around the back of the chair.

At that moment, a door along the hall could be heard opening quietly, then closed just the same.

'The light's on in my room,' Steph rasped, sounding panicked as she grabbed her brother's arm in the darkness. 'She knows I'm down here. You hide—under the table—I can pretend to use the loo—hurry—we can't have her asking questions!'

'No Steph!' He grabbed her hand sliding off his arm as floorboards groaned above in the direction of the landing. 'I've turned your light off before I came down. And closed the door. Listen.' Mum was nearly at the top of the landing now. 'She's not walked back to our rooms. If you don't want her asking questions, then don't go in that loo,' he said firmly. 'We won't have to answer anything if she doesn't find us.'

'Then quick,' Steph breathed, pulling him by the crook of the arm. 'Hide in here.'

Chapter Thirty

Cupboard

With heads stooped and pressed together, they both listened silently as the kettle boiled.

'We could have just hidden under the table,' he whispered irritably.

'The *two* of us? There wasn't space,' Steph insisted, hissing, her warm damp breath creeping down his neck. 'Now *shhh*.'

'Less space than a broom cupboard?' he argued, pushing his hip against the angled broomstick behind him.

As the kettle rumbled to a climax and Wil heard the door of the fridge open and close, he carefully shifted his shoulder further into the corner his side, silently sliding the ironing board away as far as it would go. The space was at least a foot shorter than him, most certainly not wide enough for his shoulders side-to-side but thankfully, rather deep.

'There was no other place,' his sister spat into the darkness, making the cupboard suddenly feel half its size now as she too began to shift position. 'It was either here or the loo—and what would it have looked like if she *actually* had to use the toilet and found the two of us in there?'

'Probably a bit better than this…' he muttered.

The kettle clicked off.

'I mean it, Wilden—*shh*.'

They both heard Mum make a cup of tea, and drop a teaspoon onto the hard stone floor. Pinching desperately at his side of the stick-insect knob, Wil suddenly hoped his mother would have no need for the broom and dustpan at his feet.

Finally, the sliver of light around the edges of the cupboard door disappeared. There was a faint click over by the foot of the stairs and Wil eased his sister out into the dark pantry as Mum creaked her way overhead and back to bed.

'We've got about an hour before she comes down again,' Steph said quietly, turning on the lamp again but dimming it so that it looked like the faint glow of dawn, 'unless we have another perfectly-timed interruption. Remember what I said about listening to what I have a chance to say about our lovely Aeolus as much as what I don't?' She sat in the armchair again and looked at her brother with a pointed, cautioning expression.

Just then, a phone went off.

Wil felt the noisy vibration in his pocket and hurried to turn it off.

'It's Annie,' he said as the screen glowed upwards across his face, accentuating the dark circles around his eyes. 'She wants Ben's number.'

Steph's eyes widened. 'Well, give it to her.'

Wil sent the number. 'What do you think she's gonna do?'

'I don't know,' Steph checked the clock, 'but I need to see her. It's 6 and I needed to look at a few things up in her room.' Wil took that to mean the sketches. 'And if she's awake now, I can go for my run...you can say I only just left when Mum or Dad get up... and then it won't seem out of the ordinary. Text me when they come down, and I'll tell them I've gone to Annie's if I'm going to stay long.'

'Okay,' he said distractedly, wondering if Annie had a similar interaction with Ben in the night as she had with Steph.

Steph headed for the kitchen then stopped, having apparently remembered something.

'You mustn't fall asleep, Wil,' she said firmly. 'You'll need to go for a walk,' she told him, however, his phone vibrated again.

Ben's message glowed against their concentrated expressions despite the early sunrise finally creeping into the room:

Crazy night! Can I come round? Now!

Wil wrote back,

Yes, I'm awake. Park along Wide Way. Come up through the gate. I'll let you in at the side. M and D still asleep.

As they both watched the screen, Wil wondered what exactly made Ben's night *crazy*. Had he been approached by the Anti-Aeolus of Sadie's dreams... or bombarded by any number of other Enemies?

Whether Annie was right about the consequences of dream-dragging, Wil was determined to tell his best friend everything. The minute he arrived. Hopefully, whatever happened during his crazy night would help him to believe it.

Another text.

'He's already in the village,' Wil read. 'He's just parked. He must have been on his way when he sent the first text.'

Steph gave her not-surprised expression. 'I'm going to head off then,' she decided. Quickly she went and opened the dryer, and sifted through the items until she found a pair of shorts and a top. 'If Annie's asked for Ben's number,' she said, looking for the match to a sock in her hand, 'I imagine she's trying to get him remembering like me. So don't be afraid to tell him everything you know, right along with what you don't.' Having found the sock, she pushed everything else back into the drum and changed in the loo. 'If he's going to be here with you,' she said a moment later, ready for her run, 'then text me if you end up being on your own. That, or your conversation with him turns unexpectedly dull. Somehow though,' she tightened her hair into a high ponytail, 'I can't imagine that will happen.'

Before Ben had a chance to creep up the path, she had gone. And it was in those few moments as Wil waited by the terrace doors that he wondered what precisely his sister *needed to look at*.

Chapter Thirty-One

Ben

Ben came as a black silhouette, crunching quietly along the path towards the open door. If Wil hadn't known any better, that familiar figure he believed to be his best friend may well have been a complete stranger, for the determined gait Ben exhibited there in the darkness became so starkly unfamiliar, Wil found himself closing the door slightly to the hunched form until he became certain of its identity.

'Hey,' Ben greeted from across the terrace. 'Sorry for the short notice' he whispered anxiously, slipping into the house. There was a weight there. A heavy burden about his friend Wil had not seen before.

'Pantry?' Wil suggested as he latched the door.

'Probably best.' Ben swiped his brow with the back of his hand and headed straight through. 'Geez...' he breathed. 'Looks like you've had an interesting night too.'

'What makes you say that?'

'The circles under your eyes.'

However, Ben quickly forgot about them and instead poked his head into the broom cupboard.

'Yes. Well. I can't fall asleep,' Wil said plainly. This statement however did not faze Ben, for he began walking cautiously towards the end wall there, scanning corners, surreptitiously checking behind doors and furniture. 'I mean, *I can*,' Wil corrected, eyeing his preoccupied friend more closely now, 'but... I shouldn't.'

'So Annie said,' Ben noted, still distracted.

'Did she now?' Wil tried to sound disgusted as usual, unsure as to whether Ben felt any differently about her. 'And what else did she tell you about me?'

Apparently giving up on looking, Ben's bulky frame turned slowly around. 'Nothing compared to Aeolus, Wil,' he said boldly, pointedly. Only, Wil was so relieved to hear him say Aeolus' name that he completely missed his friend's meaning.

'And here I was worried about how I'd get you to believe me,' Wil confessed as he went and gave Ben a huge hug. 'For someone who's just gone through such a transformation, you seem to be taking it all rather well.'

But it quickly became clear Ben wasn't.

'We were pressed for time. Well, Annie was,' Ben sniffed, irritated. 'One second the memories *weren't* there, the next, they were.'

The direct result was that Ben found himself accepting his old mind with a distrust of its timing.

'But we're all remembering,' Wil encouraged, not understanding. 'You should be glad.'

'I am glad, Wil. I am. But I'm not an idiot either. Think about it. *Why now?* We promised that would be the first question we'd ask ourselves when we got to this point... but of course, you can't remember that.' The annoyed tone in Ben's voice accused. 'Annie's barely been holding it together... so maybe that's the reason why,' he permitted. 'But that doesn't explain why the other things aren't falling into place. Murphy's nowhere to be found... and Annie said she's not seen him since... well, you know.' Ben threw a loathsome glance towards his shoulder indicating the past, when they forgot. 'Something's trying to stall us, Wil,' he muttered, dissatisfied and shaking his head. 'We didn't account for something... that's why we're stuck—why *you're* stuck.' He brushed by, absorbed in thought, and went towards the kitchen. Then stopping at the doorway, he realised something and came back. 'Murphy was supposed to be here,' he declared, making Wil realise that's who he was looking for behind the furniture and doors. 'Where is he, Wil?'

'I don't know... I don't even know who *Murphy* is....'

'Seriously?' The uncomprehending look on Ben's face made Wil realise this individual couldn't be more significant. 'Annie said it would take time...' he looked Wil up and down, mildly disgusted, to which Wil found himself almost not recognising this version of his friend. 'And Aeolus, well he obviously has his concerns,' Ben said flippantly, chucking his brow to the side. He then squared with Wil, intimating that he knew all about the potential Wil had to betray him, *them.* 'But I didn't think it was this bad....'

'I'm sorry, Ben,' Wil said helplessly, now understanding his meaning fully. 'I can't help what I don't remember.'

'Yes, well that's the other thing, Wil. *Why* aren't you remembering? That was the plan—the whole plan. *You.* And what good are you to us—what good are *we* to *you*—if you're now in this position?' He looked at Wil's crestfallen expression with disappointment. 'I imagine you can't even remember the fail-safe. The one thing none of us knows—none of us... but you. What good was all that now, all that secrecy and whatever it was you were doing?'

Wil looked at him confusedly.

'You said it would guarantee you'd remember,' Ben asserted. 'A *fail-safe*, you said.'

'I don't know...' Wil tried recalling something, anything. 'Annie didn't mention any of that when she—'

'—Well she wouldn't have, would she?' Ben said sharply. 'Out of all of us, she knew the least. You didn't *want* her to know.'

Of course, she knew nothing until it was already happening, Wil was acutely aware. Until it was all too late. Ashamed to have ensured that was the case, Wil slumped onto a stool.

'You shouldn't have put yourself in that position,' Ben reproved. 'You shouldn't have put *us* in that position. The least you could have done was tell one other person.'

'Maybe I did. I'm sure I would have told someone,' Wil said more assuredly, having been outwitted by his old self after trying to get Steph to tell him why they forgot in the first place.

'And who would that have been then?' Ben pressed. 'Of all the people you *might* have told... *who?*'

Wil's eyes lowered to his hands. His knees came together under the table. It was apparent to him that Ben thought there was only one person it should have been.

'Maybe I was trying to protect you by not telling you,' Wil found himself defending. 'I wouldn't have done it otherwise, would I?' But for some strange reason, Wil felt a guilty sinking in his stomach when he said those words. He could only hope they were the case.

'You never did get this into your head, did you?' Ben tried saying calmly, showing a side Wil truly hadn't seen before, or remembered seeing. 'It's easy to pick us off when we're scattered. We have to avoid it at all cost.'

'I appreciate that,' Wil acknowledged firmly, however he couldn't help see a necessary and obvious exception to such advice—the very one which restored Ben to his present state of mind: Annie. 'But we must have known some of our decisions involved risk. We must have known that allowing one of us to take a risk meant the others would have been spared. Take Annie, for instance—'

'—No *you*—*you* kept Annie from knowing,' Ben spat, now leaning and pointing his finger over the table top. 'That wasn't *our* decision. You *took away* our opportunity to tell her.'

Wil crumpled, taken aback.

'I didn't know I did that,' he admitted quietly, unable to look his friend in the face. 'I don't know why I didn't tell you... or why I didn't tell her... or why Murphy's not here...or the reason why I can't remember a thing. I don't know why any of this is the way it is but... *it just is*—and I can't change it.' He closed his eyes regretfully, adding, 'I want to believe it was for a good reason, that I had no other choice... and that if you were me....'

Ben stood there wounded, already betrayed. Then as Wil watched him sit his solid frame down, it occurred to him that this was the beginning of the dream-drag effect. Friends, turning against one another. Of course, this wasn't the mopey Ben that would withdraw in conflict. This was the Ben that had endured the very battles Annie sketched across her walls. This Ben was a soldier, Wil could see now, built like one even, and the mind he had been restored to had to be absolutely clear about who his friends and enemies were, and what he could expect of them.

'Steph might know something,' Wil said hopefully, admiring Ben just then for not walking away, for there was no way either of them could be ignorant now of the drag. 'Maybe I told her.'

This suggestion seemed to please Ben, for the strained tick in his jaw eased. Even the affronted physical distance he maintained at the table decreased a little. Maybe Aeolus was alleviating things there in Ben's head, Wil was tempted to believe.

'Okay,' Ben relented, exhaling. 'We'll talk to Steph.'

After a few minutes of preoccupied silence and the occasional glance at one another, Wil said finally,

'I miss the old you.'

'This is the old me.'

'I mean—'

'—I know what you mean, Wil. It's just…' Ben gave careful thought to his answer '…right now… I'm in two minds.'

'I understand.'

'Yes,' his eyebrows raised, 'I'm sure you do.'

Wil could not help but think of the Trojan horse just then… the chat that Ben no doubt had with Aeolus before coming here. As Wil began to wonder what exactly Aeolus said, neither he nor Ben seemed to notice the creaking above their heads that then moved along the hall and down the stairs.

'You two are up early!' Mum said in surprise from the doorway, startling them both in their extended silence.

'*Geez Liz*…. You scared the life out of me!' Ben exaggerated, beating his chest with his fist. He suddenly seemed his old self again.

'Sorry boys. I thought I heard someone downstairs a few minutes ago.' She seemed glad that this was in fact the case. 'Are you two okay? Wil you look like you've not had any sleep. What's going on with your eyes?'

Wil gave a dismissive answer, then followed Ben into the kitchen where already, Mum was cracking eggs and pulling sausages out of the fridge.

'You boys hungry?'

'Always, Liz.' Ben puffed his chest up and rubbed his stomach for effect.

This slightly dopey, uninhibited Ben now seemed odd to Wil. Fake. Especially after the exchange with the same person in the other room. But no sooner had Wil acknowledged his thoughts, he felt betrayed by them. Probably in the same way Ben felt betrayed by him, Wil recognised. Annoyed with himself, he went out to the garden.

A few minutes later,

'*Oi.* You sulking?' Ben said from the top step.

'I'm thinking.'

Wil could hear steps through the grass coming up from behind.

'About…?' Ben came alongside him.

'What else?'

'Listen, Wil. I'm not angry. There's a reason for everything. And sometimes we don't get the privilege of knowing why. In fact, sometimes the entire privilege is in not knowing why.'

'Yes, but you said I didn't give you the choice. Here I was thinking I did us all some great good, when actually, I just—'

'—Forced me to follow...?'

There was an uncertain glance between them. But then, Ben looked his own hefty rugby frame up and down, insinuating that it would be quite difficult for anyone to force him to do anything.

'Wil, the only reason I wish you had told *me*... was because I knew I'd feel this way coming out the other end. And here we are,' he hauffed, shaking his head. 'I was just letting off steam in there, that's all.'

'Legitimate steam though.' Wil folded his arms against the morning chill. 'I don't know who I am anymore—who I was. Maybe I did try and... I don't know... deceive you. Everyone.'

'Listen, Wil, there's nothing in this,' Ben tried assuring. 'You and I are best friends outside the dreams, and inside. Getting this far changes nothing. Getting this far was what we hoped for all along. We can't just throw it away because... everything's not suddenly clear.'

'It's not just what Aeolus told you though,' Wil pointed out. 'There's the dream-drag too. Did Annie tell you about it?'

'She did.'

'Well that, along with the thing Aeolus is worried about' Wil stared at the lock on the shed '...well, I get the strange feeling that you're all afraid of me. Of what I might do.' He turned to Ben. 'That you know more than you want to, and coming out here,' he threw a dismissive glance back towards the house, '...you're just trying to be careful with me.'

'Of course I am. But that's not because of the drag. I'm determined to make sure the drag doesn't affect us. But the other thing, Aeolus' concern, well I have no choice but to be careful with you, because you're an unknown quantity right now. In limbo. *And none of us have done this before.*'

'Or maybe we have a thousand times,' Wil posed, 'but we've just forgotten.'

'Maybe,' Ben considered. 'But I can't remember those times. Right now, I've only got this one. So of course I'm going to do everything I can to preserve what I believe we have.' The boldness behind Ben's words, despite the potential traitor before him, caused Wil's eyes to well up.

'I hope I never betray you, Ben.' He quickly wiped an eye.

'I hope you don't either, Wil.' Ben punched him playfully in the shoulder, knocking him sideways a little.

They stood silently at the end of the garden for a few minutes, their footprints trailing behind them in the frosty grass. Then as Wil unfolded his arms and stuffed his fists into his vast pyjama pockets, Ben brought up out of nowhere,

'Annie found my happy place amusing.'

'Your *happy place?*' Wil then realised. 'Your *Initial....*'

'Mmm. Obviously I don't remember any of it, seeing as I can't remember anything since we forgot up until this morning, but she told me all about your experience in it with Sadie. You've not told Steph about it, have you?'

'Of course not. Why would I?' Better still.... 'Why do you care whether she knows?' But Ben's tight-lipped, impassive glare suddenly moved to the frosted hills surrounding the village. 'Something happened last night, didn't it?' Wil's eyes narrowed. 'Ben? *Ben....* What did you do with my sister last night?'

'*Shhh!*' He looked over his shoulder at the house.

'Please tell me you didn't touch her....'

'Of course I didn't!' he wheezed, keeping his voice down. 'I'm not a complete idiot!'

'Then what?' Wil probed more seriously now. 'And what happened to Shellie? You got over *her* rather quickly....'

'Just *shush*, will you?'

'Then what? What happened?' However much Ben had squirmed there, Wil became acutely aware that this was not his friend's usual manner when under pressure with the ladies. Ben was, for the most part, cool. Measured. And it crossed Wil's mind that maybe his best friend just might fancy the one girl that could actually get in the way of their friendship. 'But you were so set on Shellie...' Wil muttered, confused.

'Yeah, that was until I saw her kissing a bloke in the queue for popcorn.'

'You're joking...'

'I wish.'

'And it was actually *her, your* Shellie?'

'The very one.'

'Sorry.' That inspirational rant Ben gave at the car about being more pro-active in relationships now lost its gloss. 'So what's this with Steph, then?'

'Nothing, you're making a big deal out of nothing. We had a good time and she was nice to me, that's all.'

'She was nice?'

'She was,' Ben said unashamedly, intimating that of course her brother might not readily see that side of her. 'I had literally just been going on about how amazing Shellie was, of course knowing really nothing about her... when suddenly, there she was. Standing with someone who could not be more opposite in appearance to me. Thin... tall... not a red-blonde speck on him....' Ben rolled his eyes. 'And as soon as I convinced myself they were probably siblings, or at the most friends, the gangly giant bent down and kissed her. Properly. I was gutted. And Steph was really lovely about it,' he confessed sheepishly. 'Lovely enough to remind me that there are plenty of girls out there who might actually appreciate the lengths I go to. I'm not saying Steph is one of them, but I don't want you telling her about my happy place, especially now that we're both in the know. D'you hear?'

'Okay. But surely she'll find out if we try and meet up with you or something. In the dreams, I mean.'

'No, it's changed. The Initials are all changing. Besides, shame doesn't exactly make it feel safe anymore now, does it?'

'Probably not. So that's it? No more Shellie? What about Wednesdays in the planetarium?'

'I don't see the point really, but it would be tricky to change now... especially after I came off as so keen.'

Ben had been keen. Unusually keen. And thinking on it now, Wil was assured Ben's infatuation had secured the use of the planetarium... which then prompted that determined search for Sadie... who couldn't wait to catapult Wil into the incredible world of the dreams.

'Your efforts have not been in vain, Ben. If it weren't for your hopes with Shellie.' He went on to explain the compelling dreams concerning Sadie. How their double meaning stretched to real life in the classroom... the planetarium... and led Wil to finally meet her under the tree and eventually at her house—all of which shed light on Sadie's predicament with her sister Lily and the other Aeolus.

'Why didn't you tell me any of this?' Ben seemed more surprised than hurt.

'Because I thought I was going crazy—I hardly believed it myself, much less thought someone else might believe me.'

'I would tread carefully with her, Wil' Ben said as he tried poking a garden gnome upright with his foot. 'If she doesn't know whose side she's on, you certainly won't… so assume she's not on yours. Remember? *Fret the Tret, share with the Tare.*'

Wil's head shot around and fixed on Ben's concentrating face, for the gnome he was still battling wouldn't stand upright in the patch of long dewy grass. 'That's what Sadie told me,' he pointed out. 'Does everyone say that?'

'No…' Ben said distractedly, for he was getting annoyed with the garden feature and in a moment of frustration bent down and set it upright with his hands. 'I don't know anyone else who used to say it outside you and me. When you remembered, that is.'

'Why would only the two of us say it?'

'Because I made stuff up like that all the time. Little rhymes to help us remember things. *Aeolus'll bail us…. Dream a dream of sixth sense, an Imposter full of lies, four and twenty shadows to get us through the night….*'

Wil winced, trying to focus now, for his thoughts moved to a vague, dim place. 'So you're saying *you* made that up?'

'Uh, *yes*….'

'When then—when did you make it up, Ben?'

'Back *then*.'

'And did loads of people start using it?'

'I just told you,' Ben insisted, eyeing his friend dubiously now, '*you* and *I* knew it. *Just the two of us*. It was like an inside joke or something, I don't know. What's all the fuss about it?' He looked at Wil curiously, waiting for some sort of an answer, to which none came, for Wil was trying desperately to rationalise why Sadie would use a rhyme Ben made up from over three years ago that only Wil and he knew. 'Are you gonna tell me what's going on?'

'I guess I'm just trying to figure out how Sadie knew it?' Wil explained, wondering why Ben hadn't already found that odd. *Were you hoping I wouldn't notice,* he found himself suspecting, not wanting to throw such words at his friend. *Are you hiding something from me, some connection to Sadie that started even before the dome?* he couldn't help think. *You knew where her class was,* he wanted to blurt. 'And I guess maybe I'm wondering why you didn't think it odd when I mentioned that very thing to you, a second ago,' Wil was already accusing. 'I mean, if you came up with it, then how did she know? And why did she make such a point to tell me, *more than once?*'

'Bloody hell,' Ben stepped away, defensive. 'What are you trying to say?'

Wil saw genuine shock there. The inference fully felt. And feeling a jerk for it, Wil felt a gloom leave him; its work done.

'I didn't mean…' he confessed resentfully, confusedly, feeling foolish. 'I'm sorry.'

They were silent for a few minutes as Wil imagined the drag working him.

'She could have gotten it from any number of sources,' Ben said pragmatically, indicating from his tone that he wasn't just trying to absolve himself of any wrong-doing. Indicating from his tone too that he wasn't about to let the drag take hold. 'And she could have literally had a moment, just as I did, where someone else influenced her to come up with the same thing. Now from experience, I think the real question isn't *how* she got the rhyme,' Ben proposed delicately, 'but *why?* My guess is that it was meant to cause confusion, division… which I dare say has done the trick, don't you?'

'Yes, I think so,' Wil agreed humbly, grateful for his friend's restraint.

'You know, she may be totally oblivious to where that rhyme has been, because this is what happens, Wil. The Tret—the Enemies—they take something seemingly significant, and I stress the word *seemingly* here, and they try to get you to latch onto it… to feel connected to it… but really, there's no connection at all outside the one you're actually constructing for them… the distorted story you're writing in your head to make it all fit together.' Growing frustrated now, Ben said emphatically, 'Those words mean nothing. They were an inside joke. Don't make any more of them, okay? There could be a thousand reasons as to why Sadie knew about them and wanted you to remember them. But in case you're wondering, I didn't know her before we forgot; I didn't know her in the dreams. And I certainly never told her anything.' He eyed Wil, pressing the point. 'And I have a well-enough intact memory now to be certain of that.'

Mum suddenly poked her head out the French doors and announced breakfast. 'It's a bit cold, you two all right out here?'

'Yeah, just girl troubles,' Ben called out, diffusing all suspicion of anything more.

'Well it's here when you're ready....'

'It's just the drag,' Wil said to Ben as they headed back to the house.

'Well, then we'll fight it,' his friend assured. 'One distorted story at a time.'

But after breakfast, throughout the shower and under Ben and Steph's watchful eye later that morning, Wil still felt something about those words was right there in front of him, yet completely out of reach.

'You shouldn't just sit there, you know,' Steph warned, flicking through a magazine on the couch. She shot Ben a look.

'It might be best if we go for a ride or something, Wil,' Ben promptly suggested. 'Something out-and-about.'

The way they tag-teamed....

'I'm fine.'

'It's your watch when we leave,' Steph cautioned Ben quietly while Mum and Dad were in the pantry. 'Don't let him fall asleep. And I wouldn't advise sitting *here* for much longer.'

Twenty minutes later, Mum, Dad and Steph were getting on their coats and filing into the hall.

'Do you need anything, Love?' Mum offered, her Costco list in hand.

'Nope. But we could do with one of those nice meat platters, couldn't we Ben?' Wil threw him a weary smirk, to which Mum promptly scribbled the item onto her scrap of paper.

'I won't refuse edible, free food,' Ben sneered back.

They piled out and before Mum closed the door, she called out,

'There's a package here for next door, Wil. It came this morning. Would you mind dropping it off when you have a chance?'

'Yes, fine....'

.

Chapter Thirty-Two

Vivienne

'It's not like I'm gonna fall asleep on the doorstep.'

'Yes, but what if she invites you in and offers you a soothing cup of tea? Or a bed?'

Wil couldn't tell if this was Goofy Ben being ridiculous, or Wise Ben giving him sound, albeit odd, advice.

'She won't offer me a bed, Ben. At the most, she'll just want to have a lonely-old-lady chat.'

Reluctantly, Ben went over and sat on Blake. 'Then I'll be here...' he promised, picking up a remote '...*waiting*....'

Wil tucked the package under his arm and went around to the front of the manor. He glanced up at the empty window, expecting to see the neighbour. However, at the portico, noise could be heard from deep inside the house. Someone was certainly home.

Wil pointed his finger towards the brass surround of the antique doorbell, then stopped midway. He stared at the circles within circles etched there into the metal and it occurred to him that perhaps it was best just to leave the package on the doorstep. But as he looked over the parcel, he noticed the *24-Hour Express Delivery/Next Day Service* stickers plastered all over it. Whatever was in his hands seemed important. Sighing, he pressed the brass button and listened as the bell sounded throughout the house.

'Hello...?' A parroty voice came from a small box mounted beside the door.

'Uh, hi there. Mrs Hobbes?'

'Yes….' An orchestra played loudly in the background.

'I'm Wilden Stokes, from next door. Next door at West Side…. We received a delivery for you. I'm just dropping it off….'

'Ah, lovely…. Do come in. The door is unlocked.'

An automatic click let Wil in and as he pushed the door open, the music hit him. It came from the top of the grand carpeted staircase that curved up and to the left.

'Hello? Hello…?' He waited beneath the chandelier as sublime choral voices echoed throughout the vast space.

Just then, standing there didn't feel right.

As the parcel swung from Wil's fingertips, he wished now that Ben had come.

'Shall I just leave it here…?' he called out, leaning onto his heel and looking for a nearby piece of furniture to set the parcel on. With still no answer, and noticing the entrance hall was bare, Wil felt slightly justified inspecting the room to his right, for it was the detail in this part of the house that put his own into context.

The room beside him must have been a reception room or drawing room. Without going in, he noticed the abundance of natural light. Sunlight flooded past the hearth, with its crisp white surround, and brightened a large patterned rug bearing the marks and impressions of furniture that once rested on it. There was nothing else in there. Swags and tails around the windows, but no pictures or mirrors, not even above the mantle. Wil's curiosity turned to the room behind him.

There was the same disappointing absence of furniture, making him wonder how long the rooms had both been empty for, because this second room was just as splendid as the first, with a fireplace and two large windows to the front.

Just then, the music quieted, prompting Wil to return beneath the chandelier.

'I'm here on the landing,' an unsteady voice called out. 'Would you mind bringing it up?'

'Sorry… I wasn't sure if I should come up,' he explained, trailing his hand along the twisting bannister until, as he turned at the halfway point, he found Mrs Hobbes standing at the top, beaming down on him. To see her there, frail though smiling, and animated… Wil almost didn't recognise her. Of course he identified the unmoving, cold peculiarities of the person he knew from the window as they began to fade behind the pleasant welcome of this more personable woman, but it seemed the absence of the glass which had always stood between them was what now transformed her once-ghostly form into a real and living person.

'Thank you,' she said, nodding and patting down the dated green ruffles around the neck of her blouse. It occurred to Wil that whenever he saw this woman in the upper room, she wore only grey. Or white. Pale nightgowns probably. And her hair was always like an untidy halo. However now… she wore emerald green, and a matching blue and green argyle skirt. Her hair was scooped loosely back into a walnut-sized bun, and she wore pearls at her ears and neck. She looked as though she were going somewhere. 'Thank you, my dear.'

Wil quickened his pace and held the delivery out to her from a few steps below the landing.

'My mum signed for it. It arrived earlier this morning,' he said, realising she wasn't going to take it off him, for her hands remained in a mound at the pit of her stomach, covered with gauzy, white fingerless gloves. 'Would you like me to put it somewhere for you?'

'There is fine,' she indicated against the bannister her side. Wil stooped over the top step and left the package, then retreated, intending to be on his way.

'You're just in time,' she piped up, catching him back-foot down a step. 'I just poured myself a cup of tea when you rang… and as you've come all this way on my account…. Have you got time for a cup of tea with an old lady?'

They both smiled politely at one another, but Wil was apprehensive. Not only was he thinking of Ben's parting words, but he couldn't help think of the way Gran would treat family and carers near the end, inviting them for a cup of tea… then forgetting she'd done so… only to end up screaming them out of the house like they were criminal strangers. Having no indication of Mrs Hobbes mental state, he glanced at the set-up for signs of chaos, neglect. The vast landing looked like a posh waiting room, with a green chenille two-seater and matching armchairs clustered around an antique coffee table. Along the wall to the right he spotted an under-counter fridge with a telly on top, and a small work surface next to it with a kettle and a few kitchen storage tins. Clearly Mrs Hobbes used the spacious landing like a lounge. *Mobility issues could explain this*, Wil thought. They could explain too the appearances in the window and the intercom and automatic door. Maybe even the loud music he often heard through the wall. Assured there was nothing strange here, Wil was happy to take the few steps to have a cup of tea, seeing already the steam wafting up from a teapot on a little round table between the two chairs. It waited amid a cluttered tray of cups and saucers, milk and sugar, as though she had been expecting visitors.

'Please, call me Vivienne.' She directed him to sit.

'Thank you… Vivienne.'

She poured him a drink, passed him the tiny little teacup and took a seat herself.

'I couldn't help but notice the lovely rooms downstairs as I came up. It's such a beautiful house.' He was hoping she would explain their emptiness.

'It is. It was an even better home while the children were growing up.' She took a quiet, eye-averting sip, causing Wil to notice the pale ring around the cloudy blue of her eyes. 'But everyone has moved on and with Charles gone, he was my late husband, I've given nearly all the furniture to the offspring. There's no point in keeping what you don't need and never see.'

'No, of course not,' Wil agreed sympathetically. 'And how long have you lived here?'

'It will be 40 years next summer.' The realization of that many years seemed to be sinking in for her just then, but delightfully so.

'Wow,' Wil said, astonished, 'to think of anyone these days living in one place for that long. You must love this house.'

'Indeed. All my happy memories are here.'

'So…' Wil calculated '…you would have been here before they divided it up….'

'I was here before a lot of things were divided up,' Vivienne admitted wryly.

Wil unwittingly finished his cup of tea instead of making it last as his hostess had and found himself pretending the last drips were substantial amounts. After a few breathy sips, he began to feel silly for holding the empty cup and set it a little too noisily onto the saucer.

'Sorry,' he said, wincing. 'Have we ever given you our number?' he then asked, recovering from the clatter. 'We're only next door. If you ever needed anything, you could just give us a ring.'

'Your mother may have slipped a note through in the past, but don't worry. I have help and I'm checked on regularly,' she assured, offering a little plate of digestives.

Wil gratefully took one.

He noticed the almost ineffectual sips his neighbour managed from her teacup, which was still quite full, for every time she set it down onto the saucer, she had to carefully unhook her arthritic index finger from its handle. At this rate, he was going to be here for hours. It wouldn't be long before Ben would be coming to find him. Expecting him any second, Wil gazed up at the gold plaster detail in the dome ceiling above as Vivienne too nibbled on a biscuit. Then after a long minute or so, Wil looked at his watch as though it had only occurred to him to keep track of the time.

'I really ought to be getting back. I've got a friend at the house waiting for me. I said I'd only pop out for a second.'

'Before you go, Wilden. My hands.' Vivienne put her digestive down and held out her bruised, gnarled knuckles. 'My hands won't get through that package you brought, and I can't use scissors. Would you be kind enough to open it before you go?'

'Of course.' Wil got up and brought the large cardboard envelope over to the little table. He confirmed Vivienne's approval to tear through a short end and yanked the plastic thread clean through. There was something flat and white in there. Pulling it out, it was a large, vacuum-packed pillow.

'I'm afraid you'll have to take the plastic off as well,' she said apologetically.

'Of course.' It instantly expanded.

'Lovely. Now, I know I've asked quite a lot, but I have a pillowcase ready,' she nodded towards the hall. 'It's on the bed in the first room.' Again, Wil thought of Ben's warning, despite consenting with a grin.

Wil kept a few paces behind Vivienne's stiff and slow gait as he followed her down the hall. To their right was an extraordinarily long sideboard with a CD player going quietly on the near end, and a massive collection of family photos spread out in individual frames atop the rest of its surface. There must have been a hundred photos at least, of all sizes. Wil recognized a younger Vivienne standing cheerfully with a man he assumed to be Charles. And there were other poses with children around them. Further down, there were more modern pictures of young adults and babies, presumably grand-children, great-grandchildren. Amid the large quantity of frames standing up, Wil saw that a dozen or so were oddly turned face down, making their position look intentional as opposed to accidental. Wil's eye lingered momentarily on the nearest one, and he had the sudden urge to lift it, but then something in the frame beside it caught his eye. A lad no older than Wil himself was tucking Vivienne under his arm with a warm sideways hug. They clearly knew one another well, for there was a fondness in their smiles, a genuine liking. It looked recent. Something about that lad's eyes... the hair, even, was familiar. Wanting to take a closer look, Wil suddenly noticed Vivienne had disappeared into the first room on the left.

'It's just there,' she motioned with her gloved fist to the end of the bed.

'Ah yes.' Wil went over and dutifully stuffed it into the crisp white case, only to find that when he had finished, she had disappeared again.

'Before you go, I wanted to share this lovely piece with you,' she said, shuffling to the CD player. 'The acoustics up here are marvellous. You're not in too much of a hurry, are you?'

'Not too much,' he admitted, indulging her this time.

'You know, Wilden,' she called over her shoulder while trying to read the buttons, 'I feel like I know you so well.' The jaunty tone with which she said these words sounded like pleasant surprise.

'Yes, I often see you in the window.... I imagine it's a lovely view from there.'

'It is a lovely view,' she fumbled getting the CD jacket out, handed it to him, pointed out the track with a wrenched knuckle then went back to the player '...but that's not what I mean.'

Looking blankly at the lyrics in his hand, Wil's smooth, agreeable expression slowly wrinkled with the effort to understand what she did mean then.

'Listen,' she urged with a smile, then turned up the volume and closed her eyes. '*Listen.*'

The eerie lull of angelic and haunting harmonies lilted around them, and for a few minutes Wil was enraptured.

'Bliss,' Vivienne whispered, putting a hand to her heart when it had finished.

'That was lovely,' Wil said gratefully, remembering the lyrics there in his hand.

'It's the ceiling. The landing here does wonders for whatever I play.'

'*The Seal Lullaby*,' he read aloud. 'Rudyard Kipling,' he acknowledged, remembering his module at Mulbryn. For a second, the thought of that school as he stood there reminded him of something. Only, he couldn't think what.

'Indeed. None are immune to the perils of sleep,' Vivienne said plainly, again causing Wil's brow to strain slightly, for he wasn't sure which was more confusing: what he was trying to remember, or what she meant by her remark. 'Have you got time for one more?' She didn't wait for him to decline and skipped through a few tracks. 'This next one is my favourite. Number 16.'

'One more and then I really must be going,' Wil insisted, feeling himself unable to think clearly as he looked for number 16. It ended up being the last, entitled *Sleep*.

Out of the silence, smoothly discordant voices began to stretch and pull gradually away from him... starting quietly... then working higher and higher... until Wil felt quite uncomfortable around the neck as the choir reached its mournfully peaceful climax. The resolve was a strangling murmur of repetition that forced Wil to impatiently lift his neck and sniff the air with a slight degree of panic, for it felt that these voices were working like cement, hardening the muscles around his windpipe with every elongated vowel they uttered.

Seconds later, it was silent. Involuntarily, Wil drew in a deep, desperate breath, sounding as though he might sneeze, but all was back to normal. He could breathe fine again. And as Vivienne took out the disk and turned to him, he could not find a reason as to why the music made him feel so uncomfortable, made him feel constricted and suffocated towards the end there.

'*Sleep*,' Vivienne said coyly, raising her eyebrows, implying something.

'Yes....' Wil tried catching her meaning, hoping this was just the beginning of an unfinished sentence. But as Vivienne stood there, expectant, Wil's mind reverted back to the first set of lyrics... then to these looking up at him... and his whole reason for showing up on the doorstep. *The pillow.* 'Sleep... ' he pointed out lightly, hoping to diffuse the now strange atmosphere the absence of music left behind. 'I sense a theme developing here....'

'And you should.'

Vivienne's admonishing tone cut through all the pretence they had indulged in up to now, putting Wil instantly on his guard. And quite quickly, he noted how the old woman's demeanour had suddenly changed. Instead of the smiling frail granny who enjoyed the frivolity of music and domed ceilings on her landing, she now seemed to be a serious and patronizing authority figure who asserted her puzzling conclusion by pushing her shoulders back...straightening her spine... and assuming the posture of someone intellectually superior to most, despite the irreparable shape of her hands. But somehow seeing him intimidated by this mild transformation, this misunderstanding of character maybe, Vivienne subtly changed tack. She softened, then glared at him sideways, waiting. For what, Wil did not want to find out.

'Actually, I really ought to get back,' he said flatly, setting the folded card of lyrics back onto the sideboard. 'My friend Ben is waiting for me next door. I told him I'd be quick.'

As Wil headed for the stairs and again thought of Ben's parting words—certain the old woman couldn't be trying to get him to go off to sleep somewhere—that gravelly, unsteady voice called out to him, 'Wilden, I have something to return to you,' which stopped him in his tracks. 'I'm afraid I've had it for far too long and meant to return it ages ago.'

He turned and watched her pull open a drawer from the sideboard, under one of the face-down frames, and take out a black hardbound book.

'What is it?' he asked dubiously, slowly making his way back. As she held it out to him, it did look familiar, because when he opened it... it had his writing inside. 'Where did you get this?' he asked, dumbfounded. 'This is... my journal.'

'My intention was to return it sooner. You see, I needed something that, how shall I put it... wouldn't get into the hands of others.' Her words were calculating, holding something back, and it caused Wil's heart to race.

'I ought to get back' he decided, confused and slightly afraid as he closed his diary and made for the stairs again.

'Can I not persuade you to stay...?' the parroty voice strained after him.

'I'm sorry,' he called over his shoulder, 'I've—I've *got* to go!'

Wil did not run, but strode down the hall and across the landing, skipping steps along the stairs as he caught sight of the chandelier, then the front door.

'Well, you can either hear it from me or you can hear it from Aeolus,' Vivienne shouted after him, stopping him once again, for it felt as though his heart had dropped to the floor like an anchor. 'Either way, you're going to hear it.'

'How do you know that name?' Wil called back, cautious. Her delayed answer forced him to lumber back up a few steps, dragging that anchor behind him. 'How do you know that name?' he demanded calmly, making it perfectly clear he was unwilling to go any further than the half-dozen or so steps from the top, enough that he could just see her there down the hall.

'The same way you do,' she said apathetically. 'You think you're the only one?'

'I know I'm not.' His answer was defiant.

Mrs Hobbes began walking towards him, still stiff, but less encumbered.

'Good. Then you might even know Aeolus is not your friend,' she said plainly. 'Or that maybe he is,' she posed. 'And you'll know your Initial is safe… or that maybe it isn't.'

Her familiarity with these names suggested she used them often. The old woman now loomed over him at the top step and offered him a seat on the landing with a discreet fanning of her grotesque hand.

Sighing, Wil yielded.

'Are you familiar with the psychology behind persuasion?' Mrs Hobbes asked innocently, joining him as before.

'A bit,' he shrugged slightly, unable to see how this had anything to do with her connection to Aeolus. And his journal. Or anything else for that matter.

'Then you'll know we can easily become slaves to the reciprocation rule. You brought me a package. I offered you a cup of tea. You and I both know you didn't really want to stay. Aside from a bit of curiosity…' she studied his face '…and maybe compassion…' but then thought better of it, 'or perhaps pity. In any case,' she said dismissively, 'I persuaded you to accept my offer of tea as a repayment of your delivery. We were even. The conscience likes that.' She lifted the plate of digestives and offered him one, to which he recoiled slightly, refusing this time. 'But as you

313

accepted my kindness,' she put the plate down, indifferent, 'I could oblige you to go that step further.' Here, she glanced down at the hall, towards her bedroom. 'I shall sleep comfortably tonight because of it. But I'm afraid the same principles I used, Aeolus and the others are utilising all the time. Right this very minute, even. Keeping your friend from coming to find you… keeping your family from coming home too soon…. Over and over again, they do it. Take Sadie for instance.'

Wil's eyes widened.

'You know Sadie?'

'Never saw her in my life,' Mrs Hobbes said frankly, turning the spout of her teapot away from the edge of the tray. 'She has given you an understanding of the dreams, and because of this, you feel obliged to her. When one has been given such a gift, they have the urge to reciprocate. But how would they feel if they found it had all been a set-up?' She eyed the book there on his lap. 'Would they feel so obliged then?'

'What are you saying?'

Vivienne looked at him as if to say, *is it not obvious?*

'I'm saying, *we* have Lily.'

But after a few seconds, she was the one who began to look confused.

'Did you not hear me, Wilden?'

'Yes,' he said firmly, 'but what does that mean?'

Every ounce of the old woman seemed to shrink a degree at this question.

'You mean to tell me you don't know what we're doing?'

'*We* who—no… *what?*'

All of a sudden, she began spitting the names Robert and Roselyn under her breath while agitatedly trying to use both hands to grapple the cold remains of her teacup. 'They said you met,' she insisted through gritted teeth, bobbing her head with uncontrollable irritation '… they said you *spoke!*' She gulped the entire contents in one go like a thirsty drunkard, then dumped her dainty little cup onto its saucer with no notice of its spectacular clatter.

'Please tell me what's going on,' Wil pleaded, watching her smooth her ruffles, distressed.

'We have Lily,' she reiterated, confounded. 'But what good is telling you if you don't even remember what we do—who we are…?'

Taken aback, Wil felt himself guilty of ignorance again, guilty of not having his memory back.

'Then tell me,' he urged '*tell me* to *help* me remember.'

This suggestion seemed to please Mrs Hobbes after a moment, for she regained a degree of composure and smoothed a few white strands of hair up and over the top of her head with the back of her hand.

'Very well then,' she accepted uneasily, inhaling through her nostrils, 'because there is no other way, is there? And clearly very little time by the look of that darkness there around your eyes.' She shot his dark circles a look of worry. 'All you really need to know is that *we* have Lily. In the dreams, *we* are the ones who have taken her. Not Aeolus or anyone else. *And she's safe.*'

'Why—why did you take her?'

'Because that is what we do, Wilden,' she said wearily. 'What we've always done. For well over a century. Someone has to look after the little ones after all,' she insisted. 'They're used for such unspeakable things these days… the least we can do is carry on protecting half their childhood.' The sleeping half, she intimated with a pointed look. 'So as soon as we knew an Imposter was there, we took Lily. Of course, Sadie had to deal with the consequences, but at least—'

'—Sorry,' Wil stopped her, leaning closer, trying to make sense of Annie's conclusion of the park scenario concerning Lily and Sadie's own concerns for her sister in this new context, 'as soon as you knew the Imposter was *where*?'

Mrs Hobbes eyes averted to the right, as if this was a silly question. 'Inside Lily's Initial, dear boy,' she answered, clearly trying not to be ruffled again by his ignorance. 'If an Imposter is going to move in on a child,' she said plainly, 'their opportunity is when that child is alone. And children are most likely to be alone in their Initials.'

'And was this at the park? At Vivary?'

'It was.'

Here, Wil saw a degree of credibility in Sadie's story.

'Imposters prey on the Initial' Mrs Hobbes explained further 'because children lack the skills to enter the dreamscape on their own. In fact, when the Initial begins to break down, such young minds are more inclined to simply wake up numerous times in the night and create a new one. This gives Imposters limitless opportunity to feed off fear,' she said ominously, 'as children glide from one Initial to another, on their own.' Gauging the less confused expression on Wil's face, she confessed, 'And

I'm afraid that's the very situation we found Lily in. A new Initial… on her own. Of course, our job is to keep Imposters away from children, seeing as by their very presence, their motive is to deceive, but I should hasten to add that most children are not targeted in the same way Lily had been, which is why she hit our detectors so easily.' After a beat, 'There were more than one.'

'More than one Imposter?'

Mrs Hobbes nodded once, severely.

'But why would anyone—'

'—To manipulate a child… to manipulate those associated with that child… or to pretend *to be* that child and create a malleable foundation for more serious uses in future,' Mrs Hobbes said heavily, raising her brow. 'It becomes most detrimental in the case of a young person dreaming with an Imposter looking exactly like them,' she warned, 'because without intervention, we find that when these children then approach adolescence, they end up suffering an increased number of disorders. Anxiety, behaviour… eating…. Paranoia is quite common, moving onto more serious disorders later if there has been no intervention. Of course, then there are addictions of all kinds,' she said regretfully. 'We should have known that was happening throughout history, but centuries ago, no one was caring after the child like we are now. And certainly their mental health was of no concern at all. Unfortunately, people still have it in their heads that children are resilient. That they can take the knocks,' she said blandly, 'and that feelings aren't significant until adulthood. But they underestimate a child's sensitive dependence on initial conditions. So spending every hour asleep… seeing these Imposters in many cases producing a version of you more capable, more beautiful, more successful… it's no wonder you might wake with a burgeoning disorder of some sort. Which then has knock-on effects for the entire world quite frankly.' Her eyes blinked rapidly, resolved. 'So we had no choice but to take Lily.'

'Is that what was happening to her then? Someone was pretending to be her—more than one trying to be her?'

'We don't know what they were doing, Wilden.' Mrs Hobbes seemed genuinely unconcerned with the details. 'A single Imposter alone is enough to make us move. We don't stick around to determine motive and start skirmishes. That's your job. We just remove the child and hold onto them until the environment is safe.'

'And what determines that?'

'When affinities settle.'

Wil frowned, not understanding.

'Children do not have someone like Aeolus looking after them in their dreams,' she explained. 'In fact, affinities as you and I have known them can only take hold when we've reached a biochemical threshold. Puberty,' she said dully. 'Puberty, and our minds become a smorgasbord for all sorts. An affinity war. To see if we're ripe to remember. Of course, the two sides, vying to secure such an attachment sends shock waves throughout the environment, causing rifts within relationships, emotional turmoil… identity crises…. A young person in the middle of an affinity scrum may end up quite confused. Our efforts focus on removing them until such circumstances settle, until they are more inclined to align themselves with the same affinity as those they trust most and spend the most time with. Tret or Tare, we don't discriminate,' she said firmly. 'Obviously, we wait until siblings… grandparents—anyone the child is in contact with regularly or for an extended period of time—to align, creating an ideal window with which to re-integrate them. But in most cases, there isn't complete alignment. In most cases, it is a constant swing from Tret to Tare we are negotiating. We then have to pick our moment carefully. We must pick one we think causes the least amount of conflict.'

It never occurred to Wil that there could be human minds, organised and working in the same way as the Tret and Tare did in the dreams, undermining Imposters.

'And you do this?' he asked incredulously, casting his eyes generally over the frail woman sitting before him who had to be at least… ninety. 'You take these… these children and protect them? …Where do you take them then?' Surely she didn't just have one dream full of young people… an amusement park to keep them happy for twelve hours every night.

'Everywhere. Anywhere. I oversee the operations, however I do none of the running,' she confessed. 'But they end up all over the globe, taking into account appropriate time zones, of course. You won't find a child in China with a chaperon located in Brazil—or from Delhi matched to one in San Francisco,' she said obviously, rolling her eyes slightly at the ridiculous thought, and making Wil appreciate the scale of the operation. 'And as much as we wanted to take advantage of the South American siesta… I'm afraid they're never long enough. We really only utilise them when we have an influx of little ones, those needing naps still.

It's obviously not a long-term solution,' she admitted, putting her hands around the base of the teapot, checking its temperature, 'but it gives us options. And thankfully, we can be flexible about such things, moving people around at a moment's notice, where otherwise distance might create greater restriction. With the incredibly large number of dreamers who don't remember their dreams, much of our administration and placement happens within a limitless workforce that isn't even conscious of its role, so to speak. Most dreamers, anywhere on the globe, are willing to look after a child or two without hesitation. But most importantly, all the security for these little dreamers is provided without them ever leaving their bed.' She carefully poured another cup of tea for the both of them. 'And you'd think that translation would be an issue...' she remarked, pouring the milk 'with children inevitably spread out over the continents... but there seems to be no language barrier at all. Unless the child starts to feel threatened by their new Initial. Then, most curiously, the barriers come into full swing. Reassignment, of course is immediate and swift,' she said casually, taking turns stirring each cup, 'but like I said, with such a workforce, it is not difficult.'

Wil stared at Mrs Hobbes with utter fascination. Never in a million years would he have thought this little old lady could be so involved in the dreams. For the last year, every time he saw her standing watchfully at the window, he assumed her mind was blank. But it couldn't have been. Instead it would have been full of the ugliness of her work. All that collaboration... that care.... Instantly, the patronizing authority figure Wil thought he had seen before at the CD player now transformed into something else: a wondrous rogue, doing her bit despite the Tret and Tare. Because of them, even.

As Wil watched Mrs Hobbes—Vivienne—fumble repeatedly for a digestive, he couldn't help but see those gnarled hands he had both pitied and despised earlier as marvellous mighty fists.

'May I?' He offered to help her with the plate, feeling a lump in his throat as she gratefully used both hands now to scoop up the biscuit. Then catching her eye, it was as if Wil forgot all about the dreams, forgot precisely why he had been manipulated to sit here, for he suddenly saw a familiar thing in his neighbour that made him admire her. It was unrelated to her deeds, he felt certain. Perhaps it was her humanness. Her frailty. And it was like she saw the same in him at that moment, for she appeared both fond and regretful at his presence opposite her. Maybe even sad.

'You go through a lot of trouble to protect children,' he blurted self-consciously, taking a biscuit himself, effectively lifting her sad expression.

'We do,' she pursed a smile. 'But only to undo the work of Imposters.'

'The confusion and everything,' he acknowledged, dunking his digestive into his tea.

'And much more,' Vivienne said assuredly. 'You wouldn't think it, but Imposters use fear to control our DNA.'

'My sister told me that very thing today,' he admitted, biting the soggy end of his biscuit. 'Why? Why do they try and alter us with fear?'

'Because then we are more likely to do what their counterparts desire, dear boy.' Sipping her tea, she looked over the rim of her cup with that sad look again. 'It is a relationship of interdependence, you see. Of opposites attracting... serving one another unwittingly.' The sadness moved to something short of determination as she kept her eyes on him. 'Serving until one is annihilated.'

There was a deeper meaning there, Wil felt certain, but he chose not to ask. Instead,

'Does Sadie know you have Lily?'

'She does.'

'When? When did you take her?'

Vivienne suddenly dropped her now crescent-moon digestive onto her saucer.

'Wilden,' she met him squarely, gauging his ignorance, 'we've had Lily for years.'

'*Years?*' he recoiled. Whatever hope he had in Sadie telling him some bit of the truth had completely gone now. 'Years?'

'I'm afraid so. My sources have told me you believe otherwise.'

'I don't know *what* I believe.'

'Well, seeing as we do in fact have Lily, I can assure you, she is under no stress in the dreams, Wilden. And as I said before, you can either hear it from me, or Aeolus... either way you're going to hear it. No matter what you may think of our great meddlers, they do not resort to snatching,' she said pointedly, grappling the biscuit from her plate. 'Instead, they control behaviour by manipulating dreams, then adjust whatever feedback they receive in the awake hours using a finely-tuned process. They accomplish all that is required' she sniffed 'through persuasion, suggestion and our incessant need to behold a divine coincidence. They would never act so aggressively as to abduct an actual child from within their Initial. They are far subtler than that,' she said definitively. Then waiting a beat, 'However, *we* are not above such things,' she admitted, biting the point off her digestive.

As they both drank and chewed, Wil wondered who she meant by *we*. Certainly not him and her. Humans, he understood. Humans trying to protect themselves from the Tret and Tare. And Imposters.

He put his cup back onto the table for the last time and felt the journal slip down the side of his hip into the chair.

'How did you get my journal by the way?' He placed it on his lap again. 'If you don't mind me asking.'

'Not at all,' she granted, turning the teacup between her crumpled knuckles. 'It's an old house, Wilden. Divided up. Blocked up. Stairs going nowhere and becoming cupboards and store rooms. The hall cupboard outside your bedroom leads to the landing here.' She nodded over her shoulder to a door beside the microwave, prompting Wil to look there. Sure enough, there was a door.

'That door?' he asked, trying to imagine how it matched up to his side of the house.

She put the cup to her lips and arched her eyebrows lazily, affirming.

He had heard music through that door, of course from the other side. He heard her playing her loud music as he went along the hall countless times and never thought a thing of it.

'So you just came in and... took it?' He wasn't quite sure how bothered he was by this. 'Why?'

Vivienne finished her sip and swallowed, taking her time.

'The same reason your family had to move and go to London... then ended up here, right next to me.'

They moved for lots of reasons, Wil was certain. Originally, it was because an opportunity with work came up for Dad... then Gran was dying... then the inheritance was complicated.... In the end, Dad wanted the entire family to be with him up there, instead of him commuting back every weekend.

'And what reason is that?'

Just then, the doorbell rang, startling them both.

'That'll be your friend,' Vivienne said pleasantly.

'He can wait,' Wil insisted. 'Why did you really take my book?' he pressed.

'To get you remembering, Wilden,' she said plainly, knowing this answer was far too general to satisfy him. 'Why else?'

'But I haven't,' he told her sharply, now moving to the edge of his seat.

'You will. And you will find that everything that has happened to you over the last few years has been put in place to ensure it.'

'So, *again*, why did you take it?' he asked dismissively, impatient all of a sudden.

Here, Vivienne put her cup down. She then threw him a curt smile. 'Why don't you have a little read later,' she suggested through forced calm as the doorbell went again. 'Have a little read,' she glanced at the book under his hands and stood up, 'and then get back to me.'

Wil stood up too.

For a third time, the bell went, buzzing with what seemed Ben's absolute worry. Vivienne promptly limped to the box on the wall in her kitchenette and let him in.

'Why won't you tell me—and how do you know Aeolus?' he found himself desperate to know all of a sudden. 'How did you know *I* know him?'

'Wil...! *Wil...!*'

'I'm up here, Ben,' Wil called over his shoulder, unmoving, matching Vivienne's defiance for she seemed all too pleased that there was a visitor in their midst, preventing them from carrying on their conversation. 'I'm just having a lovely chat with the neighbour here. I'll be down in a minute.'

He stood firm, waiting.

'We both know there was more to getting me up here than just alleviating my worries about Lily,' he acknowledged. 'Or me getting my memory back,' he added, knowing Aeolus was already on it, maybe even Annie. Sadie certainly had done her part. 'You said the same reason you took my journal is the same reason we're living next door to you,' he reminded her firmly. 'Now, why is that?'

Mrs Hobbes stepped away from the intercom, came around the chairs and stood in front of Wil, disarming him slightly with the effort she had made with her limp. Then looking worriedly again at the darkness surrounding his eyes, she seemed to be conjuring the most sincere answer she could afford to give,

'Let's just say I owe you one,' she said finally, causing Wil to swallow hard.

'You all right up there, Wil?' Ben called out.

'I'm fine, Ben, fine,' he said, backing away from Vivienne. 'I'm just coming.'

Chapter Thirty-Three

Dream Tactics

'Owe's you one?' Ben opened the fridge, but not before throwing an incredulous look over his shoulder first. 'I'd just steer clear of her, Wil,' he warned, pulling out a slice of ham from its packet and putting it straight into his mouth, making Wil think of their unfortunate dream together Ben had no recollection of. 'She may sound independent, but no one is really. You don't actually know who's breathing down her neck.' Ben chucked the packet back onto the shelf and went for the cheese. Then in a high-pitch voice, trying to recall, 'What was the whole point of her getting you over there now?'

'I think to tell me about Lily... to tell me Aeolus and the others wouldn't take her... And to give my journal back,' Wil figured.

'Well, she's right,' Ben admitted as he put the block of cheese onto a chopping board then fished around in the drawer for a knife. 'Tret and Tare don't take people. Everyone knows that. People take people.' Finding what looked like a mini cleaver, he pushed it into the block and held up a hefty slice of crumbly cheddar. 'You want some?' he asked, to which Wil distractedly shook his head. 'All right,' Ben shrugged, taking a bite himself. 'She didn't mention the Sheizers, did she?'

Intrigued, 'No, what are they?' Wil asked, watching his friend cut another thick slice off for himself and chew like there was no tomorrow.

'Shadow seizers. They're people, like you and me,' Ben explained, slurping his drink and swallowing hard. He then puffed out his chest and grimaced momentarily as though the half-block of cheese he had just eaten was stuck in his gullet. 'For one reason or another, they like to get you in mid transit,' he said, hitting his chest with a fist and clearing his throat. 'Like carjacking.'

Wil frowned. Neither Annie nor Steph made any mention of this.

'Yeah,' Ben asserted, clocking Wil's reaction. 'Instead of your shadow taking you where *you* want, Sheizers wait for you to join the shadow they're waiting in... and you end up where *they* want. They're just opportunistic really,' Ben said casually, downing the last of his drink and looking more comfortable for it. 'People don't know it, but that's where *sheez* comes from. You know, like *geez*. The Americans have turned our Sheizers into *sheezus*, on account of mishearing our accent and all.' Then looking up from the island surface to the ceiling, he seemed to have second thoughts. 'Then again, it could have been intentional. Either way,' he abandoned the idea, 'seeing as the practice originated on this island, and spread over there during the American Revolutionary War...' he shrugged, ambivalent 'anything adopted from these parts during that time wouldn't just be accepted as is, would it? What's more interesting though,' he pointed with the knife, 'is how the word still pops up in modern use over there.... Really, it's a testimony of how those few who remembered the dreams tried bringing elements of them into the light. Centuries on, and not everything gets washed away in forgetting,' Ben assured with a knowing sideways glance. 'It is a shame though, that after all that time, we just hide stuff like that *over here*,' he said incontrovertibly, chopping a much thinner slice into manageable cubes now. 'By comparison, the Americans have always been a bit better at getting personal things out in the open, don't you think?'

'I guess,' Wil hauffed, more interested in how to avoid anyone trying to kidnap him through a shadow than how they've maintained their nickname over centuries and continents. 'A hugely interesting history lesson though,' he mocked. 'And just how exactly do we take a shadow without running into these—'

'—Just make your own. With your hands,' Ben instructed simply, to Wil's relief. 'In the dreams, at a moment's notice, you may find yourself dashing into a dark corner, or slipping into the first black shadow you can find. I'm afraid that's an instinctive thing, and Sheizers know it. So if you can try and just use your hands,' he demonstrated, cupping his palms together like he had just caught a butterfly, 'they can't wait in there.' He eyed the small gap between his dense palms with a standoffish squint.

As Wil sat at the kitchen island and looked at his own hands, wondering what it would be like to take a shadow at all, Ben suggested in a more serious voice,

'I'm thinking you, me, Steph and Annie should probably have a little chat before tonight.' He wrapped the plastic back around the significantly reduced block of cheese and put it back in the fridge. 'Seeing as none of us really know what's going on… it might be a good idea to have a little plan in place to avoid finding ourselves alone in the dreamscape. Just as a precaution,' he maintained, arousing Wil's suspicion, for this was most certainly Wise Ben talking now. 'It's no different from how we used to do things… I mean, I don't know about you, but I'd certainly prefer not to go in on my own tonight….' Pinching cheddar crumbs together from the board, he glanced at Wil, unnerving him, for it seemed this rather light recommendation to meet up was actually a sterilized introduction to something necessary and unpleasant.

'No, I don't want to dream without any of you tonight,' Wil admitted easily as Ben swiped the chopping board clean over the sink then washed the knife, clearly in the habit of removing evidence of his fridge raids. 'I'm desperate to sleep, but as far I'm concerned, you can pretty much assume I don't know how to do anything the other side.'

'Good,' Ben said, putting the knife back in the drawer, 'because we're meeting the girls after swimming.'

'Swimming?' He hadn't the energy to swim.

'We've got to keep you awake mate! A swim… lunch… a few hours down at Lyme Regis, it'll be good for you,' Ben declared as he slapped his huge hands on Wil's shoulders and pushed him gently off the stool.

'Now go get your swim trunks on.'

Two hours later, they were along the A35 on the way to Lyme Regis, wrinkled and soggy. Despite floating on his back for the majority of the time, Wil realised the trip to the pool was exactly what he needed to feel this revived, this awake. He otherwise would have thought of his trip to the south coast as torture.

As Wil watched Ben make conscientious decisions on the road, it seemed that his friend knew exactly what was needed to get him through the day, for there was a certain awareness about Ben as he drove his gran's mini Wil had not seen before—at least that he could remember. And as it turned out, like getting a tired and reluctant toddler from one hour to another, Ben was just stretching him from one thing to the next, admitting as they waited for a parking space on the seafront that the meeting with the girls was actually at 6. 6pm with the promise of sleep to follow. Like a child, Wil felt his heart leap. But then of course, he remembered what it really meant.

A gull-infested lunch down by the pastel huts, a farcical stomp across the smooth stones to the water, and a wander across the Cobb with ice-creams took up two hours in what seemed half the time for Wil. Back in the car, as they headed up the steep hills for Taunton again, Wil flicked through the muddied and torn Dismaland programme magazine from their trip to Banksy's art installation in Weston-super-Mare. It had been sitting back there, stuffed in the footwell behind Ben's seat since 2015, when his Gran took them that day. Looking back on the experience, Wil couldn't help wonder where the Tret and Tare were in all of that. Where were they when he saw families leaving with black *I AM AN IMBECILE* balloons ironically attached to their children? Where was Aeolus when they went through the entrance into that first exhibition and decided to pathetically participate in indulging abusive staff in Bill Barminski's cardboard security checkpoint? It was all set up like a mockery, but was it?

Wil turned the page, sparking his memory of the galleries.

By the time he had passed Deitrich Wegner's literally branded baby in the vending machine and spotted his mushroom cloud treehouse beyond the unconcerned buoyancy of Hirst's beach ball, tall and ominous over the crowd of seemingly ambivalent perusing heads further down the gallery, Wil remembered the place making him feel oddly at home. It was as though the artists there had apprehended something he himself was only just beginning to. And yet, neither of them could discern its totality, despite all the apparent hours exerted in creating the works around him. Somehow, the sum of an entire gallery, even of that calibre, lacked the panorama. The whole artistic community did in fact, right along with the rest of the world. However these... these were clear, defined glimpses, Wil still felt certain, turning another page. Microscopic aspects, unto that thing.

Wil hurried through the magazine, looking for his favourite installation from the day: the woman wearing a gas mask in Paco Pomet's *Había Una Vez*. *Once upon a time*. She was showing something to a group of children huddled around her on a beach. Of course, whatever this thing actually was, it was unseen. It however had a glow the children were keen to observe and handle. The fact that they are all dressed in mere swimsuits and shorts from the 40's, and the single adult in the scene was wearing only minimal protection against something she clearly did not understand as radioactive and lethal to them all… it made Wil wonder what humanity might do if it finally had that panorama. Such a perspective would surely embolden its inherent desire to subdue and conquer, sending that benevolent ignorance over the particle-world observed there in that painting to even more devastating heights, beyond democratic bombs and popular brutality. Perhaps it was just as well the Tret and Tare made everyone forget… and the artist was left searching, only to leave fragmented impressions of the world they really lived in.

Wil shook the thought away and flipped to his second favourite work from the day: another drawing of a child on a beach. It was Bansky's.

'The world is messed up' Ben declared, glancing at the spread. Wil tilted his head, scrutinising the mother slapping sun cream onto her child in the foreground, a store cupboard of beach provisions surrounding them like a sand fort. Of course, with her back to the rubbish-riddled tidal wave, only her child could see it coming. 'We're blind,' Ben confessed. 'I'd like to say it's all our own doing…' he sighed, then gave Wil a knowing glance '…but something tells me not everything is down to us.'

Unsettled by that statement, Wil chucked the programme on the back seat and sat in silence until they got to Blagdon. His mind however could still see that art installation of Cinderella, dumped out of her ball carriage like Princess Diana in Paris. It seemed that Ben, even with his memory intact, shared none of the burden Wil suddenly did at the thought of those cartoony little birds trying in vain to pull at Cinderella's ribbons, for she was far too dead, and they were far too weak—unlike the snapping paparazzi nearby. At least they were *trying* to save her.

'You don't actually think we're powerless to the influences around us,' Wil challenged as they came down the steep, winding hill south into Taunton. 'Please tell me you don't think we're just at the mercy of the Tret and Tare—that there's no point in doing anything.'

'Don't be silly—of course I don't,' Ben insisted. 'This is about that picture of the kid, isn't it? The mum who can't see the tidal wave.' Wil's lack of an answer was answer enough, causing Ben to hauff with what seemed equal measure of both genuine amusement and annoyance. 'Listen, I see the irony just like you do. But there is something very human about not wanting to take responsibility, don't you think? I was just trying to be, I don't know, *even more ironic*. That is, considering our present situation.'

'So you were joking?'

'Of course I was, you idiot!'

Relieved, and overwhelmingly tired, Wil found himself chuckling. It was enough to get them both laughing all the way to the pizza place, where almost all at once, things didn't seem so funny anymore.

Ben pulled into Selena's spot thirty minutes later, grabbed the pizzas off the back seat and got out.

'You coming?' he urged, bending his head into the car and seeing that Wil hadn't yet undone his seatbelt. 'Wil?' He set the pizza on the roof and leaned back in. 'Listen mate. This isn't a big deal. We just want to all be on the same page,' he tried assuring. 'You'll be glad of it, because it'll mean whatever happens… you're not alone.'

'I know,' Wil accepted. 'I'm just a bit, I don't know... nervous. The closer I get to the thought of sleeping, the less I can contemplate actually doing it.'

'A step at a time, mate. So undo your belt… get out… close the door… and help me carry this food,' he directed, smiling, to which Wil obeyed easily.

'We brought dinner,' Ben said simply, passing Annie at the door and handing boxes to Steph inside.

'You look grim,' Annie mentioned as Wil came through the doorway, making him immediately aware of the constant sting grating the front of his eyes. 'My mum's staying over at Gabe's,' she said for all their benefit. 'Drinks are on the table and Steph and I have printed off a list.' And wasting no time, the three of them took a seat at the dining table, grabbed plates and pizza and began looking at sheets of paper like they had done this a thousand times.

Realising Wil was still standing at the other end of the lounge in slight bewilderment, Ben chided gently,

'This pizza isn't going to eat itself.' He grabbed a slice, dropped it onto a plate then held it out. 'C'mon. We've got work to do.'

Joining them, Wil read carefully:

Notes for Wil

Initials

You can't return without waking. Being forced to wake from an Initial changes it. Next time you dream, it will be different. Dream-dragging

Initials sometimes changes them too.

How to Use the Dream to your Advantage

Observe, observe, observe! Interact with others because they're dreaming with you <u>for a reason</u>. When in doubt—get out!!! Don't stay in one place for too long. You can travel with others, using the same shadow.

Dream Tactics

• *Senses: Tune into the uniqueness of each sense. They are your only weapon, not reason. Save reasoning for when you're awake.*

• *Objects: Ensure we connect Initials with others/join them in the dreamscape.*

• *Affinities: Not readily identifiable in the dreamscape. Consider other dreamers your enemy until proven otherwise.*

• *Point of Transition: Usually happens before waking. Involves bottleneck of dreamers, Tret and Tare who all want to influence the outcome. Avoid Transition dreamers if possible, especially if you know you can do nothing to help.*

• *Codes: Useful when eye contact with imposters is prevented. Use them every time.*

There are NO Hollywood superpowers

Words to be Familiar With:

Verger: *One stuck inside Transition, always on the verge of new affinity. Quite a dangerous person. They appear to have moral/ethical objectives one minute, only to abandon them the next. Dreamers who DON'T remember their dreams are Vergers. However they are known to navigate parts of the dreams with purpose, only to forget about it later.*

Dual: *Dual affinity. They are stuck inside Transition WITH Vergers, however they DO remember their dreams. Instead of short-lived affinities, they have long-standing connection to both Tret and Tare, with moral/ethical objectives to both. They entrench our entanglement with the Tret and Tare, maybe even Vergers' ignorance of Tret and Tare. It's in our interests to find Duals and encourage them to take a side, if not to polarize our relationships with the T+T, then at least to minimise T+T undermining human thought to such an extent. Remember, Duals remember their dreams!*

Sheizer: *Sabotages shadow use. Same affinity as yours if encountered in Initial. Sure to be otherwise outside Initial. Take palm shadows if possible.*

Substrate: *Dream infrastructure. Your emotional/mental projections. When substrate looks like people, they're not always actual dreamers.*

'We can't cover all this in three hours Annie,' Ben argued, skimming and realising there were two sides to the sheet. 'No way,' he said definitively.

'Actually, Wil already knows most of it,' Annie answered coolly. 'Unless he's lost his improved memory already.'

'Nope, still got it,' Wil assured, a crevice deepening in his brow as he tried reading.

'Listen, we don't have time to cover every unnecessary aspect of the dreams,' Ben pointed out in exasperation. 'Not right now at least.'

'Right, because you just want to focus on tactics,' Annie accused, folding her arms.

'No... I want to focus on what will get us all through the night. Codes... meeting points... what we do when we're separated or one of us is forced to wake.... Wil, I'm sorry to say it' he gave a cautious glare to Steph and Annie 'but you wouldn't know the first thing to do if something happens to all of us and you're on your own with someone who's got it in for you. You were in a fog *for a reason*. We forgot... *for our protection.*' Catching Annie's eye, it was as if Ben was just then seeking her pardon for having no part in the forgetting. 'But now we're all back,' he maintained pointed eye contact with her, acknowledging her contribution before looking around the table again, 'we can't just go in without a plan. Plenty of people are going to have unfinished business with us, especially now they know we remember. We can't afford *not* to be prepared.'

'Why do they have unfinished business with us?' Wil interrupted innocently, expecting to be fobbed off until he remembered properly. 'What was it we were doing before? And who are *they* anyway?'

The question seemed to prove Ben's point somehow, for he smirked slightly and withheld an answer, deferring instead to the other two. But it quickly became apparent that neither of them were going to say anything either.

'*We* were turning Vergers,' Ben responded finally, casting a loathsome glance at the other two. 'Turning them Tare. But the rumour was *you* were making Duals of them,' he added plainly, swallowing back what looked like something sour. 'And *they* are those individuals who still remember and disagree with what you were doing. Because *they* have a vested interest in Tret versus Tare and not some *you-do-what's-good-for-you* postmodern bollocks....'

However, none of that meant a thing to Wil, and seeing the blankness there on his face, Steph jumped in to translate.

'Vergers are those on the verge of two affinities nearly all the time.' She glanced at Ben with an air of slight defiance, for this was on the sheet. 'They're stuck inside the Point of Transition. Basically, they're the dreamers that can be Tret-governed one minute and Tare the next, having only short-lived affinities—if you could even call them that. It suits both Tret and Tare that most dreamers in the world remain as Vergers because they're just… well, pawns, I guess.' She poked a spot of pepperoni on her pizza with her finger, 'And Duals are those with both affinities, having strong ties with both Tret and Tare. Of course, these ties mean the decisions they make are perceived as ethical by them, opportunistic or loyal by the Tret and Tare, and disloyal to all of humanity by those like us.'

Rather oddly, Annie exhaled loudly through her nose, causing Steph to gauge her with a degree of uncertainty, but Steph was encouraged to continue with a pointed stare.

'The difference of course between the Verger and Dual,' Steph went on pleasantly, referring to the sheet and throwing Ben a forced half-smile as she did so, 'is that while they both occupy Transition and move with purpose throughout the dreams, Verger's can't remember theirs, and Duals can. Like someone drunk… and sober, is how I try to see it. The Verger makes decisions with reckless abandon, in the moment, only to forget later… while the Dual's constant awareness of the Tret and Tare obliges them to consider consequence with such care… they view themselves as the clearest thinkers in all of this. Now I may not agree with where they fall on the line, but there aren't many of them, and they're a good source of insider information. We've used them quite a few times in the past.' After a beat, 'And the *they* Ben mentioned… well, they're people like us.' She looked around the table.

'Is that true?' Wil asked to Annie and to Ben, taken aback. 'Is that what I was doing?'

'This is my point exactly,' Ben heated up, tossing his head back. 'He's going to go in there' his hand darted in Wil's direction 'and believe whatever someone tells him—and if they *look the part*…' he shook his head and hauffed 'God help us!' to which Annie jumped in.

'It's rumours, Wil,' she insisted. '*Rumours.* That's what was being said before you forgot.' She cast her eyes dismissively over Ben and Steph. 'Before all of you forgot. They weren't just saying it about you, Wil, they were saying it about these guys too.' She chucked Ben a derisive look then tried assuring, 'So he's just pointing out that once you get to the dreams, those things haven't just gone away because you've been in a fog the last three years. If anything, the fact that you're out now... and you're all remembering...' she caught Steph's worried face '... well, we just need to be prepared to move quickly. And you obviously can't do that if you don't remember how' she directed more to Ben than Wil now. 'So we're going to help you.'

'Wil, what on the sheet *do* you know?' Steph quickly jumped in, giving Ben no time to argue.

Wil looked over the list, still ruffled a bit. 'I know about Initials... and affinities. I'm not totally confident about these bits though,' he pressed his thumb under the heading, '*Substrate...*' turned the page over 'and *Dream Tactics*. Otherwise,' he flipped the page back and skimmed, 'most of this stuff I've at least heard of this week, if that helps,' he directed to Ben with a wince, causing his best friend's glower to finally ease.

'Shouldn't we mention The Junction,' Annie threw in, to which Steph threw a wary look to Ben.

'We probably don't have time for Substrate and The Junction,' Steph considered tactfully, handing over to Ben, who now looked relieved.

'Well then, that wasn't so difficult now, was it?' Annie piped up, souring the moment. 'And by the way, just for the record, I'm not that Annie anymore,' she reminded Ben, poking her finger into her own chest and forcing him to look at her chasing glare. 'So there's no need for the hostility,' she added pointedly. 'We're here to help each other, all right?'

'All right,' Ben agreed after a second, making Wil feel for him, for he himself had to remember the girl in Ben's face wasn't actually the same girl of the last three years—the same girl he so perversely loved to hate. 'You're absolutely right,' Ben acknowledged more humbly, wiping his mouth with a napkin and setting his own copy of the sheet onto the table. 'Sorry.' He made full eye contact with her, meaning it.

Then appearing less belligerent, he turned his attention to Wil, '*Dream tactics*, then....'

Chapter Thirty-Four

Runway

Wil sat on his bed and dutifully put the penny on his shin. He then sealed it in place with two plasters to his sister's satisfaction.

'These aren't necessary,' Steph made clear 'they're just a precaution.' She watched him do the same with two more, Ben's and Annie's, under her watchful eye.

'Just a precaution,' Wil accepted, giving her the box of Elastoplast. 'I'm happy to take precautions if it means I'm not starting off alone in there.' He pushed the leg of his pyjama trousers down and got under the duvet.

'Your ringer's set low?'

'Yep.' He looked over at his phone on the side.

'Good. You'll get there quickly,' Steph assured as she got up from the bed. 'Ben's already waiting in his own Initial. He'll join you the second you're there in yours. If everything starts coming back, you'll know how to use these,' she glanced at his knees poking up from under the duvet 'and find Ben if anything goes wrong. Otherwise, just let us do the connecting.'

'And what if it's the fog again?' Wil asked apprehensively, feeling like a child not wanting to go to sleep. 'What if he can't find me?'

'We've been over this, Wil. It might be the fog. Just try and gain your bearings. Try to remember more than what's happening in the moment.' She went and opened the door. 'Call for him. He'll be there somewhere.' She then turned out the light, 'Sweet dreams…' and was gone.

Hearing her go down the hall to her own bedroom, Wil didn't feel so reassured that he had friends and family around him anymore. And the fact that Ben was three miles away... with his head on a pillow... and his eyes closed....

Within seconds, Wil fell asleep, the knowing already taking its hold.

'Well done,' came a parroty voice beside him. 'Let's go.'

'Vivienne...' he acknowledged, confused '...where's Ben?' Catching sight of her only for a second, she grabbed his hand and disappeared ahead of him into the fog. '*Vivienne...?*' Her gnarled fingers gripped firmly around his, and Wil could see there was something not quite right about his neighbour this time, his old friend. 'Vivienne, is that really you?' He pulled back, reluctant to go any further with what seemed to be an Imposter, but she pulled even harder, making his legs feel elongated, stretching as though elastic as she persisted through the haze. 'You're dream-dragging me Vivienne—stop!' He tried picking her fingers off his, 'What's going on? Where are you taking us?'

'Stop this Wilden!' she shouted back at him. 'We must hurry!' Her shallow pant laboured against the disorientating vapour around them. 'We haven't much time!'

Wil wanted to believe her, wanted to believe she was actually his old confidant, yet didn't want the dream-drag to complete if she was an Imposter.

'You know I can't see you.... Please, just stop for a second and show me your eyes,' he pleaded, having never been in the position to doubt her identity in the dreams before.

'There's no point! You can't see anything in here,' she argued. 'Now hurry.'

Wil was suddenly worried his foggy Initial would combine with the contents of wherever Vivienne was taking them, meaning he and Ben would have to try and find one another amid twice the number of synaptic threads now. However, it seemed that wherever Vivienne was headed, there was no fog, giving Ben an even better chance of finding him, for Wil could see something ahead and gave in, allowing the obscured figure to pull him along, increasing their pace.

All of a sudden, Vivienne staggered sideways, prompting Wil to instinctively reach out and catch her.

'You all right?' he breathed, feeling her middle stiffen under his brace.

'You feel that?' She rubbed the chill from her arms and met him squarely. 'Do you?' she croaked earnestly, more unsettled by the cold than having nearly landed flat.

'It's cold...' he acknowledged simply, seeing her eyes were just as he had remembered—cloudy blue with a pale ring—for the fog was behind them now, and they were along the cloister of a historic building, a campus maybe, or a castle. There was dew on the lawn beside them. It felt like early morning.

'We've got to hurry now, Wilden!' she exclaimed, allowing him to help her to her feet. Breaking away from him, she ran with a hunched bounce, elbows out, towards the studded oak door at the end. 'Keep up!'

Wil's shoulders slumped in annoyance. He hurried past the colonnades along the quadrangle and followed her through the door, down a dim passage and up a stone stairway on the right.

'I can carry you,' he offered, hearing her wheezing now, for she weighed nothing when he caught her a moment ago.

'I'm fine,' she lied, jostling her elbows to push him away. They turned at the half-point. 'This floor,' she nodded upwards and puffed, 'first door.'

Reaching the top, something caught Wil's eye behind them. Fog. It had managed to go through the door downstairs and was clearly making its way up here. In fact, it was slowly moving up the second set of steps now, with a mind of its own.

'Vivienne...' he said ominously, drawing her attention now to the steps behind them, to which she showed no sign of panic.

'Your Initial is trying to take over,' she explained, grabbing his arm and squeezing it. 'Stop being afraid, Wilden,' she said desperately, breathlessly. 'I need you to be *here*.' She looked at the steps in dismay then left him standing there.

Wil watched the white vapour stall for a second, as though waiting for him to look away, and he wondered what he was so afraid of? What about this place... about Vivienne and this encounter made him fearful? The fog began to creep again.

'Wait! Wait for me!' Running after her, he was sure that being left alone was what he was afraid of.

'You will never be alone, Wilden,' Vivienne said plainly, having somehow read his mind as she began tucking in her blouse along the vast hall. She slowed to the first door on the right, wiped her face with a handkerchief then poked the square of thin fabric back into her sleeve. And with her chest still heaving, she then pulled at her cuffs and patted her bun, looking incredibly relieved now that she had taken hold of the handle. 'These have been my friends, and now they are yours.'

With that, her attention fell to something over his shoulder— the fog just beginning to curl around on the landing now—and as Wil caught sight of it too, she pushed the door open, pulled him in and slammed it behind them. It was as if they were in a subterranean tunnel all of a sudden, dark and enclosed, instead of the first floor of a historic building. And wasting no time, Vivienne patted him on the shoulder and led him down the winding passageway where they hurried with hands out, rebounding off the stone walls until they appeared all of a sudden in the bright sunlight... of a massive lecture hall. There had to be hundreds of people, if not a thousand, in tiered seats rising to the back, and the galleries flanking the front where Vivienne now stood. Wil self-consciously stepped back to the tunnel entrance.

'Thank you for coming...' Vivienne said to the silent crowd, her voice personable, confiding. It was the same tone—

All of a sudden, it hit Wil—*connections*—*The Junction*. His mind went back to the week leading up to him forgetting, where he and the others tried finding a way to preserve The Junction, but it had been no use. In the end, everything was destroyed. But only because it wasn't what they had thought.

'I hope I haven't caused alarm in keeping you waiting,' Vivienne said kindly, 'but I couldn't possibly show up without our good friend Wilden.' His train of thought was cut short by the sudden realisation that all eyes were on him. He sent an unsure smile in the direction of the middle section. 'Had it not been for Wilden, I could not be here,' Vivienne said rather soberly, referring to the one time Wil ever guided such a prominent figure in the dreamscape to safety. He would have done the same thing for anyone, it just so happened to be her on that occasion. Looking down at his shoes, embarrassed, he felt certain it wasn't worth mentioning. Just as he felt certain she still didn't owe him one, as mentioned on the landing in the manor. The fact that she promised to look out for little Lily when he told her he'd have to forget everything... that was payment enough.

Unsettled by the public recognition, Wil wondered what this whole event was about, for it was nothing like the Runway meetings before. In fact, the sheer numbers present... it could have been the entire

UK assembly.

'Had it not been for Wilden, my grandson could not take my place and maintain the good work you are all doing,' she said plainly, causing Wil to frown slightly at such a statement, for he never imagined Vivienne retiring, and he had no idea that he had helped her grandson—whoever he was.

'It has been a huge privilege over the last seventy years leading you,' she continued, 'because you are a determined bunch. A resilient, determined and courageous group of people. Most of you have no idea how valuable you have been to our cause. That is, not until I can remind you in your dreams,' she said more cheerfully as weak smiles went around the room and eyes averted with humility to those sitting nearby. 'I don't know many of you the other side, but here, we are like family. Here, I know every one of you like my own children, grandchildren... brothers and sisters.

'When I stand here and look at you all,' she cast her attention to every section of the room, 'I can't help but think back to the 1940's, where I witnessed what I thought at the time was the beginning of the end of what we do.' She shook her head slightly at the memory. 'It was post-war. Attitudes were changing. And you see, I had the unenviable task of finding minders like you for both Jewish and German orphans—not only the survivors of the holocaust... but the little-known Wolf children of East Prussia.

'Now, I should point out here, it has been my experience that religion and politics rarely enter the dreams of children,' she said firmly. 'Certainly not as much as desire and fear do. And as it turns out, studies completed by our partners in the dreamscape indicate that this is the case for any dreamer, whether child or adult. Desire and fear are all that we find in the dreams. Everything boils down to these.' She acknowledged Wil behind her with a half-glance, to which he then guiltily looked over his own shoulder down the passageway for any sign of the creeping fog. Thankfully, there was none. 'However... desire and fear can manifest into political and religious conceptions once awake,' she warned, 'but only when the mind matures towards adulthood.' Again she briefly looked over, apparently distracted. 'I should also point out that most of us who did this work at that time... remembered our dreams.' She pressed this point, stepping towards the front row and turned to both galleries where a broad range of young and old faces remained fixed on her. 'And because of this, *because we remembered...* the few hundred in our line of work determined that they would be selective regarding the children they took on... *prioritising scarce resources*,' she mocked. 'Essentially, they agreed to help only those they could sympathise with politically. Of course, my fellow carers were not agreeing with the political views of a child you see—for those were nonexistent—rather, they were assuming the views of a parent... a country... a country's allies, even. Yet these were children no different from those you yourselves find the courage to protect. Victims of war... victims of the outrageous political ideals of adults... victims even of those who chose to turn a blind eye until allied bombs were landing. By refusing to help, individuals in your very position imposed their wakeful ideals onto innocent sleeping minds... inadvertently reinforcing the political agenda of the time... instead of basic human rights. This,' she said sharply, 'I found a great tragedy amid the most horrific event in modern history. I was certain then that we had strayed so far from our purpose... that we would be finished within a year.

'However....' She put her head down, clasped her hands in front of her and looked among the faces. '*However*' she said determinedly, the lines around her mouth faltering, 'over the decades... you have come.' Again, she looked up to the galleries. 'All of you... who remember your dreams... you devote yourselves to protecting the vulnerable across the globe. And this isn't even all of you,' she hauffed, amazed, 'because there are hundreds more of you on this island alone, having remained over the last three years throughout unimaginable adversity. Seventy years ago, I feared there would be none of us left... and here you are....'

Vivienne held her hands out to them, grateful, crying, moving everyone in the room to tears too. Even Wil found himself blinking something away.

'You know what this crucial work costs you, and yet you are willing to persevere,' Vivienne proclaimed, incredulous. 'You... who remember, you act more justly even than our associates of the past. And it has been watching you rise as a formidable force' her voice began to crack 'that has been my greatest privilege in doing this good work.' Overcome, and nearly unable to speak now, 'Our generations are nothing without you,' she asserted, giving an affirming nod, to which the room erupted with deafening applause.

Vivienne looked over her shoulder to Wil with a wistful expression, shivering slightly as she did so. He could not tell whether she was happy or sad. She then pulled out her handkerchief, daubed her face and held up her hand, quieting the room once again.

'We all know what is coming,' she declared plainly, to which Wil found himself most curious. 'So please let me introduce you to my grandson. He has already been acting on my behalf in recent months and I think you will find him more capable and fit to serve you' she looked her frail form up and down 'than I can carry on pretending to be.' No one laughed. Not even out of courtesy. 'Please,' she held her arm out to someone in the front, her body blocking Wil's view.

All of a sudden, Wil saw him.

'Rupert?' he said aloud, confounded, drawing attention from the audience his side of the room and a passive glance from Vivienne herself. This was her grandson? Everything that had happened at Mulbryn concerning Rupert suddenly dumped into Wil's head like mountainous rubble. He didn't know where to start.

Rupert thanked her then made some sort of acceptance speech, none of which Wil heard for he was trying to figure out what Vivienne meant when she said if it weren't for him—Wilden—her grandson wouldn't be here, taking her place.

It was a short speech, and after Rupert sat down, Wil noticed a sudden movement in the front section by the aisle. It was Zara—Ben's sister. And beside her... *was Lily.* Lily was playing with something on her lap. Wil caught Zara's eye just then only to watch her pretend the little girl beside her had done something distracting. Unwilling to question Vivienne's judgement, Wil didn't know what to make of seeing Lily there in Zara's care, especially as Annie had voiced such strong views about her. And if Annie was wary, Sadie certainly would be....

Sadie....

A curling, grinding shock of apprehension worked its way through Wil's core. His eyes became distant at the thought of her, for a wash of associations suddenly fused, allowing him to remember precisely his extraordinary love for Sadie... his love that they promised one another would outlast forgetting... would surely prompt them to find one another when all the dust had settled. It was a love that they determined would overcome the fact that she was a Dual when he wasn't. *Find me,* they agreed, would lead them back to one another, no matter how much had been taken away, no matter how much had been forgotten.... *Find me....* The awareness of who Wil was—who he *had been* bled most obviously out of his face, because he remembered. He remembered everything about Sadie just then. Sadie, and Lily... when she had been so tiny, a toddler... and Vivienne.

A shallow breath came out of Wil just then, the impact of the greater things he had forgotten accumulating. His shoulders bowed with the indeterminable weight. To think that had been the plan: to remember. To prove that in forgetting, one might still choose the same path as before. Just as he had done with Aeolus this time. Aeolus every time, when given the chance. And Sadie too. He managed to love her again, despite forgetting. Love her still.

The certitude his returning memories created in him, the awareness... it was vast and precise and Wil's immediate thought was to find her, find Sadie. But he would need help. Faces then came to him, people he knew from the dreams before—people he knew only in the dreams—*Murphy*... Giovanni, Andrzej, Matheus—like *brothers*.... But the others wouldn't know half of them, Wil realised, because these were Duals. Not to be trusted. He'd have to look for Sadie in another dream, when Ben wasn't somewhere around this one.

Feeling disorientated slightly, Wil allowed his mind to catch up to the here and now. But he had to admit, while everything from before seemed intact, nothing from his time in Enemy fog came back. It was a complete void.

Raising her voice, Vivienne regained the floor and invited Wil to stand next to her.

'Before we part ways... I want to take this opportunity to thank Wilden for the work he has done in the past for us—work he no doubt has done for many organisations amid the dreamscape.' She looked to him gratefully, which caused Rupert to dismissively tug at his tie. 'However, I believe we are the ones who have benefitted most from his collaboration. We are the only group serving children in the dreamscape and had we not employed Wilden's methods to change with it—change with the minds of unconscious modern humanity—our efforts to secure the well-being and safety of millions of children would be utterly ineffectual. We are extremely grateful for your contribution to the success of our work,' she turned to him again 'so we thank you. And with your renewed memory, I think I speak for all of us here at the 360° Runway when I say we hope to work with you in the future, in the same capacity as that of the past.'

'I hope so too,' he said simply, genuinely, inadvertently glancing at Lily there in the sea of faces as he remembered just how keen Vivienne had been when they first met to protect the minds of children. She recognised that she could never reach every child, but considering how many decades the Tret and Tare had left her remembering, and that she knew more of their tactics than most, she promised to die trying. It was she who enlightened him about The Junction. It was she who helped him understand that inside the brain of all humankind, hidden amid the complex depths of memory and consciousness, inherited DNA somehow carried with it the experiences of one's ancestors. *Genetic memory,* she called it.

Seeing Lily playing so innocently there, Wil was reminded of the darker side of genetic memory. That all sensory information, every item seen... touched, every feeling felt, compounded and was passed onto the embryo in a physical manner, but was hidden along a dream thread of the metaphysical, and that sometimes it leaked out, permitting the individual to realise a particular connection with forefathers and foremothers through things other than genetics. It was no wonder Vivienne wanted to know just where this vault was buried in the mind, for it stored not just good things, but bad. She said many times how her work would be easier if she could find it. And she believed that humanity *did* have access at one point, and *consciously* so, *a daydream of answers* she told him once, but that the Tret and Tare had been forced to bury such access deep inside the unconscious dreamer. She likened the state of affairs to the biblical Garden of Eden. The inaccessibility of ancestral knowledge: banishment. The vault was not simply hidden, but locked indefinitely, for as long as the Tret and Tare were entangled with human existence. However, in those fascinating discussions with his old friend, Wil believed he found a key.

'I do hope so,' Wil said more sincerely to his old friend, in front of all those people, wondering now if her replacement in the front row knew how one lost civilisation could possibly pass the sum of its knowledge onto another... or how the experiences of nearly every person throughout history was right now hidden in the present day dreamer, revealing not just the genetic memory of one individual... but of all humanity. The near sum of its knowledge: wedged amid a single intersection of the dreams.

Returning to the side, Wil felt there was now an awkward silence in the room.

'I need your help,' Vivienne said to her listeners, drawing a hand down her arm as though feeling a draught. '*Every one of you*' she emphasised, penetrating the anonymity of the crowd, 'must go on as they have always done.' As she surveyed the room, Wil saw faces exchange wary glances, and eyes avert from their speaker. Then discomfiting her audience, Vivienne began to shiver slightly. 'Rose and Rob will continue their role,' she said with momentary distraction, then quickened her speech, 'and important decisions will follow the same protocol as before. Right, then.' She looked the room over, smiling at key individuals, nodding to others. 'I will take three final questions… and then you are free to go.'

No one raised a hand.

Halfway up the left side of the room, an arm slowly lifted.

'Matthew,' Vivienne acknowledged.

'When?' he asked, as though the question were just as daunting as the answer might be.

Vivienne put her head down briefly, then said delicately, 'Any minute now, Darling.'

Matthew crossed his arms onto his table top and buried his head as those either side of him rubbed his shoulders and consoled him.

Wil stood there, confused at the mass reaction, and found himself glancing around at the more overt expressions of sorrow and grief. He tried not to stare, but the flash of white tissues to his left and right… those sorrowfully shaking their heads… and those leaning toward others, comforting them, automatically caught his eye.

'Any other questions…?'

'I don't have a question, but I want to say thank you,' someone spoke from the gallery.

'I know how thankful you are my dear,' she answered back, 'how thankful all of you are. Your sentiments resonate here.' She put her knotted fist to her chest in earnest, both to the woman who had spoken up in the gallery and then to the rest of the room. 'But I am as thankful to you as those you support and protect are thankful. So if there are no further questions…' she glanced around the room to be sure, and there were none, 'then it is best that you now return to them.'

With that, bodies began disappearing. Wil's eyes darted to the instant absence of individuals around the room, like watching bubbles pop in mid-air, not knowing which would be next. One by one, as seats emptied, he saw hands come together like prayers... claps... or cupped like an insect had been caught. Some seemed to do nothing at all and managed to disappear. That's how Annie did it, Wil remembered. Something about the darkness behind the eyelids. She said that's how the blind did it, that it wasn't really about taking a shadow, but more getting the mind to focus through blackness. He saw the benefit in a method that required neither hands nor sight. Especially when it meant the difference between getting out of an injurious thread and being completely stuck in it. Sometimes a split second was all you had. At least half the room had vanished now. Both Zara and Lily were gone. They left at the same time.

A dozen or so still sat in the room. Just a few in the back now. Actually, they vanished too. A handful sat in the front now. Rupert... was gone... seemingly at his gran's insistence, for he tried to linger, catching glimpses of Wil over her shoulder. Four were left now, including Wil and Vivienne. A male and female down the far end of the front row. They got up and went over to Vivienne, who now looked incredibly uncomfortable as she bent over slightly and rubbed her arms energetically. Wil hurried to her, concerned, though slightly aware there was something familiar about these two.

'Robert, Roselyn...' Vivienne said breathlessly '...you two look after him, will you?'

'Of course,' Roselyn assured, bending her head to meet Vivienne's. 'Of course we will.'

'Can we hold you?' Robert asked kindly, putting his fingertips to Vivienne's elbow, drawing a permissive though pained smile from the old woman. Both of them went either side and braced her, leaving Wil to stand helplessly before her.

He watched feebly as Vivienne crumpled, deteriorating, and Roselyn kissed the top of his old friend's smooth white hair. 'What's happening?' he asked anxiously, kneeling to the collapsing form between them, seeing Vivienne's distressed face. 'Can I take your hand, Vivienne?' he offered desperately.

But just as she reached out to him, she disappeared.

Immediately, Roselyn looked at her empty arms and put her hand to her mouth, shocked. Shaking, she began to sob, sending Robert to envelop her.

'I'm sorry...' Wil uttered, still uncertain as to what actually happened to Vivienne. 'I'm so sorry....' And as Roselyn cried into Robert's shoulder, Wil began to feel utterly helpless, a spectator now imposing on a private matter.

'Rose, we need to finish...' Robert reminded her gently. Swallowing hard, she parted from him and nodded resolutely.

They turned to Wil, grieved, though determined.

'Wait a minute… *I know you*,' Wil realised all of a sudden, taking a step back as they came closer. 'You two were in my dream… in the fog—*you*—you were the bloke who heard the droning,' he insisted, pointing, eyeing Robert's cold acknowledgement of such. 'And you…' he turned to Roselyn, whose hair was in a ponytail this time instead of down, '… you were there with your eyes closed…' he declared, inching backwards, finding that even now she was acting as though she heard nothing. This… this must have been the Robert and Roselyn Vivienne cursed under her breath over tea earlier Wil suddenly realised—the Robert and Roselyn who should have told him the Runway had taken Lily.

'I'm sorry we have to do this to you, Wilden,' Robert said ominously, instilling fear, 'but it's the only way…' he looked to Roselyn regretfully, who finished his sentence,

'…To dump the thread,' she said determinedly, speaking through her sorrowful expression.

And backing Wil right up against the seats in the first row, they forced him to sit… cupped a hand each over his eyes… and he was suddenly… awake. *Awake*… and hearing his phone.

Quickly, he answered.

'What just happened, Wil?' Ben demanded. 'Everything disappeared—I ended up in the dreamscape!'

'I-I don't know really….'

'Did you take a shadow?' he pressed.

'No…' Wil insisted, but then, 'I mean, yes….' Certain Robert and Roselyn hadn't tried chucking him into the dreamscape…. 'I mean, I didn't *take* a shadow, they woke me up,' he said confusedly, frustrated, wanting to make clear that his Initial hadn't dumped Ben because Wil himself had simply decided to shadow out. 'Vivienne dragged my dream into hers—into a 360 Runway meeting, and then—'

'—*Vivienne?* Vivienne who?'

'The neighbour, next door! She runs the Runway—in the dreams—the children's rescue' Wil explained, realising that not only had he and Ben not discussed the neighbour's first name, but that Ben had no idea who actually ran the organisation. He certainly didn't know it was a frail old woman, and one that happened to live right next to Wil since moving back from London. 'She dream-dragged me into a meeting and—' he didn't want to say what he thought had happened to her 'she said her grandson would be taking over,' he recalled confusedly, suddenly appreciating why that would be the case now, 'and then the couple were there—the ones from my dreams earlier in the week—and they forced me to wake up—to kill Vivienne's thread.' He wished he hadn't used that word all of a sudden.

'Bloody hell! She was *waiting* like I was,' Ben realised, astonished. 'From next door...' he tapered off, clearly going over the events, figuring out where it all went wrong, how it all connected up. 'I'm sorry, Wil, but it's that bloody fog!' he spat down the line.

'Sorry?' Wil said distractedly, still seeing his old friend's hand reaching there in his mind.

'*The fog!* You're clearly using it to your own advantage, but she's used it to hers. She knew you wouldn't be alone tonight, and she knew getting you to take a shadow would only drop whoever was with you straight into the dreamscape... so she dragged your dream into hers without me even noticing—*because of that ridiculous fog!* Of course I wouldn't feel the stretch, would I? It would be you....' As hissy noises poured into Wil's ear, it was clear Ben was cursing himself under his breath for having been ignorant to what Vivienne was up to.

'Ben, Vivienne's dead.'

His cursing stopped.

'Dead?'

'She died right there in the dream,' Wil now understood, was dead next door now. 'I'm sure of it.' His eyes watered all of a sudden, for his chance to say good-bye had been fleeting, earlier and just now, because he had no idea. 'She gave me a cup of tea today and never said a thing, and she knew it was going to happen. And after she was gone, the couple made sure I couldn't carry on her thread. They woke me... so it wasn't my Initial propping up hers anymore. They must have been holding it open for me, for her when she came to get me....'

Ben's silence was unnerving.

'I haven't seen anyone die in the dreams before,' he uttered finally, clearly as shocked as Wil was.

'Neither have I.'

'I heard the head for the Runway was slightly crazy, all over the dreams, wasn't she? And to think she was your neighbour....'

'She wasn't crazy, Ben.' If only he knew how much she had done to help them. 'Everything we could have learned from her is gone.' Wil hated the thought of Vivienne's later years, decades of knowledge and experience, simply lost now. The genetic legacy she passed onto her offspring was composed of the years up until conception. Her last child would hold the largest cache of Vivienne's life experiences. However, not the complete. 'All of it… gone.' Wil suddenly wished he had asked more questions. Wrote down some of the answers.

'We need to get back in there again,' Ben determined, sounding as though he had forgotten Vivienne already, reminding Wil that he never even knew her. 'The others are waiting. And I don't want to *leave* them waiting if you've just had a death thread. If you were forced awake—'

'—My Initial will be different, I know.'

'Let's hope without fog this time. Now I can be there in one minute. So don't start without me.'

Wil hung up. He thought of Vivienne, there on the landing, listening to her music…. How he hated himself for not knowing what would come in that creeping cold she shivered through, ran from. He closed his eyes, regretful, opening them in his new Initial.

Chapter Thirty-Five

Murphy

Wil hurried across the carpark and up the grassy embankment, when a voice behind him called, 'Wil, *Wil...!*' stopping him.

'Pepperoni,' Ben said, jogging up the little slope, meeting him. 'Where are you going in such a hurry?' he asked, concerned, making Wil feel already as though he had betrayed them all somehow.

'Mushrooms. I thought I was late,' he admitted ridiculously, 'for my Physics exam.'

Ben scanned the campus. 'I saw the sign. *Mulbryn.* This was the last place I thought you'd feel safe in. Where is everyone?'

'Exams probably,' Wil guessed as he looked at the upper floors of the nearby English building, where students—undeterred extensions of the dream scenario—no doubt sweated over exam booklets, faithful to the authenticity of the mock-Mulbyrn timetable. 'You know, this could be to our advantage,' he suddenly realised. 'Because all the props here are so focused on academic perfection, they won't want anything to do with us, which means... anything else would stick out.'

'Good. Then take us to a place where *we* won't stick out,' Ben said gruffly. And keen to get away from the open carpark, they hurried along the path between the buildings towards the library.

'There's a table in the back on the left. By Philosophy,' Wil assured as they passed Aristotle's contemplative gaze and entered the library. Only, when they got to the Philosophy section, someone was sitting there, reading behind a stack of books. Though it was quite a large table, capable of seating eight easily, Wil and Ben looked at one another, reluctant to even take a seat there on the opposite end.

'Pardon me...' Ben whispered boldly, walking straight over to the lad behind the book, drawing Wil's attention suddenly to the fact that all dreamers were pretty much illiterate, and that if this were just substrate, the rapt studier would simply move on if prompted. 'Does affinity or Imposter mean anything to you?' And just as Ben was about to pull the book away, a familiar face looked up at both of them.

'Maybe.'

'Murphy?' Ben exclaimed, drawing glances and *shhh*'s from docile dream students studying at nearby tables. 'I don't believe it!' He punched Murphy into a standing position and then threw his arms around him. 'God I've missed you...' he gushed, stepping back, looking him up and down in disbelief. 'How long have you been here?'

'Seconds... hours...' Murphy shrugged, his blue eyes flashing. 'You know how it is.'

Amused, 'It really is you,' Ben marvelled, chasing Murphy's eyes, mocking an attempt to make sure he was no Imposter and squeezing him again sideways while clapping him on the back. But Ben's excitement was instantly restrained the second he looked over at Wil. 'Wil...' he said apprehensively, 'what is it?'

'It was you...' Wil muttered, his face now slack as Ben withdrew his arm from Murphy's shoulder. 'It was you in the end...' Wil said a little louder, causing the two there to glance at one another uncomfortably, unsure of what he was on about. But there could be no mistaking whose face that had been—a face Wil realised he had seen hundreds of times before. Thousands of times, now that he could remember.

'What was you?' Ben asked, looking concerned now from Wil to Murphy.

'You know those dreams I had about Roops, on the Thames,' Wil clarified to Ben, unable to take his eyes from Murphy's, for they set above those pointed cheeks as strikingly now as they had before, '...this is who took his place in the end.'

Ben looked at their old comrade curiously. 'You? *You* were in all those dreams...?'

'Just the one, Ben,' Wil corrected calmly, still fixed on those pale blue eyes.

'Not just the one, actually,' Murphy remarked. Brazen, certain, his dark eyebrows rose, challenging Wil's own memory of what had happened in the dreams.

Ben muttered in bewilderment, 'But Wil was in...'

'...Enemy fog?' Murphy offered, tearing his eyes off Wil and turning now to Ben. 'How then could he possibly have had any dreams at all?' he suggested, mocking, apparently guessing they were both now wondering the same thing.

'Well, he obviously wasn't fogged the *whole* time,' Ben reasoned innocently. '...But the whole point of them taking you was to stop the dreams,' he reconsidered '...to cut all those threads from Aeolus' affinity....' He seemed to have trouble with this logic and winced. 'So why would they let you out to dream all those months about Rupert?'

'Not about. *With*,' Murphy divulged knowledgeably. 'Your fog was dragged *to* Rupert's Initial, Wil. That's why no one detected you outside it those months, that's why you can remember.'

Of course... Wil realised. Dream-dragging affected fogged dreamers differently, depending on the direction they were being dragged. Fogged dreamers dragged into a normal Initial meant the two minds were essentially free of the fog, able to remember their dream together. That is, if the Tret and Tare allowed them to remember anything on waking. But drag a dreamer in the direction of the fog, like the naïve practices Annie mentioned they used to overcome the distress caused by Imposters, and neither dreamer would remember the experience.

'As far as the dreamscape was concerned, you were still isolated right up until the last night,' Murphy went on. 'And I imagine it was to see what you might do when given half a chance to get out.' This answer appeared to alleviate a significant degree of Ben's anxiety. But as far as Wil was concerned, Murphy seemed to know something neither he nor Ben knew. And being incredibly aware suddenly at how skilled Murphy was in diplomacy... how he avoided dabbling in trivial matters, which explained why, as a group, they rarely ever saw him, but when they did, he was the one who made all the difference... it now seemed no small thing that he had been there on the Thames in that last dream.

'So then... why *were* you there?' Wil asked pointedly. 'And if you had been there more than once, where were you?'

'Seriously? We're going to do this *here*.' Murphy looked about the Mulbryn Initial as if there was somewhere better, like real life—despite neither of them ever meeting there. '*Now?*'

'Those dreams had a huge effect on Wil,' Ben justified, seeing his best friend's determination.

'Yes. I am aware,' Murphy acknowledged coolly.

But knowing who Murphy really was, and trying to spare him any backlash from Ben, Wil discreetly stood his ground. 'It's been a long time,' Wil maintained, forcing a smile. 'Please. Refresh my memory.' And resigned to the inquiry, Murphy took his seat again and admitted quite readily,

'It was Vivienne's idea that I look into Rupert's recurrent nightmare.'

'Vivienne's?' Wil's eyes narrowed.

'Well you do know he's her grandson, don't you?'

'Of course,' Wil acknowledged, though still feeling a step behind.

'*Your* Rupert?' Ben interjected, incredulous. 'He's Vivienne's grandson?'

'Yes,' Wil said irritably, dismissively, but then rubbed his forehead and afforded Ben the same reaction he himself had in the lecture hall. 'I forgot to mention that earlier,' he admitted obviously, intimating that there was something more important he had just witnessed at the time— Vivienne's death, which he still didn't quite believe happened.

'Vivienne was lining him up to take over the Runway,' Murphy went on 'and she suggested that maybe I ought to turn him, to see which side made him more...' he gave an ambivalent shrug '...*charitable*. So I went in the first chance I had. I mean, it was Vivienne asking' Murphy hauffed, as if he'd do anything for her. 'And when I arrived, you were there. You...in Rupert's Initial....' He waited a beat, then looked at Wil and Ben with complete astonishment. 'Well there was an immediate conflict of interest, wasn't there?' he said obviously.

'Conflict?' Wil wasn't following.

Murphy threw them both a heavy glance and deflated slightly. 'Well firstly, apart from the fact that I consider the two of you standing here my *brothers*,' he said simply, 'I dare say everyone believes your affinity is still Tare,' he directed to Wil, 'despite all the threads that had been forcibly taken from you. Secondly,' he raised his eyebrows, suggestive, 'Rupert had Tret affinity when the two of you dreamed together. Essentially, you, a Tare—or what should have been a Tare—in a Tret's Initial.'

Immediately, Wil's shoulders fell. The only way he could have managed that was to either be Tret himself, or something of a Dual.

Basically, both Tret and Tare affinitied like Murphy. Only he was nothing like Murphy at all... not like any of the Duals he had known in fact... because he didn't have the freedom to choose when he would serve Tret or Tare purposes. What he had instead, was something like a ticking bomb, concealed inside him, ready to injure friends and family at no doubt the most destructive opportunity.

'Listen, Wil,' Ben said carefully, seeing his friend disintegrate slightly, 'we talked about this.' He gave Murphy a brief, reproachful look then went over and took Wil by the shoulders. 'We have no idea what's been going on the last three years,' he said firmly. 'This doesn't mean anything.'

'Well, it has to mean something,' Murphy said flagrantly, casually thumbing the cover of a book, showing his Tret side all too quickly. 'Vivienne wanted me to either cut the thread creating Rupert's nightmare in the first place... or simply turn him, either of which would have made him less... well, Rupert,' he said with a hint of tact. 'Now, it's risky business cutting one thread, but two?' He looked at Wil ridiculously, making it clear no person was that skilled. 'I can't be in two places at once—two minds— can I? Not only that, but you were still in protective fog, Wil. There's no way I was going to start messing around with your head while you were in there,' he justified. 'But the only sure way of doing what Vivienne asked would have been to cut Rupert's thread, which would have disconnected *you* and sent you fully into the fog. As you can imagine, the last thing I wanted to do was cut the very thing in him that allowed you those months on the edge. Being dream-dragged to his Initial was as close to getting out as you'd ever been since you got in there. And my biggest fear was that once Rupert's thread was cut, you'd go back to complete isolation with the remains of some horrible thing I had a part in. That is how they use us after all, convincing us we're doing good, only to show us how wrong we were.' Murphy shook his head as if that could never have been an option. 'And once I realised the awake proximity you and Rupert shared... that objects alone might trigger one of you to enter the dreams of the other, and that he could pick up the thread again from you... well I wasn't about to muck up the one personal job Vivienne asked me to do, now was I?'

'So then, what did you do?' Wil asked, sure he wouldn't like the answer.

'Well, as you both know, it isn't my style to turn someone outside the privacy of their own Initial,' he said indignantly, 'and it certainly isn't my style to do it in front of company,' he directed to Wil.

'What did you do, Murphy?' Ben pressed impatiently, apparently seeing for the first time an evasive side to Murphy he clearly wasn't sure he could trust—the very side Wil himself had to peel away whenever their old friend had been too long dashing between Tret and Tare territory.

'What do you think? I tried turning him, just as Vivienne asked, but the old-fashioned way. Without cutting threads, it wasn't going to be straightforward now was it? Because while I was trying to turn Rupert through persuasion instead of force, it seemed that you Wil were doing the same.' His wide eyes accused. 'Only, I couldn't tell if we were actually working together, or not.'

Probably not, Wil thought, setting his jaw askew and pressing his fist into the table. 'I was under Tret influence' Wil pointed out, hating himself for this fact, '…why would they try and get me to turn a fellow Tret? That makes no sense.'

'To see if you'd revert back to your old ways,' Murphy posed. 'To see if they'd done their work in you… to see how you do it—how *I* did it—because we did do it in the end, Wil. Rupert did turn. And it wasn't because you were dream-dragged. They know trying to set you at odds with dream-drags would undermine them turning you in the first place, because it would have been heavily influenced by Rupert's affinity, and vice versa. All too tangled,' he insisted, rejecting such a strategy.

'Rupert went Tare?' Ben interrupted, apparently relieved that both his mates achieved such an outcome. Though he looked a bit unsure as to whether he could now trust either of them.

'Well, that wasn't because of me,' Wil insisted, dismissing any part he could have played in changing Rupert's affinity. 'I wouldn't have been able to even get into Rupert's Initial unless I was on his side already,' Wil argued. 'So not only does that show it was *you* who turned him, but it shows who I really am to have been there in the first place. There can't be anything in me to turn him,' he insisted disparagingly, 'it was taken away, remember?'

Murphy frowned at Wil there at the opposite end of the table. 'I think you forget whose company you're in, Wil,' he hinted. 'Whatever happened then, *right now*… you're *here*… with *Tare* friends,' he reminded, drawing Wil to look at Ben who they both knew was complete Tare—who both Murphy and Wil knew stood there as proof that there was at least something Tare in Wil if his best friend could join his Initial like this. .

'I could still be a Dual though,' Wil argued half-heartedly.

'And what's so bad about that?' Murphy gave him a pointed look. *Nothing at all*, Wil thought to himself. But he wouldn't be a Dual like Murphy. Had he been, he could consciously choose his battles, choose which cause to join, and believe his small part was making a difference. The way he was now… probably a new breed of Dual, an experiment… he had no free will at all.

'You could be a Dual,' Ben acknowledged, 'but it doesn't change the fact that we're best friends. It doesn't change the fact that' he glanced at Murphy over his shoulder 'we're here to look out for you.'

All of a sudden, Wil gasped. 'Ben, I've only just realised—if I'm a Dual, *anyone* can come in here,' he exclaimed, horrified. It now seemed essential that they not draw attention to themselves. 'They'll all share my affinity,' Wil cautioned, looking over his shoulder, lowering his voice. 'My Initial won't keep out Tret dreamers.' He tried not to look at Murphy when he said this.

'I'm aware of that,' Ben admitted modestly, making Wil realise the risk his best friend had taken in coming to his Initial tonight. Twice.

'You know what? I am what I am,' Wil decided, looking at Ben's half-anxious, forcing-calm expression, certain he could do nothing to change the circumstances, whatever they were. 'We need to just get through the night without incident.'

'I personally don't think you're a Dual, Wil,' Murphy stated plainly, lining up the corner of book ends in front of him, 'but if you were—and I say if…' he snatched a glimpse of Wil's now concerned face, 'wouldn't it make your turning Rupert a bit odd? I mean, how does a Dual decide one should be Tare? And if you were Tret… well… odder still, don't you think?' It was a little odd, Wil had to admit. But then it could all be the ruse to undermine every decision Wil consciously made inside and outside the dreams. Because none of this had been done before. People didn't just come back and remember the things *they had been forced to forget*. All they had were those elusive threads that drew them back to their affinities, and it was from that moment—the moment they returned—that they were allowed to remember any sort of dream. *If* they were allowed to remember. 'All I'm saying is you really ought to consider your role in those dreams, because that last one—the one where you and I met face-to-face—wasn't Rupert's,' Murphy pointed out. He met Wil squarely. 'It was yours.'

'Mine?'

'You don't believe me.' Murphy shrugged, dismissive. 'For weeks I had been following Rupert's thread. Objects supplied to me through his cousins determined I'd reach his Initial, seeing as he was a complete stranger to me. But on seeing you there, I found I couldn't interact with him as I had hoped.'

'Well, he was dead,' Ben pointed out, demonstrating his ignorance in turning individuals as skilfully as Murphy could. 'How were you going to *interact* with him?'

'He wasn't dead to start,' Murphy said dryly, rolling his eyes. 'For weeks he had just walked the water's edge, contemplating. I came onto the scene when he had actually done the deed every night for months already. And I didn't realise until later that he dreamed himself dead the instant you entered the Initial. The instant you were dragged.' Murphy looked directly to Wil. 'That was when he gulped water like air and stopped fighting. So as you walked through the alleyways towards us... we were pulling him out. Of course, he wasn't actually dead. He didn't die in the dreams. Instead, he carried on in a passive role, creating the police reaction, watching as they fussed around him and told him things he obviously wanted to hear. The conversations he heard...' Murphy shook his head, appalled 'they spoke volumes about what he thought of himself.... And to think it was all a safe place in his mind, a place safe enough to visit over and over again.'

Wil hadn't considered this. It made him glad he had hounded Roops the way he had.

'The moment I recognised you, Wil, I couldn't tell if you were substrate or what, so I had to hang back until I knew for sure. I needed to be certain you not only didn't recognise *me*, but that you wouldn't try to stop me from turning what seemed to be your good friend there. I mean, part of me hoped the Initial would change, that the job would become easier somehow, but it didn't. I barely had any feedback that I was making progress. Until the last dream. Because it wasn't his. It was yours. And it was the only real dream the Tret let you have when you were with them. I waited for you to have another. I waited even before then,' Murphy assured. 'And when I couldn't wait myself, I had someone else doing it for me. But you didn't after that. You didn't have your own dream until Monday night this last week.'

'They wanted me to adopt the Initial of someone with Tret affinity,'

Wil concluded thoughtfully. 'But then, why Rupert? And why let me out for one night only?' He looked at Murphy, perplexed.

'I'm afraid I've only got guesses.'

'I want to hear your guesses,' Ben assured with a loyal nod to his best friend.

'All right then. Perhaps Vivienne knew this,' Murphy readily suggested. 'Perhaps she knew who Rupert's Initial was intended for and that its thread was already spinning inside you. Asking me to cut threads wouldn't have been just about her grandson then, would it?'

Wil couldn't help think of Vivienne's offer to look after him just then, before he entered the fog. However, he spotted a gap in Murphy's account.

'Wait a minute. You said you were there, but I didn't see you until the last night.'

'Listen, I know you both think I know more than I'm telling you,' Murphy accepted, putting his hands up, 'but when I came onto the scene, I pretended to be substrate until I knew the extent of what was going on. I posed as an officer in the tent just chatting to a colleague, and when I had the chance, I declared all the things to Dead Rupert that Vivienne wanted me to. But when I realised you were there—really there—doing the same thing, coming to identify him and saying all those kind things while he was lying there… well I saw that we sort of tag-teamed in the end until he obviously started believing being dead on a riverbank wasn't actually the safe Initial he'd once thought. Because one more dream, and I found him on a cricket field playing with his mates.'

Wil realised that must have been when Rupert packed it all in, all the excellence, all the pointless striving.

'Of course, I immediately distrusted the objects Vivienne had given me when he went from suicide to cricket overnight,' Murphy went on, 'because Rupert showed no sign of turning. He was taking the plunge right up to the night before. So when I entered his Initial on the cricket pitch, I assumed I had been diverted, that he was an Imposter. Of course, I didn't waste time finding out because that would have been valuable time lost I assumed was being used to conceal the original dream thread. I tried reaching the same thread through the dreamscape, visiting every night-time low-tide Thames shadow I could find. It didn't take long…' Murphy's eyes lost focus briefly, lowering in the direction of Wil's stomach '…and there it was. The forensics tent. Rupert would have them put it up around him once they took him from the water. So I knew it was his dream. The first thing I did was check that tent. Only, when I looked inside...' Murphy fixed his eyes to Wil's face again '...*he* wasn't in it.'

'Murphy, I saw the change in Rupert back then,' Wil insisted, wondering why his old comrade might assume the Rupert on the cricket pitch was an Imposter. 'I'm certain his affinity changed around this time—right before my last dream.' Wil couldn't help think of all those times he turned Tret dreamers to Tare, watched a Verger turn—because the rumours weren't just rumours—he, Wil, *had* been making Duals of them—it was the only way to get them remembering. The epiphanies, the character U-turns... the philosophical abandonment and conversion that remade minds... it's exactly what Rupert demonstrated at the time.

'Maybe that's why he wasn't in the tent that last night then,' Ben posed.

'Yes. But I didn't' realise it was Wil's dream at that point—I still thought it was Rupert's you see. I thought maybe he wasn't in the tent because he was in the middle of turning. I had been looking for a change in him for weeks. I felt certain the other dream had been a smokescreen, to prevent me from coming back to the river and finishing the job. So I had to find him there somewhere. But when I found you, Wil, sombre, walking through the steam of a manhole along that little alleyway.... I thought at that point he'd certainly be there, because that's when it was too late all the other times. So I went back to the tent. But again, it wasn't him.' Murphy sighed and hooked an elbow on the back of his chair. 'That's when I realised what was going on. My concern then was that you were coming. I knew exactly where you would end up, only, I knew too that you wouldn't see Rupert when you got there.'

Wil realised this was where Murphy had moved from a background role to one quite prominent, and must have taken Rupert's vacancy in the tent. However, Murphy's intimating silence, his implying frown, suggested that someone else was already there in the tent, and had been from the moment Murphy arrived until he spotted Wil walking down the alleyways.

'I'm afraid it was you, Wil,' he confessed, the lines in his face showing genuine regret. 'The substrate had *you* lying there.'

Substrate. It was just another word for the divulgences of the dreaming mind. In this case, Wil saw it as emotional proclamations to oneself.

'That night, I thought right up to the end that I should still be looking for him,' Murphy continued delicately. 'It didn't occur to me that it wasn't the same Initial until I decided to get you out of there. ...I kept thinking that maybe he dreamed you in the tent—that when I at first saw you in it, it was evidence of him finally turning. That's what made me go and look for him,' Murphy admitted, sounding disappointed with himself. 'But when I saw you, I realised you would come to that very spot, just as you had before. I couldn't let you see what I had seen,' he said firmly. 'I had one chance to sort things. Of course, the longer I was with you by the river, the more I had second thoughts—I was beginning to think it was all an ambush.' He rolled his eyes at the thought. 'But seeing your reaction to me... and knowing what you had obviously told your roommate all the other nights... I knew I had done the best thing. And when there was that feeling of dawn coming....'

Wil could see it there in his mind too, taking the gloom from the tent. The moment he woke from having seen Murphy's face there in the stony mud instead of Rupert's, he felt freed. Liberated and resolved. All those months of guilt gone because he had nothing to prove anymore. He woke feeling like a new person. Surely he wouldn't have felt the same if he had seen his own lifeless body there.

'...You turned me,' Wil uttered, the realisation all over his face. It was the only way he could have been freed of that dream. Freed so spectacularly of that unrelenting desperation for Rupert. 'You turned both of us.'

Murphy leaned forward in earnest, his chin just hovering over the books,

'No Wil. You turned Rupert outside the dreams, what I did inside... was merely return a favour.'

Wil tried imagining the dream as it was, and not as he thought it had been, and he appreciated that Murphy had taken the liberty of changing a significant element in his only Initial outside Tret fog—altered what Wil's Tret mind at the time had conjured as safe and secure.

'What did you do with it? My body?'

'Does it matter?'

But seeing Wil's stubbornness, Murphy relented.

'There was a body bag. We put it in there and moved it out of sight.'

'Where?'

'Outside the tent. The side we knew you wouldn't pass.

357

Unfortunately, anyone inside the tent could see its silhouette once the sun started rising. I'm afraid we didn't have time to move it up to street level to a vehicle. You were nearly there when we tried getting rid of it.'

Wil shook his head, aware things could have turned out so differently, had he questioned that shadow outside. 'You said *we*,' he realised, knowing how tricky substrate performing civil service roles could be. 'Who else helped you move it?'

'The police officer who offered you a taxi afterwards. That was Miles, my lookout. The moment you entered the fog, he's been on strict instruction to confirm your first Initial and then come and find me. Of course, once he detected your break that last night from protective fog and came onto the river scene to confirm it was actually you in your dream, he no doubt found himself in a rather complex situation, with two of you, and one of me. It was just as well he waited until you woke and the thread broke that he finally caught up with me on the cricket pitch. Yes, I did finally go back and confirm it was truly Rupert's Initial, once I had taken care of things with you, that is. I dare say any disturbance in those last moments would have had a completely different outcome for us all.'

Wil thought about that, thought of the effect seeing Murphy there had had on him. On Miles too probably, who would have been forced to play along until he knew what he was dealing with.

'Listen, Wil, I don't think you realise what I've told you,' Murphy stressed. 'You were turning Rupert. While you were *awake*.'

Both Wil and Ben eyed him apprehensively. The only place they knew minds turned was where they could be stripped back to simple desire and fear, just as Vivienne mentioned.

'That's why I think they tried getting you to take on Rupert's thread,' Murphy explained. 'You were clearly making so much progress outside the dreams, they tried redressing the balance inside, getting you to take Rupert's burdens onto yourself.' Wil realised he most certainly did that in more ways than one. 'Of course, they hadn't considered you still had allies like me.' Here Murphy vaguely indicating his Dual nature which allowed him to turn anyone in any Initial. 'It seems as though their plan may have back-fired.'

Nothing the Tret and Tare did back-fired though, Wil thought. As much as he wanted to show his appreciation to Murphy for doing what he did, there was something inside him that made all this feel like mere speculation. Like something worse had been initiated in that riverside foil, because the Tret and Tare were always a step ahead.

'Wait a minute,' Ben piped up, blinking wildly upwards, 'if Rupert went from Tret on the Thames... to Tare on the cricket pitch...' he sent a perplexed look in Wil's direction, 'then how could you have been in *both* Initials?' His head turned slowly to Murphy.

Wil felt something heavy drop inside him just then. He gauged Murphy for direction, but it seemed he had none this time. In fact, his slim form just sat there coolly in the chair, daring Ben to draw his own conclusions.

'You're afraid he's a Dual?' Wil argued incredulously, recalling Ben having no qualms when Wil suspected himself of it earlier. But Murphy quickly held up a hand, overriding Wil.

'I think it's time you should know, Benjamin,' he declared. 'I am a Dual' he said flatly, as if it were of little significance, especially after having just revealed his hand in turning Wil back to Tare.

'*What?*' Ben squeaked, furious. His chest puffed, his arms lifted, intimidating, and the easy manner in which he became outraged unnerved Wil as heads turned towards them from tables nearby.

'You want to know how I could get into Tret dreams,' Murphy accepted, explaining 'and how I can be here with you and Wil.' He put placating hands up to Ben who now looked like he was going to erupt. 'I've been a Dual for as long as I can remember.'

'And you *knew* this...?' Ben hissed, confounded, turning to Wil. 'You knew he was *like this?*'

Like what? Wil wanted to shout, because it never mattered whether Murphy was a Dual. In Wil's mind, a Dual's ability to play both sides when it suited them was no different to any Verger—most of the human population, actually. Awareness was the only thing that separated the two, conscious remembering of the dreams. The last thing Wil wanted to do was sound ashamed for knowing Murphy's secret—because his secret could still be his own. But as he caught Murphy's coaxing glare from behind Ben's back, Wil felt certain Murphy was encouraging him to at least *pretend* to feel ashamed in knowing.

'How do you think we knew about Donnelly,' Wil tried to sound dejected, 'or saved Zlata from Transition?' These two incidents would have ended in grievous failure for Ben personally had they not had insider information—information Wil himself obtained from Murphy. 'We wouldn't have managed any of it without his tip-offs' Wil argued half-heartedly, unsure of what Murphy was trying to accomplish here in outing himself.

'And you trusted what he *told* you?' Ben accused, making Wil realise that after all they had been through—the three of them had been through—Ben was willing to discount it because of this new knowledge, this new knowledge that changed nothing of the past.

Just then, a commotion up near the librarian's desk effectively ended their conversation and remembering where they were, they all looked at one another, wide-eyed.

Murphy stood up swiftly and squared with Ben, who instantly stiffened, standing his ground.

'Check it,' Murphy instructed, for this was how things had always been done. They always deferred to Murphy whenever he showed up. Only this time, as the three of them heard someone shouting outside the entrance doors, pounding on the glass, Wil could see Ben wavering, his trust in Murphy being tested. 'We don't have time, Benjamin,' Murphy insisted through gritted teeth. '*Check it.*'

Ben's eyes flitted from the commotion to Wil and back to Murphy until his shoulders fell slightly. 'Fine. But don't take a shadow without me.' He eyed them fiercely, to which they both nodded their heads promising, and quickly he ran up the central aisle to the front of the library.

'Now listen to me,' Murphy said hastily, coming around to Wil. 'All the Duals will forget by morning—by morning you and I will be strangers—'

'—*What?*' Wil exclaimed.

'It's our time, *my* time,' Murphy insisted, shaking it off. 'A Dual's Initial obstructs no one, so if you think about it, I've no Initials left. Besides, nothing's safe anymore when you've done what I've done. But I want to remember again, Wil,' he said emphatically. 'Like you have. I want you to try and bring me back Tare.' He grabbed Wil's elbow, urging the impossible. 'Promise me you'll try,' he demanded, unsettling Wil, for this was the first time this commanding figure ever looked uncertain— desperate—about anything.

'But I might be a Dual too!' Wil argued, despite all Murphy had revealed about Rupert's dream. '*I* might be forgetting if you are.'

'You're not a Dual, Wil,' Murphy insisted, shaking his head vehemently.

'But after you—' the last thing Wil wanted was to emphasise

Murphy's actions on the riverbank might have been exactly as the Tret wanted '… but after you turned me, I was in there another year—they could have done anything.'

'They could have,' Murphy affirmed darkly, stepping closer. 'They could have done any number of things if you weren't Tret enough for them, Wil.' He briefly eyed the students at the tables opposite then said in a hushed voice, 'Like get you to adopt Rupert's Initial… and as of this week, his school and their fog…' he trailed off, suggesting there was more to all of it than either of them could possibly know, leaving Wil feeling extremely unsettled there in the library. 'Of course they could have done anything, but they don't *do* just anything, do they?'

Squeezing Wil's arm, Murphy leaned even closer and said carefully, 'Whatever they're doing Wil, they're doing it off the back of us turning people, do you hear me?' He watched the strangers around them as though paranoid now. Those cold blue eyes looked frenzied, nothing of the resolute young man asserting his authority over Ben a moment ago. 'Since your big transition the first time, I've been turning people left and right—in fact that's *all* I've been doing. And no one seems to be doing anything about it. But why? Why let us… then do nothing about it? No one goes to the Point of Transition anymore. It's not even a place now. It's redundant. Turning happens everywhere. Anywhere. Inside Initials… outside… it's commonplace now.'

Wil couldn't imagine the Point of Transition becoming obsolete, that place in the mind where two unlikely threads crossed over. Two opposing threads. 'So then how do allies intervene?'

'They don't,' Murphy hauffed, his stare less intense for a second. 'It happens, and no one stops it. It's like they have bigger fish to fry…. Or are waiting for something to happen… some balance to finally tip.' He then thought for a second and tightened his lips, disappointed like. 'I knew they'd let me get you at the river. It felt like a set-up, you know?' he admitted, appearing a bit ashamed for saying it as his eyes darted around the chairs and tables. However, Wil was glad his friend could be so honest because it was precisely this that concerned him about Murphy's role in that borrowed Initial. Realising he was still holding Wil's arm, Murphy let go, and looking self-conscious about his state, he patted Wil distractedly on the shoulder, clumsily curbing the awkwardness, for he had been a master of discretion and strategy and now just seemed to be unravelling.

There was the noise at the front again. A dull object bouncing off a large window.

'Listen, I didn't come here to tell you that I turned you, Wil,' he hastened. 'I came to warn you that there's been a shift. The polarisation of Tret and Tare, something's happening to it. Something's happening to us and them too.' He then shook his head agitatedly for a moment as though mosquitoes were swarming about him. And through slightly clenched teeth, 'They need some of us to remember… need some of us to be Duals…' he stretched his neck to the side and closed his eyes forcefully like he was only just enduring something creeping up his back, '…and yet they don't want us aware of who we're advocating…' his jaw set and he was now wiping his chin from shoulder to shoulder across his chest '…so they're getting rid of Duals as we know it.' Having spat the words out with what seemed an incredible effort, Murphy was then resolutely focused. 'But trust me,' he said quietly, tensely 'they've got something else coming.' And there he was again, twitching, though clearly trying to overcome it.

'But that's just what I mean about *me* being a Dual,' Wil maintained, watching Murphy battle two determined sides simultaneously just then. 'Even Aeolus thinks I might have something Tret hidden in me—'

They both heard Ben warning 'Don't do it' to whoever he was dealing with just then.

'—We've all got something Tret hidden in us, Wil,' Murphy declared impatiently. 'Both sides have broken threads, hidden threads. Now promise me,' he implored. 'If you wake remembering, you know you're not a Dual—you've not been made to forget like the rest of us—so then try and find me. You and Sadie did it. *Find me.* I've already got a few things in place to help us out. *Please.* Say you'll—'

'—*Okay,*' Wil agreed, hearing Ben's urgent voice now like he was trying to speak to someone outside through the glass, for his words were loud but slow, his vowels drawn. 'Okay, but I don't even know *how* to find you…. You were always the one who found us….'

'I've got it covered. I'll be like everyone else first off. A Verger. Everyone's turning these days. So try then, when I turn Tare.'

'All right,' Wil accepted confusedly, for he needed objects and such to reach Murphy in his Initial. If any of their old threads were to be cut, they wouldn't even be able to rely on close relationships to find one another. But surely Murphy knew that…. 'Okay….' Then hearing a female voice again shouting at Ben from outside the building, 'We should go and help Ben,' Wil prompted.

'You go,' Murphy said distractedly. 'I need to see Annie, before it happens.' His eyes flickered with dread. 'Besides, I should have sent you instead. It's Sadie up there trying to get in.'

'*Sadie?*' Something vast, both heavy and light felt like it slipped out of Wil's chest just then. 'Sadie's here, in my Initial?' He turned to the aisle, his first instinct to go to her, but he stopped short and looked to Murphy.

'You know she's a Dual,' Murphy whispered, pained to have to say it.

'Yes,' Wil found himself stalled, the realisation all over his face. 'She is a Dual,' he said under his breath. And as it hit him all of a sudden that this dream might be all he'd have of a Sadie who remembered him from before… he realised too that this might be the last time he'd ever see his loyal friend standing here before him like all those other dreams. A flash of encounters went through Wil's mind just then. He saw the intense blue eyes there opposite him in situations as dreadful as this, where they couldn't be certain they'd meet again, yet every one of those times hadn't the last. This time, however, felt different. Quickly, he went and hugged Murphy.

'Listen Wil. Don't confess to being a Dual unless you know you're one,' Murphy advised, now bracing Wil's shoulders at arm's length. 'And you can tell Ben I know he'll get over it. I mean, it's not like I can hold a grudge now, can I?' he joked, his brief smile souring under the circumstances. Then taking a step back, he slowly closed his eyes and was gone, leaving Wil marvelling at how he travelled, for he took shadows the way Annie did. Pushed a thought into the darkness behind the eyelids. Never room for a companion.

Wil felt a deep sense of loss just then. And he was reminded how the dreams were only half the battle sometimes, that the other half was waiting when he woke. That's where grief piled and immobilised.

'I could use a bit of help up here!' Ben hollered as Wil rushed up the aisle to him.

Chapter Thirty-Six

Dreamscape

B en paced the lobby and threw irritable glances to Sadie outside, who appeared to be having her own little crisis. 'She tried breaking the door down,' he explained in frustration, 'then when that didn't work she started screaming... but the substrate's restricting her. You can't force it—she should know this,' he insisted, flustered and throwing a hand in the air. 'If there's anyone out there looking for us, she's just told them where we are.'

Running to the window, Wil caught Sadie's attention. 'Sadie calm down...' he mouthed quietly through the glass as she sprinted over to him. 'Please, just calm down...' he said once again, putting his hands on the glass. The relief on her face... the desperation... this was no doubt the Sadie of his past, their past. He mouthed the word *fail* to her, prompting her to mouth *safe* in return. Neither had forgotten their codes.

'She won't listen,' Ben determined angrily as she tried placing her hands on the glass, only to prompt two bursts of white to appear where she would have made contact, opaque white like paint splatters. Jerking away as though burned, she began to feverishly look for something nearby. 'It's like a seatbelt—force things too quickly and there will be no give,' Ben reminded unhelpfully over Wil's shoulder while he continued pacing. 'She tried breaking the glass doors, so of course, they're now locked. And throwing a rubbish bin at the windows... well that clearly did us some good....' Ben pointed to the other white splatters above and by the doors, places where Sadie evidently tried altering the fabric of the dream.

'She will no longer be able to make contact with the glass,' the Librarian said matter-of-factly from behind them at the desk, nonchalantly scanning books.

Wil and Ben worriedly looked at one another. They were both aware that the dream substrate should simply respond to the living dreamers within, as opposed to react. In everyday life, it seemed an ambiguous difference, but here, one was passive, while the other, most definitely aggressive.

'You still feeling safe?' Ben shot sarcastically to Wil, fixing on Sadie with serious contempt.

Annoyed now, Wil quickly went over to the door and gave it a gentle push. He then rattled the handle hard for a few seconds, drawing the attention of the librarian again.

'Pardon me,' he called to her, 'but we can't seem to get out.'

'I'm afraid it's study hour,' she said simply. 'No one gets out.' She then looked at Sadie outside. 'And no one gets in.'

'*We need to leave, Wil,*' Ben urged through gritted teeth, pulling Wil away from the door. 'We need to go to Steph's *right now*—we're not waiting for study hour to finish.' He looked over his shoulder at the now seemingly oblivious woman behind the desk and said more quietly, 'Do I have to remind you that no one can tell time in dreams. She'll keep us here *indefinitely.*' Ben was right, time was nothing in the dreams. To abide by any increment of it was merely a delaying tactic. 'And where's Murphy?'

'He's gone. Shadowed out. By the way, he told me to tell you he knows you'll get over it,' to which Ben just threw his pale, freckle-embedded eyebrows up in the air.

'What's she doing now?' Wil asked, watching Sadie roll up a leaflet from the display board outside and tighten it into a tube. She then pushed it through the book depository, her finger in one end, and beckoned them to come over. As the paper poked past the metal flap to their side of the building, she mouthed the words 'Shadow—together—you—choose.'
'She wants to get out of here with us,' Ben said plainly, as though Wil hadn't seen the same thing.

'C'mon then,' Wil decided, bending down and grabbing the end of the leaflet. 'She helped me get my memory back,' he wasn't about to mention Sadie would forget everything by morning because she was a Dual, or that before in the dreams, they hid their relationship from everyone because of this fact. 'I'm not leaving without her.'

Ben threw his head back. 'Nothing's going to plan,' he seethed, then made reluctant steps towards Wil. 'If we join that shadow...' he glared at the tube of paper 'and she takes us somewhere we don't want to be...'

'She won't,' Wil assured, looking through the glass at her. 'Now hurry up, will you?'

All of a sudden, Wil noticed the historic Literature and Languages building opposite—the one directly behind Sadie—had disappeared. And instead... the space had become... the top of a city building! It was as if a small portion of a skyscraper had been chopped off and set there... and there seemed to be an implied drop behind it for there were ambulance and police sirens blaring as though far below. Realising he no longer felt safe here, that any protective elements of his Initial were now breaking down, that the threads in his head were jolting with energy far beyond his control, he shouted,

'Seriously Ben, *now!*'

At that moment, Sadie looked over her shoulder, having seen their worried faces and saw the same thing too—the Initial collapsing, corrupting. The Tret and Tare were already there, imposing. Ben quickly joined Wil, falling to his knees. He pushed his thumb into the edge of the tube just as the courtyard outside became a vast chasm between skyscrapers, for there were more, more rooftops suddenly appearing where paths and buildings had been. Aristotle was gone and it occurred to Wil that if one of them didn't decide where to go next, Sadie would soon be precariously standing on a high-riser ledge, for she was now with her back up against the window and her arm was just barely reaching into the book depository.

'Ben...!' Wil shouted once more, waiting for them to go, and instantly, the three of them found themselves standing on the pavement, leaflet gone, thumbs and fingers pointing at one another in exactly the positions in which they left Mulbryn.

'This is our old house,' Wil recognised instantly. It was under the flight path near Heathrow. And just now, it looked like the morning rush hour. A dozen or so people, dressed in working-in-London black, bustled up the street away from them towards Feltham station.

'I saw Lily, Sadie,' Wil said in earnest, taking his first opportunity to assure her. 'She's still with Vivienne and she's fine.'

'When did you see her? Did she look happy?' Sadie asked,

concerned, for Lily was barely two when they took her to the Runway. A toddler when Sadie last dreamed with her.

But before Wil could say anything else, Steph burst out of the house shouting,

'Go-go-go! *Olives*—GO...!'

'*Already?*' Ben yelled.

'Yes!' she ran towards them. 'They've just swapped the room!'

Swaps. It was the same thing Wil had just seen in his own Initial— Tret and Tare arriving, chopping and changing whatever thread they could. Redirecting thoughts, images... the fabric of the dreams to gain an advantage. It was relatively easy to spot swaps in Initials. However, the dreamscape, where so many minds were involved, meant you had no idea who was doing what.

'We only just got here,' Ben exclaimed, 'we've got to stay longer— or we'll be out in the dreamscape with nothing—surely not everything's swapped!'

'The car then—' Steph said quickly, pointing to Ben's Gran's mini that just happened to be there by the curb. The fact that they neither knew Ben when they lived in this house, nor needed keys to get in and start the engine was of little consequence.

'It won't go in reverse,' Ben shouted, forcing the stick and sending the engine grinding.

'Just move it!' Steph instructed from the passenger's seat, flapping her hand at the car in front, suggesting he simply drive into the back of it to give them enough space to get out. Doing exactly that, Ben smashed into the back of the car then reversed for a second attempt.

Just then, he froze.

'Steph...' he said ominously, looking in the rear-view mirror, '... what are they...?'

Everyone turned around to find the long residential road... had become a strip of field, laid out between parked cars and houses... and those bustling commuters going the other direction a few minutes ago... were now a herd of black bulls coming this way!

'Are those briefcases...?' Wil thought aloud, seeing handbags and all sorts now flouncing along the length of those rather long horns.

'Quick!' Ben shouted, putting his hand out between them all, to which everyone else knew to do the same. Like a stack of pancakes, they reached. 'We're going to Annie's.' And with that Ben put his other hand

368

over everyone else's and looked into the gap like he was cosseting a flame. Only nothing happened.

'C'mon, Ben,' Steph tried hurrying him, for they could feel the vibration of hooves coming, hear the pounding.

'It's not working! Steph, you try!'

Swiftly, she took over, cupping her hands and peering into the dark spot.

'Nothing,' she said flatly. 'Maybe Annie's *awake*,' she fretted.

'We have no choice then,' Wil confirmed, squeezing Sadie's hand there beside his leg. 'They're hitting us all at once.'

Knowing the only options were to enter the dreamscape or wake up and do this all over again, 'The dreamscape it is,' Ben agreed. 'We need to split up.'

'Sadie's with me,' Wil decided as the rumble of hooves came closer, accompanied by beastly moans and bellows. 'Ben you take Steph,' he said hastily. 'Annie's always better on her own. If it's too insane, just wake up' he insisted, giving orders as though the three years had never happened.

'We'll come find you,' Ben reminded, assuring.

'Run as fast as you can,' Steph started too 'and remember that everything feeds off your perceptions. If you want to fly...'

'...I need to feel liberated somehow first,' Wil said impatiently, rolling his eyes. 'Yes, I know.'

'It's not Hollywood—' Steph declared officiously, as though completely unaware of the bovine stampede well-equipped to gore them.

'He *knows* all this' Ben bawled, the bulls a stone's throw away now, 'now let's go...!'

And they all went.

Wil suddenly found himself standing with Sadie in front of a closed shop down the bricked lane of Bath Place in town. It was dark, there was no one around.

Sadie threw her arms around him and sobbed. He too began to cry. It was the first time in three years that they were able to see each other as before. Like this.

'I'm so sorry...' she exclaimed into his neck '... I couldn't tell you—I couldn't say anything... they tormented me with an Imposter....'

'It's okay...' he soothed, shushing her, knowing she had to hide everything she knew concerning him, including her feelings, her duality, until he remembered for himself, for she had been the fail-safe Ben wanted to know about. It was her, the only person he was certain could conjure the same chemical response and renew old threads, whether he was Tret or Tare. 'You did the right thing—you did exactly as we said....'

'Only for it to change back again...' Sadie lamented close to his ear. 'It was so hard... seeing you every week...' she looked at him 'pretending I didn't know you....' The thought brought another wave of tears. 'All that work... to end up forgetting anyway... to end up with only here and now... because tomorrow... tomorrow....' Sadie's face contorted in pain at the thought of what tomorrow meant for them, and pulling her head to his chest, Wil shushed her softly, for the fear of waking—the fear of losing her again... he was incapable just now of feeling anything more than the temporary relief of having her in his arms like this, just like before. 'I don't want to forget,' Sadie said weakly, pulling away, 'you've only just come back.'

'I know. I know...' he said under his breath, leading her out of the open towards the bowed panes of the shop window. Here, he pulled her to him and pressed his cheek to her head. Then as rain began to fall, they went under the shallow shelter of the shopfront entrance, her arms tucked under his. 'We can run til we wake,' he promised. 'We can have every last minute together.'

'I don't want to run anymore, Wil,' she sniffed, looking up at him. 'I don't want our last minutes to be panic, fear. I want them to be like this.'

'We'll stay like this then,' he soothed, then kissed her.

They held one another as the night sky became darker, and Wil kept watch over her head, making sure everything around them stayed as it should.

'They told me it was an airstrip and it clearly wasn't,' Sadie said after a while, reminding Wil of what she had divulged when they were awake. 'They said you'd lift the fog and find one, but it was a school,' she said bitterly.

Thinking, Wil recounted the events of the night, mentioning Vivienne dragging his dream to her meeting, where things took a turn for the worst... and he ended up waking only to create a new Initial: Mulbryn. Then feeling incredibly stupid all of a sudden,

'Sadie, the airstrip *was* the runway—the *360° Runway*. I went straight from the fog *there*.'

As they both stood and stared at one another, dumb-founded, Sadie suddenly comprehended, 'They wanted you to see it. They wanted you to see what would happen to her.' The thought of which made him feel sick inside.

'What else did they say would happen when the fog disappeared?' he urged. 'Did they mention anything else?'

'Just that you'd get stronger... that when you were strong enough, you'd find... a runway,' she tried recalling. 'Aeolus said that threads wouldn't be broken. I don't know which ones he meant. He said that instead, they'd be tied together, some so tight they'd strangle others. The impression I got was that they're trying to make sides difficult to determine now. Not just for us, but for themselves too.'

'They are,' Wil admitted. 'Aeolus doesn't even know me the way he used to. I can see it in him. He's wary. But he wants to trust me, I know he does.'

They were quiet again, holding one another, fearing for the future as a small group of people ran laughing through the rain on the other side of the tunnel further up the lane.

After a few minutes' silence, Sadie uttered under his chin,

'Before they have a chance to find us Wil, I want to wake up.'

'Don't talk about waking,' he whispered, unable to bear the thought. But she pulled away from him a little and stared.

'We have no control what threads they leave us, Wil,' she said soberly, determinedly, 'but how we leave one another... if we could leave each other like this...' she tried convincing him as she began to weep '... not running anymore...' her voice cracked '...then we'll be able to keep something from them, won't we?' She looked like she was trying to be brave, like she was still trying to convince herself of this, knowing it may just be exactly what they wanted. Wil didn't want her being brave—he didn't want her to be anything if it meant she might go.

'Please don't leave me, Sadie,' he pleaded, putting his hands on the sides of her face. 'Please, just stay,' he begged. 'Stay til...'

'—Til they take this away from us? Til they swap our quiet moment here for fear... for chaos until we're driven awake...?'

He swallowed hard and looked into her eyes, of course not wanting to trade this for any of that. But that's exactly what was coming. She was right. It happened every time.

'We never really saw much of each other in the dreamscape,' he admitted lightly, though despairing, for it was the only place they knew each other before. Loved each other before.

'Let me go, Wil.' She could barely smile.

'But I love you.' The words came out strong, but he instantly broke down; the strength in his arms and legs drained out of him. Then hopelessly kissing her forehead, her cheeks, her lips, he promised he'd find her in the same way she had found him. 'Every night… I'll be there' he cried over her, '…I'll find a way… I'll find a way to get you back….' Holding her to his chest, he closed his eyes and thought of all those relentless stirrings inside him that could never keep him from being drawn back to her. Because until she came along, there was no one. And since, there could be no one else. 'I'll find you…' he said once more. Then hearing her muffled *I love you* against his chest, he felt her hand slide from around his back… and she was gone.

Wil opened his eyes and stared at the wretched void his arms were trying to embrace. Utterly empty, he slumped against the shop door and slid down to the wet step.

It poured. Thunder rumbled in the distance.

After what seemed a few minutes of uncontrollable sobs, Wil thought he heard a voice. Someone stood over him, speaking loudly, but not louder than the rain.

'Annie?' She was as wet as he was.

'The town's flooding,' she hollered through the thunder. Behind her was a small inflatable raft. 'Get in!'

Grief-stricken, he didn't want to. He didn't want to run. He shook his head and turned his shoulder to her, waving her on as he huddled against the door of the shop. However, Annie placed the raft beside him, grabbed his arm and started dragging. It was then that they both heard something behind them, up by the passage to the high street. A torrent of water roared all of a sudden through the tunnel there, spilling out and down Bath Place like a river, and heading straight for them. Wil scrambled to his feet and they both jumped into the raft, grabbing paddles and braced themselves there on the pavement.

The raft nearly flipped when it hit, however they were able to follow the deep crest of white down the narrow alleyway, pushing off shopfronts with the paddles. They passed the gallery and fishmonger's, and most certainly two Sheizers distorting the shadows in the next tunnel, the one with the room above. Then they carried on at speed past the Quaker's meeting hall out to the roundabout and on towards the courthouse.

With the rain still pouring, Wil noticed the raft was beginning to fill, and Annie held out her hand, offering a shadow as a bolt of lightning tore across the sky. It was the first time she had ever offered. Gladly, he put his hand beneath hers and let her take them away from there.

The brief blackness between dreams, between threads in the head, were a welcome respite of a sort for Wil just then. He wished he could stay there and not face what waited either side of the dark.

'Now, that wasn't very clever, was it?' she said flatly, standing over him as he sat in the sand. They were on a desert now, and dry. Too dry, it felt.

Wil blinked up against Annie's silhouette blocking the sun from his face. 'Mushrooms,' he said, but to his alarm, there was nothing in return. Warily, he got up. 'What wasn't very clever?' But she didn't need to answer, because the eyes told him. They were wildly active, spinning counter clockwise with grey and green swirls like a marble on a table top. 'You're not Annie,' he accepted numbly, aware he had taken the hand of an Imposter. And one with an incredible amount of energy to expend. 'Now what?' he said apathetically, unwilling to contend with the fabric of the dream.

Just then, a sand storm was upon them. With no warning whatsoever, sand blasted Wil from all sides. He couldn't see his opponent and he was forced to recognise that if he were to get out of there, he'd have to feel something. *Fear…* that was the quickest way, but he felt none of that now. *Annoyed…* he was definitely that, for the only reason he jumped onto the raft was because Annie—the real Annie—would have physically made him or sat there and watched indefinitely while he grieved. Of course it hadn't been the real Annie and now he was kicking himself for not even thinking of the eyes.

Fiercely annoyed by the hiss and moan of sand and wind now making the exposed parts of his face and arms raw, Wil felt the sensation easing a bit, becoming something else. It was becoming a violently swirling storm… of fog. The hiss of tiny grains pelting disappeared, only to be replaced by an eerie whirr of wind and white. Wil was changing it, he could feel, changing the annoyance to something more tolerable. The heat was still there and so was the Imposter, right beside him. She stood there, scanning the tumultuous white with those crazed eyes.

A voice came from the fog. Someone familiar, but Wil couldn't place it.

'Who's there?' he called out.

Suddenly, Annie—another Annie—came towards him and

grabbed his arm.

'Cheese!' she gasped, throwing her face into his, giving him plenty of opportunity to check her eyes.

The fake Annie beside them grabbed the real Annie holding onto his arm, to which the real Annie then screamed. But so did the fake one, mocking her.

'Don't let me go, Wil,' his Annie pleaded as he pushed the imposter off them, 'you won't be able to tell us apart.'

'Yes Wil, you won't be able to tell us apart,' the second one repeated with the same urgency.

'We need to shadow out' Annie instructed as she pushed the crazy Annie away, 'so get rid of this fog!'

Desperate now, the fog disappeared and Wil tried to grab Annie's hand in an attempt to shadow out, but the double was still pulling on her. '*Shadow...!*' Annie said through clenched teeth, kicking the imposter off them with her boots. '*Never mind!*' she shouted, finally breaking free. '*I'll do it!*'

Everything went black and Wil's face suddenly fell.

Despite complete darkness, he knew where Annie had taken him by its familiar smell. Cedar. Why did she bring him here? Of all the places. It occurred to Wil that in the same way she made Steph show her the dreams running up to forgetting, maybe now Annie was trying to find his version of the story.

'Have you got a light or something, Wil?'

'Just a second.' He stood there, reluctant to let her see...reluctant to show her why this place became what it did, but the lights came on despite him.

Annie sighed, recognising everything through the destruction, though floundering for comprehension.

'The Junction...?' She looked at him confusedly, pitying him. *The Failed Junction.* Taking in the windowless walls of crumbled concrete, splintered wood and broken stone, she took a step away from him, crunching broken glass beneath her feet as she did so. Everything had been here.

'I didn't mean for...' he wanted to explain why it was all like this without hurting her '...I didn't mean to....'

'You didn't mean to destroy it and not tell me,' she offered coldly 'or you didn't mean for me to find out this way,' she determined angrily, lifting a dusty map off the floor. 'So did you do all this on your own... or did you have help?'

'Ben and I, and Steph....'

'Steph?' Her expression was unbelieving, but as she wandered around the broken table and chairs for a few minutes, Wil saw something more wistful in her expression. Then in an instant, it changed back again. 'We had all of Europe,' she accused finally, 'why did it all have to stop? And why did you agree to lose your memory?'

'It was a dead end, Annie.'

'So you destroyed it? And you didn't even have the courtesy to tell me?' He wanted to. They all wanted to. 'Some of this is still useful' she insisted, throwing a hand towards the charts and graphs crumpled and torn up in the middle of the room there, darting her eyes to the places on the wall where they used to be.

'This isn't The Junction, Annie.' He blinked slowly, wearily, and took in a deep, measured breath through his nostrils, preparing himself.

'Isn't it?' She picked up a map and made sure he saw that she was doubtful. 'Why, then, could we all come here? And why would you do... all this?'

'Because three of us...' he looked at the spot and felt a wave of nausea come over him '...we could leave here through that door.' He pointed to the wooden door behind her, set in amongst the skewed and splintered wall panels.

'What door?'

'I'm so sorry, Annie....'

'*What door*, Wil?'

'The one you can't see... the one all of us can go through when you're not here... the one every person on that map there in your hands' he gave it a slight nod 'managed to walk through... so long as you weren't here.'

'What?' She squeezed her eyes closed and took another look at the wall. 'But there's nothing there' she said plainly, not seeing, for the segment of thread was non-existent in her mind '...there's nothing there at all.'

'There is, but you can't see it... because it's not the real Junction.'

'What are you talking about, Wilden?' she demanded, striding noisily through broken glass and around broken furniture, feeling the wall and running her hands up and down it. 'There's *nothing* here.'

Crunching glass beneath his own feet now, Wil went and grabbed the concealed handle and tried opening it, tried pushing it through the wooden panels it hid among, but it wouldn't budge.

'It's here Annie. I promise. But you can't see it because only a part of this thread' he indicated the octagonal room with a glance 'is shared between us. The rest...' he let go of the door and stepped soberly back from it '...isn't a match.'

Finally, realising what he was trying to tell her, that it was her voyage along this thread that proved it couldn't be The Junction... that everyone else could see and continue the thread outside the door here... she turned back to the wall and stared at it blankly.

'Had it been the true Junction, the door would exist within every mind.' He too was staring there blankly, wishing he could just push it open and show her everything he and Steph saw.... 'But the fact that it doesn't exist in yours, and we ignored it when we realised...'. The memory of being so hopeful deep down, despite the evidence, made him feel sick in his stomach again. 'We knew we were chasing a dead end. Everything behind this door was a trap. The more often we visited, the more we realised something was wrong. And yet,' he hated himself for this, 'every night, we cared a little less and found ourselves drawn back.' He shook his head, certain another week would have convinced them there was no point looking for the real Junction after all. 'It was Aeolus who reminded us that any dream contact with The Junction induces fear. The intensely strong reaction one has to something that makes them afraid is what alters our genes and ensures the next generation too learns from such an experience. Even if the lesson is subjective. Annie, we felt no fear behind that door. I can't quite explain what it was, bliss maybe, but it felt exactly the opposite.'

She looked around the room, at the remains of all that hard work, the communities covered, the nations... and shook her head.

'How long had you known?'

'Just a few weeks.'

'Yes, but weeks can feel like years in the dreams.'

'They can.' They did.

'Why did you forget then—why didn't we just start over and find a new thread—look somewhere else?' she demanded desperately.

'Because we had already trained ourselves to see nothing else,' he explained. 'We would always end up in the same place unless we started again. *Properly* started again.'

'Aeolus said a true junction should compound the genetic memory across a range of dreamers. That's anyone with Tret or Tare affinity, Duals... Vergers... anyone. He didn't say it meant *everyone*,' she argued, still trying to spare this place, even with the shambles it had become. But there could be no coming back here. There could be no repeating the mistakes they had made. Not this time.

'Annie, he said The Junction exists as a single point, hidden inside the synaptic voyage of *every* dreamer.' Her shoulders fell slightly, knowing this. 'It's a vault that can't be opened from anywhere else,' he insisted. 'One has to *be* there.' It seemed she knew what was coming, and stiffened visibly there in the middle of the debris against it. 'But you couldn't be there,' he told her delicately, surveying the remains of what looked like a tornado-stricken bunker. 'This... this can't possibly be what we were hoping for. And that...' he looked at the door '...has to be open to more than Europe. Or Steph and Ben, and me.'

Here, he stepped towards her, wanting her to know how desperately they tried getting her to see the door without ever making it obvious. None of them wanted to hurt her.

'So tell me, then,' she turned abruptly to him, stopping him from coming any closer, 'why did you all forget?'

Wil sighed, apprehensive. 'So we could start over. With you. The deep ruts created finding The Junction caused irreparable damage. Forgetting was the only way out, the only way to smooth them over and avoid deviating back towards them, towards here. All threads had to be cut. Including this one.'

'And why did you go through Transition—why did you go along with the Tret and disappear all that time? The others didn't. They didn't need to change sides.'

'That was my own fault. When it all failed,' he rolled his eyes to the chaotic quarters around them, 'when this failed, I doubted him. I doubted Aeolus. I doubted he was helping us find the real Junction... and I doubted he would give us our memories back if we forgot and started over.... I doubted even that he'd go to such lengths to ensure you were included in the next search. If there was a next one.'

'Do you doubt me still?'

Aeolus was there beside the overturned couch, against the wall.

'I don't,' Wil admitted to him without hesitation.

'Then this...' his eyes swept around the grim space of The Failed

Junction '...ends here,' he said to Wil, intimating that none of them would be able to visit this place again. 'The Tret have allowed you to keep this thread of mine, but you cannot come back.' He then said to Annie, 'You will not remember.' And with that, Wil was propelled from the dream to wakefulness by the sound of the doorbell downstairs.

Chapter Thirty-Seven

Frame

There it was again. The doorbell.

Wil sat up and looked at the clock. *6:14am.* It was a bit early for visitors he realised, only to suddenly remember Vivienne. And Murphy. *Sadie....*

'Oh Sadie,' he breathed, feeling the void just then. His nostrils dilated and stung, making the way for tears. '...Sadie....' he whimpered, anguished.

It felt as though a surreal exchange had taken place in the night: those amazing minds—lives even—for his memory, and Wil now felt it hadn't been worth it. In fact, he felt guilty and ashamed to sit there knowing the dreams as they had, but without them. Vivienne was truly gone, and Murphy.... *Poor Murphy*, he sobbed. Wil's only comfort was that his old comrade might never know he, Wil, failed him. It would be almost impossible to get him remembering. And Sadie... what was he to do to get her back? She had never been in his awake life before, but now she was in the same town, going to the same college, was in a class even. None of it was coincidence, he appreciated, yet she was further away from him than ever before. Today, the threads would be severed. She would wake with no memory of him at the park, in her kitchen. And the same thing would have happened to her mother and sister too. It would be as though they never met him.

There it was again. That bell.

'...Please ring us if there's anything we can do....'

'Mum?' Wil entered the entrance hall and saw her there in her dressing gown, holding the door open to two police officers standing in the early morning grey. 'What's going on?'

'Oh, Love...' she said sadly, 'Mrs Hobbes next door died in the night. Mrs Novak, the cleaning lady, found her just now. Apparently, there's been a disturbance.'

'Died?' he said, pretending to be shocked, feeling a certain grief he knew he couldn't express here. 'But I only just saw her yesterday. I gave her that package delivered here,' he directed more to Mum, joining her at the door.

'I asked him to take it round while we were out,' she told the officers, corroborating his story.

'I took it round and she offered me a cup of tea. It was the first time we ever spoke,' Wil lied. 'You said there was a disturbance. What kind of disturbance?'

'Nothing of great concern,' the short, stalky of the two assured.

'At what time did you visit Mrs Hobbes, Mr...?' The taller one flipped a page in a little notebook and poised his pen.

'Wil—Wilden Stokes' he said, peering at the notes the officer made and feeling quite guilty of something he was sure he didn't do. 'It was about 10am,' he looked at Mum, 'just after you guys left. My friend Ben was over,' he directed back to the officers. 'He was here while I dropped off the package and chatted with' he almost said Vivienne, 'Mrs Hobbes for a bit.'

The officer continued writing then said, 'Mrs Novak noticed a few things out of place. Like my colleague said, nothing of great concern. Nothing taken. But we do need to ask questions.'

Mrs Novak must have heard the use of her name because she came up behind the officers with a tissue to her face. 'Nothing is missing,' she assured in a faint Polish accent. 'But the photos...' she insisted '...very odd.' She shook her head, perturbed. 'And she cannot use scissors or open the post, but the package was right there—'

'Thank you Mrs Novak,' the taller officer quieted her.

'Oh, that was me,' Wil piped up. 'I opened the package for her. It was a pillow. She asked me to put it in a pillowcase. I thought it was a bit odd, but the package was next day delivery and all, she must have been waiting for it....' Feeling he had concluded too much already in front of the officers, he added sheepishly, 'I just thought it was a strange thing to ask a stranger, to open and sort it, but she said she couldn't do any of it because of her hands.' He remembered those strong hands that fumbled for the digestive, pulled him through the fog.

'Her hands?' the officer frowned at him.

'Rheumatoid arthritis,' Mrs Novak confirmed from behind the pair on the step. 'Is true.'

Wil appreciated her validation as he folded his arms in the chill.

'But ask him about the photos,' she urged in an antagonising tone that made Wil start to feel like a criminal again.

'Did you notice photos inside the house?' the officer asked, glaring from under his brow while he continued to jot things down.

'She had a sideboard thing,' Wil admitted. 'A long unit with photo frames on,' he said, eyeing Mrs Novak who was now looking rather earnest at the mention of this piece of furniture. 'There were quite a few facing down. I thought it was odd at the time, but really, that's all that I'd say stood out.' Mrs Novak looked at him disappointedly. 'I was interested in why the photos were turned over myself,' he confessed.

'Nieces and nephews,' Mrs Novak said dismissively. She shook her head again, bewildered. 'Grandchildren,' she shrugged and rolled her eyes.

It occurred to Wil that maybe one of the photos had Rupert in.

'And did you happen to notice anything else unusual about the house on your visit, Mr Stokes,' the shorter one continued.

Wil frowned and wondered what kind of question that was. 'I'd never been, so I don't know what it *should* have looked like.'

'Nothing stands out…?'

Lots of things stood out. Few of which he could mention. 'I guess it was quite empty downstairs,' he said feebly, 'but I thought that was because she had trouble getting around. She seemed to live upstairs. She made me a cup of tea on the landing. That was a bit odd.'

The officer made note and asked, 'And how long was your visit? You said you went over around 10.'

Wil had no idea how long he had been up there. It could have been an hour. It could have been half that. Ben would know. 'It was probably half an hour or so…' he guessed. 'I wasn't really keeping track. We had a chat and a cup of tea and she asked me to open the delivery, which I did, and… we just chatted about the house, how she lived in it for forty years….'

'Is true,' Mrs Novak vouched again. 'Is forty years.'

'Well I think that'll be all. If we have any questions for you Mr Stokes, we'll contact you. Thank you.'

They left a number and Mum closed the door. She appeared both relieved and unsettled by their visit as she turned the latch and put the key in the pot. 'You didn't tell me you were over there,' she started on him like he had been hiding something from her.

'I took the package over like you asked me to,' he defended. 'How was I supposed to know' he hesitated, unable to say the words 'what was going to happen?'

'Keep your voice down...' she whispered, urging him down the hall, deeper into the house.

Walking back to the kitchen, he began to worry at how all this was turning out. Not only was he probably the last one to see Vivienne alive, but her landing door conveniently led right outside his bedroom. He never even checked to see if it was locked. And whatever Mrs Novak thought was important about the photos, she didn't seem to like his observation of them. What if she thought he *killed* her? The Tret could put an idea like that in a lot of people's heads, namely police officers, and what could he possibly do to prevent it?

'I didn't do anything,' he insisted innocently, 'so why do I feel like I did do something wrong?'

'Old people die, Love,' Mum said plainly. 'I'm sure they were just trying to narrow down who saw her last to figure out when it happened.'

But he didn't feel any more reassured when Dad came down and told him the same thing before they both went off for work. Steph however saw it from his perspective.

'You told the truth, that's all you can do. We'll just have to wait and see what happens,' she advised after their de-brief from the night. 'Remember, it's Tret and Tare. 50-50. Not everyone is out to get you, Wil. Some are profoundly on your side. Speaking of which, Annie's not returning my texts. Maybe her phone's dead.' And she was out the door, in oddly good spirits, wielding toast amid lacrosse sticks, catching her ride like their lives hadn't changed at all. It left Wil feeling incredibly lonely as he sat deep in thought at the kitchen island, contemplating how different all his relationships were now, to the point that he nearly fell off his stool when the doorbell rang.

Imagining it to be Ben, he hurried with great relief down the hall. Only it wasn't him.

'*You...?*' Wil said, stunned.

'I'm sure you remember us, Wilden. I'm Rob. This is Roselyn.'

'You can call me Rose.'

Chapter Thirty-Eight

Rob and Rose

'Can we come in?' Rob asked pleasantly, to which Wil moved aside. Their arms brushed by him, magnifying the sureality of their encounter.

Rob sat comfortably on the couch with his back to the kitchen while Rose sat next to him sideways, stiff and sharp, with her eyes roving the entire length of the room. She was uneasy. Quite the opposite to her companion. Surreptitious glances went round as they waited on the couch and Wil made them drinks.

No one mentioned Vivienne. No one mentioned dreams.

'They're all the same,' Wil said as he set the tray down on the coffee table and took a seat on Blake.

Robert perched forward and passed Rose a drink, then took one himself.

'How did you find me?' Wil started, eyeing them both.

'Well you're only next door,' Rob said.

'Next door. Next door to Vivienne?' He could never assume those he met dream-side would ever be in contact with him this side.

'She's our Great Aunt,' Rose answered, then corrected herself 'was our Great Aunt.'

'*Cousins...*' Wil said under his breath as a massive shift went on inside his head, for these two had been a couple in his mind.

'Brother and sister,' Rob clarified, glancing distractedly into his mug. 'Twins, to be precise.'

There was an awkward silence as Wil watched them take a sip in near-unison.

'Listen, I'm really sorry about Vivienne,' he said sincerely. 'I had no idea what was going to happen last night...' he trailed off, not meaning to conjure what they were all undoubtedly seeing in their minds.

'You needn't apologise, Wil,' Rose assured. 'We knew you might not be aware of who she was.'

'Until she dragged my dream, I had no memory of her at all,' he said apologetically. 'In fact, I went next door yesterday and had a cup of tea with her like she was this complete stranger.' Already feeling ashamed by this fact, he picked up the last mug only to be reminded that yesterday's cup with Vivienne was their first awake encounter together—their last. Everything else had been through the dreams.

'The police were here this morning talking about some kind of disturbance,' he mentioned, abandoning his mug to the table. 'Unfortunately, Mrs Novak seems to think I had something to do with it. But I didn't.' He met them both squarely. 'I didn't do anything to hurt your aunt.'

'We know,' Rob said regrettably, 'we've been over. We've heard Mrs Novak's version and spoke to the police. You don't need to worry about anything she's told them,' he assured, looking expectantly to Rose for agreement, to which she simply volleyed a similar expression back. 'The suspicion she seems to have about Vivienne's death has been dealt with. And her anxieties over continued employment at the property have also been resolved. I think that became as big a burden as much as losing a companion towards the end there.'

'Mrs Novak's quite protective of the family,' Rose explained, 'so we'll keep her on while we're in the main house.' After a beat, 'Yes. We'll be neighbours,' she remarked. 'Rupert's family gets the money, ours gets the property. Which brings us to why we've come here today.'

She half-smiled at Rob, prompting him.

'Of course.' Rob leaned forward and set his mug down. 'As you may have guessed, Vivienne knew she wouldn't be around for much longer. She made sure her things were in order over these last few weeks and one of her wishes' he glanced at Rose 'was to give you something.'

'Me?'

Rob checked with Rose before carrying on. 'Yes, but the only problem is, we can't let anyone see us with it, and presently, it's in the main bit of the house next door.'

'Okay....' Wil eyed them both, unsure of what they were trying to tell him here.

'This is quite awkward, we know,' Rose interjected, 'but we need to access the house using your closet—the closet we used to obtain your journal.'

Wil smiled and frowned at the same time. 'Seriously?'

'I'm afraid so,' Rob said, unaware that Wil couldn't quite move on from the fact that they were the ones creeping into his bedroom to take his journal. 'It's in your interest that we get it over here before anyone else from the family visits the property this morning.'

'Sorry—' Wil stopped him there. 'It was you two who went in my room...?'

'We thought you knew,' Rose said, a little perturbed. 'Vivienne said she told you.'

'Well, she told me she used the closet off the landing... but she didn't actually say who did it,' he now found himself remembering. But as he realised the simple act of twisting open a doorknob would have proven impossible for his old neighbour, Wil saw she no doubt would have had help. But something else bothered him more just now than finding Vivienne had used someone else to secure his journal. 'What she most certainly wouldn't tell me was why she wanted it in the first place.'

'To personally gain direct access to your dreams,' Rob answered plainly.

'Yes, well I understand that....'

'So we could protect you,' Rose took her turn arguing as though it were obvious, indicating *we* by darting her eyes from Rob to herself a few times. 'Our goal was to access your Initial the second you were out of Tret fog. Of course, we needed an object to do that because you're a complete stranger to us. I mean we know who you are, but we weren't the only dreamers intent on making contact with you. Some had very undesirable intentions indeed. Your journal ensured we got there before any one of them did.'

'Only, we were so determined to protect you...' Rob said with slight indignation, 'we hadn't anticipated how keen you'd be to protect yourself. It never occurred to anyone that you'd try and block us.'

Wil visualised those early dreams and recognised the role he had made the fog play.   Not only had he instilled it to keep the twins from using shadows and take him into the dreamscape, he had also used the noise to disable them from even reasoning with him.

'Yes, the noise,' Rob said dryly. 'You were obviously wary and used it to fend us off.'

Just as Annie said. A reproduction.

'But you weren't bothered,' Wil directed to Rose, confused. 'You just stood there with your eyes closed like nothing was happening; totally unaffected.'

'We were both affected, Wilden, I can assure you,' she maintained. 'Being twins...' she hesitated as Rob eyed her cautiously. But he then relented with an indifferent twitch of the shoulder. '...Being twins' she said more confidently 'we endure one another's burdens in the dreams. In fact, we are so... *entangled* this way, if one of us changes affinity, so does the other. Only... neither of us ever shares the same.'

'Neither of you can *ever* share the same affinity?' Wil said, trying to understand.

'If one of us is Tret, the other is Tare,' she said simply. 'There's no Point of Transition for us. No threshold to cross, or threads to preserve. It just happens automatically. One minute I'm tuned into my Tret contact, the next, my Tare. No Initial is off-limits for us when we are together.'

Rose let Wil appreciate this disclosure for a moment until the astounded look on his face subsided, for he had never heard of this happening with twins.

'Effectively, we work as a Dual,' she went on, 'only neither of us is actually one. Of course, this allows us to enter any Initial together as a Dual might, and we've even found it has protected us from this last wave of Duals forced to forget. Waking up this morning, we assumed it had happened, but....' Her eyes popped, incredulous. 'It's not all free passes though. Take our experience with you, for instance. While Rob and I had equal access to you despite our differing affinities, the fact that he felt most unwelcome in your Initial meant that I would also endure his discomfort. That was the immobility part of it on that occasion, rather than the pain. We can never be sure how much of the burden our twinness will force us to share. Sometimes it's a major setback, sometimes it isn't. But our experience with you was that you wanted neither enemy nor friend in your Initial, so really, we wouldn't have had a chance to communicate with you there. We weren't just battling a compatible affinity issue, we were battling the substrate you had created. We hadn't come across that before, but considering where you had been for nearly three years, we could hardly blame you.' Rose inhaled deeply and raised her neatly shaped eyebrows, absolving herself seemingly of why she and Rob had no success at communicating with him properly in those foggy dreams. 'I'm afraid we tried numerous times, but we couldn't break through that likeness of a real fog you had clearly perfected. And unpleasant as it was,' she clearly understated, 'we understood it to be a coping mechanism in the end and devised a Plan B with Vivienne.'

'Plan B was your visit with her yesterday,' Rob said, glancing at the uppermost sections of the walls in the room like he was trying to find another route to next door. 'Initially, she wanted to tell you that not all of the Duals are disappearing.'

Wil looked at Rose, confused. 'Not all of them?' He felt slightly guilty all of a sudden. 'What do you mean not all of them?'

'Well there's us,' Rose said, turning to her brother. 'I mean I know we don't count as *proper*...' she said feebly, 'but Vivienne was certain that all the Duals *can't* just disappear.'

'And why not?' Though he still didn't understand, his hope was for Sadie.

'Because the Tret and Tare rely on the neutrality of Dual's to accomplish their purposes,' Rob said firmly. 'It's the buffer between sides. They've only been really disappearing in the last few weeks. Since Vivienne has been experimenting with some rather... delicate threads,' he said tactfully. 'So we think there's a link.'

'Delicate threads?' Knowing Vivienne, Wil took that to mean she had been looking for The Junction. Carrying on where he had to leave off. 'I always thought Duals might be the key to getting into The Junction,' he confessed, pinching his lower lip. 'And I was certain the Tret and Tare ultimately found them a threat.'

'Having greater access than themselves,' Rose confirmed with a knowing smile.

'But if they need Duals as that buffer, how can they have them and not take that risk?'

Here, the twin's faces lit up.

'By creating a *closet* Dual,' Rose said with delight.

Seeing Wil grimace slightly, she explained further.

'Basically, the closet Dual has all that exclusive information inside them, only, they don't know it until it comes time to use it. Not only does this get rid of the stigma associated with Duals at present, but they effectively become extinct. No one will know who they are... not even the Duals themselves. ...No one will see them coming like most seasoned dreamers have before... and no one will know who to go to for all the latest on our polarised pals.' Rose narrowed her eyes and gave Wil a flat look. 'No doubt, it's the price of trying to find The Junction. They get what they want and wrong-foot us in the process.'

'Then anyone could potentially be a Dual,' Wil understood.

'Potentially,' Rob accepted.

'This could make us turn against one another—*we* might turn against one another—not knowing who's who,' he could see now. 'We need to tell them then. Tell everyone who remembers what's going on.'

Rob held up his hand, 'No, Wil. We need to ride this one out a bit, I'm afraid. Besides, we've got a little matter to sort out here first. The reason we came actually.' Lowering his hand, 'If we don't get across to next door in the next half hour,' he looked at his watch, 'anyone could take what our aunt had for you.'

Chapter Thirty-Nine

Sugar

Minutes later they were in the hall closet upstairs, pushing coats to the side as Rose fiddled with the doorknob at the back of the wall in the dark.

The tight space suddenly brightened as the single bulb hummed and flickered to life above their heads.

'I thought it might help,' Wil said sheepishly, fending off their startled expressions. 'The switch is just here.' He slid his hand behind a ski jacket, showing them.

'Thank you,' Rob said, excusing Rose's stale face with over-appreciation. She rolled her eyes and fiddled again. 'Maybe I could have a go?' Rob suggested.

'What are you trying to do?' Wil asked.

Shouldering winter parkas out of the light, 'I'm trying to get this key in,' Rose huffed. 'It has to be the other one....' The sound of metal clinked and she was back at the handle again with another key. 'This is a lot easier from the other side...' she said through gritted teeth.

'I never even noticed it had a lock,' Wil admitted. 'I'm glad it does, especially when the police were here, but I just assumed the wall was bricked up on the other side.'

'No original doorway is bricked up in this house,' Rose said. 'Just locked.'

'And how did you get the key?'

'Mrs Novak. This morning.'

'Here, let me have a go,' Rob insisted, shouldering in.

Rose came out into the hall, and passed her brother the small ring of four or five keys. No sooner had they heard the sound of jagged metal rubbing, there was an unexpected *click*, which made them all freeze and stare at one another.

'Right. Until we get across the landing, I want you both to stay right behind me,' Rob instructed.

'Wouldn't it be better if I stay here, in case someone comes home on this side?' Wil suggested, having second thoughts. 'And what about the police...' he pointed out '...and Mrs Novak? She said things were disturbed... I mean, is it wise to go over there and take something, something they'll know has gone missing?'

Rob turned fully around to face Wil, hunching beneath the coat rod with his hand still on the ajar doorknob. 'Wil, we appreciate you wouldn't want an item in your house that most obviously came from next door. But what we want to get is hidden in Vivienne's bedroom. Mrs Novak has never seen this item, and neither have we. Those who remember their dreams in our family know she has it, but none of them know where she's hidden it.'

'Vivienne told us yesterday where to find it,' Rose added over Wil's shoulder 'and what to do if something happened to her.' The apparent discomfort in Rose's swallow reminded Wil that this couldn't be an easy thing for her or her brother to have to do.

'With obstacles already thrown in our direction this morning,' Rob gave his sister a wayward glance, 'I'd say it's best to get in and out of there before anything else stops us.'

'All right then,' Wil agreed, prompting Rob to attend to the door again. 'But just one more question,' he promised, cringing. 'Vivienne's not...' he threw his chin in the direction of the landing, aware of how indelicate it would be to actually say the words.

'Still there? No, Wil,' Rob said patiently. 'They took her this morning. After we had a word with the police.'

'I'm sorry. It's just....'

'You don't have to apologise,' he insisted. 'We waited to come here for that very reason.' And with that, he turned the knob and pushed the door out so that the poorly lit closet resembled the hallway passage it once used to be between Vivienne's part of the house and Wil's. Tiptoeing over the obstacles in the closet, they stepped onto the bright, spacious landing, closing the door on the Stoke's side behind them.

Wil's first impression out from the winter wear was that this place was too quiet. Looking around, everything was just as he remembered, but without Vivienne. The tray with tea things for two caught his eye on the side, sitting there clean and empty. And he noticed the packaging from the pillow tucked beside the little fridge under the microwave, and as he watched Rose gingerly walk down the hall, he noticed too that the frames were still faced down, the frames Mrs Novak was so unsettled by.

Rose took something out of her blazer and disappeared into her aunt's bedroom.

'What's she doing?' Wil whispered.

'Just collecting a few belongings,' Rob said in a normal voice that made him sound incredibly loud for the circumstances. 'Come here. You need to look at this.' He wandered over to the frames and lifted one. It was a school picture of Rob and Rose, clearly a few years back.

'You two,' Wil said, not completely surprised now.

Rob turned over a few more. They were photos of Rob and Rose either side of Vivienne on what appeared to be their aunt's 90th birthday. One was a distant photo and the other close up. Rob was now turning the other handful of pictures over, setting them on their little stands so Wil could see them all. Each was a distinct picture of Rob and Rose, or the two of them together in more recent years. There's no doubt Wil would have remembered these faces from somewhere if he had seen them yesterday.

'She turned them over in preparation for your visit,' Rob divulged, picking up a more youthful image of his aunt with her head leaning amorously against the shoulder of a slightly older man.

'So, she knew I'd come.' Wil considered the wiles of his deceased confidante who now stared back at him through the glass of these picture frames.

'Of course she knew. *Plan B*, we told you. What do you think the pillow was about? I mean, how do you think she got into your Initial if Rose and I had already tainted your journal with a failed Plan A? As personal as the book was, it was no good to her when we finished with it. And there was no time to get us sneaking back to yours….'

Of course. It suddenly occurred to Wil why Vivienne wanted him to put the pillow *into* the case. He was the last to touch it, so it became the object that allowed her to enter his Initial. And that first failed delivery attempt that meant the parcel was left with Mum, knowing Wil would be at home, on his own, able to deliver it later, was clearly no coincidence. Not when Aeolus was helping Vivienne only the night before.

Wil sighed and shook his head at the ingenuity. Then seeing a black and white photo that made Vivienne appear flawless, one that mimicked the movie star headshots of the day, he said in amazement,

'She really wanted me in that lecture hall, didn't she?'

'No, Wil. She really wanted you out of that fog.'

'Guys! In here,' Rose breathed down the wide hall from the bedroom.

The little side table beside the bed had clearly been moved to the rug in the middle of the room.

'We can't leave drag marks,' Rose told them, squatting beside the head of the bed, 'so when we put the table back, we need to lift it completely.' She then directed their attention to the dark panelled wall to her left, where Wil saw nothing. Only, as all three of them squatted beneath the dado rail with her, it seemed that maybe there could be a concealed section amid the recessed geometry of the wall. 'Put these on.' Rose handed them a winter glove each. Wil recognised them to be his own, from the closet. 'Wil, we don't want you leaving fingerprints around,' she determined, 'and probably best we don't leave too many over this particular area,' she said, putting one of Mum's ski gloves on. Then, as though she had done this a hundred times, she pressed the top corner of the panel, which allowed it to slowly lift outwards on a hinge, like the cover over the petrol tank on a car. 'She said it's heavier than it looks,' Rose reminded, getting up. She stood behind them and invited them to have a look for themselves.

The space was about half a metre square, though quite deep. And in it was a wooden chest about the size of two stacked shoe boxes.

'We've got to get over this lip here,' Rob grunted, reaching his arm deep into the blackness, and grabbing the box from the far end. 'Just lift it this side when I slide it towards us,' he directed Wil.

As it came out, Wil realised it was not actually made of wood after all, but of tarnished brass, with wood inlay. The design on the top had the symmetry and scrolling lines of Art Nouveau, curling with warm, rich tones that could only form with age. The two elements of wood and metal created a beautiful effect of movement.

'Let's get it across,' Rob decided, lifting it out completely. Rose quickly closed the panel, set the table back and they were through the closet, locking it within seconds. Downstairs, everyone stared at the mysterious box in the middle of the coffee table.

'Shall we have a little look?' Rob suggested.

'Go on, then,' Rose encouraged.

He pulled the box towards him, producing a tiny key from the inside pocket of his leather jacket as he did so. With a quick movement of his wrist a crisp little *click* broke the silence. Slowly, Rob raised the lid. Together, they saw its contents entirely. The cobalt blue velvet lining caught Wil's eye first. Then the grid of tiny vials—hundreds of them—no bigger than the butt end of a cigarette.

'What are these?' he asked, shrinking closer, to which Rob picked one up and handed it to him.

The tiny bottle, sealed with a silver lid, had a small sepia-stained label with the name *Alastair Denniston* written in miniscule script. Wil peered into the glass, looking for its contents, but there were only what appeared to be granules of some sort, like salt or sugar. Wil passed the item back to Rob and looked at the collection. A dozen or so lids had red markings on the top, like nail varnish splodges. And a handful had black markings.

'Have a good look,' Rob insisted, giving Wil free reign to inspect the contents like he himself already knew what was there, had already seen it.

The miniscule jars seemed quite old, Wil thought, as he carefully lifted a few out of their small, leather padded compartments and considered the wear around the labels. And while *Alastair Denniston* or *Alan Turing* meant little to him, an empty red vial with the letters *F.D.R.* provoked immediate intrigue. Wil put it back and lifted another with a red mark. *W.C.* He couldn't help imagine Winston Churchill. It too was empty. He tried a few more. *J.S.* With a pattern developing, he assumed that to be Joseph Stalin. *N.C.*... Neville Chamberlain. *H.T.*... Harry Truman. *R.M.* ... *W.K.* ... *M.S.* They all had granules. He started looking through the black vials. *Geoffrey Prime*.... *B.M.* ... full to the top. Wil stopped at *A.H.* Empty.

Eyeing the tiny vessel, 'This isn't who I think it is,' he said warily.

'Yes,' Rose answered without hesitation. 'It is who you think it is. Vivienne's partner, Uncle Clive, worked in intelligence during WWII. He found quite a lot of uses for objects in his line of work,' she said matter-of-factly, nodding at the vial Wil held in his hand and insinuating the contents it once held connected Clive to the Initial of Adolph Hitler.

'Obviously, we can't let something as significant as this into the hands of just anyone,' she said firmly. 'Mum can't even know Vivienne had it. She'd just end up flogging it or something....'

'What's in here?' Wil asked, switching to the full *B.M.* vial again.

'Sugar,' Rob said as he too picked up one. 'Sugar, touched by the named individual. The idea was—at least this is what our aunt said Uncle Clive did... you pretend to cough with a pinch of these in the creases of your palm and release them against the back of the head. They fall off and you collect them up with a bit of sticky tape.'

Wil tried imagining the image of that older man in the photos next to Vivienne meticulously extracting grains from this collection to...

'...Ingest one and dream,' Wil understood aloud as he lifted the glass against the natural light and turned it so the sugar tumbled around inside. 'It's so simple.' He put the vial back and let Rob close the lid. 'Are there many of these knocking around?' he wondered, staring at the strange, yet lovely box.

'As far as we know, it's the only one,' Rose suspected. 'If there are others, we won't know. You didn't exactly go around in the forties and tell your Special Service colleagues you could somehow read minds—or enter dreams for that matter. Everyone Clive knew at Bletchley Park had to sign the Official Secrets Act, which meant he couldn't really talk to anyone about anything. None of them could.'

'But surely he was feeding his intelligence back to someone,' Wil determined. 'The top, presumably. The Prime Minister.'

Rose glowered at him, disappointed in his naïveté. 'Do you really think Winston Churchill knew something of Hitler's dreams?' It was obviously a rhetorical question. 'Leaders barely get any sleep, and if they remember anything, it's the nightmares of Tret interfering with their Tare affinity—sorry Rob,' she directed his way, to which he conceded with an ambivalent roll of the eyes.

'Swings and roundabouts...' he said, taking no offence.

'The Tret and Tare make sure leaders never remember,' Rose carried on, 'because they know Theresa May wouldn't be able to stand up in front of the world and keep it together if she were consciously maintaining a private battle with them. Not only would she appear a lunatic, but no decisions would be made. And can you imagine what the likes of Hitler would have said if *he* remembered? All his henchmen in the trials later.... *The Tret made me do it*.... *The Tare*.... They would *never* see themselves as responsible for the decisions they made once in front of a jury. Yet every decision is ours ultimately. We *choose* our affinity. We choose when to listen to the voice behind it. And we choose when not to.' Her eyes averted briefly as she inhaled deeply. 'No. The box wasn't used to inform the top, it was used to inform the lower levels, or plant seeds direct, bypassing all the middlemen where necessary.'

Rose then directed her attention to the lid of the bespoke chest and looked at it with a sad expression on her face.

'Uncle Clive could never say what he knew. He certainly couldn't tell anyone *how*. But whatever he did that meant those bottles were emptied,' she shook her head at the thought of it, 'he couldn't have done it lightly.'

Wil too considered the burden it must have been to open that box and determine which vial would serve a greater purpose. Envisioning that man next to Vivienne in the pictures, not even through his twenties... extracting the granules that revealed an enemy's pursuit... the weight of such a business had to be both lonely and maddening. Every hardened crystalline block provided the sweetness of insight, yet confined it to the miniscule limits of Clive's mind. He surely bore the fear and trepidation of knowing so much, yet because of discretion, had been forced to do so little.

Rose pushed a few wisps of hair behind her ear and cleared her throat. 'He left a pile of notebooks,' she seemed to remember 'which you're welcome to. They were mostly his observations on changes in government security over the decades. He points out by the end that there's an obvious pattern with the Tret and Tare; they're so wary of one another, they adopt more skillful means of manipulating and protecting leaders, and they all just end up copying each other. Like an arms race. There's an interesting bit at the end where he poses questions about whether it was entirely the Tret and Tare initiating the changes in security, or the free minds of world leaders. But how can anyone know?' she said plainly. 'Nowadays, you don't have the access to politicians responsible for such decisions. Not like they did in the 30's and 40's.'

'No, contact with the world has changed,' Rob said, slipping the little key back into his pocket. 'Nowadays, political security is fortified by committees, panels, board members. And with everything going digital, moving online… I mean I love being in the digital age, but if we thought *this* was an extreme measure,' he eyed the box doubtfully, 'well then we haven't appreciated what the Tret and Tare can do in the world.'

'But is that actually Tret and Tare strategy, all those safeguards, or man's?' Rose posed. 'Who knows.' Her shoulder flinched, aloof. 'But to get a dependable object off the Prime Minister today, or the President….'

'I'd of said the Queen,' Rob mumbled as he absent-mindedly pulled the hairs of his sideburn and stared off to nowhere in particular.

Wil couldn't help but smile a little, for Rob's faint smirk, coupled with Rose's reproachful shaking of the head, made the two seem in perfect balance with one another. Like tidal ebb and flow.

'Anyway,' Rose said dismissively, putting Uncle Clive's chest on her lap, 'none of us can work like this anymore, gathering chance objects from influential people as this.' She pulled a bunched-up fabric carrier bag from her jeans pocket.

'They're useful when someone's alive though,' Rob granted, holding the bag open for her and carefully working the edges up around the box, 'just totally worthless if they're dead. Unless whatever's been collected was on them in the last moments.'

'The most valuable thing they used to collect was hair,' Rose admitted. 'You could get quite a few runs with hair, whether alive *or* dead, but if you were dead and bald… well, then it was nail clippings.' She put the bagged box on the floor beside her feet. 'But people don't seem to do the hair thing anymore,' she bemoaned.

'Speaking of, did you get everything we needed,' Rob asked her unpalatably, digressing, to which she promptly took out what looked like a black travel manicure set from her jacket pocket, unzipped it and opened it like a book. As far as Wil could tell, it *was* a manicure set, complete with tweezers, scissors and nail clippers… and something else.

'I did.' She held up something clear and plastic, no bigger than a sugar packet, with what appeared white threads in.

'What's that?'

'This, Wil,' Rob said as he took the packet from his sister, 'is Vivienne's hair, taken with her permission, of course.' His lips closed together tightly, dimpling his chin. 'Permission in advance,' he said in a lowered voice, intimating that such a sample had been collected this morning, after Vivienne's death.

'It doesn't matter who's touched it by the time it's been snipped off,'

Rose said with a strange proficiency as she held her hand out to have the packet back. 'That's why I like cut hair.' She stuffed it back into her kit and zipped it up. 'Thanks to Mrs Novak we didn't have the luxury of time this morning to try fibres or something less personal, did we? No matter. Now, Wil, do you mind if we hold onto Uncle Clive's box for a while? Just until things settle down a bit here at the manor?'

'Of course not.' The last thing he wanted was that object in his house right now. Especially if there were people in Vivienne's family looking for it.

'Do you have the other thing?' Rob asked her.

'Yes, of course.' She took something out from the other side of her jacket, handed it to her brother, who then passed it to Wil. It was a padded envelope with the words *FOR Wilden Stokes ONLY* written in bold black marker. 'It's from Murphy,' Rose explained. 'He posted it to our aunt. He said you'd know what to do with it. Eventually.'

Wil turned the sealed packet over in his hands. 'What is it?'

'No idea,' Rob answered. 'But don't let anyone touch it. None of us knows his address. And as I'm sure you know, it will be difficult to track him down now. He avoided social media like the plague.'

Wil nodded, appreciating the advice, though didn't like referring to his good friend in the past tense.

Just then, Wil's phone on the kitchen island alerted a text.

'You should probably have a look at that,' Rose urged.

'Probably,' Wil agreed. 'Ben, my best friend, was in the dreamscape with us last night. I've not heard from him since we woke.' He got up and had a look.

'Everything okay?' Rob asked, a faint tone of dread in his voice.

'It's my sister.' Wil stared at the screen, horrified. 'She says Annie's forgotten everything….' He looked to Rob and Rose who were staring at him with concerned expressions from over the back of the couch. 'She says Annie must have been a Dual.'

Chapter Forty

Letters

Wil watched from the landing window upstairs as the twins drove away from the manor. After the dust behind their tyres settled, he went and took Murphy's padded envelope to his room and texted Steph and Ben, hoping to find out more about Annie, but no answers came.

Waiting, Wil held the packet in his hands, wondering what his old friend could have left for him, when suddenly a vision of himself digging popped into this head. Digging and putting something in a small hole for safekeeping. It was a memory, no doubt, half there, half not. Certain it would become complete in due course, and determined just now to know what Murphy left, Wil cut the end of the package open with a pair of scissors and carefully pulled out the contents: two large Ziploc freezer bags. One had *From Annie* written in permanent black marker on the outside, while the other, *From Murphy*. And both had a handwritten letter with a lock of hair. Wil checked inside the packet again and found a small, loose note in the bottom,

Wilden, please keep these. I couldn't bear the thought of them meaning nothing after Monday. And with no time to write Annie back, having no social media presence, nor wanting one, I've replied, hoping that should only one of us be unfortunate enough to gain our memory, you'd return them on behalf of us both. The key is for me—a me who remembers. The silver box is quite rare and contains a few necessary objects I hope to make use of if I return with significant threads intact.

Wil hadn't noticed a silver box. He checked the envelope once more then pinched the protective plastic of Murphy's much heavier bag. There, hidden between the top and bottom end of the folded letter was a thin, hard object. Sliding it along the inside of the freezer bag, away from the paper, Wil saw what looked like a slim, silver, Victorian cigarette box. However, the ornate etchings were nothing of the sort. A man's head, engraved with the initials *M R P* across his brow, had fantastical dream-like visions sprawling from his head. There was a beautiful flying woman draped in a billowing dress, mountains with faces, sky maps and constellations in the background… and the half-profile of a male face, with flaming hair, appearing also as a wave crashing against a cliff. At the top of the cliff was a tiny person with arms outstretched. Gently, Wil pressed the fastening and carefully gathered the plastic freezer bag around the box so that he could see inside it without touching a thing. The two halves of the silver case held small hexagonal compartments inside it like that of a honeycomb. They were no larger than a 10p coin, no deeper than a stack of three or four of them. There must have been twenty little sections in all, all with decorative, hinged, little silver lids. One was slightly open and contained a rolled-up thread. Wil closed it properly and opened another. Then another. Hair… sand, more threads… all of it objects Murphy clearly used or thought he might need at some point to get into a dream direct, for being a Dual, he could enter any dream, but an object… an object would save him time, reduce the number of threads travelled. It did occur to Wil as he put it all back, taking care not to push too hard against the plastic bag, that maybe this was just an heirloom, like Uncle Clive's box from next door. A pocket version.

He carried on with Murphy's note,

I don't mind if you read the correspondence here. Perhaps it will help you see why I want to be back. Perhaps too, finding that all the Duals will have forgotten by the time you read this will impress upon you a greater desire to resolve your own predicament with Sadie, because there is little hope should both of you forget. But you do remember. You will remember. And you are well-equipped. Therefore, you are my hope too, Wilden. Any resolve you realise with Sadie, I dare say may be to my own benefit. So please don't forget me dear brother in your endeavours to fix her threads.

Please don't forget me. Save these items and find me. They are the only proof of who I am now, what I feel now, and know will no longer be and feel soon.

Dually Yours, Murphy

P.S. Please tell Rob and Rose thank you for passing these items on. I've already given my thanks to Vivienne.

It occurred to Wil that if Murphy knew what was to happen to the rest of the Duals when he wrote this, he might even have known Vivienne's fate when he posted this to her. He might even have known that much worse awaited her.

Perturbed at the thought, he picked up the plastic bag containing Annie's letter and began reading.

September 23, 2015

Dearest Murphy

I had no choice but to contact Vivienne. When I found out that you'd be in the last cull, in less than a week, I realised that I didn't care what being a Dual meant anymore. Vivienne helped me turn and I don't regret a moment of it. Please don't be upset with her. She tried her best to put me off, reminding me that the end for all Duals is forgetting. She warned me too that I might not have til Monday, and that there would be sleepless nights, and maybe even no chance of seeing you with the constant bombardment of unfinished business between the sides wanting to make the most of us few Duals left. But if even a fraction of this is what you were up against when all of us were remembering, it only shows the lengths you went through to protect those closest to you. You never let on your battles.

I wish I could do more than turn, and write this letter. Anything to see you one last time. Anything to apologise to you face to face, because the thought of you slipping away Monday night, without me having the chance to say how sorry I am… it makes any memory of you unbearable, even now. My only consolation is that if this letter doesn't get to you before then, I too will have forgotten.

I'm so sorry for accusing you of making them forget. I'm so sorry I turned you away in anger each time you tried telling me differently. I've spent the last few days as Dual trying to find you, doubling my chances of seeing you once more, before this apology means nothing. Before anything between us means nothing. I've never felt more betrayed by myself than when I turned you away over and over again, knowing now as a Dual what that was to accomplish. I see now that it was to create division between us. Instil distrust. Make me love you less. But Murphy I do love you. And it's because I do that I don't want to remember anything of our past if you're not remembering too. Everything I've done to try and help Steph and Wil, it's been futile. They remember nothing. You've been the only one left remembering and I chucked you away... because I found out you were a Dual—because I assumed you couldn't be trusted—because you knew that I loved you and you never told me this about you. Because I wanted you to make everything better and you couldn't. I was desperate for things to be as they were and rejected what little there was left. Being Dual now, I see how foolish I was in the end, how impossible I made it for you. I couldn't see two sides. I only saw one. Please forgive me for this.

You saved me a thousand times from myself the other side. You saved our friends. But I don't love you because of what you've done... or whose side you stand on at any given moment. I love you because you're Murphy. You may not get a chance to read this before we wake on Tuesday, but if Vivienne can get this to you before then, please know that if you come and find me once more, I won't turn you away. I will hold onto you knowing it may be the last chance I have with you.
Yours Always
Annie x
(I know you don't need an object to meet me in my Initial before Tuesday, but I don't plan on being there for more than an instant, because I'll be looking for you. The lock of hair is to save you time finding me in the dreamscape.)

Seeing the date on Annie's letter, Wil realised it was written last Wednesday, the day he heard Aeolus' voice on the train. She obviously wouldn't have known then that four days later, Ben and Steph would regain their memories. As Wil stared at her wide-looped handwriting through the plastic, he imagined that she must have regretted her decision to become a Dual once Steph started remembering. But then, on second thought, Annie's roles had never been passive, Wil had to admit. And it was quite possible that *because* she turned Dual, Ben and Steph ended up remembering. Of course, whatever role her Duality may have played, only she could know, for she managed to keep it secret to the end. That alone gave Wil reason to think she couldn't have regretted her decision. In fact, or occurred to him that last night over pizza she could have said something, confessed her big mistake if that's what she believed it to be, but she didn't. And there was the funny moment Wil remembered just now, closing his eyes regretfully at the thought, when she let out that loud sigh... right after Steph mentioned the disloyalty of Duals to humanity. That was when Steph stopped and looked across the table as though Annie might be prompting her to remember something she had forgotten to mention. But Annie said nothing. No, had there been any regret on Annie's part, Wil felt certain, the opportunity to confess Duality would have been right then. But instead, she simply sat there and encouraged Steph to carry on, listening to Vergers and Duals be compared to the drunk and sober, listening as her best friend discriminated against Duals with the very memory a Dual had restored. Annie had restored.

Wil exhaled disgustedly. 'Oh Annie...' he uttered, imagining what must have gone through her head as his sister went on unashamedly.

No, Annie wouldn't have regretted her decision. Not when she used it to prove to three of her closest friends how devoted she had been. Not if it meant she might find Murphy before the cull.

Wil put the bag down and wished suddenly that he had some sort of confirmation that Murphy found Annie in the end, after the library, for Murphy had obviously received her letter through Vivienne here, but what about Annie's own peace of mind? She deserved so much more than just to be left searching, unaware even if Murphy got her letter. What about knowing Murphy had forgiven her? As Wil thought back to last night's dream, it was a little disconcerting that Annie wasn't in her Initial when they tried joining her from Steph's, in Nan's mini... but she showed up later in the desert, and fended off the Imposter... then went with Wil to The Failed Junction. He could appreciate just now the peace it had given him in being able to tell her last night why they had to forget—*show her* why they had to start over—because of the door she would never have been able to access. Having that opportunity to show her meant even more now, knowing she woke up this morning only to remember nothing. If *he* could have that peace of setting things right, why couldn't she? Why couldn't she know Murphy had forgiven her?

Quickly, Wil picked up Murphy's letter.

Annie, I should have come to you sooner. They make it impossible for me now. In the same way you search for a SPACE in which I occupy the dreams, I search endlessly for you in a TIME. And now three years have gone. And many more soon. I waste no time in telling you that I forgive you. Please forgive ME for not coming back. I thought that maybe you'd believe me if I could find Wil and restore his memory. I thought maybe he could tell you the part I really played. But I found him in the unlikeliest of places, turning awake minds with the same determination as I turn sleeping ones. Only he was in no position to be restored. And I would only have aided those who turned you against me. I did the one thing I could, but it might have been unnecessary or not enough. In any case, it didn't bring me closer to you.

I am grateful you chose Duality. There is no difference between us now. We can merely accept what is, love what is.

It is unlikely that you will receive my letter, but yours couldn't go without a response. I forgive you and I love you. I will do my best to find you, parch my resources to remember you, and hope that loving you is my default setting after tomorrow.

Wanting to be yours, awake and asleep... always
Murphy
A lock to remember me by

Wil put the letter down and crossed his arms. Tipping his head back to the ceiling, all he could do was hope that somewhere after the library, and before ending up in the desert, Annie was with Murphy. He wished desperately she could have heard such words. Because these... Wil looked at the plastic bag again with heavy disappointment... she never received these.

Just then, a text arrived,

Steph's been keeping me posted. Nan's got blood test at lunch. I'll see you after classes. 4pm. Darlingdon Park. I told Steph to come. BTW Angus cancelled rugby. Ben

The last thing Wil could think of was playing rugby, or doing anything normal today. The fact that Steph left this morning as though nothing had changed, and Ben was his slow-to-communicate self, after everything that had happened last night and this morning, Wil was beginning to think he was going a little crazy.

Steph texted finally,

She left a note in my kit. Clearly before last night. It all confirms. Maybe she left you something? Meet you at the park at 4.

Wil was pretty certain the only thing Annie left him was the sketch in his notepad. But taking no chances, he grabbed it and had another look.

Nope. Just a picture of Aeolus. And a signature.

He slowly closed the notepad, realising that both Vivienne and Sadie had left something with him. His journal and the little envelope of clips. Remembering the futile attempts those who were afraid of forgetting made at leaving themselves clues to their pasts, clues to relationships they didn't want to forget, he couldn't help think there was something in Vivienne's insistence that he read his old journal and get back to her. Of course, there could be no getting back to her now....

Unless...

Quickly, Wil took the black book that had been missing for weeks, and started reading the earlier narrative entries, from when he was remembering. Then poem after poem from those days when he forgot, he skimmed, each one decoded slightly by a concluding line at the bottom. An hour later, he was pretty much only reading the title and last line, remembering already the contents sandwiched in the middle. That is, until he came to an entry towards the end.

Junctions.

Here, three quarters through, the binding splayed the pages outwards, prompting Wil to read the poem in its entirety.

August 15
Junctions
The place where two things meet
In space and time the same
A connection pulling threads
One never intended to reclaim
Yet here we are meeting
No space, no time, no thread
Expecting to do it again
Reclaiming the dead.
—Remembering.

Remembering what? He couldn't even *remember* writing this. The next page however, he did.

As Wil sat and finished the rest of the journal, he came back to these words, for it seemed this was what Aeolus wanted him to find, what

Vivienne wanted him to read. And getting back to her... well that could only happen if they found the real Junction. And it could never be *her* as such, rather the knowledge of her experiences, preserved amid Vivienne-shaped threads.

Unable to even think of all that now, think of why a little window had been opened for him to write this, Wil closed the book, packed away Murphy's things and tucked them into a dark corner inside the back of his wardrobe. He took Sadie's earplugs too, and did the same. As for Lily's clips, there didn't seem to be any clips when he squeezed the small grey envelope between his fingertips. It felt more like... folded paper. A letter. The realisation of this pulled the wariness from Wil's expression. Hastily, hopefully, he tore the sealed end open, finding that's exactly what it was: a small letter, smelling of lilacs.

Of course lilacs, Wil thought, pressing the folded quarters to his lips and inhaling.

He unfolded it in earnest.

> *Wil,*
>
> *Remember lilacs and Gwennap Pit? And sunset at Cheddar Gorge? I wish I could say I'll never forget them.*
>
> *I'm sorry for having to write a letter, but I can't say good-bye like you did that first time. Watching you at the Point of Transition wasn't the chance to spend our last few moments together as I had hoped. I don't want you seeing my face as lilacs and sunsets disappear, and the hollowness of forgetting takes it over. Trust me when I say the memory of it will taint anything sweet we've shared.*
>
> *I'm not afraid of forgetting. And I'm not afraid of starting all over with you. I know you'll be there in my dreams, even though I won't remember. I know you'll be reminding me of threads long broken in the hope to mend them quicker. I don't fear any of that, because you know where I live, we finally attend the same school, our paths will inevitably cross. What I am afraid of, is you not telling them. I'm afraid the hold Tret had over you the last three years may make you reconsider what you promised that first time we had to part.*

Again, it concerned the Junction and he didn't want to be thinking of it right now.

You promised that the change you'd experience in choosing to forget would ensure that you couldn't forget again. But it never occurred to either of us that I would be the one forgetting next, just as you were beginning to remember. But of course that's what was going to happen, wasn't it, Wil? Not because of who I am to you, but because I'm a Dual. Don't you see? Any shift the Tare make, the Tret react precisely to oppose it. Peaks and troughs, Wil. You may never forget, but I may never remember. You will labour over who you are serving, I will soon serve both carelessly. You knew there would be a shift and you are one of the first to lead it. Tell them why the Duals can be no more. Tell them why you have come to replace them.

Wil looked up from the letter, dumbfounded. *Replace them?* He never intended to replace anyone. But as the scented sheet slipped from his hand, it occurred to him that's exactly what was to happen.

Mutation. The new, out-surviving the old.

A flash of circles within circles shot through Wil's mind suddenly, one right after the other, blinding him. Circles within circles... at Gwennap... the dart board... the doorbell next door.... Annie's sketch then shot through his mind, followed by the giant petri dish from Monday night. The brown spots leached across his retina. *Of course*, he realised, seeing his room clearly again. What he thought was the ultimate free will—remembering—he now saw that Sadie was right. *Peaks and troughs.* The threat of forgetting was no longer there. Instead, there was the worry of who he might inadvertently be as someone again remembering. Who, after three years' exposure to untrustworthy fog, might he hurt... and never be able to forget that he did so? There was no mercy for him now. No consolation of forgetting like before. The whole reason he made his decision back then was to make access to The Junction more efficient, so all his work couldn't be undone. But what was his existence if it was full of regret... shame... and bad decisions that would no doubt be passed on as genetic memory? What was his contribution to The Junction then? When he agreed to lead the shift, seeing that his threads would no longer be broken, he had no idea it would be the undoing of Annie and Murphy... of Duals as he knew them. Was this really what she wanted him to tell Steph and Ben?

Picking up Sadie's letter again, Wil read the final lines.

They may feel betrayed when you share your secret with them, but it can be no worse than if they find out from someone else. Tell them before such a thing can be used against you... before the shift between Tret and Tare changes things further and you don't have the chance to explain.

Wil's eyes narrowed at these words, rereading them, for it seemed she was letting on that there would be more changes to come—more than Duals disappearing, more than those who had forgotten maybe remembering again... and those remembering who no longer knew what their true affinities were anymore. How much more change could there be?

You are unable to forget now, Wil. I'm sure it will feel a curse and a gift at times. I know you'll worry which side you end up serving it with. But the Tret AND Tare sides in me think you can't do much wrong if you honour friends and serve those you love. Could this be impartial advice if I have no reservations? I think so.

I love you Wilden Stokes. And I look forward to loving you again.

Sadie xxx

I'm sorry everything was so veiled between us this last week. But you understand the Dual dilemma.

Of course he understood. Sometimes the peak ended up being the trough, the blessing, a curse. It was the Dual dilemma.

For the third time, Wil went to the dark corner of the wardrobe. He tucked Sadie's little note away, not even wanting to think about why he had been allowed to receive such a thing: direct and physical instruction, from a Dual. Whatever the reason, she was right. He would have to tell Steph and Ben. But not today. Today, he felt grieved, and he couldn't think straight.

Chapter Forty-One

Roundabout

Arriving early at the park gave Wil just enough space to let his mind wander, what with Vivienne and the police… and Rob and Rose, and all the shunted thoughts from the letters and objects now hidden behind his winter jumpers. It was a great relief to see Ben and Steph finally stride across the grass an hour later.

Wil told them first about Rob and Rose, then what Murphy said to him in the library.

'He wasn't there to tell me he turned me. He said he came to warn us there's been a shift,' Wil recounted. 'He said something's happening to the polarisation of Tret and Tare—to us and them as well. And he was obviously fighting something off as he spoke to me, something that didn't want him saying anything. I know the Duals are pretty much gone, but he said the Tret and Tare need Duals to remember, but they don't want us aware of who we're serving.'

'A new Dual,' Ben recognised.

'And he said they've got something else coming,' Wil added, though he couldn't say what when Steph asked. 'I'm really sorry, that's when he had to go.'

'Murphy and Annie…?' Ben breathed, incredulous still to the fact that they both had been Duals, leaving everyone silent for a minute at the thought.

'Annie told me about the culls yesterday,' Steph remembered, joining Ben on the motionless roundabout as Wil stood next to it. 'She said they happened a few times last year, but in the last few weeks, it's been like every other day. She said no one could find a Dual anymore, and insider knowledge was almost impossible to come by. I wonder if that's what got her thinking about Murphy. She said that after all this time, she had no idea what happened to him. I think she just assumed he had been made to forget in one of the first culls.'

'If not one of the first ones, then she must have realised he would be in this last one when she entered the dreams last night,' Ben imagined as Wil only half-listened, for Wil suddenly wished that Murphy had left an address or something, not just connections to Initials, for Wil had the urge to find him, befriend him, this side of the dreams.

'Well, without proper sleep all week, she wouldn't have known til last minute, would she?' Steph reckoned. 'What I can't figure though is how she found out. How did she find out he would be in the last cull... and why would she decide to turn after we all got our memories back? She could have been standing here with us right now.' She shoved her fists into her jacket, slouched onto a crossbar and closed her eyes to the late afternoon sun, dissatisfied with her ignorance. 'That was a huge decision. I mean, she said she hadn't seen him in years.'

'He went to her last night,' Wil answered, stepping onto the corrugated platform, placing himself equidistant from the other two. 'Murphy told me in the library,' he directed to Steph while catching Ben's eye, for he wondered if his best friend might have said things differently if had he known it would be the last time they'd see Murphy as they had always known him. 'He couldn't stay with us because he said he needed to see her before waking. Before forgetting. And she didn't find out last night he'd be in the cull,' Wil divulged. 'She found out through Vivienne a week ago. That's when she turned.'

Ben and Steph looked at one another confounded, then back to Wil's weighted expression.

'She didn't mention anything yesterday about being a Dual,' Steph accused slightly, clearly bothered that her friend might have kept this from her.

'No? What did she mention, then?' Wil asked, believing it to be of little consequence anyway.

But as Steph seemed to be thinking back on yesterday, looking at her shoes as she did so, a sickening realisation appeared to take over her.

'Oh Annie...' she exhaled all of a sudden, regretting. She then turned helplessly to Wil. 'I should have known something wasn't right when she wanted all the pictures down.'

'Pictures?' Ben asked.

'The ones in her bedroom,' Wil understood, imagining what Steph was about to tell him. 'There were hundreds. They were sketches of things we'd done in the dreams before, all of it we remember easily now. Before I saw them yesterday, I knew nothing, but then something in one of them sparked my memory of the codes we used. The emergency codes.' The placement of some sketches with others, and that curling fog moving across the sheets, was a creation in itself. Taking it all apart meant one thing. 'Steph, why did she say she wanted them down?'

'She said there was no need for proof anymore.' Steph shrugged, clearly wishing she hadn't believed such a thing. 'She said if I remembered, there was no doubt you would too. And I completely forgot that we shouldn't make any big decisions when something major happens in the dreams—like getting rid of dream evidence—so without even thinking I told her she was right, and helped her take it all down. It took an hour *at least....*'

As Wil watched his sister roll her eyes, disgusted with herself for not even seeing what was going on in that hour, he reminded her that they were all taking hits. He then asked when all this had happened.

'Yesterday morning. After you and I spoke in the pantry,' she said, arching her eyebrows at him. 'I ran over there... and she was so happy. And as soon as we stopped talking about me having my memory back she started talking about Murphy and culls.... Oh how could I have been *so stupid?*'

Steph put her chin to her chest and closed her eyes.

'This morning, when she made no mention of what happened last night, and couldn't even remember what happened the night before... that's when I realised she wasn't just messing around,' Steph recounted, lifting her head, though shrivelling still. 'I figured maybe I should try and avoid talking to her about anything to do with the dreams at that point. You know, carefully see which threads were cut. So I asked about how redecorating her room was going, but she had no idea what I was talking about. And when I went back with her just now,' Steph's eyes darted sharply to the right, in the direction of Annie's neighbourhood, 'and showed her all the smudges on the walls from the sketches... and a picture I had on my phone with them in the background… she was like, *I have no idea what you're talking about.* Steph hauffed at Ben's cautioning glare, rolling her eyes again. 'I know I shouldn't have done it, but I just couldn't believe it—*I get my memory back, but she loses hers?'*

Wil couldn't help be reminded: *peaks and troughs.*

'Not only does she not remember doing any of that stuff in the sketches, but I had a good look in her room and I can't find them anywhere. *She* doesn't even know where they went. She could have chucked them for all we know and have no memory of it.' Wil was suddenly grateful for the sketch of Aeolus Annie did. There was a slim chance it could come in handy in future. 'Of course, I can't bring it up again because she's already thinking I'm pulling some trick on her, Photoshopping things into her bedroom. And I can't have her wondering if she's going crazy.'

'No, we need to be careful,' Ben agreed. 'This is exactly what she went through with us, so we've got to do our best to be as normal as possible with her. She'll be going through a major identity change right now with all those severed threads,' he said wisely, visibly curtailing Steph's anxiety. 'Let her settle down first and we can test her memory later. The most we can do at this stage is look after her in her Initial, because she's a Verger now, not a Dual, not properly Tret or Tare affinitied. She can't properly navigate the dreams, so we need to protect her from being bombarded in there by Tret and Tare—whether there's a Point of Transition anymore,' he said with eyes widening towards Wil.

'I want to go, then,' Steph quickly stiffened upright, moving the roundabout slightly. 'If anyone should be in there looking after her, it should be me. Just like she visited me all those times.'

'We can go together, Steph,' Wil assured, taking an agreeing nod from Ben. 'You shouldn't be in there on your own. You can turn her Tare at the end of the day so we can get in, and Ben and I can hang around in the background. It'll be like you're on your own, but we'll be there if you need us.'

'We need to look out for her,' Ben said resolutely, sounding like he actually understood the lengths Annie had gone to in helping them get this far. Wil imagined that Steph must have told Ben at least a bit of what Annie had been doing the last two years to try and get them remembering for Ben to be appreciating her so just now. Appreciating her despite her decision to become a Dual. 'It's just a shame we can't do the same for Murphy,' Ben added soberly, apparently meaning it.

Wil thought of Murphy's letter and object stash, his lock of hair. He wasn't sure if he should mention that actually they had a way into Murphy's Initial. Deciding that he would keep quiet about it for the moment, Steph piped up with a question that determined otherwise,

'How *did* you know Annie became a Dual last week, by the way?'

Wil decided to tell them. He told them about Annie's letter to Murphy, that she probably didn't have any confirmation he received it. He told them about the letter Murphy wrote back that Annie certainly didn't have the chance to read. And he explained what he thought happened last night, that maybe Murphy and Annie did meet briefly, before Annie then came to his—Wil's—rescue. A rescue which then allowed him to finally show her why they all had to forget, why significant threads connected to The Failed Junction had to be broken. He even told them about Sadie and how Murphy wasn't the only one who gave them the information they used in the past. He told them too what Sadie had been to him before, more than just a friend, and was still so now.

'Annie knew she was a Dual,' Steph said plainly when he had finished.

'How?' Wil asked, having no indication from Annie that she thought such a thing.

'Because you told her about Sadie dream-dragging you from your Initial to hers, then to Ben's. The only way Sadie could get to you two and share affinity with that Tret Aeolus was to be a Dual.'

Of course. Wil thought it obvious now, but when he assumed he and Sadie were on the same side… well it was no different to Murphy managing to remain undetected as a Dual under Ben's nose for years. Assumed affinity. Ben assumed Murphy was Tare and chose to see nothing else. Even when new information suggested the contrary. 'She also knew there was something going on between you two. I think she thought you just fancied her though.'

'Huh,' Ben piped up, sounding curious. 'So… that *might* explain how Sadie knew my little rhyme then?' he offered indignantly. '*Fret the Tret, share with the Tare,*' he reminded, pretending to calculate in the air with his head cocked sideways, 'because… *you told her.*'

Here, Wil threw his head back, recalling perfectly now.

'Ugh,' he said, letting his forehead then fall into his hand. 'I'm so sorry, Ben….' He looked at his best friend through the cover of his shaggy fringe and gauged forgiveness there.

413

'We'll call it even,' Ben decided gruffly. 'You didn't have your memory back when you accused me of such treachery,' he said, causing Wil to smirk. 'I take it you'll be wanting us to visit her along with Annie, then?'

'I can look after Sadie on my own,' Wil insisted.

'But none of us should be on our own right now,' Steph warned.

'Well, I can leave if there's a problem. I know how to find you.'

'But I don't *want* to be anywhere without you,' she said firmly.

'Ben can be with you while I'm gone. You wouldn't mind, would you Ben?'

'Of course not.'

'You'd be happy with him for just a little while, wouldn't you, Steph?' But that obviously wasn't the issue. 'Listen, I can't just *leave* her,' Wil said plainly. 'Just like we can't leave Annie. One visit a night—if she's Tare. That's all I need. And if she's Tret... well, I'll come straight back. One visit. That's what, five minutes out of eight hours?'

Relenting, Steph remarked that time was indeterminable in the dreams, then suggested they try Murphy too, to which Ben was the first to support,

'We can use the hair until one of us gets close enough that it's not needed.'

'But that lock of hair was for Annie,' Wil reminded.

'Yes, but what good is it if they never meet again,' Ben argued. 'A single hair is our only hope of getting them ever appreciating what they left for each other.'

Wil considered Ben's point. 'Fine, then. One hair between us.'

That evening, they did just that. They cut one hair three ways, secured it to a strip of sticky tape and hoped Murphy was momentarily Tare.

They found him on a bench overlooking the sea. This was his Initial, his safe place. Of course, without knowing Ben, Steph or Wil awake, Murphy had no recollection of who they were while he was asleep. Not with his memory taken. Their chat was discreet, strangers merely passing on a clifftop path. Over time though, they would be able to stay longer, speak of more, and come to know him again. Know him well enough to help him find his dream-aware self in the hope that he might even know his thread-severed self again.

The strange calm in the dreams compared to the night before made

414

everyone a little wary, like being in the eye of a storm, but they moved swiftly from Murphy to Annie, not needing an object, because not only was she Tare when they found her, but knowing her outside the dreams also meant none of them would have trouble getting into her Initial. They found her in a cottage garden, ambling through waist-high wildflowers, cutting zinnias and poppies into a bouquet. It was Great Aunt Margaret's house in Dorset. Wil and Ben reckoned as they sat plucking dandelions from the other side of a hedge that despite Annie spending less time at her Great Aunt's in recent summers, there must have been something about the place that made her feel safe.

'The lack of pretence,' Ben supposed.

'More like the isolation,' Wil guessed.

Whatever the reason, it was peaceful. And beautiful. The height of summertime and blossom. And Steph and Annie chatted for what seemed hours.

The eerie calm followed Wil when he split from Ben and Steph and tried Sadie's Initial. He was pleased to find her sitting under a tree. Not the tree in the field as before, but under the tree where she spoke so frankly to him at college. With her bag and books scattered around her, he knew he wouldn't be able to sit and chat, because even though they knew one another at college outside the dreams, their contact consisted primarily of everything that went on inside them. Those threads most certainly would have been severed, Wil knew, making him little more than a stranger. His only option this early on was to engage superficially. He did what he felt the most comfortable with and asked her for the time. Of course, reading a watch was impossible in the dreams, but he knew she would come up with the time she wanted it to be.

'It's 8:50am ...I think.'

'8:50am. What happens at 8:50am again?' He pretended he couldn't remember, hoping she might indicate why she chose this time, this tree.

'Psychology starts then.' All of a sudden, realising the time, she gathered up her bags, apologised for having to go, then ran off to class, leaving him standing beside the gold-tinged tree.

Wil smiled slightly as he watched her disappear between the buildings, for he knew she was dreaming of where he'd be.

Next time, he would remind her of the time, and go with her.

ONE MONTH LATER

Chapter Forty-Two

Peaks and Troughs

A month feels like years in the dreams. They have a way of making you believe anything is possible. But once you wake, reality bleeds that belief right out of you.

Peaks and troughs.

When Sadie came down the aisle to her chair that first day back, awake and with her memory lost, Wil hadn't anticipated the effect it would have on him. He had hoped she would be different. Less affected. But the aloof demeanour one adopts with forgetting, the closed-mindedness, the lack of wonder... she bled out in reality what she barely managed to hold onto in her newly threaded dreams, just like everyone else.

That first day, Wil excused himself to cry silently in a stall of the men's toilet until Ben kindly came for him when the corridors had cleared for the next class. It happened a few times again after that, after they were all forced to scoot chairs together and work on something in small groups. How she managed to be in the same room with him, giving nothing away when she remembered, when they were finally in the same town, the same school... and waiting for him to come out of the fog.... He was in awe of her. It made the vacancy he witnessed Tuesdays and Thursdays more difficult, but he told himself that if she could do it, he certainly could. He fortified his courage on Thursdays, spending time between Psychology and Ben's Communications class under the tree on the green where she always started off in her Initial. It made him feel more connected to her outside the dreams, gave him space to think, catch up on all his old journals and read Clive's notebooks Rob and Rose had given him.

'I'll find you after class,' Ben promised, leaving Wil under the tree again.

'I'll be here,' Wil sighed, not looking up from Clive's musty hand-written manuscript, for he was fascinated by the intriguing entries that explained why some things happened in the 1940's as they did. For instance, Wil learned Clive's main role at Bletchley Park was interception, and with MI5, engaging with double-crossers who fed misleading intelligence to the British. His journals explained why sleep deprivation was really used and why double-crossers would sometimes be caught and unable to confess to their captors. With instruction given in their dreams and then being made to forget altogether by Tret or Tare, they really *didn't* have an idea of what they were on assignment for when they were caught. And stopping them from going back to the dreams, depriving them of sleep made no difference. The threads had already been cut.

He explained too that when some of his colleagues forgot their dreams, they had been treated with barbiturates, truth serum, basically, to try and help recoup the information the Tret and Tare made them forget. However, no one could truly bring back the de-threaded mind with these treatments. But where the metre high stack of spiralled notebooks covering four decades really began to get interesting was when Wil grabbed the last book from the 1970's. It was almost a philosophical overview of Clive's life experiences of the Tret and Tare, and here, in the sepia pages propped over Wil's crossed legs, Clive's concluding remarks in this final notebook suggested that compassion and empathy were the only way back to one restoring their own severed threads. It was the ultimate autonomy, and the Tret and Tare undermined it in preventing populations from remembering. In forgetting one's own experiences, they forget how to appreciate the experiences of others. But embracing compassion... empathy, it was a way back to connect not only to the individuals around us, reinforcing the human identity, the human need to be connected to others... it was a way back to connect to oneself, and mend broken threads.

The Self reflects as a mirror. One cannot understand the reflection they see if they are incapable of stepping away and recognising the Self in others. Watching the Universal Self experience grief, anger, disappointment...

is the only way one can be the same again, for in doing so, in seeing the same, they begin to feel the same, rejuvenating their own threads.

Wil looked up from the notebook across the leaf-ridden green. He couldn't help but think back to that moment at Annie's, where he saw himself in those sketches, a self he had no memory of being. Yet feeling like an insect, bumping against a window, he tried imagining the person Annie portrayed. But it was only when he considered how she must have felt after he chose to forget that the glass barrier gave way and he then remembered the codes. It was as Clive demonstrated through dozens of examples: compassion and empathy, then rejuvenation.

Of course, looking back, Wil was quite aware that when he stood there in Annie's room, he *wanted* to remember. *Needed* to. However, Annie at present still had no impetus to even believe she was anyone else other than who she saw herself as now. And it was a delicate balance to advance and retreat through the dreams, much more so when she was awake, to help her find her true self again. How could one ever hope to restore threads they had no memory were severed? Where was their autonomy then?

Wil read on.

Clive's last topic was on decision making. His opening line stated that while every human had the free will to choose Tret or Tare, they did not however have the option to *hear* only Tret or Tare. They had to listen to both. Free will was then demonstrated in the thoughts and actions that followed. Wil turned the page, expecting there to be more, but there wasn't. He closed the notebook, stuffed it in his bag and got out his own journal and a pen.

His previous entry gave an account of those last few minutes in The Failed Junction with Annie, just before Aeolus made her forget. Writing it all out made him realise that she would only have known the truth for a few minutes. Barely long enough to transform the vast network of threads in her such new information would undoubtedly have affected.

Wil flipped to the next page and wrote the date.

October 29

Focusing his mind on yesterday, Wil wrote about the things he told Ben and Steph, about the possible consequences of them remembering now. That it might have had something to do with the Duals forgetting. He wanted to be sure he documented the conversation here so not to forget. However, he didn't write about how he tried making it all sound speculative, or that he felt a fraud just bringing it up. Or that if Sadie had been there, they would have rowed about how much he left out. But he couldn't write any of that, because he knew that if he did, he'd count it as his confession and never tell them. Already he was looking for ways to confess without confessing, and he was beginning to feel like that sweaty evangelist Sonya showed him, giving out useless blessings to the damned.

'Can I join you?'

Wil's thoughts stopped dead at that familiar voice. He looked up from his journal, hopeful, but immediately saw the vacancy there, unchanged.

'Of course.' He quickly pulled his bag and books close, making space for her. 'Please. *Sadie* was it…?' he pretended to guess, feeling the delight of lead-filled threads slipping right out of him.

Peaks and Troughs

ACKNOWLEDGEMENTS

This story has been a confidant and traitor, drawing me back with familiarity and anticipation, dread and disappointment, like a complicated friend over the last seven years. It could not be possible without my husband Jon's continual patience, encouragement and willingness to edit on demand. I thank him for his support. Without it, I would have given up this story long ago. I thank my children too for their appreciation and enthusiasm for the writing process. Without it, the hours I spent away from them crafting these pages might have felt a bit pointless.

I thank John, whose encouraging words made *Dreamnesia*'s publishing route not just possible, but a pleasure. Without him, the manuscript might still be stashed in a drawer.

I thank Howard for his expertise in graphic design, crowd control and for, yet again, helping me to present the darker side of one of my stories.

I thank Dr Bonnie Bassler for her research in quorum sensing (how bacteria communicate using chemical signals), and I thank Dr David Sweatt, whose pioneering work on epigenetics focuses on how we learn and store memories, and how our experiences trigger actual changes in the chemical structure of genes within our bodies—changes which can later be inherited by our offspring. Their research was the inspiration behind some of the concepts in this book, concepts that will flourish and endure throughout the rest of the trilogy.

Finally, I thank Steve Gutierrez, who, on a Hayward hill twenty years ago, motivated me to write a story. A good one. I haven't been able to shake the urge since.

Shawn Terry Upton worked in children's education in the UK for 12 years before publishing her second Young Adult Science Fiction novel *Dreamnesia: Retrospect*, the middle story in a trilogy.

Originally from California, she received her BA in English from California State University, East Bay. Her studies brought her to London, where she met her husband. Together, they live with their three children in Somerset, the South West of England. For more information on her writing and to find out about the inspiration behind her work, please visit:

www.quantalore.com

30125991R00254

Printed in Poland
by Amazon Fulfillment
Poland Sp. z o.o., Wrocław